CW00793084

WAYEL KATI

WAYEL KATI

THE QUEST OF THE SEVEN GUARDIANS

LINTHOI CHANU

NIYOGI
BOOKS

First published by **PERKY PARROT**
An imprint of
NIYOGI BOOKS
Block D, Building No. 77
Okhla Industrial Area, Phase-I
New Delhi-110 020, INDIA
Tel: 91-11-26816301, 26818960
Email: niyogibooks@gmail.com
Website: www.niyogibooksindia.com

Text © Linthoi Chanu

Editor: Stellar Quo, Arunima Ghosh, K.E. Priyamvada
Design: Shashi Bhushan Prasad
Cover design: Misha Oberoi
Cover illustration: Aaryama Somayaji
Inside illustrations: Yaiphahenba Laisham

ISBN: 978-93-91125-87-5
Publication: 2023

Price: ₹495

This is a work of fiction. The names, characters and incidents portrayed in it are the work of the author's imagination. Any resemblance to actual persons, living or dead, events or localities, is entirely coincidental.

All rights are reserved. No part of this publication may be reproduced or transmitted in any form or by any means, electronic or mechanical, including photocopying, recording or by any information storage and retrieval system without prior written permission and consent of the Publisher.

Printed at Niyogi Offset Pvt. Ltd., New Delhi, India

Contents

Note from the Author

*T*his is a fantasy, comprising tales of heroes and monsters. *Wayel Kati* is a tale that has been woven into a plot with several stories from different corners of Manipur. These stories have been preserved and carried orally for a long time, by generations after generations, in an attempt to connect with the fading past, lessons forgotten and lost knowledge. I wish to evoke curiosity about Manipur's land and culture among my readers and if, by circumstance, my readers wish to pursue more about tales from this region, I will comfort myself that I have done my part.

PROLOGUE

*I*nside the celestial hall, all the divine entities of the upper realm assembled.

The great Father God materialized as an aged hermit with a lengthy staff, with his long silver hair tied into a bun over his wrinkled forehead, his short straight moustache dropping from the corners of his mouth, his thin body covered in a starry robe and nebulous loincloth.

There was a woman beside him, with a face flickering like a star, from a young-to-aged visage in split seconds.

The horde of great gods and goddesses stood amongst the clouded floor, brilliant celestial bodies drifting overhead.

The divine beings were discussing something—chattering, arguing and some even yelling out their opinions.

The Father God, Atingkok, stood quietly. Taoroinai, the Mother Goddess, looked at him, waiting for him to announce the ultimate verdict.

Atingkok thumped his staff and the hall almost exploded from the resonance. Everyone went quiet.

'It is decided. I will be a part of it. Existence is my doing and I shall be humbled by concerning with the mortals. Our Mother Goddess will also be there. I will offer my celestial eyes. The Mother Goddess will serve with all her seven forms as necessary. The rest of the empty slots could be filled by volunteering,' the eerie voice of the Father God resonated loud within the celestial hall.

Pakhangba almost raised his hand, but Atingkok cleared his throat and said, 'Except for my serpentine son, the rest of you will be eligible for the quest.'

'I shall admit that humans are never my favourite subject but to honour my father, I shall join the quest,' Marjing moved forward, his feathered headdress and dark garments decently covering his giant body.

'I shall allow,' Atingkok struck his staff again.

'With the presence of our Mother Goddess, my participation in the quest might not be of great use, but I shall request to take part in the quest,' Sampubi said, her smoky body materializing fast into a lady with striped human clothes and a feather headdress.

Atingkok pounded his staff as a sign of approval.

'Father Supreme, I would want to be a part of the quest, but since I have a son who is filled with youthful vigour and zeal, I would want to suggest him for the quest instead,' the god of the sky realm, Korou Awangba, said and nudged a young boy standing next to him.

'The half-breed with great promise for the future, I shall allow,' Atingkok said.

'It would be my utmost pleasure to join the pantheon for such a prestigious quest,' said the young boy, a handsome youth clad in bluish cloak and loincloth.

'Father, even if I am not allowed to return to the earth realm again, I would want my son to join the quest too—my second son who is still in the middle realm of humans,' Pakhangba begged. He genuflected in his human form; sympathy was easier to gain this way.

The Father God kept quiet for a while. All the gods seemed to stop breathing altogether. There was no sound inside the magnanimous hall except for the low hum coming from the celestial bodies.

'Mother Supreme, what will be your unbiased response to your son's desperation?' The Father God asked the woman beside him. She took a deep breath and relaxed her hands.

'We have created something far beyond our control and for that we are to pay the price for eternity. My beloved son did perform his task gloriously and yet he left behind a seed of an imprecise providence. To scale the outcome of such an existence, we shall let him be part of this call,' the Mother Goddess said with a hint of uneasiness, quite unusual for a great spirit. 'A being unknown even to the gods but with promising power,' she thought as she wondered about Pakhangba's illegitimate child in the middle realm.

'Another half-breed, but the one to hold the key to chaos and creation in the future, I shall allow,' Atingkok nodded. Pakhangba genuflected, visibly grateful.

'Only one spot remains,' Atingkok reminded and the hall burst into a murmuring, confusing chatter, most of the gods and goddesses wanting to join the quest.

'I shall choose the last one,' Atingkok raised his arm and silenced everyone.

'The creator of the Night,' Atingkok announced. Everyone seemed surprised. A quiet god with a pair of sleek bow and arrows walked forward. He looked timid, surprised and worried.

'Our Great Father Supreme, I am a god-slayer, regardless. How will I ever be worthy enough to join the formidable band of gods and goddesses for such an important task?' the timid god asked, looking at the Sun God who grunted.

'We, over the upper realm, entitled as great gods and goddesses, are mere observers of our own creation. Despite our faulty pride as the almighty, none of us might be able to thrive in the human realm once we incarnate. You, as a human-turned-god, would serve us all as a caring custodian on our quest when needed. Will you honour this task?'

'With utmost gratitude, Father,' Haotangla bowed low.

THE EYES OF ATINGKOK

*Y*oung Laiba sat quietly in a corner of the spacious kitchen, observing his mother as she prepared dinner. They usually ate long after nightfall, but after the event of yesterday his mother seemed determined not to let the kitchen fire break out in the ominous dark of the night.

'Laiba, come. Bring in your bowl,' his mother said with a gentle smile, looking satisfied with whatever she had prepared.

'Mother, it's been a day already. When will father and the villagers come back?'

'Soon dear, very soon,' she answered confidently, but Laiba could sense an undertone of despair. He could easily sense these things— despair, hopelessness, loneliness and the wave of panic that had been wafting through the breeze for the past few weeks. There was a sinister affair at wake.

'Love, come over. Dinner is going to be so good. Waahh! The smell,' she sing-songed as she fanned the steam from her earthen pot and sniffed excitedly, making Laiba giggle as he walked up to her with his bowl.

The food was good, as always: the fresh fish, tender and the vegetable stew, thick with seasonings. He always loved the way his mother prepared the best dish out of any ingredients. They both cleaned the vessels in no time, leaving them all shiny and spotless. Laiba walked out towards the backyard pond to wash his hands. The sun was already squeezed between the hills, burning red with heavy clouds that blazed. He dipped his hands into the cold water and gazed at their sugarcane field that extended endlessly towards the southern forest. His father and few of the villagers had gone through the field yesterday, chasing a menacing creature that had attacked a family on a full moon night. Laiba thought about the previous night again.

He was lying by his mother when he woke up, screaming terribly in a piercing tone that didn't sound like his own voice. His mother embraced him tightly and his father came running to their room, terrified.

'Laiba! Laiba! What happened? Did you have a bad dream again?' his father asked him, patting his bald head.

'Dear, are you alright?' His mother looked at him with concern.

'I am fine, but not them. Father, the house by the brook is in danger. I just saw a creature with long hands walking up towards their house. It said it will take away all the children inside,' Laiba spoke calmly. He was not at all afraid or disturbed by the vision in his dream, but both his parents looked at each other in horror. He felt glad that they were not the ones who saw the vision or they might have fainted at the gruesomeness.

Laiba, though just nine years old, didn't feel anxious about the dream. Nightmares were regular. He had grown up dealing with such displeasures ever since he could remember.

He was different, and for that, his village found it hard to accept him. However, as Laiba grew up, he realized that it was not just his

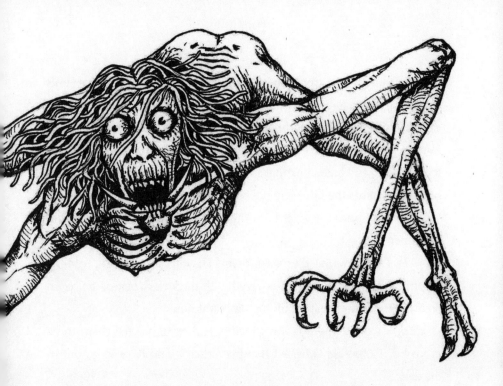

excessively pale skin and eyes that were unique but his whole self, more sensitive to unknown energy. He knew if it was going to rain or if someone was going to die or if someone was corrupted in mind. He could tell just by looking at a person. Apart from this, he could also sense an unusual dark aura that lingered in the depth of the forest at the far corner. No villagers would ever visit the forest as they believed that evil creatures dwelled within, but he knew what they merely believed were, in fact, very much real. He could sense ravenous, desperate and despicable creatures lurking in the darkness, doomed to scavenge on filth and decaying matter, as they were shielded, magically, away from the protected realm.

Laiba did not know why, this time in his dream, he saw a creature, an utterly disgusting one, with long greasy mane, sallow boggy eyes, huge brownish teeth or tusks and, most distinguishably, the front limbs that resembled human hands, only extensively long, and which seemed to grow as desired. Laiba saw in his dream, this creature extending its lengthy arms towards branches and hurling its body forward with greed and desire to haunt the first human it could find, and Laiba, instinctually, had a feeling that the creature was heading towards the house by the brook, their neighbour.

'Do you think it is what I am thinking?' His mother whispered to his father.

'Yes, I think we need to warn them.' His father grumbled, rubbing his thin face, which was half-covered with thick dark beard. 'Laiba, in your dream, is the creature on his way right now?'

'Yes, it's dark where it was moving. Father, please tell them to be prepared,' Laiba said, worried that his father would have to go out in the dark.

'Fine. I will go, but you both should stay inside the house, no matter what. I will return soon.' His father patted Laiba's head again and dashed out of the house, carrying his axe with him.

Laiba and his mother waited anxiously and it was almost dawn when they heard a shrieking cry right outside their field. Laiba jumped out of his bed and ran out, followed by his mother who cried, 'Laiba! No! Come back!'

But Laiba was already at the back door. He pushed the wooden flap open and saw the horrible creature from his dream running up with only one arm, and the other, severed and bleeding profusely. The creature ran towards their sugarcane field, followed by a group of villagers with their axes and knifes. Laiba saw his father leading the men with his blood-stained axe high up in the air. The creature managed to disappear within the dense sugarcane field, followed by his father and the other men, who chased after it without pause. Since then, none of them had come back!

Laiba snapped out of his memory of yesterday, returned to his present self and continued washing his hands at the pond. He splashed the water playfully, disturbing his pale image that was reflected on the water surface.

'Laiba, now come in if you are done washing your hands. It is getting dark out there.' His mother called out through the back door.

He stood up obediently, but paused when he heard the murmurs and footsteps coming from the sugarcane field. He looked around and saw his father emerging out of the dense maroon sticks, followed by the villagers.

'Father! What happened? Did you capture the creature?' Laiba cried out excitedly. He was pleased to see his father return unharmed.

'Laiba, go inside.' His father's stern voice slightly upset him, but Laiba didn't protest when he saw the villagers' gaze following him.

'Father is back, mother,' Laiba said dully as he entered the kitchen.

'What! When did…' She murmured nervously, but ran out and shut the back door.

Laiba could hear the murmurs and discussion between the villagers and his parents as he stood there, leaning his back on the bolted door.

'We managed to injure it significantly, but we can't just predict how many of them are there in the dark abyss. It has been so strange since the start of this week. Something is definitely not right!' One of the villagers whispered, but loud enough even for Laiba to hear.

'If not for you, my friend, I don't know what would have happened to my children. My youngest daughter must still be in pain and shock from the creature's grip. If you hadn't come in time and cut off its arm, she might have been captured by that awful creature,' another one spoke in a quivering voice.

'I am glad your family is safe now,' Laiba's father replied.

'A Khutsangbi dashing up into a house is a bold move and that was only talked of in old tales. How did they even gain the power to prowl here in the human realm? If one is capable, obviously other dark creatures must also be astir. This is a catastrophe!' another villager said a little louder.

'You don't need to jump to such a conclusion, brother. We need to learn about it in more detail. And to do that,' there was a short pause and the villager who was speaking, continued, we need your son.'

'No, I said already! Don't bring Laiba into any of this. He is just a child!' Laiba could hear his father yelling with a tremor in his voice.

'But he is the one with the gift...' the villager started to speak again, but Laiba's father interrupted with a loud sarcastic laugh.

'Hah! The gift! *Now* he is the miracle boy. Your saviour? I think it was just yesterday that you all tried to give him away at the shrine. He is my son and not communal property. I decide what he should do. He should live like a small boy of his age should, with his mother!' Laiba felt the fear in his father's voice. He had always been afraid. Laiba remembered clearly all the things his parents had gone through to keep him with them. There were always people who came to take him away because he was different and people were afraid and unsure of his presence. Forget about making friends, Laiba never even got to interact with any humans other than his parents.

Laiba walked away from the door and went towards his room, a small but neat chamber, lighted by a wooden torch in a corner. He jumped into his bed and lay still, thinking why the villagers thought it would be better if he helped. What could be done better with his help? All he could do was sense things. Laiba had no other superpowers, he was quite sure of that. He had tried to do stunts, but had never succeeded. All that he felt was involuntary—like most of his dreams, his visions and the voices in the air. The villagers must have expected him to do other amazing things, but he was sure there was nothing he could offer. His appearance was much more fascinating than his actual capability, and it always ended up with his parents struggling to keep unwanted attention at bay.

'My Lord,' Laiba suddenly heard a voice that did not belong to his immediate reality. He realized he was floating in the midst of a swirling smoke.

'Where am I?' Laiba demanded.

'It is time we reunite,' the voice whispered in his ears and a landscape appeared in front of him, like some display where he could see people and their lives. He saw a boy king being crowned on a throne and he recognized him, even though he had never seen him in his life before. Laiba knew him as an old acquaintance. The view changed and he was now looking at a group of seven people. All of them were gleaming and at the far corner stood an old man, elegant in his white garment, silver hair and beard, straight moustache dropping from the corners of his mouth. He was surprised to realize that the old man was himself. He didn't know how he knew it, but it was unmistakable. And next to him was a giant man with an intricate headdress of long feathers and gems. He was riding a winged horse and looked aggressive.

'My Lord, my other self in the human realm has just been awakened. And with it, your vision of me.' The man on the flying horse spoke.

Laiba had little idea what he was speaking of, but he nodded as he felt the man was speaking to him.

'Excuse me…' Laiba began to speak, but he stopped when his voice came out from the mouth of the old man with silver hair. It was absurd but somehow funny at the same time. Laiba grinned, looking at the old man who just said 'Excuse me' in a squeaky child's voice.

'My Lord, I shall provide you the route for your human self to find me,' the man on the flying horse said with a bow to the old man. The landscape again changed back to his house and it zoomed away slowly towards a village road and ran steadily along some snaking way until the central route was visible. The scene further magnified the central route until he saw the huge palace gate.

Somehow, Laiba could feel the urge to walk inside the gate. He immediately remembered that an important purpose was awaiting him at the palace.

'This is why I am here. I need to find the king,' Laiba murmured to himself. A memory appeared in his head of a desire he once had. It was not his present self who had the desire, but his old self before he became Laiba. The memory was of him planning to return to the human realm and reassemble the chosen guardians there. He had to find the serpent king's descendant and serve him there, he thought. Laiba was amazed at this vivid memory of a thought he had never had earlier in his life as Laiba. But he was oddly satisfied that he finally found the cause of his peculiarities.

Laiba opened his eyes and he saw his mother lying next to him. A good amount of time had passed, though he didn't remember falling asleep. It was already morning and he could hear the early birds chirruping. He stood up and tried to remember his dream from last night, and to his surprise, he remembered it all.

'Mother! I am leaving!' Laiba suddenly blurted out, making his mother spring up from the bed with terrified searching eyes.

'What dear? What is it this time?' His mother asked. His father also rushed in, just the way he had done the day before yesterday. He also asked, alarmed, 'Are you alright?'

'Yes, I am fine.' Laiba smiled and continued, 'But I need to find the king. Mother! Father! You were right! I am special!'

'Of course, you are special. You are our only son. But what do you mean you need to find the king?' His mother asked nervously.

'Mother, our realm might be in danger. Much worse than we anticipated, and to protect this realm, I have to meet the king. He asked me to find him and I found him. He is currently at the palace. I need to go to him. Mother! Father!' Laiba jumped up and down in delight and narrated to his parents the whole vision he had had. Somewhere, he had always longed for freedom, to meet people who wouldn't judge him for being himself and in the vision, he was called by an old friend. He was needed at the palace and he was to serve the Meidingu, the descendant of the serpent king, as an important man.

'Laiba, does this mean you have to go to the palace?' his mother asked with a smile, but there were tears building up in her eyes.

'Of course, he should go,' his father answered before Laiba could reply to his mother. 'He had better be in the palace than be scrutinized by the villagers here.'

'But…he is our only son!' his mother cried, burying her face in her palms. Laiba stood perplexed, looking at his weeping mother with guilt.

'Laiba, your mother is just being emotional because of your sudden decision, and you are just but nine years old! Yet you have to do what you need to. Don't worry about your mother, dear. Go to the palace if you have to. You have proven your capability more than once for me to trust your instincts.' His father spoke, evidently proud of him, but even he was clearly fighting back his tears.

'Father, Mother. I don't want to leave you alone, but...'

'Laiba, you don't have to bear the burden of leaving us. We love you and couldn't bear the thought of parting with you. So, we pretended not to recognize your true identity, but I think it is time we admit that your existence is meant for a greater purpose and we shouldn't stop you just because we are blessed enough to be your parents. It was such a great honour to be your father, even if for a short while. I think your mother here feels the same.' His father rubbed his tears away and kneeled before him to bow.

'Laiba, what your father says is right,' his mother also climbed out of bed and kneeled before him. Both his parents made a low bow, rubbed their foreheads on the cold floor, and when they raised their heads, their faces were agleam with tears.

'Do you want me to accompany you on the journey to the Central Kingdom?' His father asked as Laiba stood frozen in his spot. He couldn't find any words in response to his parents' inquiry. He had never seen them cry this way before.

'No, I...I shall travel alone,' Laiba said with a faint smile.

'As your mother, it is also my duty to make sure you accomplish what you came here to do,' his mother said with a genuine grin on her tearful face.

'Mother, Father...' Laiba whispered, smiling at both of them.

'Anyway, I think you will need some Sel to travel up to the Central Kingdom, I have heard it is very expensive there,' his father cleared his throat and stood up to retrieve his money pouch.

'And food, I shall prepare you some meals for your journey,' his mother also stood up, murmuring something about the ingredients she was going to use.

By noon, Laiba had packed all his belongings in a bundle and set out of his house with the little money his father gave him. Laiba knew his departure was painful for his parents, though they tried their best to be supportive of his decision. His mother asked numerous times if the king would accept his claim and she even revealed a small secret for Laiba to use as proof of his abilities, if the palace didn't believe him.

'Listen here, love,' his mother whispered as they embraced each other before Laiba's departure, 'if the people in the palace refuse to believe your vision and power, there is a way to shut their mouths instantly. I never told you this before, but I think it would be of great importance now. When you were a small baby, your father and I took you with us while we went to the forest and by mistake, we ran into a wild pig in the Kabow valley. We thought we had met our end, but you looked at the pig and when the pig rested its eyes on yours, he turned and walked away as calm as a turtle...'

After a bittersweet goodbye, Laiba took a wain to ride towards the Central Kingdom. The journey was smooth and relaxing—he sat on the rocking bamboo cart, leisurely feasting on the delicious meals that his mother had prepared, and enjoyed the pleasant hills and lakes that ran along the side of the road.

He finally entered the Central Kingdom at twilight. The streets were busy with people from all different regions. Laiba had to walk a lengthy

pavement to finally reach the palace gate, which was surrounded by well-armed guards, the large wooden bridge extending from the gate towards the palace island, surrounded by the brimming lake. It was late at night and the palace entrance was lit with several torches burning brightly to be seen even from miles away.

'Where are you heading, lad?' One of the guards inquried as Laiba approached the elegant wooden entrance. They didn't notice Laiba's unusual pale skin under his dark hooded shawl.

'I have come to meet the Meidingu,' Laiba replied pompously.

'Oh, child!' The guard replied with a kind smile and offered him some peanut-studded jaggery bars. 'You shouldn't be walking here around twilight. Go back to your parents, good boy.'

'I guess I have to go to the Kabow valley first,' Laiba sighed as he walked out of the palace gate.

THE TARANG LAIPAO

A flock of hornbills fluttered across the copper-glazed sky, high above the towering wooden chamber with a steep bamboo crown. There was smoke coming out of the several vents across the ridge, accompanied by the poignant hum of the priests and priestesses chanting their most important rites. They had been under strict conduct for the past few days and were performing the Tarang Laipao, the oracle of the cosmos.

The royal guards outside the wooden chamber shivered at the eerie choir tickling their skin even though they had been hearing it for a while now. The priests and priestesses were declaring a cataclysmic prediction. They were not accustomed to it yet, and could sense a maddening urge to run away from the compound and hide from whichever dark future was being prophesied and never return. But the king had given his orders to guard the royal shrine and for that, they had to endure the sickening smell of burnt black eggs, pine woods, crane feathers and many other things indistinguishable but equally foul. The chants got more intense as the darkness of the night engulfed the rest of the kingdom. The royal guards had been standing on duty for long and their legs wobbled while they stood. Few torches began to flicker at the far corner where the king's chamber was. Maids and servants rushed in and out, executing their chores, while the guards wished they could trade professions for a while. Honour and prestige all melted away when they could hear the apocalypse blaring in their ears, with disasters and nightmares being predicted. They looked up and saw the constellation of Khongcholnubi blinking, despite the despair below, and they prayed for hope and sought to know their purpose in life. The star-studded sky, though thousands of miles away, was the only sight that comforted them with a promise of a better tomorrow.

Meidingu Iwanthanba sat uncomfortably on his wooden throne inlaid with cotton and thin velvet, idly receiving the evening conduct. The feather-fly whiskers and cotton fans didn't help much on his sweaty face; there was a look of utter displeasure reflected in his young features, with his droopy eyes fixed on the floor and not on the colourful fruit baskets which were being offered by the servants. The cup in his hand was tilted, the contents about to spill, the flowers were held high towards his face, but he seemed to fail to pick up the rich aroma. Slender and lethargic, he looked like his spine was missing. With lineament that carried the refinement of his mother, the queen, combined with his father's darker complexion, silken locks under his laced headdress, a dark mole on his sharp chin, twitching fingers and pursed thin lips, he was distracted, the displeasure vivid on his exhausted face. The throne room with its usual gloom didn't help with the situation either. The layers of white *thakal* flags that hung from rectangular bamboo frames were the only items that brought serenity. The wooden walls were tiled with huge skulls of different wild catches, such as tigers, jaguars, bears and several mountain buffaloes. And underneath were the royal guards in their black attire, with their viciously long spearheads.

It was quite obvious that the king didn't notice, but his council of 10 ministers, Pongba Tara, sat facing each other on two straight rows of reed mats right beneath his spacious wooden dais. None of them spoke since the king didn't, but they all understood that the young king had not yet woken up. His innocence at a pleasurable age of 16 was marred by his destiny to the throne, but there was no pity to be spared for the boy king. They wanted to turn him into the great emperor as they always planned, at all costs. They couldn't let the death of the late king foil their ultimate dream to rule all the high mountains and the rich river basins.

It appeared that Meidingu Iwanthanba had decisively declined the truth in front of him. It seemed like only yesterday that he ran around the palace compound with little care about his life, safe from all blunders and not having even the slightest worry about the fate of his kingdom, a responsibility possibly resting on his young shoulders in the near future, but not yet. Without leaving much time to grieve or mourn, within a week, his father, the king, was dead, his mother had vanished (or was possibly kidnapped) and he had been crowned as the new King of Kanglei, the Meidingu. As a Meidingu, he was deemed to carry a mythological legacy of his great ancestor, the Serpent King, who founded the very kingdom of Kanglei. But, with chaos and innocence as his excuse, he didn't even start his training of kingship except that his ears had been pierced at midnight on the day before the coronation. He blindly followed the fervent head priest who ran around like someone possessed when the news of his father's death was announced by the ominous thumps of the royal drum on that peaceful summer morning.

His father's death was most unusual. When the news arrived for the first time, everybody refused to believe the sole witness of the tragedy, well until they found all the bodies. The king went out for his usual ride, hunting game in the southern forest with his troops, only to run into a baffling misfortune. The only survivor spoke of spotting an incredible creature, a deer with golden antlers and silver fur, which dashed within the dark wild. The king chased the deer deep into the forest until it jumped into a swamp nearby. Quite instinctively, the king and the rest of his huntsmen plunged into the same swamp following the creature, leaving only their wine bearer on the bank. The Yu bearer, the only living witness of the tragedy, tearfully narrated the whole incident to anyone who came to inquire:

'The deer lured us into the swamp. I felt it. It was an evil spirit in disguise. It lured us deep into the forest and into the swamp, and it walked through the fence as if the water was only knee deep, but when His Majesty and the rest lunged in, the swamp suddenly seemed as treacherous as the ocean, with tides and currents hurling them to the bottom. Oh...master, oh Meidingu, oh...'

The king and all the huntsmen drowned in the marsh and lost their lives on the spot. Their bodies were found days later at the bottom, carefully preserved under the thick layer of dirt. They all looked as if they were asleep when the soldiers unearthed them. The image of his father's dead body remained raw and sour in Meidingu Iwanthanba's mind. It was just two days ago that he had performed the final burial rites; the pale king, in his gold and silks, was lowered into the cavernous grave and showered first with flowers and then with red clay.

'Your Majesty, the head priest has arrived,' the guard announced from the doorway, bringing back the new boy king from his reverie. He nodded nervously and stirred in his seat.

An old stooped man in his late nineties walked in as slowly as he could, supported by his long cane, dressed in all white cotton— white headdress and a large white cotton cloak that dangled over his wrinkled arms. His silver beard with two short moustaches drooping from the corners of his mouth gave him the look of a wise prophet.

'Greetings to Our Majesty,' the old man bowed before the king.

'Welcome, Epu Maichou (the enlightened one),' Meidingu Iwanthanba replied, his disinterest obvious in his voice.

'Your grace, the Tarang Laipao ended this evening, and with it came several prophecies from the greater realm.' The old head priest paused for a moment, expecting a bit of response, but the boy king just blinked at him; so, he continued in a grim manner, 'It rendered greatly on the lost scissor, Your Majesty...'

'The scissor again! We are not here to discuss such myths,' one of the ministers replied.

'My royal minister, since when did we become unnecessarily valiant in the face of our infamous gods?' Epu Maichou, the head priest, answered with a smile.

'This is not about being against our gods or other funny enterprises of the priest's guild. We just lost our great king who has left his beloved son, our prince, to continue his legacy and to follow the path of the great empire he envisioned,' the minister retorted.

'Yes, I agree with Minister Nongthomba. We need to discuss more urgent and important matters like the marriage alliance with the Takhao kingdom. The Ahom princess is our only chance for our future endeavours...' Another minister spoke reverently, but the boy king interrupted,

'Does the Tarang Laipao say anything about my father's death?'

The old priest chanted some ancient proverb and Meidingu Iwanthanba raised his eyebrows, waiting for an explanation.

'Your Majesty, the oracle spoke of your succession to the throne as an event of the celestial order. The lost scissor of divine origin was prophesied to be restored only when the seven chosen guardians would unite. And for this to happen, the king, your father, was destined to die and you were to succeed the throne as the king.'

'So...so he died so that...isn't this murder? He was killed by fate for my destiny? What kind of destiny? How is that even possible?' the young Meidingu flared up.

'That is not for me to answer, Your Majesty. We humans merely live to serve the way of the greater realm. If it is to be this way, we stand with no possibility of carving out a different path, rather we anticipate the miracle and see how the prophecy unfolds.'

'No, wait. What do you mean by it is not for you to answer? You answer to your king, is it not? Who stole the magic scissor? Why did my father have to die? And why is nobody discussing my mother's disappearance?'

There was an uncomfortable stir among the ministers, but the old man didn't shift his watery eyes away from the boy king. He perceived the bitterness in the boy's tone. His mother, the queen, had not been genuinely loved in the palace since her arrival. Being a Khuman princess, she was only queen for the fear of her maiden house, the only clan capable of war against the Kanglei throne. The ministry hated her more for they couldn't bring themselves to trust the queen with the many Khuman emissaries that had been filling the palace since her arrival. The king respected his wife and they had less of a say, but now with the tragedy and her suspicious disappearance, the ministers were all out to openly criticize the lost queen of all foul deeds for which they so wanted to accuse her. There were indeed rumours flying about a possible murder of the late king by the Khuman, in conspiracy with the queen. There was also another rumour of the queen eloping with her close cousin from the Khuman clan, who was spotted regularly near the queen's quarters not so long before the incident. However much the old priest pitied the poor queen, he could not do much at the moment. He walked a little closer and began, 'Your majesty, it is a firm decree for a head priest to always provide an answer to the king.' He smiled weakly and then bowed to continue, 'The matter of your father, our late king's death and the unusual disappearance of your mother, the queen should be answered by the head priest...'

'So, tell me. What is happening? And I don't want complex words here. Just tell me in a way I can easily understand!' Meidingu Iwanthanba cried out. He had grown impatient with fragments of information and the old man who just kept on playing with words.

'As I said, it is not for me to answer that,' the old head priest licked his lips to suppress, possibly, a grin.

'Please! I need to know what is going on here! You are the head priest!' The teenage king was surprised by his own loud voice thundering across the throne chamber, all the ministers and the guards gawping at him in utter dismay.

'No, not anymore,' a sweet voice, giggly, responded to the king's uproar from the wooden doorway. All eyes immediately searched for the mysterious intervention. Meidingu Iwanthanba was taken aback and searched for the speaker at the entrance.

There he was, among the black-suited royal sentries, a small boy of eight or nine, with a tiny bald head and puny body, but wearing the sacred cloak of royal head priest over his inner white garment. The sight was so bizarre that none of the people inside the throne room could let out a word out of their mouths. The king sat frozen on his throne, his eyes on the mysterious boy who hopped towards him in a typical manner—he was unusually pale, with thick ashen lashes, and thin snowy eyebrows and striking eyes; one eye had a searing reddish yellow iris and the other, his left eye, a gleaming, calm, silvery gray. He hadn't seen such mismatched eye colour before. Only the old head priest turned and gave a sigh of recognition when he saw the young boy at the entrance.

'Ah, Maichou Laiba! You are here already. Please...welcome, welcome. His Majesty was about to be informed, but since you are here, why don't you introduce yourself?' The old priest gestured for Laiba to come closer.

Laiba, in his oversized white cloak with black floral and animal motif, strode up with a bright smile across his glowing chubby face. The inner white garment was proportionate to his small skinny body but the cloak was dragging on the floor as he skip-walked towards the king's throne above the pedestal.

'W-what, I mean who is he?' Meidingu Iwanthanba recollected himself and asked the old priest. But the small boy was already near his feet; so, he asked hesitantly, 'Who are you?'

Laiba had to repeat that he was the new Maichou several times for the king to process his statement and ultimately yell, 'WHAT? W-what is this? What kind of a joke is this?'

All the ministers bowed their heads when the king sprang up. The old priest gently gestured for the king to sit down and tried to explain, but the young king scolded, 'At this crucial and painful hour, Epu Maichou, do you think this form of practical joke is entertaining?'

'Your Majesty, our former head priest, Epu Maichou, is not joking, but telling you the truth. I came here to fulfil my destiny; the oracle of the cosmos, the Tarang Laipao also predicted so. I am here to serve you.' Laiba answered with a wide smile plastered across his blushing face.

'Alright! You speak terribly well for your age!' the king spoke after a moment of silence, glancing up and down at the tiny boy.

'Well, I was taught to tell you that, Your Majesty,' Laiba looked pleased with the comment.

'So, as I said, Your Majesty, Lord Laiba here is one of the guardians that the Tarang Laipao talked about. I was diverted earlier from narrating the whole prophecy to you. So, please listen carefully, for all the answers His Majesty seeks might be in it.' The old priest took a deep long breath and continued, 'As I said earlier, first it predicted for us the ominous future where we lost our grip to chaos. It presaged the disappearance of the *wayel kati*, the magical scissor of justice that guards our realm. But it did not foretell the complete decay of our realm, for the cosmos had already sent the chosen seven guardians to restore the *wayel kati* and bring back balance to the realms. The Tarang Laipao spoke of the missing *wayel kati* as being removed or stolen (very unlikely even in either cases),' the old man continued, 'and for the second part of the prophecy, it spoke of the seven chosen guardians. The first one is about you, Your Majesty. It talked of you. Your father's death was no accident but a fated one for you to step out of your disguise from an ordinary prince to that of the king of destiny.' The king fought his urge to intervene with several inquiries and nodded while the old priest continued, 'Your father's death served the purpose for your legitimacy as the chosen one, and I also believe his death could bear no more reasons than this.

Tragic, but necessary in the eyes of the cosmos. And the second one is right in front of you. The all-seeing eyes of Atingkok. Take a closer look at Maichou Laiba's eyes, Your Majesty.' The old priest made way for Laiba to walk up and Meidingu Iwanthanba nodded in response. The eyes were already something he found most bizarre. It even diverted the attention from the fact that the boy also had an excessively pale complexion.

'What is this?' the king whispered grimly.

'The eyes of Atingkok, the Supreme Father of the Universe, Your Majesty,' Laiba replied excitedly.

'Yes, the all-seeing eyes. The eyes that shine alternately in our sky as the sun and the moon. More baffling is that the cosmos decided to choose Maichou Laiba, our young friend here, to host such immense power.' The old man gave a gesture of slight bow towards Lord Laiba and continued, 'The prophecy mentioned the fruit of destiny, when instated on the laps of his rightful serpentine throne, the eyes of Atingkok will wake up from slumber and the bearer will find his way to his companion to serve the rest of the celestial guardians.'

'What?' the king asked, blinking in confusion.

'It means, when your father died, you became the one prophesied and with you on the throne, it triggered my eyes to show me my path. I was to serve you and be your advisor and help in assembling the remaining five members of the seven chosen celestial guardians,' Laiba spoke, his plumped lips fluttering as he recited the words like a poem he learned by heart. There was a deep silence in the throne hall again. The king dropped his jaw again. The ministers were fixed on their spot throughout the session like they were mere stone statues. The old man, the king and the strange young boy who claimed himself to be the head priest seemed too absorbed in their discussion, and quite obviously no one wanted to interrupt when the young king was yelling or stupefied most of the time. The silence lingered for a while until Meidingu Iwanthanba grunted out sarcastically,

'Hoiney! So, my father died or was killed by "the cosmos" (he made a dramatic emphasis for the space above his head with his arms) for me to rise up on this throne to fulfil my destiny and this boy here gained an incredible power out of my misfortune and came in search of me to offer some service. Very convincing. So, let me rephrase for convenience! There are more people like him to gather?'

'Yes, Your Majesty. The lost scissor of justice could only be restored when the seven chosen guardians unite.' The old priest answered.

'Do you seriously believe a child with some strange eyes could be that special? You are the head priest, Epu. He can't replace a wise and experienced man like you,' Meidingu Iwanthanba was furious when he spoke to the old priest.

'Umm…excuse me, Your Majesty, but I think I need to show you what convinced the former head priest that I wasn't lying,' Lord Laiba interrupted the king's murmur.

'Oh, can you? Go ahead then,' Meidingu Iwanthanba answered annoyingly.

Laiba bowed to the king, while continuing to smile, and walked away towards the exit. He nodded to the ministers on his way out, who only blinked at him with confusion writ large in their stares.

'Your Majesty, in troubled times like this, the only wise word I could suggest to you is to follow the path of the cosmos. They gave us this realm and we merely play along with their instruction. Destruction or creation is up to their whims and fancy. If we were to serve in a way, it would be much more glorious to acknowledge the charted destiny,' the old priest smiled at the sulking teen king.

'Epu Maichou, the reason why I asked you to perform the Tarang Laipao is to find the answers, not to freak ourselves out with more confusion and fear of some impending catastrophe! My mother vanished after my father's funeral rites and we all are yet to treat it as an adversity...' Meidingu Iwanthanba knew this subject was the most controversial, but he wanted to see the old man's reaction. He already knew that the ministers utterly despised his mother, but the learned Maichou wouldn't be someone clouded with vanity or suchlike.

'Your majesty, our Mother Queen is one so gentle and composed. She loved her family dearly and that is something we would dare not doubt. But her disappearance was one most unexplained and also not at all mentioned in the prophecy. Any further details if you so desire should be forthcoming from Lord Laiba and not me.'

Meidingu Iwanthanba didn't answer and continued to lay back over his throne. His thoughts raced back to the early morning when the ominous news of his father's death was announced in a low mournful hum. He was inside the horse shed, playing with his favourite white horse named Yangba. It was quite early for him to wake up and the sun was not out yet, but Yangba was more like a brother to him, easing the loneliness of being the only child in a huge palace. He usually spent more of his time in the horse shed than in his chamber.

Out of the far corner, the drum began to beat repeatedly—not a war alert, but something more awful and startling. He left his horse and ran out instantly, and on the edge of the queen's chamber, he saw his mother, the queen, covering her mouth with her hands and looking straight towards the southern forest. He remembered how his mother had fainted on the floor. He had run up to her in tears. She woke up hours later and refused to speak with anyone. Convinced that the sudden tragedy was too much for the queen, they left her undisturbed in her chamber. At the funeral, she was there, standing at the edge of the sacred lake, covered in black attire, stripped of all jewels and flowers from her long silky hair. Iwan saw his mother confused and lost in her own thoughts. She stood still, looking blankly up towards the sky. The next morning, she was nowhere to be found. It was hard to believe that their queen had just vanished and the guards had looked around the palace expecting to find her inside one of the shrines. When she didn't return to her chamber for the whole day, the ministry had issued a full-scale search for the queen throughout the kingdom; but no one found any clue to her whereabouts. The palace went into an abrupt turmoil of possible war or conflict. The Khumans came with their own accusations over the lost queen, probably not so loved as their daughter but more as a catalyst to their power hunt. The Kanglei Ministry was also ready to point towards the queen as the possible murderer of the late king and also an adulteress.

Young prince Iwan was so preoccupied with the abrupt chaos that neither the death of his father nor the disappearance of his mother ached him. He simply waited for the supposedly wise ministers to suggest how to break the tension in the palace which was also slowly spreading out into the kingdom. Iwan sat quietly in the middle of the council where all the ministers bellowed at each other. The rest of the events were all raucous and vague. He was asked to bathe at the sacred lake; he remembered its icy water, a new costume, receiving clan heads, accepting hill chiefs, piercing his ears, conducting rites, crowning, hosting guests, giving away rewards and titles, and before he knew it, he became the Meidingu. And just a week into his reign, he begged the priest's guild to perform the Tarang Laipao, one of the strongest forms of prognostication, hoping to find some answers to few of his greatest dilemmas. The Tarang Laipao, which went on for days, instead of providing answers to his worries, had him tangled with a huge load of riddles and a suspicious child with strange eyes claiming to be his advisor. He sighed and rubbed his forehead, wondering if the head priest was ridiculing him, as was almost everyone else in the palace, because of his age.

While Meidingu Iwanthanba sat drifting in his thoughts, Laiba walked in happily, with his typical skip-walk, towards him. He sat up straight and looked at Laiba's hands, but they were empty, and to his horror, something huge and heavy followed the little boy, not so far behind. Meidingu Iwanthanba let out a weak scream when he saw the furious face of a wild boar. All the ministers shivered in their seats; they dared not run out of the hall without the king's permission, but their faces made it all too obvious that they wanted to run for their dear lives. The old head priest grinned toothlessly.

'Your Majesty, may I introduce our adorable piggy…' Laiba began but the king let out a yelp.

'Piggy!? Isn't that the Bloody Boar from the Kabow valley?' Meidingu Iwanthanba exclaimed. Everybody recognized the enormous crimson boar with its vicious tusk that had been considered as the monster of Kabow—the wildest, most violent and gigantic. Many brave warriors had lost their lives trying to capture it or testing their strength in hunting games. The Kabow valley had been considered a suicidal vale because of the Bloody Boar's presence, for no creature had ever lived after encountering it. For such a creature

to stride leisurely inside the throne chamber filled with people was unimaginable. It snuffed out, and almost everyone present inside the hall jumped on their spots. Laiba seemed quite impressed.

'As I told you, Your Majesty, Laiba came well prepared to prove his worth. When he was denied meeting you by the palace guards, he went to the Kabow valley and brought this beast as tame as a kitten to demonstrate his ocular power. It responds only to his command and even allowed him to ride on his back,' the old priest spoke with a wide grin, looking admiringly at the mighty beast from time to time. It stood close to Laiba, wiggling its short tail like a loyal dog.

'My mother told me that I should catch this piggy if Your Majesty refused to believe me.' Laiba giggled, lightly patting his giant friend.

'Well, O…alright. This boar. Okay, I am convinced. So, what can your eyes do? What kind of help are you offering? Can you see where my mother is? Where the magic scissor is?'

Iwanthanba expected a miraculous answer, but the boy pouted his lips and refused to talk further unless he was fed. Regardless of his exploding annoyance, he had to nod. The small boy skip-walked away through the exit, followed by his colossal hog. All the ministers let out a sigh of relief. Some were wiping their sweat away from their forehead.

'So, Your Majesty,' one of the ministers immediately began, as if he had been desperately waiting to speak out, 'I am convinced that the young boy claiming to be our head priest has some tricks up his cloak, but that doesn't mean he should be given a post as prominent as the royal head priest.' A few of his fellow ministers nodded their heads vigorously.

'In fact, we cannot heed an oracle and decide over our grave political matters of urgent importance. This is no time for mysticism and suchlike. We are at the brink of war and the best way to save our kingdom is your marriage with our powerful ally. We need to secure our power and not waste our energy in some divinity that talks of a nonsensical lost magic item and heroes, like in fables,' another minister lectured.

'I couldn't agree more. The best and most important thing that Our Majesty needs to do is to prepare for the marriage,' another minister approved, looking at other members in his vicinity for endorsement.

'That will be more grounded in reality than tales and unpredictable divine orders. We are not even sure if this Wayel Kati exists for real. It was mentioned only in some ancient tales of how it brings Divine judgment and protection against the chaos. And if it really exists, who on earth would remove or steal such a magical item, let alone search for it or recover it,' another minister spoke assertively, giving a swift glance over the king to observe his response. Meidingu Iwanthanba turned his eyes towards the old priest who stood quietly stroking his long beard.

'I served the throne as loyal as the ministry did and our guild is the most revered of all for so many reasons. It was recorded in ancient scriptures that the Wayel Kati was kept inside the Central Palace to defend us from all dark entities, to protect our realm from chaos. If the celestial order is for our king to look for it, he might be destined to do it whether we like it or not,' Epu Maichou spoke ever so calmly, still stroking his beard, but thinking hard.

'We will defend the kingdom in case of any trouble, but the king shall not leave the palace to seek such a mysterious thing as the Wayel Kati without any preparation. We are talking about risking a nation. What if other kingdoms wage war upon us? What if our political condition gets even worse? We cannot throw him out there. We are here to protect him and this throne!'

'And that you can do it as long as the divine will permit,' the old priest smiled as the ministers' faces reddened, so disturbed with worldly troubles that they could probably explode, like a ripe pomegranate, anytime soon.

The young king pursed his lips, his ministers began to get louder, discussing and agreeing among themselves.

'Enough. My dear loyal ministers,' Meidingu Iwanthanba began softly, but Minister Famthakcha, the lanky one of all the brawny ministers interrupted, 'While we discuss the matter of real importance among ourselves, His Majesty shall rest and prepare for the evening ceremony.' The words were said with all due respect, but the weight of authority rested heavily over the young king's head. He stood up obediently and all the ministers bowed as he walked briskly out through the door. The old priest slowly followed behind him, leaving the ministers to murmur among themselves.

'Your Majesty, you should rest for now. Lord Laiba will be here with you shortly,' the old priest called out as Meidingu Iwanthanba strode up towards the scholar's guild, a large wooden edifice with triple-thatched roof surrounded by low shrubs in a wide circle that stood a few metres away from the throne hall. Meidingu Iwanthanba walked through the familiar dark passage absentmindedly. The compound was not well lit, but the elongated bamboo windows of the guild were shining brightly with flickering torches and they could hear the rumbling of several scholars inside.

'Your Majesty, you don't need to be present here at this moment. Maichou Laiba will visit your chamber at any hour and I can consult the scholars on your behalf. It would do you great to retire for a quick nap before dinner. You had been conducting duties all day,' the old priest finally caught up with the king, as he of all people knew how anxious the boy was.

'Oh Epu Maichou, I need to think quickly. You heard the ministers. You can sense the fear in their voices when they speak. I need to resolve all this before everything falls apart. I can't be a boy king. I need to do something. Something quick. I know they think something else about

41

my mother's disappearance. I need to find answers quickly. I need to think and act quickly.' The king murmured furiously, more to himself as he paced up and down in the guild's front lawn. The old man listened keenly, with gentle eyes looking over the boy with concern.

'Majesty, peace of mind is also essential rather than immediate decisions which could bring regrettable choices. I advise you now, as a friend, for you to return to your chamber and rest for a while,' the old priest offered his hand and Meidingu Iwanthanba put out his, after a moment of hesitation.

The old priest led him back to his compound through the dark passage, talking gently about the upcoming ceremonies and festivals as if the world was entirely ordinary, as ordinary as last week. Iwanthanba wished he could cry all his suffocation out, but decided not to. He bit his quivering lip and walked on quietly.

THE SEVEN GUARDIANS

Meidingu Iwanthanba felt like he had just fallen asleep when the royal *feida* (attendant) woke him up with the annoying conch hooting in the early morning hour; the *penna* musicians also came in following the morning hymn singer. Last night, he retreated to bed late after spending long hours with his horse. He rubbed his eyes and yawned sluggishly, contemplating the things he would be doing once he stepped out of his comfortable bed. The attendant stood up and offered him his morning clothes and brought in the wooden platter on which a cotton towel, water and a pot of cinnamon twigs were carefully arranged.

After his preliminary cleanse, he walked down towards the backyard pool and prepared for morning ceremonies—bathing with icy water over the stone basin, changing into an elegant royal attire (uncomfortable starchy garments made of silk and cotton fabric), paying homage to the shrines and finally taking a light meal of fruits and soft rice before he walked towards the throne chamber. He did all this half-asleep, half-uninterested, barely listening to the several instructors who securitized his every step to make sure he did everything correctly and enjoyed sympathies for being young and naive when he muddled a few of his duties.

Followed by a handful of attendants holding a giant white parasol, circular fans, feather fly whisk, water pitcher, wine pitchers and several other baskets, Meidingu Iwanthanba arranged his heavy feather headdress as he walked through the large wooden entrance. His ministers were already inside the courtroom and bowed when he passed them. He gave a nod to Maichou Laiba when he saw him comfortably seated on his futon near the throne. He looked quite out of place. Meidingu Iwanthanba was not at all used to seeing the head priest's seat occupied by a small and underdeveloped lad, instead of a wise old prophet.

'Your Majesty, what did you have for your morning meal today?' Laiba asked, peeling a banana to devour it completely in one go.

'Rice and... I don't think it concerns you,' Meidingu Iwanthanba murmured as he quickly settled on his throne and gestured at his ministers to raise their heads.

'Today is Thursday,' Laiba said after he forcefully swallowed the whole banana, 'you better get a bowl of beans. The scriptures say they bring energy and luck!'

'Everyone knows that. Now, allow me to address my ministers, high priest.' Meidingu Iwanthanba looked at his agitated ministers and delivered his greetings which they all returned in unison. Meidingu Iwanthanba announced, 'My beloved subjects, loyal servers and intelligent members, here with me is the new head priest. Maichou Laiba has proven yesterday that he has the eyes that have celestial powers, and unto him we shall rest our trust and expectations and seek spiritual guidance.'

It was obvious that he himself was uncomfortable to heed and depend on a nine-year-old boy, but he understood that he needed to make it formal after the prophecy. Moreover, he realized that he too seemed as incongruous as Laiba, in being a king. If his ministers were truly to respect him as the ruler, he needed them to accept and trust Laiba as the lord of royal prophets.

'Your Majesty, we have seen Maichou Laiba's unique...feature with our own eyes and that he has this blessed talent of whispering to wild animals, but that does not prove anything. The house of prophets, the priest's guild, is the most revered, just as our Maichou said yesterday. It shall not be under a young lad, some nine years old. And we also need to study more about the oracle if Your Majesty had decided to give it any importance at all.' One of the ministers interrupted, making him feel frustrated again, just as the day before. The ministers would not have dared interrupt if it had been his father speaking. With all the flowery praises and gentle pieces of advice, there were some of them that still looked at him as a mere prince. Meidingu Iwanthanba calmed himself to conceal his worries and replied,

'Yes, there shall be that too and other things, but him being the head priest is his foremost prophesied task. Our former head priest has already resigned as of yesterday and has rendered his blessings to our new lord of the prophets, his successor. And he shall be revered for his title and not for how he appears in our eyes.'

'A remarkable announcement, Your Majesty. I truly admire your faith in the prophecy.' Another minister, Minister Nongthomba, spoke, a man with a broad face, not at all proportional to his thinner frame. He continued, 'Which we all should. With the power and the allusion of the prophecy, we should decipher what our future beholds. With our Maichou Laiba's ocular power, we can trace where our queen has eloped.'

Meidingu Iwanthanba pursed his lips and forced a smile, but no words came out this time. His competence was under doubt and he knew it. The ministers were the backbone of the throne and when it was occupied by someone as young as himself, it was natural for them to be suffocating and overbearing if given an opportunity. Even as a king, he couldn't protect and defend his own mother's honour when insulted so openly. He was repeatedly failing at it. His eyes became moist.

'Your Majesty, deep apologies for the misfortune of our kingdom, but…' Minister Nongthonba began, but Meidingu Iwanthanba didn't let him finish and cried out, 'My mother could be in danger.' The anger was evident in his voice.

The ministers instantly spotted the young boy's protest.

'Your Majesty,' Minister Famthakcha, another one of the officious gang with layers of jewels and silk, spoke carefully, rubbing his fidgety hands, 'with all due honour, may I suggest that we refer to our new head priest for his aid in finding our lost queen? We can also marvel for what his eyes could reveal. It would be great if we could hasten the search; I certainly mean rescue, of course.'

Meidingu Iwanthanba replied after a moment, 'I think you are right.' Minister Famthakcha was the only one who was more of a thinker and the mildest in the whole of the ministry. The king decided to calm down and said, 'Maichou Laiba should provide us…' He turned towards the head priest's seat to speak, but found the boy fast asleep over the thick futon surrounded by huge cushions. At any other time, the sight might have been adorable, but with the present stress and serious worries, Meidingu Iwanthanba could hardly control himself.

'Wake him up!' He yelled at one of his attendants and turned his face away. He wished the cosmos had chosen their host wisely for entrusting such important powers.

'Your (with a big yawn) Maaaaajesty?' Laiba stretched his little legs from under his white garment and mooed.

'It's early morning! Do you think it is right for you to sleep here?' Meidingu Iwanthanba hissed, but made sure that his ministers didn't see his angry face.

'What, I just took a naaaaaaap,' Laiba let out another wide yawn and answered.

'Alright, now sit straight! I am about to address you here.' Meidingu Iwanthanba snapped as he turned back to his ministers to speak aloud,

'Here, Maichou Laiba, terribly exhausted but still with us to our advantage, my ministers and I have decided to request for your kind assessment over the mystery of our Queen's disappearance. With your immense ocular power, we couldn't help but have a strong expectation of learning the whereabouts of Her Majesty, which are currently unknown.'

'Yes?' Laiba asked, flashing an excited look, but also oblivious about what was just said.

'Use your power to look into my mother's disappearance. See if you could conjure up a vision about her whereabouts. Tell us if you can pick out signs of where she might be,' Meidingu Iwanthanba softly whispered back, nervously smiling at his ministers.

'I can only see things that the cosmos wants me to see, but I have not tried looking for the queen. When did she vanish?'

'Five days ago,' Meidingu Iwanthanba answered shortly.

'Five days…if done the star count… Alright…uh huh…squeeze squeeze…' Laiba closed his eyes, pressed both sides of his head with his tiny fingers and murmured funny words, a reason that made Meidingu Iwanthanba shudder in his seat. He couldn't help but worry about Laiba embarrassing him. If not impressed in a divine scale, revering an immature child could further complicate things and that would reflect a lot on his royal exercises.

'Your Majesty,' Laiba finally opened his eyes, and Meidingu Iwanthanba instinctively leaned over to his side, but he said, 'I see nothing.'

'What? W-What do you mean you see nothing?' Meidingu Iwanthanba stared searchingly at Laiba's dazzling eyes, ignoring the murmurs among his ministers.

'I told you I can only see what the cosmos wants me to see,' Laiba whispered apologetically.

'What!? You said your eyes are the most powerful thing. You should answer at least a basic inquiry such as my mother's whereabouts. You should...' He began whispering furiously, but the presence of the ministers didn't help him much, so he sighed, 'We need to talk in private. Let me deal with my ministers first.' He turned back and faced his ministers sitting in two perfect rows, a little away from his wide dais, 'My respected loyal ministers...'

'Your Majesty,' Minister Nongthomba interrupted the king effortlessly and the boy king gulped weakly without a protest. The minister continued, 'The divine powers are the most mysterious and we seldom know how to reciprocate justly, especially when they are vested on young people like yourself with less experience and worldly knowledge. I believe it would be in the best interests for all of us to carefully supervise Your Majesty over the Tarang Laipao.'

Supervise? The kingdom might get plagued or worse, and his minister is taking about authority again. Iwan faked a smile and wondered innocently, 'How so, minister?'

'Let young Lord Laiba and His Majesty spend more time in the scholar guild while we prepare our nation for possible calamities as the oracle predicted. You can rest assured. Study the oracle first. You need not hurry and go on the quest with less knowledge of what you would be looking for. Learn about the scissor first. Meanwhile, we, the Pongba Tara shall defend our realm in your honour.'

'What about my mother?' Iwan asked, with a frozen smile.

Minister Nongthomba was stunned for a moment, as the boy king threw in the uneasy question.

'We will continue the search for the queen until we find her safe and sound,' Minister Famthakcha came to the rescue. None of the ministers doubted the queen's involvement in the late king's mysterious death. They just didn't want the innocent boy king to get involved, but Iwan, though, meek and obedient, knew more than they thought he did. He rose from his throne and began,

'It is a profound delight to receive all of your valuable suggestions and advice. As you all have often recommended, we shall never overlook the virtue of patience. I would like to conclude our morning session here and ponder over several other problems, along with our reverent head priest, Lord Laiba, and decide a favourable verdict in solitude...'

Laiba rested his tiny bald head on his palm and looked at the teenage king reciting several intricate phrases to disperse the gathered ministers. The attendants and guards were conducting their usual obligations peacefully, but the 10 ministers sitting on the long parallel straw mats were murmuring uncomfortably, some unimpressed and some nervous as the king repeated dismissals from the hall, of course, in a flowery vocabulary. They stood up reluctantly, one after another, and bowed to the king as they walked out of the hall. When all the footsteps died down completely, Meidingu Iwanthanba turned his head swiftly towards Laiba and yelled,

'Now tell me! What do you mean by you see nothing?'

'I see nothing,' Laiba replied, rolling his eyes, intentionally avoiding the king's stare.

'Yes, I heard that. What does that mean?' Meidingu Iwanthanba retorted sharply.

'It means I see nothing—it's blank. The cosmos doesn't allow me to venture into your mother's path. I don't know why. I cannot see everything I want. I told you that already. I want to go home. You are mean!' Laiba protested, cheeks blushing deeply.

'Oh guardians!' Meidingu Iwanthanba rubbed his forehead vigorously and stood up from his throne to walk around the platform. Laiba sat on his futon, almost crying, and he covered his head with his cloak in protest.

'I don't know what to do. The ministers are already questioning my conduct and a head priest, who should be my divine support, being a cry-baby wouldn't help much. I am sorry if I am pushing you too much, but that's what I was supposed to do! To look up to you and heed your advice and soothsaying. They always do that. My father would never go to war if his head priest predicted bad omens. It was always like that. It is your duty to provide me divine answers when needed and guide me spiritually. But look at me, I am an underage Meidingu, already judged for my immaturity and, to make matters worse, I have to babysit a toddler in place of my powerful former head priest. I feel so defeated already! I don't know what to do and I hate not knowing what to do!'

'You are still mean!' Laiba yelled from under his hood.

'Well, forgive me but I'm telling you I can't help it. There are still so many things to do here. Rescue my mother, solve domestic crisis, resolve inter-clan conflicts, get married, conquer all of north and west... and now recruit five more incredible members to look for a lost scissor that we don't even know exists or prepare for some chaos—God knows what kind! The list goes on and I don't even know where to begin!'

'You already started. You asked for the Tarang Laipao. The prophecy is the divine clue you seek. You will send your best warriors to find your mother and meanwhile, we will gather our chosen guardians and head out for the quest before it is too late. What is it that makes you so confused? Are you frustrated with your ministers? But aren't you the king, small or big?' Laiba popped up his head and demanded, crossing his skinny arms around his inflated chest.

'Ye...I mean yes,' Meidingu Iwanthanba mumbled, embarrassed by the reasonable rebuke he received from his young companion. He realized he might be paranoid about the whole situation a bit too much instead of deciding on a reasonable action. He breathed slowly to calm himself and retreated to his throne. 'The Tarang Laipao—I still have to learn about the full prophecy. What does it say about the rest of the chosen guardians?' Meidingu Iwanthanba asked gently.

'The first one is you, and with your coronation comes my label and the third one is the golden egg,' Laiba said, pricking his nose as he wondered if he remembered correctly.

'Golden egg? Care to explain?'

'Golden egggggggg!' Laiba emphasized and rolled his eyes, 'Who else is referred to as a golden egg? Who delivers or is believed to deliver a golden egg other than one obvious divine entity?'

'Yes, I know. It is the serpent king and his offspring, but explain how this third chosen guardian is related to my great-great-...I don't know how many "great"-s...grandfather?'

'He has nothing to do with your great-grandfathers or your line of royal blood. Yes, you are a descendant of the serpent king, but the one

prophesied is the golden egg himself, coming forth to serve you in retrieving the scissor.'

'That,' Meidingu Iwanthanba blinked absently and wondered, 'that didn't...I mean, does that make any sense? The golden egg refers to my ancestor, long deceased, the serpent king's only son, who ruled as the second king in our kingdom a very long time ago. How is he coming back?'

'I told you that he is not related to you! He is not the ancient golden egg, your ancestor, but a new and presently alive one.'

'Hold on, is he just referred to as "the Golden Egg" like some kind of title?'

'No, he is the real deal. One with the divine blood of our serpent king coursing through his sacred veins.'

'Don't make me ask again or I will lose my mind. Explain in detail! Everything!' Meidingu Iwanthanba demanded impatiently.

'The serpent king must have somehow, I don't know how yet, managed to father another offspring, other than the one he left on this throne hundreds of years ago. A recent birth, it says, I forgot the exact words of the prophecy, but it says a new golden egg coming to help you,' said Laiba, imagining a funny image of a shiny egg rolling happily towards the palace. He sneaked a smile, but cleared his throat, when he saw the king narrowing his eyes, and cried, 'I am just nine. I cannot recite the whole prophecy. I said it in a way I understand. If you don't get it, then it is your problem. There is nothing to get confused over either. It spoke of another offspring of the serpent king who would be coming to help you. Don't look at me like that.'

'You ought to know more. It's your job to solve this puzzling prophecy. I told you, just fancy eyes wouldn't do!' The Meidingu snapped.

'Our first king is the one most mystical and is always shrouded in many mysteries and legends. Some said that he lived on for a millennia after the end of his human existence and some said he turned permanently into his divine form, the dragon-headed giant serpent. One thing is for sure, that he didn't die a human death, so another of his offspring being alive today is not so strange. Our former head priest also said so. Your slowness in digesting facts is not my problem,' Lord Laiba said dryly.

Meidingu Iwanthanba gave up and sighed, 'Alright, so the third one is the golden egg. We will discuss it later. Now tell me about the fourth one.'

'The prince of heaven and earth, motherless since infancy, regerminated entirely as a human to obey his celestial father, to serve as the chosen guardian, yet he seeks the one that was once lost.'

'Didn't you just say you are nine and can't remember the exact prophecy?' The king snapped.

'Yes, I just learned this part by heart to test your intellect. You are an idiot,' Laiba giggled and added playfully, 'Your Majesty.'

'I shall pretend that I'm not offended.' Meidingu Iwanthanba faked a smile and grunted out, 'Now, what does that mean?'

'An incarnation of the sky prince, Khoiriphaba, as known in the valley,' Laiba grinned when he saw the look of utter delight on the king's face as he uttered the name.

There was no need of further explanations since Meidingu Iwanthanba could comprehend the prophecy when the name was mentioned—Lord Khoiriphaba, of course, the prince of heaven and earth. His mother was a human princess who married the sky god, ruler of heaven. The tragic tale of Princess Tampha who fell in love with the sky god was one of Iwan's favourite bedtime stories. His mother would narrate the lovely tale until he fell asleep. A legend of two lovers crossing the forbidden boundary to be together. The tale was about a beautiful princess who met Lord Korou Awangba, the god of the sky disguised as a human. They instantly fell for each other, and Lord Korou was determined to marry Princess Tampha.

They were aware of the strict order against the marriage between gods and humans, but Princess Tampha chose to be with her beloved and vowed to marry the sky king and never set foot on earth. The married couple happily ascended up to be in their sky kingdom and lived happily for many years. In time, Queen Tampha gave birth to Prince Khoiriphaba, adding to the moments of happiness in their lives.

The story might be considered to have a happy ending if it had stopped here, but it continued and took a drastic turn. Due to misunderstood circumstances, Queen Tampha broke her vow once and returned to earth. Despite her husband's strict warning, she walked away from the golden ladder that led to heaven, and instantly it vanished into thin air. As per the legend of Queen Tampha, she was doomed to remain on earth forever, separated from her young son, and died grieving. The sky king shared the same grief. He condemned the humans for luring his wife into breaking her promise and showed his anger with thunders and lightning. Prince Khoriphaba was just a crawling baby when he lost his mother. There were stories of several gods and goddesses taking turns to take care of him when he'd cry and demand for his mother. This demigod, prince of heaven and earth, was believed to mature into one of the strongest divine lords, rising in status and being included in several important rites.

Meidingu Iwanthanba couldn't believe that such a powerful demigod would be joining his team, to protect his kingdom. He found himself excited to meet him, this manifestation of Lord Khoiriphaba. For him, it would be like meeting a celebrity of some sort. He admired the demigod deeply.

'So, now we have me, you, the egg and the prince of heaven and earth.' Meidingu Iwanthanba could hardly control his elated voice, 'He is really joining us right?'

'Yes, he was sent here to join us,' Lord Laiba said dully.

'So, how are we supposed to assemble?'

'Some will find us. Others, we need to go and convince.'

'Yes, there are more, right? So, what about the fifth one?'

'An archer.'

'An archer? What kind?'

'An archer, a sun-slayer. This one still needs to be reciprocated. We have so many well-versed archers here but a sun-slayer is the baffling part. I have no idea what it means. Our former head priest brought me few ancient texts, which he thinks might be helpful. I will look into them and tell you if I find more insights.'

'Then tell me about the sixth one, if you know anything.'

'A lady, it spoke of a maiden favoured by the Boulder Lord or the king of rocks or some sort,' Lord Laiba said doubtfully.

'It's going to be hard to prove the prophecy. I mean the Boulder Lord? Never heard of one. Any details other than that?' Meidingu Iwanthanba wondered.

'Seems like a girl with incredible strength. The prophecy suggested something about her being the Queen of the Hornbill Forest and someone who provides for and protects the northern mystic range.'

'Strong—sounds good. We need strong people and not people like you and me.'

'I disagree. I don't know about you, but I think I am really an important person. My parents said so,' Laiba said dryly, feeling offended by such a remark from Iwan.

'Hornbill Forest? But hornbills are in most forests. It might mean someone from the northern mystic ranges, but which clan?' Meidingu Iwanthanba mumbled, oblivious of Laiba's grumble. He turned towards Laiba after a moment and asked candidly, 'Anyway, what about the last one, the seventh one?'

'Most interesting and also the one who would be handling the scissor, once found; she is none other than our seventh guardian, the Supreme Goddess, Leimarel Sidabi. She incarnated herself to serve as the seventh chosen member.'

'The Supreme Goddess? For real? Can she do that?' Meidingu Iwanthanba widened his eyes and cried out.

'What do you mean by "Can she do that"? Of course, she can do that! She can do a lot of things. She is the ultimate Mother Goddess. She would be joining us shortly,' Lord Laiba answered lazily, scratching his bald head.

'The sooner they find their way here by themselves, the better,' Meidingu Iwanthanba said excitedly, 'But most importantly, we can relax a bit with the powerful demigod and the Supreme Goddess on our side. I think our squad might not be as bad as I imagined.'

'Hehe… Your Highness, don't let your ministers know this, but you are really an idiot,' Laiba grinned again.

'How so?' Meidingu Iwanthanba answered, not feeling insulted at all. It seemed like he had already accepted heeding the head priest, quite unconsciously, but was slowly becoming aware of Lord Laiba's exceptional ability of perception.

'We are all, I mean all the seven chosen guardians are manifestations of seven powerful gods and goddesses. You and I included. We have not been randomly selected with a dice.'

'Me and you? But look at us. You have at least fancy eyes, but me? I am just a boy king. Always frustrated and impatient. You don't seem so divine either, no offense, and you are also just a kid, though with a unique complexion and some fine eyes.'

'Do you think the cosmos just chose me randomly to host these powerful eyes? No, I am the supreme father god,' Laiba whispered, displaying his adorable smile, but somehow disturbed, now that Meidingu Iwanthanba had heard what he just said.

'You are what?!'

'Yes, I am the supreme lord. I am the great nothingness, the Atingkok.' Laiba sang with delight, 'The cosmos didn't grant me these eyes. These are *my* eyes. Pretty, right?'

'You are talking nonsense!' Meidingu Iwanthanba struggled to keep his face straight and argued, 'Then why did you say that your eyes can't see everything? Like you failed to look for my mother.'

'I, in my human appearance, am different from my original god form. My powers are limited here. All of us have the same trouble— you, the egg, the archer, the demigod, the warrior lady, our supreme goddess—are all powerful gods and goddesses, but we have little or no idea of our true forms since we vowed to serve the human realm as humans, before we came here. We cannot just run around using all of our super strong charms whenever we want. It would lead to chaos, against the holy law. We were to follow the way of the human realm as a sign of respect and for maintaining balance. That is why (you will understand later) some of us would be completely unaware of our real identity, just like yourself. One of the major tasks for me as the bearer of these eyes is to knock some sense to any guardian who begins to lose himself or herself in this human realm. Trust me, I have to deal with a lot of you who have already convinced themselves that they are "ordinary" or "just lucky" and will try to escape their destiny as the chosen one. Boring, no?'

'I didn't try to escape though. I believe the oracle. I want to save this realm!' Meidingu Iwanthanba said defensively and continued in a gloomy tone, 'It's just that I just can't imagine myself as something more than a helpless teenage prince whose father died and mother disappeared recently. If I am all special and godly, I might have done something. It is just ridiculous. I can't even trace my own mother.'

'That is the price we all paid to walk in the human realm, to experience those human qualities which make them so unique in the first place. It's a courtesy to share this very essence of living mortals,' Laiba said, prophetic, his golden and silver eyes gleaming calmly.

'So how do you know all this? Did your eyes allow it?' Meidingu Iwanthanba asked innocently.

'Know what? That I am the Atingkok?' Laiba grinned again, 'Hehe…my parents told me if I were a god, I would definitely be the most important one and when I received the sign, I could see all seven of us in our original forms, proving them right. Me, the Supreme Lord. Pretty neat. Wonder what my original self could do with these eyes. It must be one absurd power. Everything is me!'

'Alright, and to focus back to our main plan,' Meidingu Iwanthanba shook off the uncomfortable image of the Supreme God being a nine-year-old boy and spoke seriously, 'You mentioned that two of the guardians are already on their way here. Do you know when they will arrive?'

'The egg is still rolling, might take more time since he seems to live somewhere far, but our seventh guardian might be here tomorrow. I had a short vision yesterday. It showed her near our palace.' Laiba flashed an excited grin across his pale face, 'Oh, I can't wait to welcome her. She is the one I really want to meet.'

'Oh, why? Is she pretty?' Meidingu Iwanthanba asked mischievously.

'No, but she is my wife,' Laiba replied bluntly making Meidingu Iwanthanba almost choke on his own mockery.

'What? When did you even marry?'

'Like I said, you are a real idiot, Your Majesty. I said I am the Father God and she is the Mother Goddess. Now, do you get it? We were a couple in our divine forms. Your ministers were right. You need some serious schooling alright. Atingkok is everything but the whole existence of senses and meaning is hailed as the Mother Goddess. We both are one but dual in existence. This is sophisticated philosophy, perhaps. Don't the scholars always discuss and chant verses about this?' Laiba raised one of his snowy eyebrows.

'But to consider her your wife is still not right.'

'I didn't! The humans did. They think we are parent gods. The male and female mode of creation. So hypothetically, she is my wife!'

'Uh...whatever. So, she is on her way here, right?' Meidingu Iwanthanba asked calmly.

'Probably, but I don't get unnecessary visions. So, she might be already in the Central Kingdom by now. Note it.'

'Can you really recognize her immediately? She might look a lot different from her real form.'

'I can distinguish all of you with just your mere presence. And besides, I will be the one who claims our seventh guardian as the one being prophesied. She would desperately try to deny it since she has very little knowledge about anything other than cooking a pot of rice, and she is not as brave as her original self.'

'I hope you are prepared in case she refuses us,' Meidingu Iwanthanba said, struggling with the thought of the Supreme Goddess coming to his palace as an ordinary human with little to no knowledge of who she actually was.

'Yes, don't worry. I know my work,' Laiba said, brimming with confidence.

'Good, we should discuss the rest of the members after her arrival. Until then, you can try to decipher more information about the archer and the boulder lady. And I will work on my mother's search,' Meidingu Iwanthanba returned a quick bow as they both stirred in their seats.

'Whatever I do, I will do it after I feed my piggy. Boy, he must be hungry...' Laiba stood up and stretched as he walked out of the throne hall. 'Your Majesty, I shall take my leave.' Laiba made a low bow before he disappeared behind the wooden exit.

Meidingu Iwanthanba sunk back in his throne, breathing in deeply to calm his mind. His attendants came up to serve him drinks and fruits, but he waved them away and closed his eyes. The hall became quiet and empty; the guards and attendants became extra careful to not let even a slight sound escape while their king took a nap. Meidingu Iwanthanba was not asleep though. He had just closed his eyes, but his mind began to work faster now that he was resting alone. His mother... she must be somewhere and he wondered if she was safe.

THE WAKE OF TAOROINAI

On the night of Lamta Thangja, the first Saturday on the month of Lamta, the most ominous day, Phenmei was struggling to deliver her ninth child. The wet nurse, Mayoknabi, who came to help with the delivery, told her that this child would be no ordinary one and that she must patiently endure the pain, but Phenmei screamed, 'I care no more! Oh! Just take it out! I don't care. I want this to end soon! I better not die giving birth to babies who wouldn't even live longer than a week!'

The wet nurse struggled trying to give the job her undivided attention in spite of the dimly lit, suffocating old cottage that smelled of wood smoke, her tired face dripping with sweat, her hands feeling the slimy baby and the obnoxious mother screaming more than she should.

'Oh, here is the baby. I told you she will be a girl! Welcome my dear.' The wet nurse smiled down at the baby, as she skilfully cut the umbilical cord and carried it towards the bathtub containing warm water. Yes, the baby looked tiny and weak, but she was blinking intelligently and even seemed to smile at her, which the wet nurse assumed must be due to the dim torchlight playing some trick on her eyes.

'Oh, look at her. She didn't even cry. I never had a hunch this strong ever before. I know she is meant to do great things. Why don't you name her now? Have you thought of a name for the little one?' The wet nurse beamed over her shoulder.

'Nonsense!' Phenmei lay exhausted on her straw bed, 'We can celebrate only if she survives more than a month. That's what they do. They don't want me to be their mother. She will soon join her brothers and sisters.' The mother grunted out distastefully; her soul had turned sour after the bitter experiences of her eight previous children dying in her arms even before tasting a grain of rice.

'What a thing to say, dear.' The wet nurse's nose flared in annoyance, 'What did I tell you? She has come to stay. Phenmei, you must take a look at her. Here.' She brought the baby, now covered in a soft cotton blanket, and held it out towards the mother.

Phenmei refused to touch her, but lay her eyes for a moment on the alert baby and saw a pair of dark eyes much like her own, ogling around. She muttered, 'They all look the same.'

'At least give her a name for the Guardians' sake!'—the wet nurse sighed impatiently.

'Okay, okay,' Phenmei said, and answered immediately, 'Sana!' which means gold, an item she often thought about and that is how it always popped up in her head as she lived a life of utter misery.

'Sana,' the wet nurse muttered with a smile. 'Yes, it is a beautiful name. Do you like it dear?' she spoke softly to the baby who, to her great surprise, smiled at her again.

'Phenmei, she smiled. Ohh, good Guardians! I have never delivered a baby like her before. She is special. She is…' the wet nurse continued with her murmur and walked around the room, rocking the baby in her arms.

Phenmei wiped her black bushy hair away from her sweaty face and lay still. Her husband, Poinu had dozed off in the far corner on top of their wooden chest. He had, as always, made sure to celebrate the birth of a baby by drowning himself in a few litres of liquor and had been lying stoned throughout the labour and birth. Phenmei wished she was as sedated as her husband through the delivery.

Late at midnight, Poinu woke up finally, gaining consciousness, and looked around at their small cottage that could collapse any moment. There were several holes in the timber of the ceiling, the mud walls creaked, with several pots that were fermenting and had a pungent smell of fermented and smoked fish. His wife and possibly the newborn were sleeping in their only bed, a soft cotton mattress on top of layers of straw. The wet nurse was no longer present. She might have left, he thought. Poinu stood up and stretched himself after an uncomfortable and long nap on top of a wooden box. His head was still wobbly, but he wanted to go out of the house before his wife woke up. He shuddered at just the thought of hearing his wife's shrill voice cursing him for wasting money and being useless. He stood up and prowled towards the other side of the hut, where a small wooden chest lay, semi-concealed under a large fish net. His wife was bad at hiding anything, he thought to himself with a greedy smirk. He ruffled through the tangled net, making as little sound as he could and took it out. He opened it and, much to his delight, saw some tarnished coins inside. It was not much, but enough for him to be welcomed again at Wangleikol, the tavern.

'That is for this baby's birth ritual, you fool!' Phenmei grunted, breathing heavily, as she lifted her head from the bed to look at her husband.

Poinu almost jumped, but quickly recovered. Acting sober, he spoke assertively, 'Huh, another stupid birth ceremony, is it? Wasting money! Let me use it for a better purpose, instead of spending on a useless ceremony. That baby will die too.'

'Better purpose? Do you think rotting yourself in liquor all day with my hard-earned money is the most ideal goal in life? You useless scum!'

Poinu didn't have to stand and listen to his wife, especially when he had already got the money. He walked out of the house, leaving her screaming behind him.

Sana didn't have a birth ceremony since her mother didn't have the money or the will to welcome her in her life. She grew up wearing a pale cotton robe as her mother couldn't buy her anything. Her mother ensured that there were no items around the house after her previous baby's death. But, Sana absolutely survived her infancy and grew up into a healthy girl! She had thick long hair, now trimmed with layers of fringes as she turned 13—rich honey-kissed complexion, tinted plump lips and sparkly brown eyes. Even though her mother was not an affectionate companion, Sana learned to love her mother dearly, since she was all she had. They lived in an extreme corner of their hamlet where there was not even a single neighbour. She learned that long before her birth, her father was caught for robbery in a nearby village and since then, they were outcasts and lived as far as possible from the community.

'Sana! Eat your dinner before your father comes back,' Phenmei snapped at her daughter from the kitchen. 'That insolent baboon might come back tonight.'

'Yes mother. What is for dinner tonight?' Sana came running from the bedroom.

'Fish! We always have fish! Why do you have to ask every day?' Phenmei fumed, irritated at her daughter, as she passed her a plate filled with rice and watery stew.

Sana sat at the corner and ate without a word. She also didn't want to be awake when her father returned since it was always a disaster. Her father, a drunkard woodcutter, never really returned home unless he had money troubles, but her mother was not a wealthy lady who could leisurely sit in her house to dole out bags of coins. Her mother went to the market and sold fish and could barely meet even the basic needs. When her father returned home, it only meant one thing—a night with her mother shrieking and cursing while her father broke things and physically fought with her mother, looking for something of value in the house.

Sana took her plate and walked out towards the backyard to wash the dishes and clean her feet. She tried to be done with it quickly in the dark, not wanting to spend more time in the bushy wilderness that stretched next to the small muddy pond. Thousands of fireflies were flashing here and there, accompanied by the loud noises of insects and bullfrogs. She left the chorus of the marshland to retreat early into her bed.

Sana had just closed her eyes when she heard the front door open with a bang. She jumped on her bed and sat straight. It was her father—drunk out of his wits and yelling incoherently. She covered her head with a thick blanket and closed her eyes tight. The usual uproar began while the world was asleep and her parents were close to killing each other. More noises of crashes, heavy thuds, screams, curses and cries seemed to go on endlessly. Sana could feel her teeth chattering on their own and she curled her frozen toes in fear when she heard her name being mentioned amid the furious caterwauling. And true to her horror, she could hear footsteps rushing up to the bedroom.

'Sana! Come out!' her father yelled as he walked in, wobbling.

She climbed out of her bed and stood shivering in front of her father. Her mother also ran in and forcefully pushed her father aside.

'Don't you dare talk to her! You dog!' Phenmei clutched her husband's untidy hair and pulled with all her might.

Even though Poinu was drunk, he skilfully twisted his wife's hands and freed himself from her clutches. Phenmei screamed some more, as her hands got twisted at an odd angle. With tears streaming down her face, Sana kept running around, calling out to her father and to her mother to stop their violent clash. But both were oblivious to the desperate calls from their daughter.

Poinu finally managed to give a hard blow to his wife's head that sent her twirling on the other side of the wall. She fell on the ground and sat still, groaning in pain. 'Come, we need to go!' He yelled at his trembling daughter and dragged her out of the room and towards the front door.

'Father! Where are we going?' She cried out, struggling to stay behind, looking back repeatedly at her mother who was unconscious now.

'Just walk, child!' Her father yelled, fanning her face with his putrid breath. She wrinkled her nose and resolved not to speak a word and just follow him, wherever he took her. It was not the first time she had undergone such terrifying trips with her father. Once when she was just six years old, he took her with him and asked her to pretend to be sick so that he could ask his friend for some money. She was young at the time and was not even aware of what her father was doing. All Sana could remember was that her father took her to a huge well-maintained cottage and introduced her to a family. While her father was busy explaining a non-existent sickness that Sana supposedly had, she walked around the house to admire the riches inside the home—a huge fish casket dangling from the ceiling, rows of dried corns, mushrooms and meats, metal wares and fine crafts made of cane. She came across a small room where a girl was sitting alone in a cane chair. Sana approached her and to her disbelief, she saw half her face covered with a heinous form of leprosy.

'This sickness shall go. You shall be cured,' Sana slowly lifted the scarf and placed her soft palm over the girl's infected face, quite involuntarily. Much to her surprise, Sana watched in awe as her finger slowly rubbed away all the blistered skin, revealing soft and fair skin just like the uninfected side.

'What did you do?' the girl cried out, standing up as she felt her face with her fingers. She ran towards the corner where there was a small mirror and let out a cry of delight when she saw her face. It was no longer half raw with skin that was filled with pus. She now had a whole beautiful face.

The rest of the events were unclear and Sana remembered wishing she had never gone into the girl's room. Her father received a good amount of money for curing the daughter, but instead of feeling good about it, Sana realized that she had made a big mistake. After that incident, Poinu took his daughter to village gatherings and openly claimed that Sana possessed mystic qualities and had the ability to cure gruesome diseases. Desperate people with various types of illnesses came to Sana and her father asked her to cure them, but she couldn't as she didn't feel the same way she did for the girl. All she saw was greed, hatred, corruption and envy. It actually frightened her enough to make her faint seeing the depravities all around. Sana had to endure long days of punishment from her father for embarrassing him in front of all the people. He used to ransack the house, asking her mother to pay for his disappointment, asking for money to refund all that he took from the sick people, promising to cure them. Her mother had to sell two of her fermenting pitchers to settle the matter, but since that day, neither of her parents seemed to forgive her for the blunder.

Sana quietly followed her father in the darkness, the bitter memories playing on her mind. For hours, they seemed to walk, but slowly she could see the faint torchlight flickering at the far edge of the wood. She was shivering from head to toe, partly from the chilly night air and partly from the unknown that awaited her.

'Father, I am scared.' Sana sobbed and looked around desperately, but everything was pitch-black except for the flickering light ahead.

'Shudup, wer hea. Yol be stayin hea fom t'day,' her father rumbled, dragging her vigorously through the coarse lane.

'Stay? I don't want to stay here! I want to go back home!' Sana protested but her father didn't stop and she had no choice but to still follow him. An old bamboo hut, lighted by a single burning torch, came into view and on the side of the hut was a sign that said something and under it were numerous carved images of gods and goddesses feasting.

'What is this place? Father, please take me home.' Sana tried again, but her father acted like he was deaf and went straight inside the hut. It was a room filled with wooden chairs, futons, reed mats, straw seats and thick timber tables.

'Tam'ba! Tam'ba!' Her father called out roughly, peeking through a small wooden door at the far corner of the hut. After a few moments, a light flickered on the inside and the heavy door was opened by a heavyset man with a long bushy beard. He was not so tall, had a significant belly, blunt nose and small narrow eyes.

'Poinu! What the hell are you doing at this hour?' Tam'ba spoke rubbing his sleepy eyes.

'Wellll...., I wan yoh't kep'er,' Poinu spoke uneasily.

'Keep her? What has gone into your rotten head! Poinu! Isn't she your daughter, you donkey!' Tam'ba roared. Sana wiped her tears away and stood closer to Tam'ba than to her father.

'I've no Sel, friend!' Poinu yelled and dropped face down on the floor.

Sana stood with a blank look on her face, looking at her unconscious father and then at Tam'ba, who stood looking at her father with evident disgust.

'I thought you just enjoyed my liquor but you are neck deep in filth. What a foul creature! You fool!' Tam'ba murmured.

'What was your name again?' Tam'ba asked Sana gently, with an apologetic smile.

'Sana,' she replied and bowed.

'Did you have your dinner, Sana dear? I got some cold meat, but I can reheat if you would like some,' Tam'ba asked as he walked towards the door.

'I already had my supper. Thank you for your kindness, Uncle,' Sana replied timidly.

'Oh, well then.' Tam'ba hovered around his door awkwardly, but took a chair nearby, 'Well then, you can have a seat here. Sorry dear, but you will have to wait for your father to get up before you can return home.'

Sana sat down on a futon nearby, resting her face on her knees.

Uncle Tam'ba sat quietly, perhaps thinking for ways to comfort her, smiling at her awkwardly from time to time. Sana innocently asked if she could stay. It came out as a bit of surprise for both. As a child charmed by curiosity, she never knew she would want an escape.

Tam'ba laughed and suggested her that she should be spending her time running around, playing. Uncle Tam'ba found it hard to believe when she revealed that she was never allowed to leave her house. He seemed to feel pity and consoled her that she could stay as long as she liked, suggesting that a tavern could also be a place to learn, as it was a room hosting various people from different regions. Sana accepted the offer and he led her inside the cottage to arrange a room for her stay.

Sana opened her eyes and was lost for a moment when she found herself curled up on a velvet futon, in the middle of a small room filled with wine barrels and other stock of earthen jars. Vertical beams of dusty sunlight casted down from the vents near the roof. It barely lit the room, but was enough to make Sana remember why she was there. She stood up hastily, rolled up the futon and placed it in the corner. Hearing the faint chattering of people somewhere in the front, she chose to skulk out to find the backdoor. She realized that the tavern house was much bigger than she had anticipated. There were several more rooms for storage, raw meats dangling in a few of them, rice sacks in some, water pitchers of significant sizes and small dark cabinets for storage that smelled strongly of pungent wine. She finally reached the backdoor and pushed it open. It swung out easily, revealing a refreshing view of a bamboo forest right across the backyard, congested, the long papery leaves susurrating. Several birds also cooed from within, but were concealed safely by the impenetrable giant tubes. The backyard pond was clear, sparking under the morning sun, some wild chickens ran here and there, crocking as they plucked out juicy herbs by the side of the pond. She walked down the narrow bamboo wharf. Sana washed her face with the refreshing icy water, careful not to wet her dull white bodice. She wished she could just swim around the tempting water, but refrained herself when she heard heavy footsteps, probably of Uncle Tam'ba.

'There you are, lass! I was a bit worried when I didn't find you in the room,' Tam'ba said when he saw Sana returning from the pond. 'Your father is up and good, but I told him you could stay here so he's about to leave now. Come, dear. Say goodbye to him and send good words for your mother, so she does not worry.' Tam'ba gestured Sana to follow him.

Sana quietly followed, walking back into the cottage and towards the front hall where she first met Uncle Tam'ba the other night. She could already hear the mumblings, but when Tam'ba opened the small wooden door, a confusing chatter of people immediately burst out from the hall. Sana stooped shyly and took a peek first. She shivered when she saw many people, sitting around in groups having food and wine. They were all talking, with no clue as to who was listening, and Sana saw her father dangling from a high bamboo stool at the far corner.

'Father, I think Uncle Tam'ba already told you.' Sana whispered to her father.

'Yes, stay. Earn some money. You wouldn't die, if you have survived till this day,' her father sounded sober but distracted, his hands drumming at the edge of his chair, gulping and ogling at people who drank from their tumblers.

'Please tell mother that I am fine and that…'

'I ain't talking to that devil! Now go and do what your Uncle Tam'ba tells you to do. Don't be stupid and ruin my name again.'

'Alright, I thought you were leaving. So, I came to say goodbye.'

'I leave when I want. You go do your thing, child,' her father grumbled and turned away towards the blank wall. Sana walked cautiously through the crowd and stood beside Tam'ba, who was busy pouring several bamboo cups with foaming milky rice wine.

'Uncle, father told me to help you,' Sana said, rubbing her hands with her cotton dress.

'Oh, you dear lass, you don't have to do anything tedious,' Uncle Tam'ba said looking up at Sana, 'but you can help me with these tumblers. Take these over there, yes, to those musicians. You see those drum bags, right? There. Take these and serve them on their table.'

Sana took the drinks to the allotted table where a group of male drummers, four of them, were chatting. They didn't see the drinks being served and carried on with the gossips. It seemed like one of their friends had disappeared after he had met a woman. They felt betrayed and were accosting him for choosing a lover over friendship. Sana didn't pry further and left.

However, it became a curious case for Sana as the musicians visited the tavern again with the same story. They now seemed to have lost another friend in the same manner. Every visit became similar.

A few more days passed and she began to notice that there were just two musicians out of the five who visited the tavern regularly.

'Phew! Hope he reaches his home safely,' Uncle Tam'ba murmured after helping a client and turned to the last customers present, the two musicians still seated at the corner. They had been there all day, but their wine cups were still half full. 'Ah, Master Kharam and Master Tarao, where are the others? They already left?' Uncle Tam'ba asked and Sana stood curiously to know their answer. She had been covertly worried for their distress, as yet unknown to her.

'No, it's just the two of us today. All three of them might not be joining us from now,' said Master Kharam, a sound of melancholy evident in his words.

'Is it so? What happened? I have never seen the five of you separated ever since I opened this tavern. Is my wine not as good now, Master Kharam?' Uncle Tam'ba asked, taking a tumbler of wine from Sana's hand and sniffing.

'No, no! It is not your drink.' Master Kharam spoke with a tired smile, 'It's my friends who are getting busier by the day. Time changes people, I guess.'

'Not me. I thought of forgiving them, but now all the three are acting the same way. I somehow felt I shouldn't. It hurts, you know. You can't just disappear from your friends' lives just because you found the love of your life or whatever. They are not young boys to be this mad about a woman,' said Master Tarao, his muscular arms resting on the cane table.

'Woman! Is it Master Tarao?' Uncle Tam'ba said with an apologetic smile, 'I know a thing or two about women. Some are so exceptionally good with how to woo men that they change them.'

'But we can't blame the lovely creatures, can we? It is those idiots who value ephemeral beauty over their friends. I will make sure they regret ignoring us just because they were lucky enough to run into some pretty faces.' Master Tarao cried angrily and stood up to leave, 'Come Etao Kharam, you better not be like them. It is just us two now. Those three will surely regret not saying a word to us.'

'No way. You know I love my drum more than anything,' Master Kharam stood up and followed his friend out of the tavern hall, 'We shall take our leave, Tam'ba.' The two musicians smiled sadly and walked away, murmuring something to each other.

'It is a bit strange. They have always been together since I have known them. Hmm, women,' Uncle Tam'ba sighed and turned to Sana who had already finished cleaning the floor, 'Oh dear, sorry. Let me help you with the tables. You should go and wash yourself for dinner. We will have fermented bamboo stew and some chickens.'

It was another humid day at the tavern. Sana prepared the usual items to serve the early customers. There were not many people early in the morning except for the travellers. They were not regular visitors and just sat around, counting their coins or checking pamphlets.

Out of nowhere, a man burst into the tavern and Sana looked up, half expecting to see her father but was relieved when she saw the familiar face of the musician whom she had served a drink just yesterday, Master Tarao.

'Master Tarao, so early today. Can I get you anything?' Sana asked, bowing her head out of courtesy.

'No thank you, little child, but can you get me your uncle? I need to talk to him. Tell him it's urgent,' Master Tarao ruffled his long silky hair with his thick fingers and paced up and down the hall looking distracted and worried.

'Please have a seat. I will get uncle right away.' Sana ran towards the backyard and called Uncle Tam'ba, who was quick to follow her.

'Master Tarao! What is it?' Uncle Tam'ba asked as soon as he sat down next to the brawny musician. Sana also sat near them, having nothing much else to do.

'Something is wrong, Tam'ba,' Master Tarao said, pushing his hair away from his sweaty face.

'Yes? Tell me, what can I do for you?'

'I don't know what you can do, but I thought I need to speak about this to someone without making myself sound like an idiot. My friends, I think something is not right about the disappearance of my friends. I am not jealous or anything, but something is definitely not right.'

'Where are they?'

'That is what I am trying to figure out. I went to their house and none of them were home or had been home for the past few days. Even Kharam. I walked him to his house last night, but today his family told me that he went out to meet someone around midnight. He never leaves home that late. So, I began to worry and thought of asking my other friends, but none of them were home. Their families have no idea where they went and they started asking me about them instead. I also went to our musicians' guild, but nobody saw them there either.' Master Tarao spoke nervously and buried his terrified face in his palms.

'They must be somewhere then. They can't just disappear, can they? Have you checked the women's houses that your friends usually talked about? Maybe they are with them,' Uncle Tam'ba suggested hopefully.

'I don't know any of them. None of them talked about who they meet or from where their ladies are. Those fools just talked about them being beautiful and attractive. The rest might be with their ladies, but I am more worried about Kharam. He never goes out, never late at night,' he said.

'Master Tarao, why don't you calm yourself a bit here? You can come and sit at my backyard to relax for a while and then we can think of something. You look worried sick right now. Come, more customers will be here soon. You need to rest in some quiet for a while. Come to my backyard,' Uncle Tam'ba stood up and tried to help Master Tarao to get up, but he sat still, not moving a muscle, casting his eyes absently ahead. 'Master Tarao? Are you alright? Can you please get up?' Uncle Tam'ba asked, bending his head towards Master Tarao's face. He didn't answer, but flashed a wild smile at the space in front of him.

'Master Tarao, please go to the backyard with uncle,' Sana spoke gently and went closer to the musician to help him up, pulling his arm from the other side.

'...I can't forget her.' Master Tarao faintly whispered.

'Forget who? Did you say something, Master Tarao?' Uncle Tam'ba asked confusingly.

'Yes, what a lovely face. Oh, my dear love. She told me to meet her by the forest,' Master Tarao spoke again, this time more clearly and passionately, grinning with his face blushing deeply.

'Who? Master Tarao? Can you please get up? I think you need to rest.' Uncle Tam'ba said, now looking anxiously at the musician who was muttering away.

'My love...she told me to meet her by the woods. Oh...she is calling me. Oh, princess, my lady, she is calling me...' Master Tarao groaned and giggled.

'Okay, Master Tarao, you need to get in right now,' Uncle Tam'ba yelled, looking around nervously.

Sana grabbed the musician's hand and tried to pull him up, but stopped when she saw a strange blotch on his wrist. 'What is this?' she muttered and looked closer at the veiny scar. It was like an imprint of fingers, four skinny lines on the upper wrist and one small line on the lower part, but the strange thing was that it was not just an imprint from a grab but a deeply burnt one, violet veins bulging out on the red fleshy strips where the mark ran deep. 'Uncle, look here. Master Tarao's hand seems injured,' she whispered.

'What? Where?' Uncle Tam'ba looked from the other side and examined the wrist which she held up to examine.

'There. Looks like an imprint of fingers, but it seems rather like a painful burn. Isn't it?' Sana said, cringing as she imagined the horrible pain he must have felt when he received it.

'What dear?' Uncle Tam'ba looked around the wrist, unimpressed and said, 'It seems alright. His arm is alright. Did you imagine something? He sure is talking a lot of nonsense that even I am getting a bit confused here'—he murmured tiredly, but Sana couldn't believe that her uncle couldn't see such an obvious scar on the pale wrist of the musician. She looked at it again and it was unmistakably there, becoming more and more distinct.

Sana had to ignore it anyway and help her uncle drag the mumbling musician towards the backyard instead. Master Tarao kept struggling to run away.

'Emaiiii…wait, Master Tarao. Where do you think you are going? You have to stay here. Sit down, sit down.' Uncle Tam'ba forcefully made Master Tarao sit on a nearby wooden bench. 'Sana, you look after him; don't let him go anywhere. He is not himself. I will go and get some help. Please look after him while I am gone.' Uncle Tam'ba then turned towards the others and asked them to resume their tasks.

Sana stood by Master Tarao's side and gently talked to him, but he didn't seem to hear what she was saying, murmuring desperately that he needed to walk away.

'Where do you want to go, Master Tarao?' Sana asked nervously.

'I am on my way, love. Please wait for me. I am on my way…' Master Tarao whispered, struggling to free himself from Sana's grip and to walk away towards the bamboo forest.

'Who called you? What happened to your arm?'

'…Yes, my dear beloved. I love you more than anything…' Master Tarao became much more agitated and jumped up, and Sana stood up, terrified. She tried to force him to sit down, but stopped her struggle when she heard an eerie cry.

Laaaaaaooooooooooooooooo…

It came from the bamboo forest nearby. She turned around and, to her horror, saw something approaching from within the crowded bamboo forest—a person or a person-like something; with long glossy filaments drifting mid-air, resembling long hair wafted on a windy day; white acorn face with a thin line that cut across where the mouth should have been; two large gelatinous eyes, pure black and no pupils, filled up half the face; and it had no distinct nose. The creature walked upright like a human and was wrapped in a translucent white cover over its sticky figure, just like a regular sarong and cloak, but one thing that sent a deep chill down Sana's spine was the creature's hand that stretched out, pointing its slender fingers at Master Tarao as a gesture for him to follow. The fingers were like twigs, dark, skinny and slender, exactly like the hand imprint on Master Tarao's wrist. Sana looked around at the wine makers near her, but to her surprise, none of them seemed to be aware of the strange presence within the bamboo forest.

Master Tarao finally freed himself from Sana's grip and ran inside the dense forest as if his life depended on it. Sana screamed for help, but no one even looked up. She had no choice but to follow the musician to make sure he was all right.

Sana squeezed herself within the bamboo rattans and followed Master Tarao who slithered easily between the little spaces, almost like drifting towards the creature who kept on gesturing to him to come forward.

'Master Tarao! Stop! Please!' Sana screamed, her fear surpassed by the desperate need to keep Master Tarao safe. She really didn't want her uncle to be disappointed.

'Eeeeeemmmmmaaaaaaaa...' a long screeching sound came out of the creature's mouth that opened like a cloth being torn, its eyes seemingly on Sana for a swift moment.

Sana had an instinctual feeling that the creature was intolerably disgusted by her presence and was angry that Master Tarao didn't come alone. She couldn't move further, both her feet having frozen from fear. The creature began to flicker like a torch and kept appearing and disappearing alternatively in and out between the dark bamboo groves, screeching ominously with contempt. Master Tarao, mourned like he couldn't breathe and stretched out his hands hungrily at the creature that seemed to drift away further every time it reappeared.

It was all dark and unrecognizably cold inside the forest, so much so that Sana was no longer sure if she was still right outside the backyard on a warm sunny morning, the rustling sound of bamboo leaves somehow deafening. She could feel her eyes leaking and her breaths becoming heavier, but with the little courage she had, she called out again for Master Tarao. He was a little ahead of her but crawling on the rugged floor, spiky bamboo shoots stabbing on his hands and knees, his clothes getting soiled and tattered, constantly groaning but struggling forward. The creature was going farther away and Sana somehow felt like it was terrified of something. She didn't understand the noises it made, but it was a clear sign of disapproval. The more the creature wailed in contempt, the more it reassured Sana that she wouldn't be in danger and she walked a bit closer. Finally, she reached where Master Tarao was crawling, and instinctively, she grabbed his wrist where the mark was burning hot and bloody. She closed her eyes and a familiar chant came to her mind, 'Release...my minions of the dark abyss...release...'

Sana didn't understand a single word that she muttered, but she somehow knew what it meant. She looked down on Master Tarao's wrist and saw the scar boiling up into a scarlet bubble and vapourizing, slowly disappearing as if washed by water. With the scar gone, Master Tarao had stopped groaning and passed out flat on the floor, right at her feet.

'Master Tarao! Can you hear me?' Sana cried out, but he didn't answer and lay still. She checked his pulse and was relieved that he was still alive. Sana looked up and realized the creature was nowhere to be seen and that the forest was not as dark and ominous as it was a moment ago. She stood up, gaining little courage after the incident and decided to ensure that the creature was really gone for good. She moved a few steps deeper within the bamboo staffs and was relieved that the creature was no longer hovering around.

'Sana! Master Tarao...'

Sana almost screamed with happiness when she heard Uncle Tam'ba's loud voice thundering across the forest. She heard footsteps and after a few moments, Uncle Tam'ba appeared followed by a handful of people with long sticks and clubs.

'Good Guardians! Sana! Are you alright? What happened?' Uncle Tam'ba ran up to Sana.

'I am fine, uncle. But Master Tarao didn't seem so well. We need to help him.' Sana pointed at Master Tarao who lay still, stiff as a log.

Uncle Tam'ba asked his companions to carry Master Tarao and they all walked out of the congested bamboo forest with much difficulty. Sana narrated the whole incident to her uncle and he listened attentively to every detail, looking worried and terrified. They reached the backyard and Sana was shocked to learn that it was already dusk! She thought that they had been inside the grove for just a few moments, but time seemed to have passed without her knowledge.

'Sana, whatever you just told me, I do believe because you both were gone for the entire day and I have been searching the area repeatedly. It just seemed like you both just appeared out of nowhere. These are not ordinary circumstances and I have a strong feeling that the rest of Master Tarao's friends are also in a similar danger,' Uncle Tam'ba whispered at Sana while other people were busy nursing Master Tarao, who was still unconscious.

Sana covered her mouth with her hand when she realized what her uncle just said. Indeed, Master Tarao came searching for his friends in the early hours of the morning and he had been telling them that they too had mysteriously disappeared, claiming to have found their lovers. From what Master Tarao did in the morning, Sana could understand her uncle's assertion. She looked back at the bamboo forest and, to her surprise, heard one last familiar shriek. The creature's call that somehow resembled the word 'Mother'.

Sana gestured at Uncle Tamba towards the voice and he nodded as if he understood what she meant. He immediately called his fellow friends and went towards the direction. It took just a few moments for them to return with the demented musicians dangling on their shoulders, flailing as if wanting to escape back into the forest. Sana asked her uncle to leave the musicians inside the backyard cottage. While the crowd was busy, trying to refresh themselves with drinks and snacks after the eventful day, Sana secretly sneaked inside the cottage and used the same charm she had used on Master Tarao. All of them fell unconscious at her feet.

She finally let out a breath of relief and sat down on the floor, exhausted, leaning her back on the wall.

'Sana, is everything alright?' Uncle Tam'ba whispered and entered as quietly as possible, but stood perplexed when he saw all the four musicians lying unconscious on their spots. 'You...you... They look exhausted, but free from the madness. Sana, are you alright?'

'Yes, uncle. And they will be fine too,' Sana said with a tired smile.

Uncle Tam'ba walked into the room and sat beside Sana, looking nervously at the musicians lying in front of them.

'Sana, can I ask...I mean...you don't have to tell me if you don't want to, but how did you do this?'

'I don't know, uncle. But this is not the first time I have done something like this. I don't understand exactly what had happened to the musicians, but they seemed possessed. All of them had been marked. I told you in the morning, right? I saw a strange mark on Master Tarao's wrist, but I don't know why you couldn't see it. When I was with him inside the bamboo grove, I sort of knew how to remove the mark. I...I started speaking in some strange language. I know this doesn't make any sense, but I think it was my gut telling me to do things. I think I have a strange gut.' Sana looked at her hands, soft and small.

'Hmm, I think it is a lot more than just gut if you were able to notice a mark made by Helloi,' Uncle Tam'ba spoke weakly.

'Helloi? I saw a creature today...is that it?' Sana widened her eyes and asked her uncle in awe.

'I desperately wish I am wrong, but this type of madness can only happen when spirited away by a Helloi. The baffling part is that no human can see a Helloi except a bewitched man,' Uncle Tam'ba said grimly.

'What! But I saw the mark and I saw the creature. It looks like human but...' Sana blurted out but Uncle Tam'ba winced like he was in pain and interrupted her.

'Keep it to yourself, child. I am sorry, but I don't want to know what a Helloi really looks like. They always take the form of the most beautiful lady as desired by the one whom they mark, and they only mark men. They are creatures who dwell deep in the forest, but as we can see here, they have done a terrible deed to our people. I am really surprised that you could actually see one of them and can even rescue their victims.'

'One of them? Are there more of th...those?' Sana asked, gulping down at the absurd information.

'Seven. Helloi is a band of seven spirits, the seven sisters. But what disturbed me the most was how they boldly took five men as their victims. It only happened in dark ancient times. We were supposed to be protected from them as long as we lived a virtuous life within this sacred land, or so the legends once said.'

'Maybe they were corrupted,' Sana said but looked apologetically at the unconscious musicians.

'Helloi don't hunt only those who are corrupted and spare the ones who aren't. They were once docile spirits, but have now turned into fetid creatures of the dark that would feast on any man they can find. Helloi existed in some old tales and we were supposed to be protected by a powerful magic. But it is not the case at the moment, is it? I think we might be in a lot more trouble now, knowing that one just vanished from my backyard.' Uncle Tam'ba grinned but there was a deep fear in his voice.

'I hope they don't come back and hurt more people,' Sana whispered, half-heartedly. She could not shake off the feeling of danger looming around.

'But more importantly, Sana. About your peculiarity...' Uncle Tam'ba said after a moment of silence.

'Yes?' Sana sat straight, staring at her uncle who smiled kindly.

'You said something about speaking an unknown language.'

'Yes, I felt like I talked with the Helloi, somehow, speaking a language...'

'You need to travel, lass!' Uncle Tam'ba jumped up.

'What? Where? Why?'

Uncle Tam'ba was quite convinced that Sana needed to travel towards the Central Palace and learn about her gift from the royal shaman. She was supposed to travel as a participant in the royal wine ceremony. It took her hours until she decided to travel, finally realizing that her unknown intuition needed some answers.

That night, Tam'ba dragged Poinu out of his chair and pinned him up against the wall and gave his orders to him. Poinu was terrified that his friend was desperate for him to accompany his daughter to the palace. Poinu yelled, 'Alright! Alright!' and freed himself. He saw his daughter standing timidly at the corner and for the first time, he felt a bit embarrassed because someone else treated her better than he ever did. He mentally decided to impress his daughter a little, for a change, during the journey.

Sana went back to her home and met her mother who came running out of the house and immediately locked her up, an act of defending her girl from her husband. Sana had to make a lengthy speech about where she had been for the past few days and how kind her father's friend was and the supposed service she had to perform for the tavern master and all other tiny details to her mother until she finally agreed to let her go. But it was not her speech that changed her mind but her father who brought a small tattered bag of coins and tossed it to Sana as an allowance for her stay during the 'yu' ceremony in the palace. Sana's mother, not even in her wildest dreams, thought she would witness such a moment. With the father finally coming back sober to offer her daughter a trip to the Central Kingdom, Phenmei could not say much about the change. She never really considered herself any better than her husband as far as Sana was concerned, and thought it was for the better that their daughter was now moving on her own path in life.

Pongba Tara

Meidingu Iwanthanba didn't say anything to the group of soldiers who returned from their assignment, greatly disappointed that there was still no news about his mother. He had expected at least a clue, a tiny detail about the queen but they didn't bring him anything even after searching for one whole day.

'Please retire for today and continue tomorrow,' Meidingu Iwanthanba gave a reluctant nod and dismissed them.

The soldiers gladly hustled away, leaving him to sulk alone with his horse in front of the shed. He suddenly realized it was already late afternoon and Laiba didn't even visit him after their brief meeting during the morning ceremony.

'Yangba, that kid, I need to go to him. I am sorry that we can't spend time together for long these days. Please do eat your fodder well. Alright?' Iwan rubbed his horse's nose gently and whispered lovingly in its ear, 'I promise I will ride you out at the inner field tomorrow. We will play all evening. I promise.'

Yangba seemed to nod, rubbing its head on Iwan's shoulder.

Iwan pursed his lips and ran out towards the newly erected chamber at the far corner near the palace shrine, the place allotted for the new head priest. Just as he entered the small compound, he could hear Laiba's giggle from the backyard. Meidingu Iwanthanba barged inside

the earthen hut and then went straight towards the backdoor. He saw Laiba playing with his giant wild boar at the backyard pitch, rubbing the beast's belly like that of a cat.

'Having a good time, aren't you?' Meidingu Iwanthanba thundered, but Laiba didn't even look up and continued playing with his beast. 'Lord Laiba, I think we need to do more important things here,' he said, struggling to keep his calm.

'Yes, and we will,' Laiba said, but was not sure if he was answering Meidingu Iwanthanba or just mumbling to his giant pet.

'We will do, sure. But what? You said one of the guardians is coming but I don't see anybody coming for the past two days and all we do is just wait here, doing nothing. You know I hate doing nothing!'

'I said what I saw. She will come when she comes. Your frustration is quite unnecessary,' Laiba replied, annoyed.

'Unnecessary? We need more of those powerful guardians to help convince the ministry if we want to go for the quest and save the realm!'

'Yes, we need to do that. So, shall we go and wait at the gate?'

'I am a king, you little twig. I can't wait for anybody at the gate! When is she coming?'

Laiba was smirking when he felt a sudden wave of goosebumps, his eyes pulsating for a moment.

'She is here...' he muttered.

'Where?!' Meidingu Iwanthanba jumped up and looked around.

'Not here, idi… I mean Your Majesty. Maybe almost at the gate now. Still not welcoming a supreme deity because you are a human king?' Laiba walked out of the chamber and washed his hands in the nearby pond.

'No, changed my mind. I am going to seek her blessings.'

Meidingu Iwanthanba absent-mindedly fixed his headdress and followed Laiba, who skip-walked out of his small hut and onto the long passage towards the western gate. They passed several people who bowed and began to follow, but Meidingu Iwanthanba gestured for them to leave. He was more than anxious to meet this particular chosen guardian for she was hypothetically the Supreme Goddess. Iwan didn't speak of it, but he wondered how he should behave towards the lady. He now knew that Laiba was the Supreme God, but he had been exposed to him as a boy before he learnt about the fact and was used to seeing him as ordinary. It was different with the anticipated visitor. He had been curious for the past two days since Laiba had mentioned her possible arrival. The more he thought about her, the more nervous he grew.

'Maichou Laiba, are you sure she is coming now?' Meidingu Iwanthanba asked anxiously.

'You are supposed to trust me, remember?' Laiba said plainly, walking straight ahead towards the large wooden gate at the far end, the wide moat visible as they approached the wooden bridge.

'I trust you, but...okay,' Meidingu Iwanthanba gulped and bowed back at the guards who kneeled when they saw him walking up along with the head priest.

Laiba stood still at the edge of the bridge and looked out at the other end where several people passed by, the noise of the Central Market lingering far beyond. A few people walked inside the palace, but not the one he anticipated. He saw the Meidingu rubbing his hands and pacing up and down anxiously, but ignored him. He knew the king was most impatient. Nothing really calmed him for long.

After long hours of waiting, Laiba finally noticed a peculiar visitor crossing the bridge. It was a girl and a grown man, carrying a wine jar each. He let out a smile and nudged the Meidingu and said in a whisper, 'Your Majesty, she is here. I don't know who she brought with her but that girl over there, yes, she is the one. One of our guardians, Leimarel Sidabi, our Mother Supreme.'

'What! Where? Oh, there!' Meidingu Iwanthanba arranged his shoulder scarf and his long feathery headdress, his hands moving rapidly for no particular reason. He saw the girl approaching—a young lady, with smooth cinnamon skin, long, lustrous hair falling free behind her, well-trimmed fringe, slender body and wearing a plain white cotton bodice and a dull red phanek. She clutched her pitcher and looked like she was on edge herself, shifting the container from one hand to the other, staring at him and Laiba with suspicion. The man who came with her didn't pay much attention and quietly led her through the bridge, ignoring the guards who slowly gathered around Meidingu Iwanthanba in defence.

'Please stand aside, my dedicated royal sentries, and escort the guest over there towards me,' Meidingu Iwanthanba spoke gently, maintaining his stiff monotonous voice when he ordered. The guards bowed respectfully and walked towards the bridge to conduct their duty. Iwan saw the look of confusion and fear on the faces of the two guests as the royal guards slowly encircled them. They seemed to enquire, but also obediently followed them towards the Meidingu.

"We just came for the wine ceremony. We didn't cause any trouble. My daughter…' The man pleaded, looking around at the guards and then at Meidingu Iwanthanba and Laiba for an explanation, his eyes flashing with fright. The young girl didn't say anything but stood still. She seemed amazed by Laiba's unusual appearance.

'Hail Your Majesty, the king, our great sovereign, lord of the seven realms and protector of the nine mystic ranges,' the guard blared, bowing stiffly at Iwan who was busy scrutinizing the daughter.

'The king? Oh, good Guardians!' The man gawped at Meidingu Iwanthanba for a while, but immediately dropped on his knees and pulled the girl, whispering loudly, 'Sana! Bow before your king! His Majesty is right in front of us! Sana, kneel right now!'

'You don't have to, my lady,' Meidingu Iwanthanba almost yelled. He wouldn't want the Supreme Goddess to kneel in front of him. And quite untimely, Laiba giggled loudly, making Iwan wish he could drown him in the pond nearby.

The man and the girl stared at him in disbelief, not moving a muscle but expecting an explanation for his unusual remark. Even the guards gawked at the girl and then at him.

'Pleased to welcome you to the palace, most esteemed lady. I, Meidingu Iwanthanba, and my faithful companion Maichou Laiba, the royal head priest, has been waiting earnestly for your arrival.' Meidingu Iwanthanba bowed before the girl and she retreated unsteadily.

'Forgive me, Your Majesty, but I think you have mistaken my daughter for someone else. We came here to conduct a simple ceremony at the royal shrine. Please bless us with the opportunity to participate in the ceremony,' the man spoke meekly, pressing his forehead on the floor and extending both his arms towards Meidingu Iwanthanba's feet.

'Daughter? Oh, so you are the father. May I know your name, father?' Laiba asked in a professional voice, rubbing his chin as if in deep thought.

'My name is Poinu. And she is my only daughter, Sana,' as Poinu said that, he gestured for his daughter to kneel.

'Sana? Beautiful name, befitting for our lady,' Laiba grinned playfully, looking at the stunned people around him, the Meidingu, the guards, the father and the girl who dropped her jaw long time ago without remembering to close it.

'I think you are mistaken, great lord. We just came for...' Poinu began but Laiba interrupted,

'Yes, for the Wanglei ceremony, but I am not mistaken, Father Poinu. Your daughter—we have really been waiting for her. Our Meidingu, here, nearly killed me with his impatience over the past two days. Why didn't you send her here sooner?'

Speechless and petrified, Poinu looked at the small boy as white as a cotton ball, who gazed back at him with his strange eyes, oddly mismatched and sparkling.

'Is my daughter...what about my daughter?' Poinu whimpered, his body shivering as the Meidingu and the head priest looked at his daughter like she was some special guest.

'Father Poinu, we have been waiting for Sana's arrival. She is of great importance to us and her arrival at the palace is our utmost providence. I will do my best, everything in my power, to treat your daughter exceedingly well, as well as she deserves, during her stay here,' Meidingu Iwanthanba said before Laiba could answer, so he nodded in agreement.

'Excuse me,' Sana spoke for the first time since her arrival in a soft whisper, 'I don't understand...'

'We will explain later, once we get inside, Lady Sana. I will explain everything myself if you want me to, but it is true that we have been anticipating your arrival for quite a long time now. Please come.' Meidingu Iwanthanba bowed at Sana again.

Poinu slowly got up and looked at the teenage king and then at the small white boy. Things made very little sense, but he was sure of one thing—that his daughter was an important guest to the Meidingu.

Poinu didn't waste his time in turning the event into a bargain, quickly summarizing a list of things he needed the king to pay him so that he could allow his daughter to stay in the palace. Sana looked upset, returned her small money pouch to her father without a word and left quietly with the royal guards who took her towards some guest chamber. Poinu ignored her and, instead, narrated a long tale of his misery, which was quite fruitful as the Meidingu accepted all his needs, and he walked away with four carts, full of rice sacks, wine, salt caskets and metal presents when he finally left the palace at twilight.

Meidingu Iwanthanba was more than relieved to send the father away who kept on extending his needs, emphasizing his decision to take away Lady Sana as one most devastating for the family that somehow seemed to depend a lot on the young girl.

'One strange father, alright. He didn't even bid his farewell to his beloved daughter,' Iwan wondered aloud as Poinu vanished from the palace gate.

'I don't know that but he left and fortunately without his daughter, who is our main priority! We finally have one more of the guardians with us and I don't really care about anything much besides. Just four more to go and then we can do our thing,' Laiba said, laughing for no particular reason.

'Yes, Lady Sana. What do we tell her?' Meidingu Iwanthanba asked feeling suddenly tensed as they approached the wooden cottage where two black sentries stood guard at the entrance.

'We tell her the truth,' Laiba answered matter-of-factly and surged ahead.

'Yes, the truth. That is what got me worried. She will go mad if we pour out the prophecy. We need to carefully divulge our plans to her, so we do not confuse her too much,' Meidingu Iwanthanba stopped Laiba from entering the cottage.

'What? Come on. Everything will be fine. I am here,' Laiba shook his hand away and entered the cottage. Lady Sana instantly stood up from where she was sitting on a polished bamboo chair in the middle of the empty hall.

'A very pleasant evening, Lady Sana,' Meidingu Iwanthanba said with a light bow and Laiba also followed his gesture. 'I hope you would allow us to explain the circumstances. Very peculiar but of great importance.' Lady Sana seemed too distracted by Laiba and his non-stop grins to hear what the Meidingu just said. She did not reply; her eyes remained glued at the small, incredibly pale boy with dazzlingly deviant eyes.

'As I was saying, Lady Sana,' Meidingu Iwanthanba tried again forcing a smile as he picked his words, taking utmost care not to startle the already-lost-looking lady, 'I was recently crowned as the new Meidingu and many tragedies have befallen my family. In order to find some answers, I instigated the oracle. It didn't provide answers to my personal problems, but did shed some light about our realm and foretold great calamities, but what is hopeful is that it spoke of seven chosen guardians who would save our realm by restoring a significant divine tool called "Wayel Kati", the scissor of justice, which was stolen or lost from its original safekeeping here. Lord Laiba here and I are each one among the seven guardians and so are you. That is why we knew you would be coming (all glory to Lord Laiba's ocular power, of course). You are one of the seven chosen guardians.'

'Yes, Your Majesty?' Lady Sana enquired, bemused.

'I said you are one of the chosen guardians, Lady Sana. You are to work with us in restoring the scissor of justice.'

'Chosen who?' Sana asked grimly, already anticipating something ominous, 'Do you know about me? My intuitions, weird ones?'

'Yes,' Meidingu Iwanthanba looked at Laiba for some help, but the pale boy kept grinning. Annoyed, he decided to handle the talk alone. He repeated again, 'Yes, we know exactly who you are. You are here to work with us. This may sound strange right now, but we will tell you everything so that you can gradually take it all in. Even I got confused the first time I got into this.'

'As long as His Majesty will give me some answer about my peculiarity, I will do anything to help you, if I could, that is,' Sana spoke shyly with a weak smile. She didn't notice before, but the young king's pricky nose and the dark mole on his chin was glossing with sweat. He looked more nervous than her and could feel the all too common sensation of panic that comforted her in this otherwise odd discussion.

'Wait. I will tell her...' Laiba pushed Meidingu Iwanthanba aside and moved closer to Lady Sana and whispered, 'You are my wife.'

'Your what?' Sana gaped. 'Please don't tell me, I am supposed to marry this small child,' she cried out at Iwan, alarmed. Sana remembered a talk in the tavern about young children being married off to spiritual people or a deity for some religious reasons. She cringed in horror.

'What? Marry? No! Not at all,' Iwan answered hastily, he turned at Laiba and shouted angrily, 'You little...you are making things more confusing.'

Sana tried to walk out of the door. She could no longer trust the royal lunatics and she was the one who faltered easily.

'No, No!' Meidingu Iwanthanba almost screamed out before Sana could reach the door. He ran up to her and said, 'He didn't mean what he just said! A huge misunderstanding!' Meidingu Iwanthanba turned furiously towards Laiba and gave a hard knock on his bare head. Kok!

'You think that was funny?' Meidingu Iwanthanba thundered.

'Ouch! That was painful!' Laiba cried, rubbing his head.

'As it should be! Explain to her before she runs away from us! Explain, you...' Meidingu Iwanthanba looked around and murmured, 'Don't let me lose my calm, the sentries might hear us!'

Sana stood still and looked at the pair fighting and bickering with each other. The scene was like two siblings involved in an argument. Laiba was now on the verge of crying, his plump lips pouted and eyes thick with unshed tears.

'Lady Sana, I am terribly sorry for the misunderstanding. You are not his wife or anybody's. You are here to help us in our most important task. I said that already. We need you to find a lost item and save the realm,' Meidingu Iwanthanba pleaded desperately.

'Save the realm?' Sana whispered, now wondering if the teenage boy was really the monarch.

Meidingu Iwanthanba gestured that Sana should sit on the bamboo chair and she idly followed his request. He began abruptly about a long and very important prophecy delivered by the royal shamans regarding an impending catastrophe and the need to assemble seven select members in a troop of which, the Meidingu convinced Sana, she was a crucial member.

'I am one of the guardians?' Sana murmured after she had heard out the Meidingu completely. Laiba was at one corner, sulking alone with his bruised bald head.

'Yes, Lady Sana. In fact, Lord Laiba said you will be the most important one,' Meidingu Iwanthanba spoke confidently. He let out a reassuring smile and Sana realized that the Meidingu was perhaps charming in a special way. He was adorable and his silky dark locks were bouncing as he nodded while he spoke. He seemed to have a habit of nodding when he spoke seriously.

'But how? Is it why I have this strange feeling all the time?' Sana asked grimly.

'Strange? Might be. Everything about this is strange, so that might probably be,' Meidingu Iwanthanba said with a nervous grin.

'So, what do I do? How do we find this lost scissor? Where do we begin?'

'Well, that,' Meidingu Iwanthanba thought and added nervously, 'we can figure out soon.' He turned towards Laiba and spoke loudly, 'We will need Maichou Laiba to be done with his whining.'

Laiba threw a nasty look at Meidingu Iwanthanba and turned away angrily.

'Maichou Laiba, I am sorry I misunderstood your statement. I am sure you have a reason for saying that,' Sana gently apologized to Laiba with a kind smile.

'What I said was true. You are the Supreme Goddess and I am the Supreme God, we are husband and wife. You all are stupid! You don't know your own self, but I do,' Laiba retorted, looking angrily at Meidingu Iwanthanba while he rubbed his nose with his sacred priest's cloak.

'Don't smear your fluid over that expensive sacred cloth!' Meidingu Iwanthanba snapped, but Laiba didn't even bother and blew his nose on the cloak again, quite on purpose.

'We don't know that for sure.' Sana murmured, she felt like laughing out every time the Meidingu or the head priest spoke of her as an embodiment of this Supreme Goddess. She could easily rule them out as insane.

'Oh, I am very sure!' Laiba looked deep into Sana's eyes and for the first time she realized the eyes were much more than just the strange colour, they seemed to gleam.

'Your eyes…' Sana whispered and Laiba turned away.

'I host the eyes of the Atingkok but these are my eyes. I saw myself in my original form and I was the Supreme God and you, the Supreme Goddess, my wife! Well, it would be wrong to address you as my "wife" here but at least, hypothetically, you are my wife, born as a human girl. A silly one!' Laiba now crossed his tiny arms and stood between Iwan and Sana.

'I am sorry I didn't believe you before,' Sana said, more out of pity, not that she bought any of what was said. 'So, I have some peculiarities alright but I doubt I would be as useful as you both are hoping. I mean, I don't want to disappoint His Majesty or our head priest.'

'No. Don't worry. I am also a pathetic young king. We will figure this whole thing together, Sana, I mean Lady Sana. I will always try my best to support you and our destiny through this madness.' Meidingu Iwanthanba grinned at Sana and she returned a warm smile. Just a year or two older, the Meidingu was the kind of warm person that Sana had been wishing all her life to meet. Laiba was adorable and she would love to trust the two with whatever bizarre things they had been telling her since her arrival.

'So, Lady Sana, if you could accord a bit of your attention to your divine husband in celestial order, may I know what sort of peculiarities you think you have?' Laiba asked, pressing his hands over his tiny hips.

'Well, there were few incidents where I did some strange things very involuntarily,' Sana muttered hesitantly.

'Like?' Laiba urged for more details.

'Like that one time when I was young, I cured a blistered face with just my hands, and then, at another instance, I could see a Helloi mark and even rescued five of its victims by speaking some unknown language.'

'Helloi?' both Meidingu Iwanthanba and Laiba exclaimed simultaneously.

'Yes. They almost abducted five musicians in my village.'

'Helloi lurking out in the settlement and the Khutsangbi in my village. The dark entities are already awake,' Laiba suddenly gave the look of an aged hermit, casting his eyes with sadness over the slowly darkening evening sky through the window.

'Whatever we need to do, we should do in a hurry. Lady Sana, the creatures of the dark are rising against our sacred realm. And the oracle said we are the chosen guardians,' Meidingu Iwanthanba murmured half-heartedly, somewhere wishing what he said was not true.

'Like I said, I have strange intuition but it's mostly involuntary...' Sana looked at the gloomy faces around her.

'Lady Sana, you have already rescued not one but five victims from a Helloi. Among us three, I think you are the most brilliant guardian so far. Your presence already gives us hope that we might turn out fine too. Isn't that splendid?' Meidingu Iwanthanba gave another smile with his thin lips curling up, 'I think you should rest for today and then we will discuss our plans further tomorrow. I shall arrange for your chamber. Come. Laiba, let's go.'

'Did you just call me "Laiba"?' Laiba turned his face away from the window and gave a nasty look to the poor Meidingu who giggled and said, 'Apology. Lord Laiba, old sage, we shall walk out of here and take our lady towards her chamber.'

'You can't make fun of me...' Lord Laiba pouted again and the Meidingu waved his hand irritatedly.

Sana quietly followed the two, but suppressed a smile from the squabble.

As soon as Sana walked out of the guest room, she was received by a group of royal maids headed by one Hanjabi, lady-in-waiting. Iwan and Laiba went away to attend to their duties and Sana obediently followed her new assistants. They took her to a neat wooden bedchamber where a soft cotton bed was prepared, surrounded by a week's worth of fruits and drinks displayed nearby. The ladies tried to help change her clothes, but Sana insisted on doing that alone so they quietly left her room.

After changing and filling herself with quick refreshments, she rolled around the bed. I am in the palace, Sana reminded herself. The king and the boy want me to be special, but am I really what they said I am? What if I fail them? What is this scissor they are talking about?

While she was drifting in thoughts, a gentle knock alerted her. She immediately sat up, but was anxious about how to respond. The knock was repeated.

'Please come… I mean, who is it?' Sana asked nervously.

'My lady, it is I, your royal assistant, bringing your meal for the night. May I enter?' a lady spoke in a soft voice from beyond the door.

Sana jumped out of her bed and opened the door. What she saw made her jaw drop again. There was her lady-in-waiting at the door, a pretty woman with a dark glossy fringe, clad in royal attire just like her fellow maids along with another prominent-looking lady, a bit older than the rest, in the age group of early forties. With a gentle smile on her face, she had her hair tied on the back of her head and was clad in a starchy cotton stole and striped phanek. Behind the ladies was the actual line of amazement, food platters gleaming in the flickering lights of the torch bearers.

As Sana didn't welcome them inside, out of bafflement, the lady-in-waiting walked in and led Sana back inside her chamber, 'My lady, we are here to serve your meal, personally arranged by Phourungbi, head of the royal granary department.' Sana moved away and the elegant lady came forward and bowed to her with a smile, 'My lady, it is certainly my pleasure to personally arrange your dinner as my deepest regard to our king. I hope it suits your taste.'

Sana vaguely nodded and Phourungbi motioned her hands towards the food bearers. The lady-in-waiting took all the pots and bowls from the servants and neatly arranged them in front of Sana. Sana was still staring at the elegant woman at the corner. She was around her mother's age, but very neat and undeniably resilient.

'My lady, please enjoy the dinner that we humbly prepared with care,' the lady-in-waiting reminded Sana to start.

'Everything looks delicious,' Sana spoke absently, but she didn't touch any of the pots or bowls.

'My lady, even a king never skips his rice for anything. The power of rice is something our civilization is built upon. In this time of chaos, we put our faith in each grain of rice in our platter,' Phourungbi spoke most diligently as she lifted the lid off one of the pots. Smell of boiled greens and fermented fish assailed Sana's nostrils and she picked up her rice plate obediently.

Long after dinner, Sana still couldn't close her eyes. She had feasted on a luxurious royal cuisine, had maidens serving her from left and right, but the more she received such uncalled-for attention, the more she was reminded of the impending task. I am here for a reason and all these moments are the calm before the storm, she thought. She heard about Laiba and the incident of the Khutsangbi running out of its habitual abyss. She had witnessed a Helloi directly and the Meidingu told her of the prophesy of chaos if the divine scissor was not restored. She was to help them defend the kingdom and if she made those terrible mistakes like the ones in the past, she knew it would result in a lot more than just the bitterness of her parents.

Sana hardly slept that night but as soon as the morning drum began, two royal guards came and informed her that her presence was immediately requested by the Meidingu in the courtroom. Sana reluctantly followed the tall bulky soldiers and entered the large courtroom where several attendants in white, matching attires served the Meidingu and the head priest at the throne platform. She looked around and realized that a couple of reed mats where five middle-aged men sat were the priority seats. All 10 of them in heavy sets of jewellery, velvet shirts, cotton shawls with their own clan's insignia and white feathery headdresses, were staring at her without blinking. She bent to make a low bow but Meidingu Iwanthanba almost screamed from his throne,

'Lady Sana, you are welcome to my humble courtroom and kindly take your seat that I have had prepared for your comfort.'

Sana widened her eyes and stood questioningly, but a maid ran up to her and guided her towards a soft cotton futon at the far corner, right above the place where the 10 gentlemen sat, with their legs folded and spines erect. Their eyes followed her wherever she moved, like their eyeballs were attached to her nose!

'To my faithful ministers, here with us, on my right, is none other than one of the prophesied guardians. She will be the one joining us in our quest of finding the Wayel Kati,' Meidingu Iwanthanba announced with a worried look at Sana, who was busy staring back at the ministers with equal intensity.

'A girl your age, Your Majesty.' Minister Nongthomba said with an uneasy smile.

'May I have the honour to inquire about our new guardian's age? Minister Famthakcha asked with a troubled smile.

'I am 13,' Sana promptly replied, but added nervously, 'and will be 14 next summer.'

'And 15 by another summer,' Minister Nongthomba said but quickly added, 'and your clan?'

'I...I don't, I mean my father is an outcast, Loi,' Sana answered innocently, but all the ministers cried together, 'What!' Admitting some folly, she hurriedly added, 'But my mother once said something about one of my maternal grandparents being the Thangal. My father was long outcast, because he had stolen a black hen, and few other things... and...I mean...'

'A social leper in the royal court hall!' Minister Nongthomba cried.

'Please calm down, Minister Nongthomba, our king requested her presence. Spare her of dishonour,' Minister Famthakcha raised his hand and said.

'Minister Famthakcha, I do not mean to dishonour anyone, but you of all people must know this could bring trouble to our utmost important affair.' Minister Nongthomba was nearly in tears.

'What affair? Minister?' Iwan asked, clueless.

'Your Majesty,' Minister Nongthomba jumped out of his allotted seat and genuflected near Iwan's feet. He shrinked back in fright. Laiba sighed, but didn't say anything. The minister cried, 'Your Majesty, we didn't want to burden you with our intricate political affairs and so decided to keep this matter to ourselves but as you have asked today, our marriage proposal of the Ahom princess with you was not some plain move, but what would change the very course of our kingdom's fate. The Ahoms are new in their own kingdom, but unmatched in their valour and my insiders in their court sent word of their prosperity. We are grand as a nation in ancient history, but not anymore with too many autonomous provinces corroding our collective power. We need to win the hand of the Ahom princess and to do that, we cannot be dishonoured by the presence of disreputable people in a royal court hall...'

'She is my guest, Minister Nongthomba. How dare you humiliate her!' Meidingu Iwanthanba thundered. Sana looked down without a word.

'I am not trying to humiliate her, your Royal Majesty. Never. I was just worried that this could be misunderstood. I am just...well...

we need to act smart and lend some help to the Ahoms in their times of need, while they are in their infancy. This is the time when they will appreciate help and that will make them owe us some good favours in return. We should always be careful to enjoy grand goodwill in our plan for future subjugations.'

'Subjugations? We can hardly control our own little kingdom, minister. I know I am young, but why is there a need for conquering more land? More war?'

'My king,' Minister Nongthomba spoke clearly, 'We are a grand people, people of mystic origin. You, my divine king, are still too young to understand our sentiments, but your late father entrusted his throne to us, to make you as grand as he wanted to be himself. I will make it happen even at the cost of my life!'

Iwan sat quietly for a while. Sana nervously played with her hair. Laiba rolled around on his futon without a care for what was happening around him.

'Minister, I understand that and I shall never question your loyalty, but since time memorial, our kingdom has been regarded as one built on mysticism, just as you said. We live with strict divine codes. We fear divine predicaments. My father,' Iwan gulped and continued, 'Even my father's death was most unusual...'

'Our beloved king was murdered! I am sure of it!' Minister Nongthomba thundered, but genuflected again as an apology.

Iwan clenched his fist, but didn't say anything. He looked down and tried to calm himself.

'Your Majesty, what our good, devoted Minister Nongthomba wanted to say is that your marriage with the Ahom princess is our most valued priority. We bear no disbelief for the oracle, but the presence of Lady Sana inside the court hall could be easily misunderstood by the Ahom delegates, if they came to know of this. The outcome wouldn't be favourable. It could ruin our hard work and lucrative plans.' Minister Yaiskul Lakpa, the most silent of all ministers, said calmly.

'But, she is our Supreme Goddess incarnate.' Meidingu Iwanthanba answered weakly.

'Ministers, my loyal ministers, the great Pongba Tara, have any one of you seen the beauty of the Helloi spirits?' Laiba sat straight and asked playfully.

The mention of such an unrelated question stupefied everyone. None in the hall spoke for a while, some blinked, confused. They murmured.

'He...Helloi?' one of the ministers asked.

'Yes, those beauties. Have you seen them?' Laiba cupped his chin in his palm and smiled, his golden eye beaming bright while the silver one seemed to dim.

'No...no. I haven't. Who would be here anyway if we saw one?' The minister tried to smirk, but seemed too nervous.

'Lady Sana rescued five men from Helloi back in her village.'

Sana sat uncomfortably with all the eyes suddenly resting on her.

'Helloi attacking random people?' Another minister wondered aloud.

'Not just Helloi, I saw a Khutshangbi in my village. My father cut one of its arms while it tried to grab a child,' Laiba spoke dully and threw out an amputated arm, much like a human arm, but bluish, veiny and with claws.

The ministers let out a collective scream. Sana was too shaken to even utter a word. She widened her eyes and stared at the arm without blinking.

'Is this...?' Iwan whispered in horror at Laiba and he winked. Iwan sneaked a smile. He somehow felt glad to have the kid by his side.

'It cannot be true...' One minister wept.

'It is. The sacred scissor is gone. There is no balance or defence from chaos. A battle might even be expected, though not with any mortal enemy, but those creatures lurking out of the dark and we do not know yet what they are capable of. The way of ministry and policies wouldn't be of much help, I think!' Meidingu Iwanthanba spoke calmly, satisfied to finally render few knowledgeable words of advice to his know-it-all ministers who kept cross-questioning him for incompetence.

None of the ministers spoke a word, but there was intense thinking and judging going on, which was quite clearly visible in some raised, some squeezed eyebrows.

'But with all due respect, Your Majesty, that confirms the worst. You are yet to master the art of kingship; you have never been trained under the scholars. You have been crowned in such haste and with all due honesty, you are but a child. You know nothing!' Minister Nongthonba thundered above all the confusion. He had been serving the throne for 30 long years and never expected the prophecy to throw in some children to be all high and mighty, goddesses or not, and ruin his grand scheme. He wanted to be as relevant as he always had been. The sense of panic caused by divine grants to incompetent juveniles seemed intolerable.

Iwan gulped, looking defeated at such an insult in front of the whole crowd. 'I don't want this either,' he mumbled.

'We understand that the prophecy is the divine intervention, but we want to do our duty as protectors of the throne. You cannot be out there without better knowledge of what is what. We are ready even for dark creatures if that is really what is happening,' Minister Nongthomba said with a deep breath. He stood up and walked backwards to his seat.

'We do understand the divine obligation, but as for our part, our priority is not the fear of gods or divine punishment, but to protect you and safeguard your throne. His Majesty shall learn more about the scissor before making any hasty decision,' Minister Famthakcha said and the rest nodded in agreement.

'For our lively morning conference, we shall conclude here. Deep gratitude to my royal ministers for your valuable guidance and advice,' Meidingu Iwanthanba bowed swiftly and turned away to drink his herbs. He gave up on continuing with his stubborn king-sitters.

The ministers stood up and walked away briskly after a light nod towards the Meidingu, more urgently than usual for some reason.

'Are they always this annoying?' Laiba asked after a yawn.

'I know,' Meidingu Iwanthanba answered weakly.

'I already caused some sort of disaster, didn't I?' Sana spoke, but her eyes were still fixed on the severed arm.

'No... No! Not at all! It is definitely not about you. You heard them,' Iwan said, crossing his hands.

'And, Lady Sana, that arm is fake. I had it made yesterday,' Laiba winked at Sana.

'Oh...is it? But...'

'But the story was true. My father did cut the creature's arm alright.'

'I don't think we will be able to get out of the palace without the ministry's approval. And you heard that Minister Nongthomba yelling at me. If it was my father, his head would have been decorated at the western Luphou stone by now.' Iwan clenched his fist.

'You can do that too. What's stopping you?' Laiba fell back on his futon.

'Well...well... I need to find my mother first...' Iwan cleared his throat.

'Yes, Your Majesty. You can't just kill all whom you don't like, even if you are a king.' Sana said, impressed with the king's benevolence.

'You are one soft king. No wonder your ministry acts like a bully.' Laiba said with a giggle.

'Whatever, but we can't trick the ministry with a fake arm for long. We need to think of something. Laiba, Epu Maichou, how many of the guardians will be here?'

Laiba sat up and closed his silver eye with his hand. The golden one shimmered brighter. Sana watched in complete awe.

'He is getting closer. The golden egg. The rest are running wild on their own, completely ignoring their divine calls. We need to go after them,' Laiba said dully.

'Golden egg?' Sana asked.

'Another guardian, just like us.' Iwan said with a faint smile, 'He is supposedly the son of our serpent king.'

'The serpent who?' Sana asked bluntly.

'This one, our first divine king, the one that ruled this very realm,' Iwan turned back and looked at the enormous wooden ouroboros installed behind him. Sana widened her eyes when she noticed the intricate rectangular pattern made by a serpent with a dragon head that bit its own tail. A beautifully carved woodwork.

'Hope he or she doesn't disappoint you as I did,' Sana said with a guilty smile.

'You disappointed no one, Lady Sana. Rest assured. Our quest has not even started yet. We have a lot of work to do before our actual task. Most annoying task of gathering those clueless guardians. God bless me,' Laiba grunted, gesturing at an attendant nearby to bring him his pineapple cubes.

'Yes, we need a plan,' Iwan turned to Laiba.

'Plan? I hate plans, especially when they don't work as planned,' Laiba pouted his lips again.

'Then what do we do?' Iwan yelled.

'I am eating pineapples!' Laiba turned his back to the king, took his platter of pineapple cubes and chomped.

'Maybe, Maichou Laiba will figure something out,' Sana said, reminding herself that no matter how smart Laiba looked, he was still a child. 'And you too, Your Majesty. You must be tired. I will go back to my chamber for now. I hope everything goes well.' Sana bowed and walked out of the hall.

She returned to her chamber complex and loitered around the garden.

'What if I am of no use? Those ministers did seem scary,' Sana spoke to herself.

'Greetings to our Supreme Mother, queen of all queens, mother of all creation.' Sana jumped at the sudden cry from behind. She turned around and found an old stooping man with a long staff.

'Greetings, who…I mean… Do I know you?' Sana asked with a nervous smile.

'No, Mother Supreme,' the old man bowed low and spoke with a content smile, 'I am the former head priest. Since Maichou Laiba is here, I am in retirement and had been eagerly waiting for you since he told me about your arrival.'

Sana nodded, still smiling awkwardly.

'Blessed is my existence to have this opportunity to meet you personally,' the old man came closer and continued, 'I shall leave my beloved young king under your care.'

'Are you going somewhere?' Sana asked innocently.

'I have done my time, used my blessed ability to guide and to serve, and have also failed terribly, but I hope I am forgiven since you are already here by our king's side.'

Sana didn't understand anything but nodded out of politeness.

'Fear no more, your grace,' the old man walked closer to the pond nearby and said with a teary smile, 'Don't let the vessel conceal more of who you really are. What more could I ask for when I will be travelling back to our subterranean birthplace through your divine elemental path!'

Sana wondered if she should continue smiling. She just didn't understand him at all.

The old man walked down the pond and as if he were a grain of salt, dissolved into nothingness. Sana ran up to the pond, but the water was crystal clear with no old man in sight.

'What...what just happened?' Sana cried out.

Her assistants ran in.

'An old man, I mean, the former head priest. He just, he just vanished inside the pond and...' Sana tried to narrate the incident.

'Calm down, my lady,' Hanjabi embraced her and spoke gently, 'The head priests are always of a mystic order. They can perform grand magic and charms. I hope whatever happened is nothing to be worried about.'

'But I need to tell the king or Maichou Laiba...'

'Neither the king nor the maichou will be able to host my lady until evening. They will be on their royal duties now. I shall inform you when His Majesty visits the pavilion for the evening refreshments. Please rest assured.' The royal attendant was so gentle in her way that Sana decided to heed her calm advice. She waited the whole day, walking up and down her complex, worried about the old man who had vanished, worried about the lofty expectations and all the grand treatment she received as a powerful goddess.

It was already twilight. Hordes of royal servants marched around the vast palace, busy running the errands of the day. The young king came out with his head priest after their usual ceremony and conferences.

'...I tried my best. The fake arm did prove somehow effective anyway,' Laiba said with a giggle.

'Yes, they now seemed a bit cautious. Even Minister Nongthomba didn't cross me immediately,' Meidingu Iwanthanba admitted.

'Yes, only if we can smash them with something wilder than the arm to completely shake the gang.'

'I can't think of anything for now, I just hate...'

'Your Majesty, why don't we relax for a bit. Your ministry is surely a big pain in my...well...in my behind, but we need to calm ourselves too. You said you have that horn and the flutes,' Laiba said, jumping up in excitement.

'Flute? Now?'

'Yes, I want to play for a while. I am tired, you know. Or else, I better go and chill with my piggy...' Laiba pretended to leave the pavilion.

'Wait...' Iwan sighed and gestured at one of his attendants.

Sana ran towards the pavilion shining at a distance with bright torches and a small crowd. As she approached, she saw Laiba trying the brass horn and Meidingu Iwanthanba rolling in laughter, an elegant white horse curled near him. The attendants were busy bringing in more musical instruments and food and wine for the two.

'Your Majesty, I have news,' Sana cried.

Both Iwan and Laiba stopped and stared at her.

'An old man, supposedly the former head priest, came to my chamber complex and vanished inside the pond!'

'What?' Iwan stood up, devastated.

Sana had already shed a few tears, knowing it was some more tragedy for the young king.

'You both please calm down...' Laiba said calmly, 'Our former Maichou went elegantly. He was waiting for Sana for the past few days. We talked so much about it.'

'What do you mean?' Iwan asked.

'You of all people should know! We, the maichous, are mystic people and when we complete our earthly task, we want to leave in style. That is what our former head priest did. He went in style, using Sana's blessing.' Laiba explained.

'I didn't do anything.' Sana confessed, rubbing her tears away.

'No, my lady. Our former head priest departs our world into the underworld by the way of water. That's all. Not your doing! You just blessed him. That's all,' Laiba patted Sana's shoulder.

'Now that you mentioned it, Epu did come to me last night and he said a lengthy farewell. I wondered where he might be going,' Iwan took a deep breath and looked at Sana's chamber complex far away.

'I thought I did something...' Sana fell on the floor, relieved. She was impressed by how one can leave the world so peacefully, modest with death; only the most enlightened must be capable of it.

'Now, you two. Calm your nerves while we can, because we might be leaving anytime soon,' Laiba took up his horn and blew a sonorous 'pooooooooooooo...', which sounded like a healthy flatus and Sana couldn't hold back her laughter anymore.

Meidingu Iwanthanba relaxed and said excitedly, 'And Lady Sana, meet my little brother, Yangba,' he rubbed the white horse that stood beside him.

'Oh brother? He is such a handsome one,' Sana ran her hands through Yangba's soft mane.

Laiba was struggling to blow the brass horn, pouring all his concentration, closing his eyes shut and inhaling deeply before he blew another 'pooooooooooooo...'

Both the lady and the Meidingu giggled again.

'Mother said that Yangba was gifted to me by one of the southern clans at my birth ceremony. We grew up together,' Iwan said with a smile.

Sana saw the look of affection in the king's eyes as he stroked his horse.

'That is lovely. I always wanted such a friendship too. I used to have a kitten once.' Sana said, 'Only my mother went and abandoned her at the forest after she ate my mother's smoked fish kept for sale.'

'What?' Meidingu Iwanthanba widened his eyes in disbelief.

'Y...Yes...' Sana realized she was ruining the mood and quickly changed the topic, 'Anyway, what is this?' Lady Sana asked holding up a bamboo frame with several holes.

'A flute. I don't know how to play it, but it gives a good soothing sound,' Meidingu Iwanthanba said, pointing his finger at the holes. 'You can try if you want, Lady Sana.'

'Your Majesty, please call me by my name,' Sana said with a smile. The whole 'lady' business always made her uncomfortable in some way.

'Alright,' Meidingu Iwanthanba said happily and then added, 'Then the same goes for you. Iwan will be fine.'

'But you are the Meidingu, Your Majesty.'

'If we are to be friends, this has to be fair,' Iwan smiled and Sana could see the delight on his face. It made her heart warm, and he looked more gorgeous when he was relaxed and acting his age, rather than sulking and worrying on an oversized throne.

'I never had any friends before,' Sana answered warily.

'Really?' Iwan sounded surprised, but added, 'Well, me too. Just me and Yangba.' He looked at Laiba and smiled, 'Glad I am not alone anymore, even if chaos breaks loose. I'm genuinely glad.'

Iwan nodded his head, his curls bouncing softly without the weighty feather headdress. He was glad that Sana came out for a short while. Laiba, as if to distract him from his worries over the unsuccessful quest for his mother and feuds around his ministry, suggested trying out the sacred musical instrument and got him laughing for the first time since his coronation. Sana's presence made him even more comforted.

'Me too. I mean, to be honest, I was scared to stay here at the beginning, but had to stay, so that my father wouldn't punish me again...' Sana laughed nervously.

'Punish you?' Iwan widened his round eyes.

'I don't know. Parents are very scary, right?' Sana suggested, 'Are yours not so?'

Iwan thought for a moment, but before he could reply, Lord Laiba suddenly dropped his brass horn with a loud thud. Both stood up in awe and realized something strange was happening. Lord Laiba's mystic pupils were oddly dilated, the silver one glowing brighter. He stood stiffly, facing the eastern forest.

'Meidingu! Your attendants and servants! Tell them to shut themselves in! Now!' Laiba let out a piercing scream.

'What happened, Laiba? Maichou Laiba?' Meidingu Iwanthanba grabbed his shoulders.

'Hurry, Meidingu. All palace lawns are naturally enchanting. Tell them to lock themselves up in their respective complexes for protection. He is coming,' Laiba whispered calmly.

Though Meidingu Iwanthanba had less of an idea about the cautious suggestion, he immediately dismissed all his attendants and ordered them to lock themselves up in their respective chambers. Sana looked towards the eastern forest which Laiba stood facing, like a stone statue.

'He is coming? Who?' Meidingu Iwanthanba yelled.

'The tiger-man,' Laiba said, clearly showing fear and uncertainty in his words.

'The WHAT?' Meidingu Iwanthanba cried.

'Hurry! And also get your horse out of here for safety.'

'Are you sure? Tiger-man?'

'Yes him, rushing mad. He wants women. He wants...' Lord Laiba didn't finish his sentence, but looked grimly at Sana.

'H...H...He wants me?' Sana stuttered.

Iwan and Laiba stood in front of Sana as if to protect her, quite intuitively. They all looked towards the dark eastern passage. The breeze was calm and the moonlight was shining softly above the stone pavement.

THE SERPENTINE DRAGON

Deep in the cold dark swamp, Keibu Keioiba, the half-human–half-tiger crawled towards a rotting piece of flesh. He poked the unappetizing meal and grunted.

'Not so hungry? Keioiba?' A squeaky voice teased from above the skeletal trees.

'Mind your own business, Loudraobi!' Keioiba roared irately. His human legs were terrifying with beastly claws and his striped tiger torso and head gave him the look of a walking nightmare. His muscular hands, were coated with dried blood and dirt.

'Well, I thought of sharing some good news, but I guess I will have to wait until you are in the mood to enjoy it,' an amused Loudraobi retorted.

'Good news?' Keioiba halted instantly with both his ears straight up with attention. A piece of good news was expected and he was desperate for it. He had been waiting his entire life for it.

A stooping body covered with a thick mossy coat came down from one of the blackened skeletal trees. The creature had a mass of hair or dried weed on its head, resembled an old human, was wrapped in a tattered garment, had skinny legs and arms covered with flaky, severely wrinkled skin. The face was not visible in the mass of the mane, but its thin crinkled lips were open and one could see the set of yellow teeth and the distinctive thorny tongue that flashed out repeatedly.

'Yes, good news.' Loudraobi smirked and wiggled its tongue again, 'From the human realm. The place where you once received one of your greatest embarrassments.'

'Tell me the good news!' Keioiba roared impatiently, 'One more unnecessary opinion and I shall tear up your annoying tongue.'

'No, not my tongue, you naughty boy,' Loudraobi nudged the tiger-man playfully, 'It is my tongue that kept my lovers bound to me eternally. None of my captured lovers ever left me like in your case.'

Keioiba almost bit Loudraobi; he jumped and strangled the creature, roaring bitterly.

'Calm down, my boy. I am just teasing your cute little temper.' Loudraobi didn't seem scared even though she was pinned under Keioiba's claws on the ground. She smiled, 'The realm is no longer a sanctuary. Not even the palace, and there, a woman of great promise for the future, has recently arrived. You can woo her before she matures to her true power. Your long-lost bride is waiting for you at the palace, lucky chap! You are suggested to seize your rightful bride from the palace.'

'The palace! Hah! You think you can fool me?' Keioiba groaned in anger.

'Years of imprisonment in the dark realm must have dulled your intellect,' Loudraobi extended her thorny tongue and curled at Keioiba's claw that pinned her. Keioiba immediately retreated in awe. Loudraobi stood up, ruffled her mossy coat, and spoke matter-of-factly,

'The scissor is gone and we are free yet again. We are back to the fair and undivided. Just like when we were created. The deal that bound the thread of balance has been breached at last. We are free to go and have our way. Everybody wins.'

'Then why don't you go first?' Keioiba retorted, 'Were you planning to say "Eheyyyyyy" after I got killed in the enchanted defence.'

'How adorable you are when you act like a little kitten, curling your tail between your legs and whining in fear,' Loudraobi smirked with her thorny tongue wiggling around.

'I am not afraid,' Keioiba roared, 'But I shall not be fooled by the likes of you. The realm can never be infringed. The palaces more so. Every dark entity knows that!'

'Yes, till the recent past, but not anymore. The boy king in the serpentine throne is not even capable of cutting his own nails. The royal institute of priesthood is in jeopardy, currently under a mysterious nine-year-old boy, may be special but not so for now. And more importantly,' Loudraobi moved closer to Keioiba's ear and whispered, 'your bride... Didn't you always want your bride back? The humiliation? The betrayal?'

Keioiba grunted at the painful memory. He had once kidnapped a maiden, but she fooled him and escaped from his lair. Oh! How the crows mocked him terribly. He was doomed to the dark abyss with the shame and betrayal after the maiden's seven brothers defeated him. How could he forget such a painful scar?

'Your lady...they said she would be troublesome if not taken care of.' Loudraobi continued, 'If you visit the palace by tonight, the lady would easily be your bride and for us, a grave foe removed. What do you say?'

'Tell me about her,' Keioiba purred.

'Lass from the marshland of our eastern realm, long charcoal black hair, skin as smooth as a newly moulded earthen pitcher, thick-tinted lips. Her round eyes adorn a pair of kangkhil eyes, yes, as large and dark and shiny as that seed. Delicious, isn't she?'

Keibu Keioiba left the dark swamp for the first time since his defeat. It must be thousands of years ago when he used to walk in the realm with ferocious power and freedom, kidnapping women for food or as a bride.

At first, he was reluctant to cross the blazing smoke that divided the dark realm from the sacred one. He timidly extended his hand and to his surprise, he punctured right through the mist and nothing happened. Earlier, he would be screaming in pain after touching the enchanted shield, but now, except for a mild sting around his arms, nothing hurt. The tiger-man roared in laughter and raced through the forest of the sacred realm.

Keioiba realized nothing much had changed since his glorious days. The eastern forest was still thick and dark, favouring his energetic leap towards the palace not so far away. The flickering lights of the Central Kingdom became visible once when he had raced through the vast valley out of the forest. He closed his eyes and saw his imagined bride, the lady screaming when he clutched her with his clawed hands. It thrilled him and he leapt, grinning and becoming even more feverous.

The lake, pathetic and god-made, surrounded the palace and was shimmering under the moonlit night, water rippling in a calm breeze and the wall torches burning in long rows.

Knowing the intractable palace, which was constructed by the divine king himself, Keioiba stood at the lakeshore and contemplated the risk. From his view, he could already see the outer Lairiren complex—tall, carved wooden edifices, the garrison of cardinal guardian deities of directions, picketing the palace from dark creatures like himself.

Keioiba made a supple leap, crossing the water and falling neatly inside the Lairiren grounds. A tingling sensation wobbled his body for a moment but the charm was too weak to trounce him. He stood up and breathed deeply. Nothing happened. No surprise guardian attacked. The palace was still as quiet as the lake. Keioiba couldn't help but smirk. Not even the gods could stop him now!

Crossing the Lairiren frontier without a scratch buffed up Keioiba's confidence and he began to walk leisurely around the palace. The place looked beautifully deserted. He then came across the second frontier of Tilliren, the garrison of human guards where there were several huts and chambers. All of them were bolted shut and he could easily smell fear from within, full of people who panicked. But Keioiba was not interested in any of those puny humans. He just wanted his bride.

Meidingu Iwanthanba saw the bushes rustling gently and Lord Laiba clutched his cloak tightly. He was glad the nine-year-old Laiba didn't run away in fear. Both could hear Sana's heavy breathing, she was sniffing and her teeth were chattering.

Out of the dense shrubs and trees, came the towering beast with its frightening tiger-head, striped torso, muscular arms with sharp claws and thick human legs—the tiger-man, Keibu Keioiba.

Sana could sense the abusive scrutiny from the pair of glistering emerald eyes fixed on her. The beast grinned, his yellow fangs protruding out of his mouth.

'Back in my days, my presence always called for hordes of warriors to defend against me. What a downfall! Now not even a full-grown man is ready to consider me as a worthy opponent?' Keioiba smirked.

'You don't belong here!' Iwan spoke bravely, but his voice trembled.

'Oh, I didn't know that,' Keioiba slowly walked up towards the pavilion. Iwan and Laiba stood closer to Sana. She didn't move, barely breathing, her eyes staring straight at the beast without blinking.

'I don't think she belongs here either,' Keioiba almost drooled; he could now sniff the scent of the lady, a sweet honey scent.

Keioiba stepped inside the pavilion; it pleased him to see the king was visibly terrified, but the small, strangely pale boy was quiet and clearly not afraid of his presence. He wondered if he should just take the lady or play around with the little human cubs. The idea was tempting. He had been banished to the cold dark abyss for millennia. He thought he deserved some fun.

'You unappetizing boy, you must be...' Keioiba started at Laiba, but he couldn't finish his sentence because the pale boy just kicked him in the most vulnerable area of the body, his loins, and quite unexpectedly too.

The tiger-man covered his crotch and roared in pain, but Laiba immediately jumped up and pulled his ears. Iwan was lost for a moment. He thought Keioiba had attacked Laiba, but it was Laiba climbing up the tiger-man and pulling his ears. Iwan dragged Sana and tried to run out of the pavilion, but the tiger-man threw Laiba away from his face as if he were an irritating insect and tried to grab Sana.

Iwan pushed Sana out of his reach and let himself get caught in the tiger-man's powerful grip. It hurt terribly, as his bones got crushed, but he tried to endure the pain.

Sana ran towards Laiba, who had fallen on the ground, but didn't move.

'Maichou Laiba, are you alright?' Sana cried, picking up the fragile boy in her arms.

'Lady Sana... Get out of here. He wants you. Not us!' Laiba pushed Sana away and stood up, evidently in pain. Iwan was struggling in the tiger-man's grip, flinging and punching helplessly. Laiba ran inside the pavilion and jumped towards the tiger-man's arm and bit him with all his might.

The tiger-man let out another painful yelp and set Iwan free, but caught Laiba by his waist and threw him hard on the ground.

'Noooo,' Sana screamed when Laiba fell unconscious, but the tiger-man remembered his actual purpose. He leapt right in front of Sana and clutched her with both his hands and slung her up on his shoulder. Sana cried out helplessly, flinging her arms.

Meidingu Iwanthanba stood up despite his injuries and ran towards the monster, shouting, 'No!'

He was crying; he could hear Sana's screams. Have I failed already? Iwan thought bitterly.

Out of the corner, a sharp spear flew through the pavilion and hit the roof near Keioiba's head. He turned around and saw the royal warriors encircling the pavilion.

'Hahaha! So, you all decided to save your baby king at last? Welcome to the revelry!' Then Keioiba's laughter resonated through the compound.

Multiple long spears flew through the air and some even struck the beast and made him roar in anger. Sana took her chance and escaped the monster's claws while he fell on his knee and injured himself.

Iwan looked around and saw his ministers carefully administering the soldiers for long-range attacks. He felt grateful, but at the same time, mortified. He quickly crawled towards Sana, who was desperately trying to awaken the injured Laiba.

'Will he be alright?' asked Sana with teary eyes.

'Laiba, Lord Laiba?' Iwan gently nudged the boy but he lay still.

'Oh Guardians!' Sana cried helplessly and looked around the chaotic battle between the soldiers and Keioiba.

Iwan rubbed his tears away and tried shaking Laiba to consciousness. Startlingly, Laiba abruptly opened his sparkling eyes and cried, 'We will be fine! God! What a coincidence!'

While Iwan was struggling to inquire about the bizarre revival and the remark, a bright golden object hurled across the sky and fell right at the centre of the demolished pavilion. Everyone halted their busy battle for a moment, even Keioiba, who turned around to look at the mysterious light.

Iwan narrowed his eyes to look closely at the blinding piece of gold and, to his horror, realized it was a gigantic golden serpentine dragon with antlers, claws, wings and mane.

It immediately turned towards Keioiba and began to wrestle with the creature stubbornly. Keioiba looked small for the first time. The dragon was huge and majestic, covered in glistening golden scales. Its lengthy body curled and twisted while it fought with the tiger-man. Keioiba tried his best to put his feet on the ground, but the enormous dragon that came out of nowhere began to overpower him. Realizing that his chance at abducting his bride would not be fruitful in the presence of the dragon, he turned towards the eastern forest for escape.

Keioiba leapt away and the dragon flew behind him. The soldiers also followed, more from the desire to witness the unnatural battle between the two. Knowing that the beast was retreating, the dragon slowed down and shrieked a triumphant cry, but he realized he had made a terrible mistake. Keioiba, before leaping away through the forest, captured a handful of soldiers and ran off into the dark. The dragon howled regretfully, but Keioiba was already gone with the soldiers into the dark abyss.

The golden dragon flew back to the destroyed pavilion and landed heavily over the rubble.

'What is this?' Iwan murmured, his eyes stuck on the divine beauty.

'The golden egg,' Laiba replied weakly.

'One of the guardians?' Sana asked, but nodded as if replying to herself.

'Our fourth companion,' Laiba smiled.

The dragon stared at them and then, with thick smoke emerging out of its long nostrils, began to transform into a young boy of around Iwan's age. Another young boy!

The teenage boy was fair, with long silky hair, slim face, dark beady eyes, pink, plump lips and a thin body. He was a lot taller than Iwan, and most noticeable about him were the pair of golden earrings dangling heavily from his thin earlobes—a *chommai*. He wore a beautiful cotton loincloth with tiger and python motif, laced cotton shirt crossed over the chest and a single but large string of gold and stone neckpiece. He smiled at Iwan, while receiving an awkward one from him in return.

'I am Lungchum! You can call me Lungchum!' the boy said, running up to the flabbergasted trio.

'Incredible...' Laiba said and grinned.

'What... I mean, who are you?' Iwan struggled.

'I am Lungchum, the crown prince of Moirang, King Kongding's adopted son,' Lungchum answered as excited as ever.

'You can turn into a dragon?' Sana gaped.

'That was new, but the Moirang royal seers performed some rites and I was able to turn into this giant creature, a golden serpentine dragon.'

'Understandable...' Laiba nodded, still grinning.

'Understand what? Wh...why...how can he turn into a dragon and not me?' Iwan protested.

'Really? That is what you are thinking right now?' Laiba snapped, 'After all this?' He pointed at the debris left by the battle a moment ago.

Iwan wanted to argue, but the ministers ran up to inspect both the bizarre dragon boy and the rest of them. Sana stood timidly with Laiba still in her arms. Lungchum smiled and waved at everyone.

'Incredible...what...how...' the ministers circled the dragon boy, impressed with him, revering him instantly.

'Where are my soldiers?' Meidingu Iwanthanba thundered.

The distracted ministers took some time to realize the missing soldiers. They circled around in search of the missing troops.

'Sorry. They are gone,' Lungchum looked away guiltily.

'Gone?' Iwan cried. The ministers looked down in shame. The boy king did order them to stay inside their own complex, but the tiger-man seemed strong and they only wanted to protect him.

'Your Majesty, you are injured. You must be tended to at once,' one of the ministers suggested.

'I am fine! We lost our men! Keioiba killed them,' Iwan cried bitterly.

'Keioiba killed them?' The ministers broke up into a chatter.

The very next morning after the battle with Keibu Keioiba, rumours began to spread in every part of the kingdom. Several of the institutions in the palace were closed down and attendants were sent home to stay safe in their own houses. The markets and palace streets were deserted, and food and drinks were being accumulated as everyone prepared for a catastrophe in the near future.

Iwan walked out of his room to visit Laiba and Sana, but saw his ministers holding their own conference. Iwan decided to ignore the annoying bunch. He briskly walked past the hall, but something caught his eye through the window and he stopped for a closer look.

To his surprise, he saw the newly arrived Lungchum, the dragon boy, chairing his Pongba Tara's conference. The boy was at the centre, speaking, and his ministers were nodding in agreement. He burst inside the hall. All the ministers immediately bowed low, but Lungchum waved at him with a smile and called, 'Brother!'

'Greetings,' Iwan smiled uneasily and looked at his ministers questioningly.

'Your Majesty, you should be resting to regain your health for now,' one of the ministers spoke with a bow.

'I am fine. But is there anything else you might want to tell me?' Meidingu Iwanthanba asked sternly.

'We are being advised by our Moirang Prince about the upcoming battle. We made a terrible mistake by using our soldiers,' the minister spoke sadly.

'Battle?' Iwan asked Lungchum.

'Yes, our royal seer said there is some foretelling here too. I received this call to go on some quest and suchlike.'

'How much do you know about it?'

'All I knew was that I should be here as fast as I can and to heed the small white boy,' Lungchum said with a gleeful smile, his silky hair falling straight from the high ponytail.

'What about the battle?'

'Judging from the creature we fought yesterday, I assumed that we might be dealing with something a lot worse.'

'Intelligent conclusion,' one of the ministers nodded.

Iwan turned and gave a glaring look at the minister. He had been saying the same thing all along!

'His highness, Prince Lungchum had advised us to dissolve our council as well as every other department until the recovery of the scissor,' Minister Nongthomba spoke as calm as a tortoise.

Iwan raised his eyebrow questioningly. His ministers were such a persistent and annoyingly loyal troop and for them to easily heed a provincial prince, that too as young as him, irritated him even more.

'Nonetheless, we will be here to safeguard the throne with our life,' Minister Famthakcha said and genuflected.

'Alright. I shall have a word with my new friend here then. My good ministers shall take their leave,' Iwan bowed. His ministers departed one by one, most of them showing admiration towards Prince Lungchum.

'What did you tell the ministry?' Iwan asked sternly.

'That I am the serpent king's son...' Lungchum grinned and looked at the back where the huge wooden serpentine ouroboros was installed.

'I can't believe my father used to sit here once,' Lungchum looked teary-eyed, but was still smiling.

'Can you turn into...a dragon any time you want?' Iwan asked curiously.

Before Lungchum could answer, Laiba burst inside the hall, munching on a cob of corn.

'Laiba, are you alright?' Iwan asked, worried.

'I wouldn't be munching if I was not. I am fine and you?' Laiba took a seat next to Lungchum and took out another steamed corncob for him. Lungchum quietly accepted it and took a bite instantly.

'Yes, I am fine too. What about Lady Sana?' Iwan asked, looking through the door, expecting her to follow in.

'She is alright, but it is better to let her be by herself for some time. She needs some peace after last night.'

'Then what about this guy here? He can turn into a dragon!' Iwan spoke, as if Lungchum was completely invisible between them.

'He is our golden egg. I don't know how he was able to turn directly into a dragon, but it is understandable since he is the direct descendant of the serpent king. Obviously, the golden egg is known for its divine powers.'

Iwan looked at Lungchum chewing corn absentmindedly and sighed. He didn't want to admit, but he could feel that the Moirang prince would be his least favourite among the chosen guardians. He made him feel pathetic; he seemed manipulative and more importantly, too jubilant to be serious, always flashing this annoying smile on his face.

'Imagine what would have happened if Prince Lungchum didn't arrive in time yesterday? We should be thankful,' Laiba spoke calmly and patted Lungchum's shoulder.

'So how can he turn into a dragon while none of us can do anything amazing?' Iwan asked, drumming his fingers on the low wooden table.

'Maybe, you are waiting for your own dramatic battle...I don't know. What we need to discuss is our quest,' Laiba said, scratching his nose with the cob.

'Alright. We need to act now. The ministry wouldn't pry anymore.'

'The ministry? You finally handled them?' Laiba asked with a proud smile.

'No. Lungchum dismissed them,' Iwan said, giving a look at Lungchum who sat clueless, chewing his corn.

Laiba was quiet for a while but nodded, 'Alright.'

'Thank you so much for everything, Prince Lungchum,' Laiba bowed with a kind smile.

The dragon prince smiled back and nodded. Iwan sat unimpressed and stared at Laiba as if he had betrayed him. Laiba saw the look and said, 'You two wait here and I will go check on our lady.' Laiba stood up and walked away, probably sensing that the two would need to spend some more time together.

'My king, we are like family,' Lungchum said, getting closer to Iwan.

'Ye...yes, in a way,' Iwan moved away and faked a smile.

'I mean, I grew up all alone, wondering who my parents were.'

'How did the Moirang King adopt you?'

'He came for me. My mother was his concubine. After she died, the Moirang seers found out about me and got to know that I was alive. Having no heir, he decided to find and adopt me. Before that, I thought I was an orphan.'

'Really? The Moirang King is incredibly humble then,' Iwan said, genuinely impressed. No king would go about looking for some concubine's child.

'I am just fortunate. If not for him, I would be out there in the Moirang market, scrapping over leftovers now.'

Iwan nodded, feeling a little sympathetic for the first time. 'Aren't you angry that your mother abandoned you?'

'Had she been alive, maybe, but she is already dead. It's not like I can dig her grave and swallow her now.'

Lungchum said it with a smile and Iwan was confused if he was just messing with him. He nodded nervously.

'Anyway, my father—Moirang king—told me to express his gratitude. He was more excited than I am about this whole adventure; he told me that we should really support each other as real brothers. I vowed to protect you.' Lungchum smiled again. It did hurt Iwan that he was taken as someone who needed protection.

'I think I will be fine anyway. I mean we all are some or the other powerful gods and goddesses,' Iwan said uneasily.

'Sure, sure, brother.' Lungchum nodded and said, 'Will you please take me to my father's shrine? I want to pay my homage.'

Iwan was confused, but realized that Lungchum wanted to visit the shrine of the serpent king, his real father, the celestial lord.

Sana sat quietly near the pond. The event of yesterday seemed like her fault. The monster was after her. It hurt her friends and she was helpless there. She was always causing one trouble or the other.

'Sana, are you up?' Laiba asked, walking inside her complex.

'Laiba, I think I shouldn't be here...' Sana began.

'What? Sorry?' Laiba came closer and sat beside her.

'I mean...' She began to sob, 'I am no divine lady. I nearly got you all killed. I mean, the monster was after me. Wherever I go, there is always some disaster. I bring real bad luck. Laiba, I better leave before things get worse and I don't have any power like the new prince, I mean...'

'Calm down, my lady...' Laiba patted her head, but she yelled, 'I am no lady! I can't...' She cried, pouring her eyes out.

'My king, our Meidingu, lost his father and then his mother disappeared. None in this palace, except for a very few, actually love this boy genuinely. When we came here, he began to collect himself, refrained from mourning and instead, stood by the oracle and by our side, hoping to save his people. If anyone could do with a breakdown, it is him,' Laiba said, staring deep into Sana's eyes. She sobbed, but wiped her tears away.

'How did his father die? And... I mean, is his mother really missing?'

'Yes, the former king died under mysterious circumstances and the queen, being a princess from another intimidating province, was accused of treason, after which she mysteriously disappeared. Instead of looking out for the missing queen, there is conflict brewing within the provincial governments blaming her. As a son, our Meidingu should be mad with grief by now, but he isn't. He might not know it himself, but he is being incredibly valiant, putting his people forward, the welfare of the kingdom first.'

'I am sorry...' Sana said guiltily.

'No, I understand how you are feeling right now, but wouldn't it be better not to blame everything on ourselves? A great part of our journey is still unknown. You still don't know what you will be capable of,' Laiba smiled faintly.

Meidingu Iwanthanba walked in casually and called out, 'Sana, are you feeling alright?' but noticed her puffy eyes and added, 'Were you crying?'

'No...just...' Sana rubbed her eyes and patted her face nervously.

'Where is Prince Lungchum?' Laiba asked.

'I left him at the shrine. He wanted to pay homage to our serpent king.' Iwan sat next to Sana and tried to take a closer look at her face. She turned around, embarrassed.

'What happened?'

'Nothing, it's just, Meidingu, I wish I was as brave as you,' Sana said, trying hard not to cry again. This time, thinking about Iwan. The poor king suffered a lot himself and yet was being caring towards her.

'Glad you think I am the brave one. After last night, I am finding it hard to think it that way,' Iwan laughed, genuinely glad to receive such praise.

'No...I didn't know anything before...but, Meidingu is really brave...'

'No, you are brave. If I were you, after last night, I would have run home for good...'

'Will you both...' Laiba was about to say something, but both his eyes suddenly pulsated, his hair follicles tingling all over his body. He felt his eyes with his hands.

'What happened?' Iwan asked, noticing the familiar act.

'I sensed another one, another guardian!' Laiba cried out.

'Now? Here?' Iwan stood up. Sana searched around.

'He is almost flying towards us at an incredible speed. Good Guardians!'

Iwan instantly looked up at the sky.

'Wait...wait...he is walking away. What is going on?' Laiba yelled like mad.

'Walking away?' Iwan repeated. Sana stood observing the two screaming at each other.

'I am...I am feeling...wait, not just one but there are two guardians so close to the palace a moment ago, but they both moved away somewhere. We need to go after them!' Laiba cried, his pale face sweating profusely.

'Two of them? Yes, let's go!' Iwan almost ran towards the gate.

'Wait...wait. Meidingu, calm down,' Laiba said, taking a deep long breath.

'But why?' Iwan demanded.

'You shall go and get Lungchum and tell your ministry to send the equestrians for public announcement. You need to order the citizens to stay inside their houses until we complete our quest. We need to perform a rite to strengthen the protective charm. Sana, please go and arrange for some horses. Your assistants will help you. I will go and check the protection rite first. Meet me at the gate. We will leave before twilight.'

Sana nodded obediently, but Iwan asked, 'Protection rite?'

'I have already initiated the protection rite with a hundred priests and priestesses standing around the periphery of the palace lake. It will protect our people from the dark entities while we are on our quest for the scissor, well at least as long as they stay inside their homes,' Laiba explained. 'Now you both, please go and do as planned. I will be at the western gate.'

Laiba ran towards the western gate and checked the large spread of items like different types of grasses, water pitchers, eggs and salt gathered in preparation for the rite. A hundred priests and priestesses clad in white cotton dresses stood half-immersed in the lake. All of them stood at equal distance from each other and chanted the same verse with their eyes closed and hands holding the white veil that covered their heads.

THE SKY PRINCE

The woman was in her early forties. She was running fast, but also in an enjoyable manner. She smiled so warmly, her slender hands and fingers lightly touching the tips of the wild flowers. Her dress was soiled, but it must have been once the most beautiful piece—striped silk phanek in gold, white and black, starched translucent veil with a golden border. Her long hair tied into a huge low bun decorated with black and white feather crown, gold and bead necklaces, jingling gold earrings, bracelets and rings. The woman was about to leap from a cliff…

'No!' Gothang screamed awake. He was sweating profusely, like always. He tried to hold his breath, but his heart was racing as in the dream—recurrent dreams of his mother—haunting him again.

Gothang rubbed his forehead with his hand and looked through the small bamboo window. Dawn was breaking. He lay back on his straw bed, but was afraid to close his eyes again. This strange dream of his mother had been recurring for the past few days. His mother running through wild terrain, heading somewhere dangerous. He knew it was a sign. He always knew his mother was somewhere, even though his late father never admitted to her existence. He knew his mother was alive and somewhere. Now, his mother was giving him a sign to find her. Gothang just wondered when and where to start the search.

'Mother...' Gothang murmured, feeling the pain in his heart. He always wanted to meet her, since the day he could remember. He had always missed her.

'Pa, I want to see mama,' Young Gothang used to nag his poor father, usually during mealtime, a small lone child desperate for his mother.

'Gothang, what did I tell you?' his father would speak in a dramatic regal voice, 'You are no ordinary child. You do not have a mother. I found you by the side of the brook inside a casket made of cloud! You were drifting in that golden-lined cottony cloud! My son, you are a hero. And heroes usually don't have a mother or a father. Now, eat your meal well and one day, you are going to defeat a monster or slay an evil king or save a kingdom...' his father would go on with loud satisfied laughter in between.

Even though Gothang grew up handsome and clever, his father never changed the story. Every time he asked about his mother, his father gave the same reply, that he never really had a mother. Gothang knew his father was lying for a very good reason. He obviously must have a mother. Everybody has one.

When Gothang turned 18, his father fell ill and never recovered.

'Gothang...' his father whispered on his deathbed.

'Yes, father. Tell me,' Gothang whispered back, his eyes filled with tears.

'You are no ordinary man, son. I found you in a casket made out of cloud...' Gothang wailed terribly when his father was laid to eternal rest. His last words were still the story he had made up.

Now, Gothang was 24 and ravishingly handsome. He was taller than most of his clansmen, tanned and with long silky hair that he usually tied into a high bun with a feather pin. The only thing depressing was that he was dirt poor!

Since the death of his father, Gothang was lost and did not know how to make his living. His father usually didn't let him mingle with the other children of the clan who were mean and often picked on him for being a motherless child. Even as grown adults, they all seemed to resent Gothang. None of them ever invited him to join their squads and, if he approached them, they simply ignored him.

The only thing favourable for Gothang was his looks. He recently found out that he was quite popular among his female clan members. The chief summoned him after his daughter's suggestion and gave him a minor job of herding his pigs.

For a small hut and regular meals provided for, Gothang happily took up the job. But not so long after his new job, his strange dream began to haunt him. Gothang began to miss his mother more than ever. The dreams were vivid. His mother running through a forest, sometimes a field, sometimes a swamp, but she was always running. Gothang looked around his quiet hut and sighed, 'Mother, I want to find you, but where do I start?'

A gentle knock came from outside and Gothang sprang up from his bed and went to the door.

'My lady,' Gothang immediately knelt on the ground when he found the chief's daughter, Lady Kilungshi, standing outside his hut, along with her friends.

'Oh, still so formal with me, Gothang? Rise, please,' Kilungshi rolled her eyes and her friends giggled.

'To what do I owe the pleasure of your early visit, my lady?' Gothang stood up and asked.

'Yes, my father wants to perform his Chon ritual this year with the biggest swine in our clan. I hope you already have just the right one in your mind?'—the lady spoke authoritatively, but looking admirably at Gothang's messy morning hair and sleepy eyes, his muscles bulging fine and his black and white striped loincloth covering only the essentials. That he was a dashing man, the ladies always noted.

'My lady, I shall prepare for it right away,' Gothang answered humbly, eyes on his toes as the ladies scanned his bare chest. It was their unnecessary giggling that made him blush; he felt uncomfortable all right. Girls were the least of his desires. He was smart enough not to daydream about such an expensive enterprise as courting a woman. There was no way he could earn enough for the grand list of bridal gifts.

'Ladies, please behave. How would you feel if our clan's men start staring at you like that all the time?' Kilungshi snapped at her giggling friends. She always defended Gothang, even though she barely saw him in the clan. He noted her excellent benevolence and fairness.

'Gothang, I will talk to father for your Sa-ai next year. You are the only one left to conduct the ritual now. I won't let you be left out,' Kilungshi smiled kindly.

Most young men of his clan performed several rituals, offering grand feasts and drinks for the whole member as a sign of their bequest to their community. But, as a poor orphan, Gothang had to fight every day even for a meal and being able to afford an Ai ritual was far away from reality. Lady Kilungshi was being too generous to suggest help for such an important personal ritual.

'I shall not trouble my lady with such a matter that depends on my competence. I will earn on my own and promise to perform many Ai-s as a dignified community member of our clan,' Gothang answered politely.

'I know, you will one day,' Kilungshi smiled and added, 'For whatever you need, know that I am always here for you. And don't think of this

as mere sympathy; I wouldn't say so if I didn't think you are capable. Hope you prepare our swine on time. I will go inform father that it will be ready.'

As soon as the women left his hut, Gothang took his herding staff and went through the backdoor towards the vast slope of the grassy mountainside, where the herds of pigs were kept. Skilfully, running though the enormous giant trees around the gradient, he hopped inside the bamboo fence to greet his livestock.

However, his calm face turned hot with fear when he saw the stains of blood all over the compound, few pigs heedlessly cannibalizing the pieces of their brutally severed members. He nervously started counting the pigs and realized four of his pigs were missing, including his prized swine, the biggest one. Someone or something had attacked his animals. Predators on this side of the slope? He wondered at the absurdity. Why would a wild animal encroach this deep into the clan's periphery? It had never happened before. The wild animals usually never crossed the brook downhill where the actual jungle began. Human territories were the most feared, especially higher on the slope. A buzz of flies invaded all over the place, pieces of carcasses here and there. Gothang walked fretfully around, nearly in tears, breathing heavily and even more traumatized when he finally found his prized swine left half eaten, only the torso left on the muddy ground with the rest of the body parts gone, guts out of the open half. He sat down to examine and instantly caught the claw marks near the pig's eyes. Predator! A big one. He stood up at once, a bit scared, wondering if the thing that ate his swine was still inside the compound. It did not seem so. His pigsty looked calm.

Gothang rushed towards the chief's hut. The old man in his late seventies was sitting with his warriors when Gothang rushed inside the room. A sentry blocked him, but the chief welcomed Gothang promptly, seeing his urgent manner.

'Allong's boy. Come in, come in,' the chief gestured for him to sit on the wooden floor.

Gothang kneeled and answered shakily, 'Honourable chief, I have a terrible news to share.'

'Tell me,' the old man seemed to prepare himself, his relaxed face suddenly crunched with seriousness.

'My pigsty, well, it was attacked.' Gothang lamented.

'Attacked? By which clan?' The chief asked angrily.

'No, I don't think it's human. A predator. I saw claw marks.'

'Predator? On our ranching slope?' the old man asked slightly doubtful.

'Even I was confused, but it is the only explanation. And it seemed like a big one. The claw marks were big. Enormous,' Gothang shuddered at the thought of it.

'Are you sure it's a predator?' one of the warriors asked as the chief sat silently in deep thought.

'I think it is. My swine, the biggest one was torn into half,' Gothang answered sadly.

'Well, you know it is very unlikely. And moreover, aren't you hired to guard them? Didn't you fence them properly?' the warrior asked coldly, his eyes narrowed at Gothang with distaste.

Gothang saw the stare and he didn't reply. He knew the look. The warriors hated him.

'A heartthrob, but can't even properly carry out an assigned task,' another warrior joined in.

Gothang took the abuses, but the warriors didn't get the chance to continue as the chief raised his hand and spoke,

'The more I feel apprehensive, the more I feel something sinister is awake. The very reason why I wanted to perform the Chon ritual with utter care,' the chief thought for a moment and said, 'Will the Thimzin era be really revoked again?'

'Thimzin?' Gothang asked innocently, but the warriors seemed to get what the chief meant. They seemed afraid of the very word.

'Ahh... We humans fear what we do not know. Thimzin, the era of darkness.'

Gothang finally remembered the tale of ancient calamity. The era of Thimzin brought total darkness for seven continuous days. The world shrouded with dark entities, sucking the life out as soon as one bats the eye. Yes, his father once narrated the story of people sticking sticks to their eyes to not bat them or to fall asleep, as they knew that they would die if they did. How people beat drums and utensils, shut away in their houses during such dark days, madly praying for the era to be over.

'The ancient legend! I remembered, chief,' Gothang said gladly.

'Yes, legend. It should be a legend,' the chief tried to smile, but continued with a serious face, 'Allong's boy, since you said it might be a predator, I want you to capture it. Rewards will be handed as deserved. You may leave.'

'Duly noted,' Gothang genuflected and left the room for good.

As soon as he reached his hut, Gothang didn't think twice, but reached for his favourite weapon, a *dao*, and dashed out towards his pigsty. He cleaned the carcasses and planned out his trap. Calculating the size of the claw, he estimated the size of the predator and dug up holes; constructed artistic bamboo traps all over the place. Now, all I have to do is wait, he thought.

As the sun began to set, he waited behind a bush with his sharp *dao* and ivory shield, ready for anything. His breath became slower, his eyes fixed on his traps ahead. The pigs were clueless, munching on their fodder blissfully.

It became dark; the night sky was drizzled with stars and Gothang was yet to spot his prize. He waited patiently, sipping from his wine gourd from time to time, but alert even to the slightest sound and movement of the wild leaves around him. It was almost daybreak and yet there was no sign of any beast. Gothang began to lose hope of catching the animal anytime soon. He decided to call it a day, gathered his weapons and stood up to leave. As soon as he stepped out of his hiding spot, he began to notice something. He saw the silhouette of two children standing right outside his traps and the pigsty.

'What are these children doing here at this hour?' Gothang muttered and to his surprise, the shadow vanished. He felt fear; his hair follicles tingled. He moved closer towards the spot where he thought he saw the children, but there was no one. Nothing.

Next morning, Gothang rose early and went back to his pigsty. He walked faster than usual, quite afraid of finding his pigs missing or attacked again. He reached his farm. True to his horror, his pigs had indeed been slaughtered by the predator yet again. His traps had been destroyed; imprints of paws were everywhere.

'No, no, no...' Gothang cried helplessly, 'Not again. Not again.'

He took care of more than 20 healthy pigs, but after the two attacks, just three of them remained. The predator seemed ravenous, clean and somehow more intelligent or just lucky. Gothang had set up nearly 10 traps and all of them had been destroyed.

With no creative solution for his misfortune, Gothang, quite unwillingly, went back to his chief's court hall.

'Allong's boy, did you catch the notorious beast?' the chief asked as soon as he set his foot inside the hall.

'I am terribly sorry, chief, but the creature attacked again. I lost more swine. I am terribly sorry for failing you,' Gothang genuflected.

The warriors who were standing behind the chief's throne mumbled amongst themselves. They were satisfied with Gothang being miserable, some even smiled triumphantly. Within a close and dependent community like theirs, none celebrated the isolation of Allong and Gothang and his unknown origin.

'You failed?' the chief asked doubtfully.

'Yes, I failed to catch the beast and it attacked yet again,' Gothang answered weakly.

'Incompetence at its best. You have taken our chief's generosity for granted,' one of the prominent warriors stood up and chided him.

Gothang didn't reply.

'Gothang, wasn't it your name?' the chief inquired calmly.

'Yes, respected chief,' Gothang answered with a bow.

'Hmmm, listen Gothang. Your father, Allong, was one of the best hunters in our clan. You see that jaguar's head and the bear? Yes, right over the first row? Your father's first kill. He must have been 14 when he conducted his Sa-ai ritual. My father honoured him right outside this hall with a grand feast by the fire.'

Gothang raised his head, utterly surprised. Sa-ai, a ritual to overpower animal spirits, could only be performed by a reputed individual, mostly grown men with exceptional hunting skills. He couldn't believe that his gentle father would be such a prodigy that he'd perform Sa-ai in his early teens. He never really knew his father though. His father was as much a loner as him. He never joined any gathering of his clan members. He stayed quite isolated from the clan's main complex, minded his own garden for food and refused any invitation for festivals. It was just Gothang and him taking pleasure in the little things of life. His father was quite a cheerful man, encouraging Gothang for everything, trivial or grand. Gothang remembered his father showering him with praises for accidentally releasing the fish when he was a kid. 'Yes child, we only take what we need but the rest belongs to nature.' His father used to say. He was a peculiar man who didn't mind the caterpillars feasting over his cabbages, talking to the birds who came to feast on the caterpillars as if he was delighted by the whole food chain, calling all of nature's creatures by funny names. For such a man to be once the greatest huntsman of the clan was unimaginable for Gothang. He didn't know about it at all.

'My father saw great things in Allong and he always wanted him to lead our warriors someday. Always asked us to look after him, to hunt together and even to offer my sister's hand for marriage. If that had happened, your father would have sat right here,' the old chief smiled as if remembering more. 'But, it didn't. Did it? Right before the announcement of his title as the warrior commander, he brought you. A child out of nowhere. Nobody questioned Allong's loyalty to the clan, but my father wanted an explanation. He refused to give a sensible answer. He made up the most hilarious story he could think of, that he found you in a casket made of cloud. A hero was instantly turned into a lunatic. It broke my sister's heart and my father's expectations.'

Gothang was quiet. He knew the chief wouldn't lie. Why would his father do that?

'Chief, if am allowed to say something, my father never talked of the past. I know very little of him and nothing at all about my mother.'

'Yes, the most baffling part was your mother. We never expected your father to hide information about her. He kept on repeating his ridiculous story. Knowing how much he valued our clan's reputation, the only explanation is that your mother must be some maiden from the defeated clans.'

Gothang felt a sting from the chief's remark about his mother. He felt even more betrayed that his father refused to talk about his mother just because she was from an inferior clan. He didn't interrupt and let the chief continue.

'Whatever the circumstances, my father was ready to forgive him, but he was the one who didn't return. He didn't leave the clan, yes, but he was never the Allong we knew, ever again. You somehow changed him. He left his prestigious existence, gave up his clan duties and went to a corner to raise you.' The chief took a sip from his wine gourd and gave a sad look, 'Gothang, shouldn't I be expecting something from you? You are Allong's boy! He must have taught you well. I know you have it in you. Don't let your brave father down.'

'I wouldn't disappoint you again, Chief,' Gothang promised.

'Gothang, I entrust you to solve this problem and bring peace to my aged mind. Our clan is big and mighty, but I have been bothered lately. Our southern ranges seem not as serene as they used to be. And now with the thought of a predator lurking in our ranching slope, it only makes me feel worse.'

'Chief, thank you for trusting me. Thank you for telling me about my father. Let me take my leave and I shall deliver on your expectations,' Gothang bowed his farewell with gritted teeth.

The story of his father changed something in Gothang. He wanted to keep his promise to the chief and to make sure that the predator that caused so much trouble was put to justice.

The slope got covered in traps, and Gothang sat down behind the bush for another wait. This time, he made sure he brought enough food for three days. He wouldn't be leaving without the beast at any cost.

The sun went down and the few remaining pigs in his farm loitered around without a worry. In complete darkness, Gothang lay parked on his spot, his eyes fixed ahead, ready to catch on any sudden movement. The whole night went without anything exciting happening. The beast somehow refused to turn up.

The day started to break in the eastern sky. His eyes were stung from the sleepless hours, but Gothang didn't want to move or rove his eyes away. He wondered if the beast was indeed intelligent.

A soft something wafted around Gothang's left shoulder. He suspected a branch and looked up but what he saw threw him out of his hiding spot, screaming for his life. A mountainous beast, reddish brown fur, wolf head but with two giant antlers, one silver, one gold, and with a thick furry tail were looking down at him. He lay petrified on the ground. The giant beast looked at him with its bright red eyes and a smiley mouth opened slightly where its brilliant white fangs were visible.

'What in the world...' Gothang cried weakly, but he couldn't finish his sentence as something else began to move behind the beast within the wild bushes. Another one came out, a twin.

'Not one but two?' Gothang surrendered as the two giant beasts stood together with a grin near his feet.

He closed his eyes and waited for the beast to embed its fangs on his flesh, but a soft wet tongue licked Gothang's trembling face. He timidly opened his eyes and saw both the beasts kneeling right beside him as if they were his pets. Their thick tails waved excitedly. He sat up and the beasts responded with excitement as he moved, so he stayed still, his eyes searching for his *dao*. He saw it lying near his hiding spot. He felt helpless. He took a closer look at the identical beasts and was sure that they were unusual and that he had never seen such creatures before. They looked like overgrown wolves or bear-wolves with fancy antlers. Gothang ignored the beauty of the beasts. He wanted to make sure that both the beasts made it to the skull collection inside the chief's hall, right next to his father's jaguar head and the bear.

'So how do I get my weapon?' Gothang wondered. The beasts were looking at him as excited as ever, panting heavily and rolling out their pinkish tongues. He stood up slowly, the beasts circled around him, sniffing and panting, but they didn't seem threatening to him for some reason. If the beasts wanted him dead, he would be dead already. He began to move ever so slightly towards his hiding spot. The beasts didn't make a move but their ruby eyes followed him.

'Don't look at me. Don't look at me,' Gothang found himself praying.

Little by little, he was about to reach his hiding place, where he could actually see his thick shiny blade resting neatly on the grass. Just a few more steps, he thought. The beasts still didn't move or attack him, but were intriguingly observing everything; one was even tilting its head in curiosity. Gothang felt their eyes burning up his back as he tried extremely slowly to get near his spot.

When he finally stretched out his hand to retrieve his *dao*, he heard the beasts move. He wasn't quite sure what happened, but he felt the sharp fangs scrapping his bottom as a beast picked him up by his loincloth and dragged him out of one of the bushes. The rest of the journey became a blur. One of the beasts was carrying him away. He screamed helplessly as he swung around the beast's mouth as it took him to an unknown place. The beasts ran and ran; mountains and lake scenes rushing past them. Gothang tried to look around but the beast ran fast and everything was blurry. After hours of travel, both the beasts slowed down and finally stopped in front of a large water body, a lake. They dropped Gothang gently on the ground and waited for him to stand up. He grunted at the uncomfortable trip, his back hurt from the swing and his head still felt wobbly.

'Why did you bring me here?' Gothang managed to speak as he struggled to stand up.

The beasts gave a satisfied howl and retreated towards the forest.

'Wait, wait. Wait! Where are we? Take me back. Where...' Gothang tried to follow the beasts, but they disappeared fast within the forest nearby. He turned back to the lake for a clue. He realized it was not an ordinary lake but one that surrounded a huge island. He also realized that the lake was lined with people half submerged and covered with a white cloth, chanting something together. He stood quietly, observing the unusual site, but a loud horn alerted him. He looked towards the sound. An equestrian was announcing something,

'...to safety. Listen, O Listen! I bring you the royal announcement. The royal ministry has ordered every citizen of this kingdom to stay within the protected periphery of their compound until further notice. Everyday duties and conducts...'

Gothang stood clueless. He saw a confused crowd at the far end where a patch of cramped settlement was seen.

'Am I in what they call the Central Kingdom?' Gothang began to understand. He had only heard about the Central Kingdom in the news. He was sure the Central Palace was known for its impenetrable water defence that surrounded the palace island.

'The Central Palace? That's weeks away from my hill,' Gothang murmured at the absurdity. 'Why would the beasts drop me here? How did they travel such great distance within such few hours? Did anybody see them? What is going on?' His head was bursting with thoughts.

'Excuse me, young handsome man,' a male voice said in a soft tone. As Gothang turned, he noticed a well-built man in his thirties, carrying a bundle, dressed in a bright multi-coloured robe and sarong, exquisite feather headdress around his unevenly long hair, with thin facial hair, a gold earring on the left ear, and a pair of dark brown eyes looking admirably at Gothang.

'Me?' Gothang answered nervously.

'Yes, you,' the man giggled, 'How many men as handsome as you do you think there are?' He gestured at Gothang to move aside, 'You are in my way.'

'Sorry. I am new here,' Gothang replied shyly.

'Oh and you have an accent. Hmmm, southern man. I see,' the man observed Gothang's loincloth and nodded.

'So, what...' Gothang wanted to ask many questions but didn't know where to begin or if he was asking the right person.

'You heard the gong, right? The world is ending. I would suggest you not to stand here for long. Even I am heading home now,' the man bowed to leave.

'Please, I don't know anyone here. I just reached here and I am completely lost,' Gothang cried out, frustrated and a bit scared.

The man seemed to think for a bit and then replied, 'Well, you can come to my place and then we can discuss matters.'

The Ominous Foresight

'And that fish goes well with the bamboo too,' Lungchum chattered as the four of them galloped idly on their respective horses towards the Luwang province. Except for Yangba, the other three horses were black, carefully selected from the royal horse shed. They got the strongest ones, the ones that must be ready for combat.

'Is he planning to discuss food for the whole journey?' Iwan murmured so that only Laiba could hear him. Sana was riding her horse as if she were a statue, probably worried sick of what might happen.

'What do you want him to talk about?' Laiba asked, giving a bored look.

'Well, there is a lot he could speak about. About the rites that turned him into a dragon?' Iwan hissed.

'Ask him then. Got a problem? You address it. That is how humans solve problems, I guess,' Laiba pulled the reigns of his horse and galloped a little ahead so that he rode at the same pace as Sana's.

Iwan rolled his eyes and moved his horse closer to Lungchum and interrupted the happy chatter, 'Prince Lungchum, I was wondering if you can give details about the rites that turned you into a dragon.'

'Yes? And just Lungchum, please. We all agreed to keep the formalities aside. Didn't we?' Lungchum seemed happy that Iwan had finally spoken to him. He smiled and answered, 'Our chief seer received the great prophecy too.'

'And?' Iwan raised his eyebrow impatiently.

'And, we conducted several rites to make me competent for the journey. Since I am the son of the great serpent king, the charm was easy and I was able to morph into a divine being and embarked on my destined journey.'

'But you have also got wings and legs, and those are very different from the serpentine dragons we know of, the Nongda Lairels.'

'Obviously, I don't belong to the Nongda, the celestial origin; so, my form is different. I am just a mortal son of a divine father.'

'Yes. It's still hard to believe that you are a real son of the serpent king. He ruled this kingdom hundreds of years ago. As far as I know, after completing his human reign, our serpent king turned permanently into a monster serpent and suddenly disappeared from the great lake which used to be his dwelling place.'

Lungchum looked at Iwan and said, 'Since I was abandoned in my childhood, there is a part of my story that is not clear.'

Laiba didn't pay much attention to the talk, but his eyes began to pulsate as he started witnessing a dreamy vision:

A maiden was walking through a mountain trail, swaying her axe on the low branches off her face. She was humming gently, a soft creature to look at, but the size of her axe and the movement of her arms were enough to rethink about underestimating her strength. She was beautiful with long dark hair, honey-kissed complexion and bright almond eyes that roved around the woods, searching for fruits and nuts. She picked wild fruits, nuts and chopped some firewood, then tied it all together into a bundle and turned around to return. As she walked down the slope, she stopped at a cliff where she saw the view of the vast lake underneath. Loktak was gleaming golden under the twilight sky.

She stood staring at the mighty waters for long, while a gentle breeze refreshed her sweating face. Quite abruptly, she dropped her bundle and ran down the slope, towards the lake. Breathless, she ran towards the shoreline, not worrying about the mud and the dry fens staining her clothes.

There was no one, just wild birds fishing over the shallow water near the shore, but they all flew away in fright when the lady ran towards the lake. She stopped when she got near a body, the body she had seen from the hilltop.

'Are are you alright?' the lady nudged the body. It was a young man, probably a drowned victim washed ashore.

'Lord, he is still breathing,' the woman murmured in relief and pulled up the unconscious man out of the muddy shore and towards a flat, giant boulder nearby.

She pressed the man's chest, breathed in through his mouth and repeated the process quite earnestly. The man coughed out a bit of water and opened his eyes. They looked at each other without exchanging any words for a while. (The vision shifted).

The pair was running around an orchard, embracing each other, the man put flowers in the woman's hair, while she giggled. He also produced a golden staff and gave it to the girl with a kiss. (The view got distorted and shifted again).

Then came the view of a cottage. An elderly man was angrily shouting, a sickly lady was on the floor. It was the same woman from the previous vision. Now she was kneeling on the floor with a swollen belly. Tears gushed out uncontrollably and the elderly man pushed her out of the house. The woman walked away, holding a golden staff to support her heavy body. (The vision flickered and changed again).

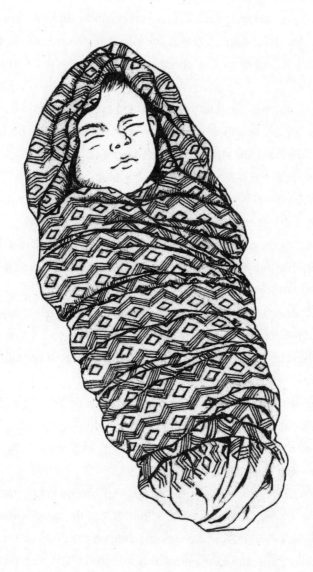

The lady now held a small baby in her arms and walked around in tattered clothes, ignored by all on the busy street. She seemed starved. Her once dark hair was covered in dust, her clothes were soiled and her small bundle was carefully wrapped in an old piece of cloth. The child was sleeping peacefully in her arms, a fair child with dark silky hair. Then came the man who pushed the woman away; he seemed to talk to the woman, grabbing her by her hand and pulling away. The woman struggled to free herself, 'Let me go! I don't want to return home, father! Let me go...' Laiba could hear the woman.

(Another flicker and the view shifted back to the cottage). It was a moonlit night. The man lurked out of his own house with a bundle and ran towards the nearby forest. Laiba's vision seemed to follow him. The man looked around sneakily, left the bundle under a rotten tree and ran away without turning back. Laiba took a closer look and realized it was the child.

In another flickered vision, the man told the woman, 'Your son got lost and died. I searched for him everywhere.' Bitter cries filled the room. (The view flickered again). Now the woman was clad in a royal attire and dragged out of her house by the father. He pushed her inside a decorated palanquin and asked the men to carry her away fast. The woman didn't protest anymore, but was crying uncontrollably.

Another change in the view and Laiba found himself inside an elegant room or a space dotted with several celestial objects.

'I need to go back, father!' A man was crying.

Laiba turned around and saw the serpent king in his divine form, crying; there were tears in his eyes.

'You cannot. Your time in the human realm is over. Say no more of it.'

'But I left a son and a wife! I need to go back! Just this once. Please... please...' the voice cried, but Laiba saw himself closing the celestial door with a loud thunderous sound.

(The flickering visions changed faster now). Young Lungchum running around the forest as a wild being, scavenging in a market place, chased by the royal guards near the great lake, bringing him towards the king's cottage, grooming the tiny boy into a royal child, Lungchum being surrounded by the Moirang seers, the king handing him a golden staff. Then there was smoke and he turned into a serpentine dragon—all seven of them united and seen laughing together as if they had succeeded in their quest...

The vision intensified with blood-red clouds and cries of war breaking up everywhere. Laiba was confused for a moment. He felt like he was standing on top of a mountain. He could see the whole kingdom smothered with smoke and fire. There was a terrible screech from the sky. He looked up and saw Lungchum going rampant in his divine form. He seemed angry. The realm was infested with unknown powers, alien schemes and manipulated faiths...

Laiba's eyes came back to normal, but he found himself shivering on his horse. Sana didn't seem to notice. He turned back and looked at Lungchum, happily talking with Iwan. A possible future with Lungchum succumbing to hatred, Laiba thought. Somehow, Laiba seemed to conclude that the Moirang prince was not supposed to know of his past. Maybe, the divine order wanted him to intervene, he wondered. Or else, why would he get the vision now?

'Prince Lungchum, I just received a vision for you,' Laiba turned back and said with a faint smile.

'Yes?' Lungchum asked excited, 'What was it about?'

'Come closer. I will show you telepathically. I can do that with my ocular power,' Laiba gestured for Lungchum come near him. Lungchum rode up with a nervous smile.

Iwan and Sana observed quietly. Laiba held onto Lungchum's shoulders and his golden eye gleamed on him. Lungchum stared deep into Laiba's eyes, not moving a muscle. Iwan knew that Laiba was rendering a vision for Lungchum. He found it unfair. Laiba failed to give any vision for his missing mother, but gave one for the dragon boy. Things seemed annoyingly easy for the Moirang prince, everyone so ready to respect him. He left the group to ride ahead. Sana saw the look of disappointment in his eyes. She followed him and called out, 'Iwan, we don't know the way. We should wait for Laiba.'

'Let them be. They seem busy. I will be here.' Iwan stopped his horse a little ahead and decided to wait for the group. He looked back at the Moirang prince and his head priest staring at each other. He looked away, sulking with a 'Huh!'

Lungchum saw the vision where his mother and father met for the first time at the shore of the lake. His father gave a golden staff to his mother. He saw his mother becoming pregnant and giving birth to him. He saw his mother going through a rough jungle path with him on her back. A wolf came out and chased her. She ran fast but her Nahong, the baby carrier cloth, unfastened by mistake and he fell on the ground. He could hear his mother scream, but the wolf took him and ran away. Lungchum instinctively noted the pattern of the cloth his mother used. It was woven in a tiger motif. The vision began to flicker and Lungchum came back to his present self as if woken up from a dream.

'So that was what had happened,' Lungchum smiled, 'and all this time, I hated her without knowing anything...I always thought she abandoned me to marry a king,' Lungchum spoke calmly. Laiba nodded, looking down at his hands, mentally convincing himself again that his altering the vision was what he was supposed to do.

'The first vision we saw, it was my parents. Weren't they? So in love,' Lungchum said with a smile, his eyes were sparkling, the corners wet.

'Your mother found him, but didn't know he was the monster that everyone was so afraid of. Our Lord Pakhangba, the first serpent king, turned human only few times after his eternal exile and he was fortunate to meet your mother. She fell in love, had you, but then your father completed his service in the human realm and was ordered to return to his celestial abode right before your birth.'

'You saw your parents?' Sana asked, interested to know what transpired.

'Yes, they met near the great lake. They were so in love, but not so lucky. And my poor mother lost me to a wolf. I feel bad now that she died thinking I was dead,' Lungchum said bluntly, but Laiba knew the Moirang prince was deeply moved despite his calm face.

'Your father, our serpent king, fought hard to return to you. It's just that he couldn't,' Laiba said, omitting the part where he shut the celestial door.

'I know,' Lungchum humbly replied, 'My father is a god and a very kind one as I have always heard. He wouldn't just abandon me if not for some important reason. My mother probably died of grief, but I am just glad that they are at least together now. Or are they?' A familiar smile coursed through his pale face as he looked at Laiba for comfort.

'Yes, your mother is actually our first queen, reincarnated. She will always be by his side. That's the reason why they were united again and had you. Gods are strange. I must be strange too.'

'It must have been hard for you.' Sana said softly.

'Childhood was hard. Life in the street was not common, so I had to be constantly roaming within the forest for a living. When the Moirang king began searching for me, I thought he wanted to kill me. Didn't know that the seer prophesied my existence after the death of my mother...'

They all rode their horses to join Iwan who was waiting impatiently ahead. He saw the group approaching him and decided to act aloof, but their conversation caught his attention. Lungchum was speaking in a calm and clear voice, but looked a bit grave for the first time. Iwan couldn't help but wonder what made the irritatingly cheerful boy look so. He pulled his horse near Lungchum and listened as he spoke.

'My stepfather is very kind to me. That golden staff that father gave to mother, he actually gave it to me. I soon realized it was magical and it helped me through a lot.' Seeing Iwan raising his brows in question, Lungchum added, 'Yes, it was a magical staff. I used to do a lot of amazing things with it.'

'So then, where is it now?' Iwan asked eagerly.

'The Moirang seers took it and used it during the rites to turn me into a dragon,' Lungchum smiled.

'I am glad you learned about your parents,' Sana said, genuinely happy for Lungchum.

'Thank you. You are also very kind,' Lungchum bowed to Sana.

'I have been doing fine without any magical staff, just saying,' Iwan said, puffing up his chest for no apparent reason.

'Story time is over. We are in the Luwang province now,' Laiba interrupted before Lungchum could respond and all of them had to focus back on their track. The long dusty road snaked all the way through its crowded settlement. It was just houses, though. No one was seen in spite of them arriving at the bright hour of a beautiful afternoon.

'You said north-west right?' Iwan asked again.

'Yes, this way,' Laiba galloped his horse forward and led the way.

They crossed the market street, which was deserted. All the houses and shops were bolted shut. They could hear people inside a few huts and cottages, but it was just some whispers and murmurs.

'Sure, everyone has panicked,' Sana admitted, riding a bit behind with Lungchum.

'They will be fine if we find the scissor soon. Don't worry,' Lungchum tried to cheer her up.

'I hope so,' Sana replied with a smile.

'Yes, smile more. You are beautiful like that,' Lungchum spoke so bluntly, but Sana was already blushing red. Iwan saw the duo when he turned back. Pathetic, he thought.

'Laiba, I think our dragon is flirting with your wife,' Iwan leant forward and murmured to Laiba, who was busy trying to lead them towards the exact location.

'Like I care, Your Majesty. I am trying to locate our guardians, so will you please excuse me and shut up?' Laiba turned towards Iwan and he almost fell out of his horse when he saw Laiba's pupils glowing. The eyes were always hard to get familiar with.

'God, Yangba, did you see his eyes? Sometimes the yellow one seems bigger and sometimes the silver one. His irises seem to change their sizes according to their use. Don't you think? And now they are glowing, strange...' Iwan bent and spoke to his horse instead.

'Sana, according to the prophecy, I believe you are the incarnation of our Mother Goddess, Taoroinai, the Mother Dragon of the universe, the Supreme Goddess, Leimarel Sidabi?' Lungchum asked as they leisurely followed Laiba and Iwan who led the way.

'Yes, but I just found out about it from Lord Laiba and our Meidingu,' Sana answered as timidly as always. 'Seems unreal.'

'But, my lady, the prophecy can never be wrong. Especially, an oracle like the Tarang Laipao. Our Supreme Mother is both fear and love incarnate. You are a combination of the very best of both. I do await your awakening,' Lungchum continued his never-ending smile.

'Awakening?' Sana wondered, thoughts of her being close to anything great was quite unimaginable.

'The moment I left my kingdom for this journey, all I thought about was meeting you. My shaman talked of you with the highest regard. He even reminded me not to forget to bow before you, but our first encounter was perhaps a bit confusing, and I missed my chance to do so. I hope you have forgiven me,' Lungchum bowed his head slightly.

'What is there to forgive, Your Highness?' Sana flustered, 'Please, every time I think about the Goddess and me as one, my head begins to wobble.'

'You may have your reason to remain dormant for now. But, my lady, you are no doubt our Supreme Queen. Unmistakably. She is also known for her beauty, and you prove it right.'

'Oh! Ahehehey...' Sana giggled awkwardly, but looked at Iwan wondering if he heard Lungchum. Did Iwan also think so? She wondered.

Iwan turned back when he heard the giggle, 'Lungchum roasted Sana's face.' He delivered the news to his horse. Laiba would have heard him, but the boy was busy pulling his horse towards a thick dense forest, their journey becoming more and more isolated within the thick woods of the Luwang province, his eyes and mind delving deep into another realm of the unknown for guidance.

Iwan noticed the dark canopy above, streaks of the afternoon sun bouncing around the waving leaves. They saw a few reed huts scattered around, but all of them looked forsaken and left to rot for a long time.

'Do people still live here?' Iwan wondered aloud.

'It seems pretty deserted,' Sana answered doubtfully. She pulled up her horse to be closer with Iwan.

'Oh, Sana. What weird things was Lungchum telling you?' Iwan asked aloud.

'No...no, nothing, Your...ah Iwan,' Sana avoided looking at the Meidingu.

Lungchum replied from behind, 'Nothing weird, brother.'

'It's getting dark. I wonder when we will finally be able to meet the other guardians. Lord Laiba, you were sure of them both, right?' Sana tried to change the topic.

'My visions are never wrong, my lady. It is just that they don't come out as often as I would want them,' Laiba said apologetically.

'Pretty much like a fart, Laiba,' Iwan began to giggle.

'That one was funny,' Lungchum joined in the laughter, but Iwan stopped, annoyed.

'So, Maichou Laiba, we know of our sky prince, but do you know anything about the other guardian?' Sana continued with her inquiry and Laiba tried to answer to his best, with all that he knew of the guardians so far.

The three continued with their chatter and followed Laiba deeper into the woods.

Napa-yanba Macha

'Shall I carry your bundle?' Gothang asked politely. The man's belongings seemed heavy on his shoulders.

'Humble gesture, but I am fine. Not so far from here now, my home,' the man replied.

They had walked a long way from the Central Province and were now approaching a thick forest. Gothang had introduced himself, but was yet to know about his generous host who was odd enough to let a stranger like him to tag along to his home. He knew he could get into a dangerous situation if the man turned out to be troublesome, but something told him that the man had dignity. It might be because of the manner in which he spoke, his way of dressing or his caring nature that reassured Gothang that there wouldn't be anything rough. However, he also noticed the abandoned huts and the slow feeling of isolation as they walked deeper into the woods. Sounds of rustling leaves and mountain cicadas filled the air; dragonflies and beetles frequently whistled past their faces.

'You live alone?' Gothang asked, unsure.

'Alone? I guess so. Yes. Now, I am alone.' The man confirmed, a sad twinge in his voice.

'What happened to the huts around here?'

'They left. Things are different now.'

'Different?'

'To be honest, people are scared. So, they packed their things and just ran away.'

'Scared of what?' Gothang asked nervously. He sensed something scary, alright.

The man stopped and rested his bundle on the ground to wipe his forehead; he did it so elegantly.

'Here, at least let me help you with this. You were kind enough to welcome a stranger like me to your place.' Gothang took the bundle and hung it across his broad shoulders before the man could protest. Good Guardians! Gothang almost cried out when the bundle crushed his shoulder. It was incredibly heavy, like it was filled with rocks. He wondered what was inside, but was polite enough not to ask the man.

'Oh, you are really such a nice gentleman. Not just in your looks, but also in your mannerisms,' the man smiled gratefully.

'So, what are they are scared of?' Gothang asked, as the subject did disturb him. What if the creatures that dropped him in the Central Kingdom were the culprits?

'It's the *lanmei thanbi* in this forest. Lately, we have seen it a lot.'

'What?' Gothang couldn't understand. 'What's that?'

'*Lanmei thanbi*. You don't know?'

Gothang shook his head.

'They are the floating fire spirits of the forests and the swamps. It is part of legends and myths, but now we see so many of them floating around our woods as soon as midnight approaches. I have encountered them many times, but never thought they were reason enough to be so scared that I leave my only home. Some of them are even adorable.'

'Adorable floating fires?' Gothang asked, a bit confused.

'I mean they are usually small and bluish green or sometimes even pinkish orange. They float around the woods as if they were decorative balls of torches. I find it appealing to watch them.'

'Yes, it sounds attractive when you say it that way,' Gothang admitted. Brilliant, coloured lights in the dark of the night sounded pretty.

'But you see, they were not supposed to loiter around the human realm; so, people took them to be the spirits of the dark realm and despise encountering them.'

'Do they attack people?'

'No, not really. They sometimes mislead hunters, as the legends say, make people lose their way and such, but you see, they are just balls of floating fire. You will lose your way if you were stupid enough to follow them.' The man said matter-of-factly.

Gothang nodded in agreement.

'Oh, by the way, we are almost home now and I still haven't introduced myself properly.' The man stood proud and announced, 'I am Leisatao of Luwang, the famous dart-maker.'

Gothang stood blinking for a moment, but it quickly hit him that the moment needed some kind of applause, so he threw in some wonder in his voice and said, 'The dart-maker?'

'Oh well, my name might have not reached the ranges yet, but here I am peerless in my art. All of the royal darts, any size, come from my humble cottage over there,' Leisatao pointed ahead, where a hut came into view at the far corner of the tiny glade within the forest. 'Each meticulously designed and handcrafted by my own hands. *Arambai*, one of the most prestigious weapons to wield, the most accurate and vicious of all darts.'

'I know *arambai*.' Gothang realized that the heavy bundle he was carrying might be supplies for making darts. It explained the weight. He knew *arambai* well. The various provinces in the valley were known for their notoriety with these weapons. Moreover, none knew the technique to make one except a few brilliant artisans and he realized Leisatao might be one of those talented few.

'Of course, you know it,' Leisatao beamed.

'I heard it is very popular here. Undefeatable.'

'A little exaggerated, but yes; none could wield it as effectively as these valley warriors, and also it is suited to the terrain. There is even this popular saying: "Never chase a valley warrior who retreated."' Leisatao stopped and cried, 'We are home. My sweet home. Come, come.'

Gothang saw a neat cottage above a thick wooden plinth in the clearing, poorly fenced by small bamboo groves standing in scattered clusters. The house had tiny windows with embroidered fabric windowpanes, woodcrafted windowsills and doors, flower motifs around the vents, evenly trimmed thatched roofs—it was a house worthy of an artisan.

'Beautiful. And that too, right in the middle of the forest,' Gothang said admiringly.

'Thank you. And yes, my bundle. It must be heavy. Rest it here, quick,' Leisatao hastily opened his door and they both walked in.

Gothang not only dropped the bundle but also his jaw. The inside of the cottage was painstakingly decorated, in fact, much more than it was on the outside—feathers and shiny metals moulded into miniature animals and dolls of all tribes and clans were kept as display pieces inside wooden cabinets. There were also long and tall rows of urns and sealed crocks, probably a collection of hand-prepared lethal solutions for the darts. Silks and finely woven cotton fabrics hung on the walls as huge drapes. Cane and bamboo furniture filled the space with matching tables and stools. A huge table, noticeably a worktable set at the centre, was full of tools and supplies, alongside a tall heap of exquisite feathers gleaming in their vibrant shades, and few unfinished pieces of the acclaimed dart weapon, *arambai*.

'You must be rich,' Gothang concluded.

'To fight loneliness, perhaps, I acquired too much of wealth for fun. Embarrassing, but nobody minds it here,' Leisatao said sadly.

Gothang didn't respond to the deep and pitiful words. He just roved around the rooms and observed the decorations. Even the kitchen oven was made of huge rocks and was arranged neatly into a triangular pit. Must be heavy to move, he noted. There was the regular bamboo back door on the right, opposite to the pit. With the bedroom filled with velvet futons and cotton sheets, there was an unmistakable taste for luxury.

'Rice wine?' Leisatao asked, bringing in a pitcher to the bedroom.

'Yes, please,' Gothang bowed and extended his hand for the pitcher. 'I shall do the honour.'

'Here...' Leisatao passed the container and he brought out two bamboo beakers.

As the younger affiliate, Gothang served the wine to his host and also poured himself a generous amount.

'You must be thirsty. I have several batches of the fresh ferments that will last throughout the year, so drink as much as you like. Alright?' Leisatao pampered his guest.

'Sure,' Gothang drank the whole portion in one go.

They both sat quietly and drank until the pitcher was empty and it was time for a refill.

'More?' Leisatao shook the pitcher lightly.

'No, I am fine. We can continue later,' Gothang replied.

'I am glad you are here,' Leisatao began. 'But, why at the Central Palace? Want to meet someone?'

'I...I was abducted,' Gothang couldn't think of a better way to explain his bizarre adventure.

'What?' Leisatao cried out dramatically, flipping his long hair in disbelief.

Gothang realized he shouldn't share the details of his bizarre incident to the kind stranger and changed the subject instead. He asked about the commotion in the Central Kingdom.

'Oh, that,' Leisatao cleared his throat and continued, 'It seems that we are in some trouble now. The Meidingu initiated a Tarang Laipao and it came out bad, it seems. Quite understandable. It prophesied an impending catastrophe and that we should refrain from crossing the protected periphery of our house until some divine problem is solved.'

'Really? What kind of catastrophe?'

'I don't know the details. I went to deliver supplies and heard some news here and there, that's all. But it does seem serious. I saw people panicking in confusion.'

'Wouldn't the Meidingu inform the greater clans in the ranges for alliance?'

'He should. I don't know. The new Meidingu is said to be young. However, no worries. It's the royals and their business. I just live, make darts and will die one day. Catastrophe or not. So, didn't care much. You seemed worried. Anybody back home that you shall be reuniting with soon?'

Gothang kept quiet for a moment, but answered, 'No one.' Nevertheless, he sure wanted to return home and search for his mother. He had recently become very sure she was alive, running somewhere.

'No one?' Leisatao stared back at Gothang.

'My father died years ago and since then, I am practically alone. I live as a swineherd at my chief's farm. No friends, no one. Just me and my pigs.'

'Welcome to the guild, then. I lost my parents too. I probably killed them,' Leisatao said glumly.

'For real?' Gothang almost jumped.

'Hehe...not directly. But, they died because of me alright. My parents were Luwang nobles. I grew up in the Luwang royal court. But you see, I am...well...I am me. My mother accepted me for who I am, but my father didn't. Long story,' Leisatao drank another tumbler of wine in one go. Gothang didn't say anything, but was ready to hear the lonely man out. He had been lonely too.

'Can you believe it? Even before I was born, my father promised our Luwang king for a wedlock for their children. Our king had a princess and my father got me. They were happy with the alliance. It wasn't my fault the way things turned out. I am their child, you see. Even our princess was fine with me being *me*! My father went mad when he realized that the marriage cannot happen. I confessed so honestly. Bravely. Bowed to him a thousand times. But my father said, a promise is a promise. Without a thought, my father went to our king to offer his head as well as my mother's as a payment for the shame. It happened when I turned 27. Ten years now, to be exact. Been so long, but still feels so painful.' Leisatao stopped drinking and looked up, as if in thoughts. He had witnessed his father slitting his mother's throat. The Luwang king begged forgiveness and asked him to stop the madness. But Leisatao's father didn't stop. He gave one last bitter look at the shrieking Leisatao and slit his own throat. It was the last time Leisatao ever set foot in the Luwang court. He had exiled himself inside the deepest part of the woods since then.

'I am sorry,' Gothang wasn't sure what he should say after such a talk.

'Why should you be sorry? This is the first time I have talked of this to anyone. I feel incredibly light now. Back in the Luwang court, I am known as the Napa-yanba Macha, father-slayer. They wouldn't understand my side of it, so I never talked. Despite all this, our princess is still kind to me, but for other people's sake, I avoid her for her own good. This pain had been buried deep in my heart for long. Meeting you, a complete stranger, gave me comfort and helping you out would give even more pleasure,' Leisatao smiled after a loud hiccup.

'I am glad I could be of a little comfort to you, brother,' Gothang smiled back.

'You can leave for your clan tomorrow, but with bad news around and with your abductors still at large, why don't you stay here for a couple more days?' Leisatao sat up and asked kindly.

'Will you be alright with it?' Gothang had no plans to stay any longer, but he didn't want to be rude to the kind stranger with his kind offer.

'Absolutely,' Leisatao sprang up in delight, 'I will arrange a bed for you right away. We will also have a nice dinner of roasted meat and black rice today. I haven't had any guests before. This is exciting for me. You shall wait here. I will make the arrangements, don't you dare move. Rest here while I go and arrange for things.'

Leisatao ran out from the bedroom and shuffled around in his belongings. Gothang heard the kitchen fire being lighted and the scrapings of pots and pans. He lay down on the bed and waited patiently, as told.

After a few moments, Leisatao came in wearing a simple cotton shawl and sarong, his long hair covered with a wide scarf and said, 'Boy, you can wash yourself in the pond at the back. Dinner will be ready in a moment. I have also hung fresh clothes by the bamboo line near the pond for you to change. Do be quick, alright?'

Gothang went to the pond, freshened up and wore the fresh clothes. He was glad with the new cotton shirt and the loincloth provided instead of his old one with huge holes around the buttock made by the beast. I had been walking almost naked the whole day, Gothang realized as he examined his traditional fabric before tossing it away.

Inside, Leisatao had already arranged the meal at the small cane table, lighted by bright torches in a high wooden stand nearby. There were several pots and bowls filled with vegetables and stew and in the centre was the huge piece of roasted meat sitting above the mighty heap of sticky black rice.

'A feast!' Gothang exclaimed with a smile.

'Don't be silly,' Leisatao waved his hand shyly, 'this is the least I could do.'

'Shall we?' Gothang offered to serve as they both took their seats.

Before Leisatao could answer, there was a knock at the door.

'I think someone just knocked...' Gothang noticed Leisatao's frightened face.

'I know,' he answered grimly.

The knock was repeated.

'You said you never have any guests here.'

'I know,' Leisatao stood up slowly and retrieved one of his *arambai* from the work table. He gestured at Gothang to keep quiet and went to the door.

He slowly pulled the latch and peeped outside.

'Greetings,' a happy voice greeted him. A bald child, incredibly pale, with snowy eyebrows and lashes and bicoloured eyes, one sunset yellow and another silvery gray. Strange little creature.

'Smells delicious,' another tall boy who stood behind the bald child remarked in the Moirang accent. Big round eyes and clear porcelain skin, the boy wore some fancy clothes.

'We need to greet them first,' a timid girl mumbled at the tall boy and made a quick curtsy to Leisatao, who was just gawping at them without a word. She looked neat and poised.

'Can we ask for water now? I am literally dying here,' complained another boy who was standing farther behind. He was a lean boy with a distinct mole on his chin and head full of curls.

There was a group of children with horses and torches in the dark of the night.

KAMATEI, THE BOULDER SPIRITS

*A*cadaverous figure came, dragging itself out of a bush—a man in red loincloth, body covered in black tattoos, gem-studded bone earrings and hornbill feather over his high hair bun. His parched tongue stuck out as if to collect vapours from the air to quench his thirst; he seemed possessed by the demon of hunger. His sunken eyes roved tiredly, but the view was something that made him breathe faster, his legs trembling with too much happiness. The man cried, but with a big smile. In front of him was the spread of a beautiful garden nested betwixt the low hills. A garden filled with voluptuous squashes, creepers netting the ground with hardly any space to walk. Each and every rise of a tendril nurturing huge-sized pumpkins, gourds of all kinds and low shrubs stooping with ripe fruits—oranges, berries, tomatoes, so much so that the greens of the garden were interspersed with a heavy dose of all delicious colours.

The man, who had probably walked in dying of fatigue for days, ran up to the wild crop and feasted to his heart's content. He stuffed his mouth, squeezing the berries that exploded with a tangy elixir, chewing diligently almost anything that his hands could pluck.

Stuffed with the bouquet, he looked around for water and found a tiny pond with clear water nearby. 'Didn't even see this one before,' he said to himself, distracted as he was with the foods. However, there was no time

he could lose. He had a family to feed at home. He just ran into a treasure trove of supplies that could last them a lifetime and was delighted at the thought of finally being about to feed his family in abundance, something he had not been able to do in quite a long time. He looked about and saw the plantain grove decked with ripe clusters of bananas.

'How convenient,' he muttered and went to pull down a few of the huge leaves to make a basket.

After a few more moments of work, he was sure to carry sufficient vegetables and fruits from the strangely abundant wild garden patch. With years of failed harvest, the man had been trying to scavenge through the mountain forest to fight the hunger, but with little luck. Up until now. He was on the verge of giving up, but then he found the most fertile patch of land that grew almost anything delicious.

'Wait until my wife gets to hear about what I found. We could all come and settle here. My children could establish their own clan here.'

The happy man carried the basket over his head and walked out of the garden to return home. It was around noon. The sun was right above him, his cracked feet stomping on his shadow. He hummed his favourite festival song and walked the long journey in good spirits, conjuring up an image of his happy family circling him when he told them the news. For hours, he walked, but the path did not lead him to his familiar route back home.

'Did I lose my way?' The man thought doubtfully, as he knew the ranges well enough to travel blindfolded. He must have taken a wrong turn in excitement. Just as he realized he may have taken a wrong path, he noticed the same garden lying ahead.

'God! So, I had been going in circles. I sure am an idiot.' The man made sure that he marked his track this time, so that he wouldn't make any idiotic wrong turns again. As he went, he left a mark on the tree trunk that stood at the crossroads leading to the garden.

For hours, he walked again, but still the landscape didn't seem to change much.

'Wait, this is strange.' The man realized something was odd. He walked slower, looking around the path for an explanation. There came the crossroads again, and he dropped his basket and ran up to the tree.

He began to breathe faster, perturbed.

'No, no, no. This can't be...'

He lifted his trembling hand and scrubbed the mark on the tree that he had made hours ago. He seemed to be going around in circles.

'What in the world,' he cried out, anxiously looking around the thick forest. And for the first time, he realized he was the only moving creature. Not even a tiny fly was present, a humming silence ringing in his ears. He screamed in horror and to add to his misery, he saw his feet still standing over his shadow. The sun hadn't moved an inch.

Ningrei gave out her last catch to the group of young siblings who had been standing in the long line outside her hut to end their starvation. They were the last in line.

'My lady, what about your meal?' her attendant whispered sadly.

'I will be fine. We still have a few tubes of dried cassava, don't we?' Ningrei answered confidently, her eyes following the siblings running away with the meat.

'We shall pass this, my lady. We definitely will,' the attendant said, nodding her head, self-assured.

'I hope so,' Ningrei wished aloud. She gazed at her small clan, spotted with tiny huts with yellow fire blinking through their window holes.

With years of famine, the earth seemed to turn into ashes, waiting to devour everything in due time. Their slow impending death loomed closer with each passing year, but she wanted to do the best she could.

It all began with the failure of the crop and then the forest becoming unwelcoming, wild fruits and nuts becoming rotten as soon as they ripened, the trees swarmed with stinging insects, the field infested with unknown pests; the clan was at the brink of collapse. Ningrei knew this was her fate and that she was meant to protect her people regardless of what came. She earnestly hunted for food, ran deeper and deeper into the forest every single day, trying to find at least something for the children, even if it meant shortage of food for the adults. She wanted to honour her deceased parents by protecting her clan at all costs. She couldn't idle away as a helpless teenager.

Ningrei was about to retire to her room, when one of her clan members came running. She came crying, informing that her husband hadn't returned from the Lam forest. She knew it was something to be worried about. A lot of people had been reported missing in this forest. She decided to discuss the matter with her grandmother. Inside the council hall, her grandmother and chief waited for her, sitting in the middle, surrounded by their strong and high-ranking warriors.

'Ning-Ning! Who cried?' Her grandmother, an old but elegantly dressed woman, called out in a worried tone. She had her hornbill feather crown over her head complemented by crafted ivory pieces. She was a tiny little woman who had aged with grace, wearing a brightly dyed cotton robe and sarong, but her full-body tattoo patterns was unrecognizable in the folds of her wrinkles.

'It's sister Chon,' Ningrei answered after she bowed to her grandmother.

'Is the matter serious?' her grandmother asked sadly.

'She informed that her husband went missing in the Lam forest. He has been gone for a week now.'

'Another fool venturing into the eastern forest alone. People should have the basic common sense by now that the forest eats up people. Our Lady Ningrei should be looking after the folks, while we men hunt as our forefathers had!' Ranpui, the head of the warriors said. His bitterness at Ningrei's rejection in marriage and his dashed expectations of becoming a chief reflected in his tone every time he said something to her.

'I do look after my people,' Ningrei defended herself, 'but people are growing desperate. We haven't harvested a single field of paddy for the last few years. What we are doing and what I am doing are not enough. They want to try their own luck now. That is the reason why I am helping you men with the hunting. How much did you catch today? I hope enough to feed the children.'

'Ning-Ning. Do me a favour and pour my wine,' the chief asked a fuming Ningrei.

'And to my warriors, go back to your home and rest for the day. Night is long and we shall rise early before dawn.' The old chief sent the warriors away and turned to her granddaughter, 'Ning-Ning, my dear. Do not lose your cool over petty complaints of men.'

'But they think I am better off weaving in spite of providing food for our people at this crucial time. Haven't I proved to them time and again that I am not any less than them?' Ningrei flung her royal scarf, the Ruirim that once belonged to her father. This scarf, made with greige cotton, tiny black stripes near the wide scarlet border, was supposed to be worn only by the future chief. Since she came to know the significance of this piece of cloth, she had tied it tight across her shoulder and around her waist, determined not to let anybody else touch it. And more to her amusement, she also recently found out that it made her rival Ranpui mad, even though he wouldn't dare ask her not to wear it.

'You are not less than them, you are not less than any of them. You are far better. Come here, let me comb those dry leaves and twigs off your hair.' The chief took a bamboo comb and gently pulled her granddaughter close to her lap. Ningrei didn't protest and sat quietly. Her grandmother hummed a lullaby and gently stroked her hair, pulling out dirt from her soft long hair.

'Why would you even bother about their opinion? You are matchless in your hunting skills, and beauty, and every inch of you is like a divine measure of perfection. You shall not frown and allow your smooth honey-glazed skin to be lined with stress.'

'But that Ranpui is the one I hate more than anyone else! He is always looking for a way to make me feel a lesser leader,' Ningrei protested.

'Hate is a strong word dear. Especially for a remarkable child like you.' Her grandma plucked out a feather from her hair, looked at it and resumed her combing as well as her speech, 'And for Ranpui, you must understand that a man's weakest spot is his pride and you have dishonoured him by rejecting his proposal. It will be this way until he finds himself a woman worth his title. Try not to take it too personally for now.'

'I wouldn't mind much if we were not involved in our present scenario, but Apai, I sometimes wish I could tell them what I could actually do. My true power!'

'Hush!' her grandmother dropped the comb and instantly covered Ningrei's mouth with her hand, 'I told you that is profaned to eternity!'

Ningrei pushed her grandmother's hand and protested, 'But Apai!'

'No buts here! You see that Atuchaga Kamatei, the holy stones, will not hear your call once people know of your bond with them.'

The fact that this was shared only between the two of them was too annoying for Ningrei at times. She wanted the warriors to know of her divine link to her guardian boulder spirits. She knew Ranpui would crawl in fear if he knew about it. However, she couldn't tell anyone!

'I know!' Ningrei stood up, ran out of the hut and towards the gate, and further up the slope. She ran past the tall grasses waving in the breeze as if there were a vast ocean tide, the rustling blades looking silver by the moonlight.

At the hilltop, Ningrei could already see the giant silhouette of the monolithic crown. The hum could be heard in her mind and the voice came out distinct, a strong husky tone.

'Daughter, welcome.' Million tiny echoes followed the word.

'Father King, your daughter is here and I bow to you,' Ningrei bowed in front of the huge boulders towering over the blunt hilltop. She walked inside the structures, lost in the warren. From the outside, the boulders seemed lesser in number, standing not so congested, but once she entered them in the vicinity, it somehow seemed as if she were entering another world. The boulders were spread everywhere, standing in countless rows in uneven files. She remembered when she entered this place for the first time when she was young, six or seven years old perhaps, crying because she thought she would forever be lost within the confusing labyrinth. She smiled to herself at the memory and looked up at the sky, clear and dotted with zillion stars as always.

'Angry?' the voice continued.

'Yes. Let me rest here for today,' Ningrei said.

'We hear you,' a feminine voice whispered and the wind howled a little stronger ahead as if leading her path. She continued walking through the columns and not so far ahead, she noticed a flat rock lying as if it were a bed, covered by thick moss and tiny flowers. With a smile, she ran up and lay atop the cushiony surface. The breeze carried the usual hum as if singing a lullaby. Before she closed her heavy eyes, she remembered the first time she heard the call from the Kamatei, the holy boulders, the husky voice that mesmerized her as she entered the megalithic realm, 'Mortal daughter with divine exemplar, protecting you, our eternal oath.' Back then, she didn't know what the words meant, because she was but a child. Feeling stuck, she cried, but the stones sang and cast beautiful shadows of flowers and birds. She remembered playing to her heart's content. She found layers of stones as if stairs for her to climb and slanting flat surfaces for her to slide. Her laughter echoed through the stones that day...

Ningrei woke up and realized the sky was already stained by the morning sun. She bowed at a random direction and ran out towards a path, which she believed was her way back home. She came out of the megaliths quite fast. Again, you never know the exact distance or ways around the stones. They seemed to make their way out of there, when needed, and if not, anyone would be stuck inside. Lost forever. That is why, the megalithic site was known as an ominous place for other clan members. It was only Ningrei who could walk in and out of the stones, who could converse with the spirits of the stones.

She dashed towards her clan and saw the hunters already ready for departure.

'Wait! I am coming.' Ningrei ran inside her house, hastily picked up her spear and shield, tied her silken hair into a bun with her hornbill feather pin and came out with her small creel of essentials slung across her head.

'Alright. I am ready. Shall we go?' Ningrei led the group of men.

'Where have you been at this early hour?' Ranpui inquired. He noticed that she came running back from the forbidden hilltop where the labyrinth of giant boulders stood. Every clan member knew better not to walk even near that path.

'Sadly not your business, Lord Commander,' Ningrei answered irately.

Ranpui grunted aloud but followed the pack, vanishing quickly within the thick jungle.

Ningrei looked back to see if her troop were at a safe distance, she needed to make sure that what she was about to do was not witnessed by any mortal soul. As her companions were busy walking through the jungle, she made a quick jump up atop a tree and looked for her hidden servile ones—giant boulders resting at random places throughout the forest. Though covered with creepers and ferns, Ningrei knew they all were just waiting for her command.

'My liege, to a new path,' Ningrei closed her eyes and prayed.

'New path, we shall.' A hum of whispers returned her prayer and Ningrei could see the giant boulders almost levitating and rolling, making clear, connected paths through the forest. Ningrei jumped down from the tree and ran back to her companions who were sneaking around the bushes with utmost care.

'Warriors! I found a path ahead. It will save us more time,' Ningrei announced triumphantly.

'Again?' Ranpui asked doubtfully. 'Forests are not supposed to have paths. Is it not suspicious? What if it was a trap set up by our enemy clan?'

'We better go or slither here with less luck. Can you even hear a buzz of a bee here?' Ningrei openly retorted, 'Our forest is dying. Even if we run into an enemy clan, we have no choice but to fight. Follow me!'

Everyone looked at their warrior commander, nodded as a sign of apology, and then they all willingly followed their lady, who by all means, always brought them some sort of luck.

Ningrei ran through the long path without much curiosity, but Ranpui couldn't help but notice the huge boulders that nestled on every turn of the path were as if forming some kind of a checkpoint. True, the stones were huge and looked like they had been sitting in their spot for ages, all covered up with mosses and ferns, but he knew the forest well and he had never come across a path like this, all cleared up and convenient. He was suspicious also because Ningrei always ran up ahead and found random paths within the forest.

They ran through the path that ended with a view of a shallow stream running slow but wide.

'We need to cross and try our luck beyond,' Ranpui ordered as he saw his companions slowing down with the hope to rest for a while.

'I don't understand.' Ningrei thought to herself. The path was supposed to lead them to some kind of a hunting spot. It always does. With the forest dying and infested with strange insects and pests, she had been relying on the blessing of her Kamatei father to help hunt at least something each day. The boulders always made sure she returned with a trophy. Yesterday, she performed a secret miracle. When nothing was found in the forest, Ningrei secretly called the Kamatei. The stones replied to her call and whispered back. With an eerie breeze, huge rocks began to jut out of the ground like a staircase and Ningrei jumped over them towards the lofty heights where the stones were assembling. At the end, the stones lifted Ningrei towards a tall mountaintop where there was a crowd of beehives oozing with honey. None would have been able to harvest such nests, which were stuck at the impossibly steep side of the mountaintop. But for Ningrei, the boulders had made her a comfortable stairway and she collected a basketful with ease. After the harvest, the rocks descended back to the ground and disappeared as if nothing had happened. Ningrei prayed and thanked the boulder king and queen. Everyone was surprised when she showed her basket. When

Ranpui suspiciously asked how she managed to harvest the hives from such a lofty height, she smirked and replied, 'I flew up, of course.' Every stone in the realm obeyed the Kamatei and the Kamatei had pledged its services to Ningrei for some inexplicable reason. She deeply believed that it was her deceased parents who had returned to the stones to protect her.

'Lady Ningrei, shall we?' the warriors asked as Ranpui already went ahead to cross the shallow water.

'I am tired. I shall rest here for a while. You go ahead with our commander,' said Ningrei and sat down on the grainy bank. She watched as her troop followed their beefy commander towards the dark jungle ahead.

Ningrei stood up as soon as her troop was out of sight. She prayed again, 'My liege, please guide.'

'Dwellers of the flowing,' a distant whisper in a familiar rasping voice filled her head.

She opened her eyes and began to wonder, but it didn't take long for her to realize what it meant.

The water began to ripple violently as if beginning to boil. Ningrei stepped back, observing carefully as to what might happen and how. A huge something emerged out of the stream, and to her surprise, it was actually a huge plane rock with a little concave surface in the middle, where she could see a few fishes splashing in a puddle. She ran up towards the levitating rock surface, brought the fishes out of the puddle and stuffed them inside her creel. She ran back towards the bank and as expected, the huge rock fell back inside the streambed with a huge splash of water. Ningrei could feel her back wet and dripping from the impact.

She turned back and saw the stream running as calmly as before, as if nothing had happened.

Not so long after, Ningrei saw her troop running out of the jungle and crossing the stream to come towards her. She saw disappointment on Ranpui's tattooed smug face.

'Nothing?' She asked the commander with a smirk.

'Unfortunately,' Ranpui answered defeated but added sarcastically, 'but I am glad our lady is resting well.'

'Yes,' Ningrei removed her creel and threw it on the ground, the contents spilling all over—her small dagger, her dried-fruit lunch, small drinking gourd, spare feather pins, ropes, dried herbal leaves and four large river fish. 'And also enjoyed myself a fun fishing time.'

The sight of the fish excited all the warriors beyond control. They bowed towards their lady, kissing her hands and feet in gratitude. Ranpui stood perplexed, staring at the fish and then at Ningrei. She collected her belongings and slung the creel back across her head. She turned away happily to return with her companions. Ranpui saw her back; it was wet and dripping.

'My lady! What have you done?' Ranpui thundered.

'Done what?' Ningrei turned back, a little offended that Ranpui still had the nerve to question at her.

'How come only your back is wet? Do you fish backward?'

Ningrei was quick with her wit.

'Yes, and I caught four. You try your style and see if you can catch more,' she snapped and turned back quickly to walk with the troop.

'You are not being true to us. Mother spirit will punish us more if we lie to each other. Lady Ningrei is not true to us,' Ranpui shouted bitterly, but the troop didn't wait and followed their lady instead.

Not knowing where to release the frustration, Ranpui turned to the stream and looked around. He saw nothing alive in it, just algae-coated flat rocks at the stream-bed. 'She is not true to us,' he muttered assertively.

Being arrogant was enough. The added meddlesomeness just makes it way worse, thought Ningrei as she walked back to her clan, escorted by her happy clan members. However, she knew that Ranpui was saying the truth. They were bound by a vow to be always true and loyal to one's own clan and she did break it in a way.

'But, I am helping my people. Why would mother spirit punish me for it?' she reasoned and comforted herself.

As soon as she entered her clan gate, a scream filled the entire compound and Ningrei had to drop her creel yet again and rush towards the cry.

'What happened now?' she demanded, pushing the gathered folks away.

'My lady, our brother! He is untameable,' a horrified young girl cried out and moved so Ningrei could have a better view of what exactly was happening. She saw a boy, around her age, tied up with ropes but flinging on the ground violently as if he were some captured prey.

'What happened to him?' she looked around and asked. She realized all the gathered people were the youths from the Morung compounds, the residence of the youth.

'My lady, he had been acting strange for the last few days. And, now he is acting completely like a dog, peeing with one leg up, licking from his bowl, howling and much more, sniffing around everything,' a fellow young boy tried to explain, breathless and worried.

'Did he complain of any sickness before this happened? Anyone who can explain this in detail?' Ningrei scanned through the group of young boys and girls who stood circling their possessed dorm-mate.

'My lady, he is my brother and we share a bed at the Morung,' Another young boy who had been quiet the whole time spoke up shyly.

'Good. You shall come with me. And, the rest shall return to the dormitory,' Ningrei ordered the youths to disperse. Quite obediently, they all moved back to their huge cottages without delay, whispering and discussing among themselves.

Ningrei brought the boy inside the chief's hall and her grandmother interrogated him. She learned that the siblings belonged to the Mangfu house, the house of hounds. After asking for careful details, she let the young boy return to his dorm.

'Apai, how do we treat the boy?' Ningrei asked.

'I don't know, Ning-Ning,' her grandmother sighed, 'but of all people, you know better that we can't let any kind of panic spread among our people. Our clan is at the brink of falling apart. Nothing is going in the course of nature. We will do what we can to tame the boy, but you see, our land is the podium of all mystics and charms. It took thousands of years to separate the chaos from nature to run in a course that we, mere humans, can understand today. And in chaos, we sacrifice both the enchantments and the clout of magic. We vowed to stay unsoiled from such encroachment.'

Her grandmother gave a weary smile and continued, 'Which, I deem, is no longer so true now. To begin with, you, yourself, are the best example of something extraordinary. At the age of seven, the Atuchaga Kamatei spirits summoned you, and not only that, the holy boulders also vowed to be your protector. I know that your blessing is an auspicious outcome, but it could also entail dire affairs. Legends say we used to have the power to turn into animals which belong to our houses, and that boy is acting like a hound, a wild thing. People are going missing. Something is completely wrong; something or someone disrupted nature. I fear this could be something much bigger than our clan's misfortune. Ning-Ning, I fear this might be a lot more worse than we think...'

'Respected Chief and Lady!' A warrior ran inside the chief's cottage and bowed low.

'Anything urgent?' Ningrei inquired.

'It's Ranpui,' the warrior said nervously.

'What about him?' Ningrei asked, already irritated.

'Lady, I request you to come with me, look into the matter personally and deal with him accordingly.'

'Alright. He had better not be stupid enough to cross his line this time. Come, lead me, brother.'

Ningrei ran out of the chief's hall along with the warrior.

The old chief sat preoccupied in her own thoughts. She began to remember more bizarre events related to her only grandchild.

'My Ning-Ning. Time had made me oblivious of the past, but I did make the terrible promise once. Will this be the time for payment?' She seemed sad, but still forced a smile through her wrinkled lips. A proud smile.

THE NORTHERN MOUNTAINS

'So, what you are telling me, us, is that we are some kind of chosen ones, we are the guardians?' Leisatao asked again to make sure what he just heard was right.

'Exactly,' Laiba answered, as confident as ever.

'You are the head priest?'

'Yes.'

'And he is the Meidingu?'

'Yes.'

'And this is the prince of Moirang province?'

'Yes.'

'And this girl is the supreme incarnate?'

'Yes.'

Hahahaha! Leisatao laughed, loud enough to make everyone startled.

Gothang smiled but stopped when he saw the look of disappointment on the face of the thin boy with fine curls of hair. For some reason, the boy acted inspired and an admirer of his existence since their arrival. He didn't want the boy to change that notion about him.

'Gothang, these children are all muddled up in their heads. Poor children, getting lost in the woods and running scared,' Leisatao rubbed a tear away from the corner of his eye and playfully rubbed Laiba's bald head, still giggling.

'But, respected uncle, I mean brother, what our head priest said is true,' the meek girl, Sana, said in a tone of protest.

Leisatao stopped giggling and looked at Sana for a while, 'Sana, right?'

'Yes,' Sana nodded her head.

'Listen sweetheart. I heard the news. There is some sort of chaos or whatever, but I am a dart-maker. Nothing more. *Arambai* is my life, and that's it. I have neither superpowers nor intelligence, if those are the things you are expecting me to have. And I live a very regular life. The only atypical thing I encountered in my 36 years of existence is meeting this man, here, Gothang, today.'

'Truth to be told, I am equally disappointed that you were one of the guardians,' Iwan snapped, but he realized he had just made a terrible blunder. Great! I just dishonoured a guardian. Incredible move! I couldn't be more stupid. Iwan looked down, his face a shade of red.

'Please don't mind our king. He is a spoiled brat,' Laiba said monotonously as if he expected something like that from Iwan.

Everyone stood quietly for a while. Leisatao didn't expect the smiley anxious boy who had been trying to impress Gothang with all the strange bowing and offerings of wine to offend him so easily.

'Forgive us, but I think you have mistaken us for someone else. We just met and I do not even live here. I am a southerner,' to ease the tricky situation, Gothang spoke for the first time since the arrival of the children. He had been listening to the pale boy, asserting that he and Leisatao were some sort of protectors—gods? They were asking him to join in a quest to find some sort of scissor, if he heard it right. The small boy who claimed to be the head priest in the Central Palace did sound convincing. Even though he was just a low-lifer, just another swineherd, he was sure that such a prestigious position as a head priest was not for some child. But then again, strange things had been happening. The boy did look odd; his pale complexion aside, his eyes were too sparkly even in the dim torchlight.

'Yes, southern brother!' Laiba cried with a huge grin flashing across his tiny face, 'I believe you enjoyed a smooth ride towards the Central Palace? Good Guardians! I wish I received a vision of how you came to the Kangla fort. Something very fast brought you here, wasn't it?'

Gothang stood up at that instant, 'How did you...'

'Now, convince our archer. We will wait!' Laiba took a futon from the corner and sat with a relaxed smile.

'What just happened?' Lungchum, who had been busy admiring the glittering display around the room, turned back to inquire.

'Yes, Gothang. What did this strange child mean?' Leisatao looked at Gothang for an explanation.

'I don't understand,' Gothang mumbled, 'I am sorry Brother Leisatao, but I lied to you about the abduction part. I wasn't abducted. I was...umm...I was carried here by some sort of a beast, a strange-looking beast. There were actually two of them...'

'Wait!' Leisatao fanned his hand, and then dramatically continued, 'Are you serious? Now, you are going to join their little fun and story time?'

'No...' Gothang tried again, 'I don't know about the rest of the children here, but this boy—he knows stuff he shouldn't be knowing. I think we need to hear them out first.'

Leisatao didn't want to doubt Gothang. He thought for a moment and rested his eyes on Laiba, 'Fine, young man. Do me the honour and explain why you think I am who you think I am, again.'

'The prophecy spoke of an archer, and you are a dart-maker. An excellent one at that. Perhaps, you might be the only guardian who learned to put his "gift" to good use. No wonder you have wealth spewing all over,' Laiba said and the rest of the children nodded with an 'Ohhhh...' at the reasonable assertion.

'Fine,' Leisatao placed his hands on his hips and replied, 'good point, but you see, I am a dart-maker. I make them. I don't use them. I hardly use them anywhere. I don't even know how to...'

'Why don't you try then? See if you can hit this target.' Laiba stood up and took a finely made *arambai* from Leisatao's work table and said to Sana, 'My lady, please put that roasted sweet potato piece on top of Lungchum's head.'

'Why my head?' Lungchum protested, but Iwan was quick to put one on top of his head.

'Children, this is very dangerous. You see, an *arambai* is not a toy. It might...' Leisatao began hesitantly.

'Yes...I agree. This *arambai* is no toy,' Lungchum nodded his head, making the sweet potato fall rolling on the ground.

'Quit it, dragon boy. This should be nothing to you,' Iwan picked up the piece and put it back on top of Lungchum's head.

'Why don't we try some other target?' Sana tried, but nobody paid heed.

'Just throw it, brother,' Laiba said with excitement, handing the *arambai* to Leisatao, 'Our friend here is a dragon. It will be fine even if you miss your target. But you wouldn't.'

'Listen, dear children...'

'It's going to be fine,' Iwan smiled as Lungchum waited anxiously with a sweet potato on his head.

'This is not safe...the poison, a single tiny scratch...' Leisatao tried, but the children were getting noisy—some excited, some worried.

'I don't like this, dragon or not, poison is poison,' argued Lungchum.

'Don't be dramatic,' Laiba pacified him.

'We should try some other target, please,' appealed Leisatao.

'It's going to be fine, brother. Hit your target,' said Laiba.

Leisatao got confused. He had never been so crowded with such annoying clatter before. He looked at Gothang and, to his surprise, saw him looking expectantly for some sort of stunt from him.

'Alright! Here!' Leisatao screamed to shut everyone up and threw the dart with his eyes closed.

It must have been Sana who screamed next, louder than everyone else. Leisatao opened his eyes, doing a little prayer to a Guardian deity. He let out a big sigh of relief when he saw the Moirang prince still standing, 'My goodness! This brood!'

'And here is our answer.' Laiba picked up the dart with a piece of sweet potato fully inserted on the tip.

Everyone gawped.

Leisatao picked up another *arambai* from his table and aimed for the pot on top of his tallest shelf. It flew right through it, making it fall to pieces. He took another and aimed for the tiny hook of his tall drapes on the wall. The drapes fell flying when the dart cut them at the hook. He took another and looked around for a more challenging thing to aim.

'I think you got our point, brother,' Laiba smiled.

'Yes, please stop darting at your decor,' Lungchum pleaded.

'Incredible,' Sana sang in excitement. She had never seen such an accurate flight of darts before.

'I...alright...sun-slayer, hmm,' Iwan slurred, perhaps too awestruck that it left him with less to say.

'Well, that is indeed something,' Gothang had to admit.

'Alright, one thing you children got right is that I do have this hidden talent for shooting too,' Leisatao cleared his throat.

'Want to know more?' Laiba ran up and held his hands, 'I was waiting for this. Here are all the answers...'

Leisatao saw the golden shade of Laiba's eye and it flashed a blinding light. He squinted hard and, to his surprise, saw his own self, taking aim to shoot the sun. He was trying to shoot the sun with a sturdy bow and arrow. He shot it and heard a scream. The bright sun fell off the sky and his vision got blurred.

'What just happened?' Leisatao woke up on his bed, surrounded by those odd children and Gothang. There was sunlight coming in from the vents.

'Are you alright? Shall I pour you some water?' Gothang asked worriedly.

'I am fine,' Leisatao said quite honestly. Contrary to all the concerned looks from his companions, he did feel much better than before. 'So, why was I shooting at the sun? Is it some sort of a dream? How did you do that?' he asked Laiba.

'It is my ocular power, but I can do such a display of a vision only when it is granted by the greater realm. That vision you saw is not a dream but a piece of your memory. You once shot the sun. Remember that story...once we had two suns? A hero killed one of them to create night? Turns out, you are that hero. Reincarnated as one of the guardians.'

'The sun-slayer,' Iwan rubbed his forehead. 'Why didn't I think of that. That's the most common tale!'

'But that was a myth. A legend.' Leisatao couldn't help smiling. 'Anyway, if I am this sun-slayer. What about him? Who is Gothang?'

'The sky prince, son of our Sky Lord,' Laiba announced bluntly.

'I am a huge admirer of yours, lord brother,' Iwan extended his hands to bow towards Gothang again.

'Brother is fine,' Gothang pressed Iwan's shaking hands to save him from another of his bows.

'A prince, no wonder,' Leisatao was impressed and was about to rattle on in his excitement, but he stopped when he saw Gothang looking not so thrilled.

Gothang knew the children were not having fun with the stories. If the pale boy said he is a sky prince, he decided it was true. Gothang knew less of the myths and ancient stories; so he asked, 'Do I have any strange power?'

'Not that I know of for now, but according to the legend, you are unparalleled in strength.'

'My father said he found me in a casket made of clouds...'

'Would love to give you a vision, but I haven't got any related to you for now,' Laiba said apologetically. Gothang seemed restless with curiosity. He had been fidgeting.

'So, you came in a casket? That is splendid. None of us came in such a godly form. We all have our own human parents here,' Laiba added excitedly.

'I had my father, but as it turns out, he was an unlucky bachelor who picked me up and was kind enough to raise me. He was telling the truth all along.' Gothang answered poignantly, but asked with some interest, 'If my father is supposedly the sky god, then who is my mother?'

'You seriously don't know the popular tale of their love story?'

'I am sorry. Southerners are known for being reclusive. Tales or news from the valley rarely come to us.'

'Alright. Your father is the god of the sky, Korou Awangba, and your mother, Goddess Tampha, is a human princess. And that makes you a demigod. In the story, however, your mother, our Sky Queen broke a vow and for that, she was doomed to live on earth for eternity.' Iwan felt a sense of honour, narrating the tale of his hero to the hero in person.

'Do you mean she is here?' Gothang couldn't hide his excitement and it was already too late. Everyone in the room noted his interest at the news of his mother.

'Your mother is long gone,' Laiba didn't smile when he answered the question. He stared straight at Gothang as if to warn him about what he was thinking of doing.

'Gone? Isn't she a goddess?' Gothang asked, his inner child torn apart by the declaration. Everyone sat quietly. They all knew his story. They pitied him.

'Yes, humans honoured her as a goddess for she once ruled as the queen of the sky realm, but your father revoked his vows and with it, she lost her godly ties. She died long ago.'

Gothang sat staring at Laiba. He felt a pain in his heart. He wanted to revolt, because he had been having this dream of her and none of them knew of it.

'She could be alive. Legends are not so unreal anymore...'

'What makes you think she is alive?' Laiba interrupted, studying him curiously.

Gothang wanted to speak about his dreams, the recurrent vision of his mother running around in different places, asking him to follow her.

But the dreams were too precious to just share with anyone. He wanted to keep this beautiful piece of experience for himself. He was sure his mother was waiting for him somewhere. They had been separated for ages. He was meant to come to earth and find her. That is why his mother appeared in his dreams. He faked a smile, 'I was just wondering. I know it is some ancient tale.'

Laiba didn't say anything, but gave a look that made Gothang uneasy. This boy sure is suspicious, Gothang thought.

'I am sorry, Brother Gothang,' Sana tried to cheer him up. 'We can all visit her shrine once this whole thing is over.'

'Is there a shrine?' Gothang almost jumped at the news, 'Where!?'

'It's...' Sana was about to answer, but Laiba interrupted, 'Yes, the shrine is a huge tree that grew out of her mortal remains. We can all visit the site after all this is over. Until then, we need to focus on the immediate danger. The lost scissor. Now, all six of us are already together, all we have to do is recruit our last lady warrior and go find the scissor.'

'Go find the lady warrior? What do you mean?' Leisatao protested unpleasantly at the added information.

'We already told you, we were seven in number and in order to restore the scissor, we need all seven of us to work together. We have to go north and find our last lady.'

'Why don't I wait here with Gothang while you four go and recruit her?'

'It doesn't work that way. We need all the help we can get.'

'So, are we going north?' Leisatao repeated grimly.

'Yes, we can leave early tomorrow.' Laiba said and the rest of the people began to move.

'Excuse me, children. You cannot just come here and dictate what to do,' Leisatao cried, pressing both his hands on his hips.

'But brother, I even showed you the vision. We don't have much time,' Laiba tried calmly.

'But the north is treacherous. You young children will not know, but you see, there is a political situation up there. The Central Province had been nasty to them. Forgive me Meidingu, but your father is not so popular there, is he?'

Iwan looked blankly at Leisatao as he did not know of any political problems. He knew almost nothing about the kingdom or his father. 'I... ah... Is he not so?' He tried looking guilty.

'Meidingu Iwanthanba, Luwang is different. We serve the Central Province, but we are also the most peace-loving province. News of wars and treaties are always discussed here. We stay loyal to deserving leaders and despise those who don't. Your father's untimely death was not so delicately mourned here, and the northerners didn't send their condolences. I am clueless myself, but I grew up in the Luwang court and also, as a travelling businessman, I have a bad feeling of travelling to the north with you. Your head priest might have easily convinced me of some divine duty and suchlike, but I don't think anyone from the north will easily take this absurdity as a service. I recently heard that our northern brethren are bitter with the Central Province's negligence in times of calamities. Will they be really happy to discuss charms and magic and quest?'

'Are they facing calamities?' Iwan asked innocently.

'I heard it that way. In olden times, your kingdom was supposed to lead us all and protect the ranges. Meidingu is the lord of the seven realms and the protector of the nine ranges. Now, not many provinces are interested in serving and maintaining the traditional ways of conduct, but instead are selfish and greedy. And it's more of a pity and our misfortune that your father is no longer with us to solve all these or be repentant.'

'I think we better leave the political feuds aside and focus on our divine duty.' Lungchum intervened, noticing the blushing cheeks of Iwan as he stood clueless about such a serious matter. Iwan looked down, defeated, his curls covering his eyes.

'Yes. We better carry out our divine duty first. I am here for solving all the problems,' Laiba agreed with Lungchum.

'Laiba darling, your king might be in a lot more mess if you are not careful. This comes from a person who has seen the sun and the moon a lot longer than you; so consider it as a humble advice. I don't or perhaps can't doubt your powers, divine or whatever, but you see, if we go up there and get caught as political prisoners or if we get hunted down as the enemy, we might be in trouble. You can't just fight back or attack them, give vision to the bitter warriors, turn a dragon on them. Think, children.' Leisatao made the children quiet and then he turned to Gothang and asked, 'What about you? Do you want to travel north with the children?'

'I...I... I am honestly here out of choice. I better go with the majority?' Gothang looked around.

'You are with us then.' Lungchum raised his hand up in the air.

Leisatao looked at the children and thought hard. They obviously have no idea of the troubles other than the magical quest they had been trusted upon by the greater realm. Even if he refused, the children would definitely leave. He saw the vision. Their magical powers couldn't be questioned, but will they stand up to the worldly troubles? Will it be really a sound decision to follow the children up to the north? He stood wondering.

'That scissor, *wayel kati*, is it?' Leisatao asked the group of gloomy children.

'Yes,' Sana answered.

'The divine tool from the legend... So, it really does exist.' Leisatao nodded, 'Who would have thought that the Central Province would acquire such a tool and so effortlessly lose it and lead to chaos. If not distracted by other strange happenings, even the other clans might revolt for war. I can't believe that the oracle entrusted a duty as important as restoring the scissor on only the seven of us. And half of you, just naive teenagers.'

'My head shaman reassured me of glory,' Lungchum said, optimistically.

'And I trust my vision. We just need to reach our last guardian before it is too late,' Laiba added.

'I didn't know my father was not liked. I am too naive,' Iwan looked troubled.

'Your Majesty, we can try fixing one thing at a time. Don't get distracted. Maybe restoring the scissor can set most things right.' Laiba consoled his king and then turned to Leisatao, 'Please, Brother Leisatao, let us go north. We will heed your advice and be careful.'

'And you, you can turn into a dragon?' Leisatao asked Lungchum.

'Yes, but not for a very long time. My head shaman advised me not to exhaust my divine form much, but I can turn into one anytime I want,' Lungchum nodded.

'We will go in disguise,' Leisatao said and Laiba looked up in utter delight. He seemed surprised but happy.

'We will not wear anything that will give us away. We will do the recruitment as calmly as possible and then go after the scissor, for which I am already expecting a decent plan from our head priest. I don't want any trouble and all of you will behave with whatever abilities you have, regardless. I don't want to deal with unnecessary attention from any of the northern clans. Sana, love, do you understand?' Leisatao asked with concern.

'Me? You don't have to worry about me at all,' Sana smiled nervously, 'I can't do much.'

'Aren't you the Supreme Goddess incarnate?'

'Yes, the oracle said so and Lord Laiba confirmed it, but I am yet to know of my true power.'

'But be on guard, our Supreme Goddess is one who is most feared if she unleashes her wrath. She tore up giants, drank blood, crushed skulls...'

'Huh?' Sana dropped her jaw and Lungchum chuckled, 'Yes, our Mother Goddess is also known for her temper. But, no worries, not all of her seven forms have those traits.'

'Anyway, Gothang, I hate to say this, but we better get going with the children right now, because we need to cross the northern river before dusk. We will avoid settlements as much as we can...' Leisatao began to instruct the preparation for the journey. Despite his nagging effort to convince Iwan to leave Yangba behind, the boy king refused to part with his horse and they had to prepare with two horses for the journey, however inconvenient.

The group crossed the northern river before dusk as planned and they slowly began to travel up the northern mountain. All of them were clad in simple black attire, Sana and Leisatao covering their long hair with an additional black hood. Lungchum left only his eyes uncovered and his high ponytail sprouting out of his thick black scarf. Laiba didn't change his priest clothes, but agreed to cover himself with a huge black cloak that swept the ground as he moved about. Iwan and Gothang wore matching black clothes and a long robe, their hair covered with a black headdress. Gothang didn't speak much as usual, but followed the troop obediently, helping with the horses and carts on the rough mountain path. As a brawny man among the group, he proved most helpful.

'What would have happened to us if not for you, brother?' Iwan would shower him with praises every chance he got.

Gothang would just smile as usual, but his head and heart were somewhere else. With every path they took, he would look around for more familiarity. Since the moment they crossed the river, he had been feeling disturbed. The landscape looked much like the one he once saw his mother running through, in his dream. It excited him incredibly, but he didn't express any of it before his companions. As night fell, the group decided to light a fire and settle within the forest for the night. Chatter soon filled the air along with smoke from the fire, with potatoes being roasted, dried meat and fish being shared and feasted upon. Laiba was constantly asked about the lady they were about to recruit, but he didn't or couldn't provide much details except that the lady loves rocks or big stones, which didn't make much sense.

'All of us can't go off to sleep; one has to stand guard,' Leisatao said as they finished their meal by the fire.

'Lungchum, you can,' Iwan said, licking his fingers.

As Lungchum nodded, Gothang interrupted, 'No, I will guard for tonight. It used to be my job, remember?'

'Well,' Iwan looked at Gothang and smiled, 'I will guard with you then. I am not that tired either, brother. We three can guard. Yangba, you and me. You know, Yangba is really so vigilant that sometimes I wonder if he was a dog in his previous life.'

'No, no,' Gothang insisted, 'I can do it alone. You both should rest. We are not so high up on the mountain yet. I don't think we need to worry much.'

'I will stand guard with you,' Laiba had been sucking a boiled water-snail when he noticed Gothang's unusual desire to stay on guard for the night and intervened. Gothang turned at him and they looked at each other for a while, the bonfire reflecting Laiba's bright eyes, the silvery gray prominently sparkling.

'Oh, you all can guard us then. Sana dear, let's go and sleep over there,' Leisatao rolled his eyes and stood up along with Sana who followed him to the corner where they had arranged their sleeping mats.

'It is fine. I will stand guard with Brother Gothang. Our royalties can get their beauty sleep,' Laiba stood up and washed his hands. Tired and not being used to hard labour, both the young royals didn't protest and went ahead to rest for the night.

'Brother Gothang,' Laiba said with a smile, but Gothang didn't return it.

'So, have you not yet changed your mind?' Laiba asked, artless.

Gothang looked around worriedly and hissed, 'You need to understand something...'

'Your mother is already dead,' Laiba whispered apologetically.

'Listen, Laiba, Lord, I know you are special, but what you say will not give me peace at heart. I need to find her.'

'Why did you agree to join us if this was your decision?' Laiba asked disappointed.

'Well, I changed my mind. I know I am some guardian or something, but I think I need to find my mother first. I need to...'

'You are selfish and that is pathetic as a demigod. Our king lost his mother too but here he is with us, trying his best to follow his destiny. It is our obligation and you are being cruel here to leave us.'

'You are the selfish one, always invalidating our feelings for your quest. I knew this path. I saw it. I saw her running through this path...'

'What are you talking about?' Laiba began to wonder about something. His eyes were restricted from a certain matter, but he began to wonder if he could logically decipher some more mystery without using his divine powers.

'She must have been here, this path...'

'Hold on,' Laiba got more curious. 'Have you seen her? Is there something you are not telling us?'

'Laiba, I am so sorry. You need to forgive me,' Gothang bowed to Laiba.

Sana woke up before anyone else. She saw Leisatao snoring loudly near her. Both the boys were sound asleep a little further near the fire pit. The horses and the cart were as they had been parked. She looked around for Laiba and Gothang. Neither of them were to be seen anywhere; so she stood up and began looking around the woods. She spotted Laiba and cried out, 'Lord Laiba! What happened?'

Laiba was tied up around a tree with his mouth bound by a cloth. Sana's frantic scream awakened the rest of the guardians and they all ran in her direction.

'Where is Brother Gothang?' Sana cried.

'Mmmm mmmmmm...' Came the sound from Laiba's mouth muffled by the cloth, as he rolled his eyes.

Sana quickly removed the cloth and Laiba let out a breath and said, 'That rascal! He ran away!'

'Ran away?' Iwan shivered at the betrayal, 'Gothang? Brother Gothang?'

'Yes, that idiot thinks his mother is still alive. What is wrong with him? What is wrong with everybody?' Laiba yelled.

'What about our quest then? What about our last lady? Shall we go after him first?' Lungchum asked, readying to turn into his dragon form. He extended both his hands as if wings.

'We will be just wasting time and we don't have much time left. We will go after our lady first. This is a disaster!' Laiba threw down his long black robe on the ground.

'Poor boy, I knew he seemed disturbed, but he should have told us nicely. I would have understood him. I would,' Leisatao looked at the far view of the valley seen from their spot.

'Laiba, are you sure his mother is dead?' Iwan asked weakly.

'If he came as a human like us, I would have thought of his human mother, but you heard him. He came directly from up there, riding those clouds and stuff! I think the prophecy even warned us of him. He still seeks what he once lost. He might be having reminiscences of his deceased mother. But she is dead for sure! He is all confused. Stupid demigod!'

Iwan followed his companion, but his thoughts kept racing back to the bitterness of Gothang's betrayal. He couldn't bring himself to hate his hero either, but it was frustrating to realize that they might be in bigger trouble because of him.

'Your Majesty, we are already inside the northern realm and I am feeling closer to our lady too. Once we convince our lady to join our quest, we will go and find Brother Gothang,' Laiba said carefully. He even added, 'Or who knows, he might be on his way to us already.'

Iwan nodded, but didn't say anything. He had been pulling up his horse on the steep mountain, sweating and breathing hard, but with his mind clobbered with uneasy thoughts, he had been uncomfortably quiet for the first time.

'Iwan, we will find him for sure. He was destined for this,' Sana also joined in, hoping to cheer him up. She sincerely missed the jovial Meidingu. Iwan nodded again, but pulled his horse more sternly. Yangba gave a loud neigh.

'Sorry, brother,' Iwan apologized shortly to his horse and continued moving in silence.

Leisatao and Lungchum were ahead, taking turns in pulling the horse cart. Lungchum turned back and checked on Iwan.

'He will be fine, dear,' Leisatao said with a kind smile.

'I can take my dragon form and go after Brother Gothang.' Lungchum suggested again.

'But that would be more inconvenient.' Leisatao said, 'I agree with Laiba here. This is the north. We will go after him once we leave from here.'

Lungchum obeyed and continued pulling the cart up the slope. The group stayed close, avoiding settlements and crossing only forest paths. The low clouds and chilled air assured them they were in the higher part of the northern mountain. Leisatao found it strange that the ranges were calm and quiet. There were many big clans and villages scattered everywhere. He was expecting to encounter a warrior sometime soon, but it turned out, they no longer cared about outsiders. Strange.

They crossed the mountain and slowly descended towards the gorge, still with a plan to avoid clansmen. From there, they planned to follow the stream towards the upper north as Laiba suggested. He felt that their lady guardian was somewhere in one of the upper clans.

The gorge was deep and difficult to walk with their cart and horses. It was Leisatao who made sure that his belongings and the children didn't slip and fall to their death. He kept checking the ropes and the stone steps where they all climbed down under his lead. Lungchum grabbed Sana's hand quite absently, as they walked and she let him without a word, for she knew what would happen if her foot slipped and she fell off the edge of the steep rocky steps.

They reached deep inside the gorge and decided to settle there for the night. Leisatao still managed all, but Iwan began to sulk away on his own. Sana tried to console him, but he ignored her meanly, leaving her teary even. He went away towards the small stream nearby and sat with Yangba. Laiba decided to leave the cranky king by himself and instead discuss plans with Lungchum.

Iwan saw the group helping each other and trying to settle for the night. He realized that he was being immature again, but with a little bit of twisted pride, he decided to stay alone until someone came up to him with comforts on a platter. He took a peek at Sana, but she was busy helping Leisatao with the meal. Lungchum and Laiba were chatting as if he didn't exist. He turned away disappointed. He even considered firing Laiba once the quest was over. Head priests are supposed to be overtly loyal to their kings.

'Perhaps you are the only one I can always trust,' Iwan said looking at his horse drinking a huge amount of water, 'You must be tired too. I am really sorry. But look at these people, camping and feasting...'

To distract himself from the annoyance building up, Iwan gazed around at the dark mountain forest nearby. For a moment, the scene was pleasant but something caught his eye. He saw something staring at him through the wild bushes. The figure walked out with his long spear. He wore the hornbill headgear and intricately woven loincloth with jewelled bone earrings, fur knee-guards and was tattooed all over. It was a northern clansman. A warrior.

Iwan stood up startled, but the man was quick; leaping over the stream, he knocked Iwan out instantly with a skilful blow of his fist.

DEITY IN THE MOUNTAIN

Ranpui sat alone, cursing. He was a warrior commander, but all his warriors had left him as soon as they learned that their lady had got food. Yes, they were a desperate lot, but he couldn't believe that they were stupid enough not to notice the strangeness of their lady. She was definitely hiding something. He had been suspicious of her for a long time, but he couldn't doubt the possibility anymore. He had seen the lady hovering near the infamous labyrinth of boulders over the western hilltop. What was she doing there? Was she practising dark magic there? He felt more and more frustrated.

'No point sulking here. It's dusk already. I better confront her personally,' Ranpui stood up to leave the stream bank, but his sharp eye caught a faint trail of smoke rising up from further downstream.

'Someone deep in the gorge?' Ranpui knew better about wandering alone, but he couldn't help it. 'An enemy's head will restore my pride alright,' he said to himself and followed the smoke through the forest to try his luck.

The stream got shallower while the smoke grew more visible, but the mountain chasm was also getting narrower as he ran deeper downstream. Ranpui smirked at the possibility of Ningrei finally acknowledging his strength after seeing an enemy head. With famine and unknown diseases spreading around his small clan, it had been long since they had earned a head.

Ranpui arrived at the spot. He could already hear the faint chatter and to his utter delight, he got a whiff; he could smell delicious food. Not only enemy huntsmen, he had found some supplies too. If I can defeat them, this will be my golden ticket to chief-hood, he thought excitedly. He carefully hid behind a tall bush and took a sneak peek towards the gathering. The view was bizarre. There were no huntsmen. They were children. Children? Deep in this terrain? Ranpui was confused for a moment. He took a closer look. One young boy was sitting right ahead of him near the stream bank with a gorgeous white horse. Few other children and an adult were near the fire a little further. He wanted to go a little closer and observe them some more. They were also dressed in all black; it confused him further, thereby preventing him of making any reasonable guesses. While he hesitated, the boy by the bank saw him. He had no choice but to run up and silence him before he could alert his companions.

Ranpui ran up and leapt beyond the narrow stream and hit the boy hard on his head with his fist. The boy was knocked out instantly, but the horse neighed angrily. Unavoidable as it was, his companions became aware of Ranpui's presence. They all stood up facing him. The adult man was screaming together with the young girl, while the other boys were preparing to defend themselves. The boys looked strange. The smaller boy even more so. He was too pale and had a pair of mismatched eyes. Ranpui hadn't seen a child like him before. The taller boy seemed to grow bigger, or was it his imagination but then he heard the small boy shout in the valley dialect, 'Lungchum, not now. He isn't here by coincidence.'

'From the valley?' Ranpui roared, flashing his spear carefully at the pale boy.

'Yes, I am Leisatao from Luwang. You can't take our heads without your chief's verdict. Can you?' Leisatao asked, with a look of relief. He knew about the northern laws.

'Laiba, I will handle this. Let's do as he says and we will be fine. At least until we meet the lady,' Leisatao looked at his crew and cried, hugging the younger girl in his arms.

'Meet who?' Ranpui was confused, but decided not to buy their nonsense. 'I don't care. You all die today!'

'Warrior brother of the great northern range, we are from the valley, the Central Province. You cannot take our heads,' Leisatao spoke again, trying a painful smile.

'Cen...Central? Clever, funny-looking man. But you all are still liable to be taken as prisoners to my chief for entering our territory uninvited,' Ranpui answered in his northern accent.

'Oh, we all surrender then. Take us to your chief. In peace,' Leisatao thrust out both his hands as a sigh of surrender and spoke to his companions. 'Offer your hands, children. He will have to tie us up first. It's alright. Do not panic.'

'I don't like him though. We are not even the enemy and he is already obsessed with our heads. Anyway, he will be useful, so I shall oblige,' the small pale boy said dully.

'What did you say?' Ranpui retorted.

'Please, please, please forgive him. You know, kids,' Leisatao tried to smile again, showing his perfect teeth.

All the members of the group seemed obedient to the elegant man. They didn't resist as he took their rope and tied them up with it in a line. While tying Leisatao, he pulled the black hood in annoyance and revealed his long uneven hair ornamented with shiny pins. The man looked sort of beautiful, Ranpui had to admit.

'That was really unnecessary, brother. I would like to have my hood back,' Leisatao nagged.

'Shut up, ridiculous valley people! Prisoners should walk with their faces exposed,' Ranpui turned to the shivering young girl and ordered, 'You too. Remove your black hood.' The girl obeyed. The taller boy with high ponytail looked at the boy who had fainted by the bank and asked, 'What about Iwan? Is he alright? Can I go and check on him first?'

'No, he will be fine. Give me your hands,' Ranpui snapped and tied him up along with the rest of the members. He then went towards Iwan, who was lying by the bank, to load him over his own horse nearby, but the horse threatened to attack him when he tried to get close to the boy.

'Excuse me but let my friend, here, help you with loading our Meidingu onto his horse. Yangba wouldn't let you touch his master after you knocked him out.' Leisatao said and turned to his companion, 'Lungchum, please go and load our king onto his horse and bring them here so that our captor can lead us at ease.'

Ranpui looked at them suspiciously, but since he was alone, he had no choice. He let Lungchum help him. The white horse allowed Lungchum to touch the unconscious boy and even willingly lowered itself, so he could carry him.

'Alright, come back here. I will tie you up,' Ranpui spoke dryly to Lungchum and he obediently came back.

Ranpui loaded everything that looked edible back onto the small horse cart that they had somehow managed to drag all the way up into the mountains and began to haul it all together.

'Now, you all walk in front of me,' Ranpui ordered.

'Wait, are you alone?' The pale boy asked, surprised. He seemed to realize that no huntsman travels solo.

'None of your business. They are waiting upstream. Now move,' Ranpui lied and pushed them forward. He didn't need to reveal his embarrassing situation anyway.

'I am Laiba, the royal head priest of the Kangla Palace of the Central Province,' the pale boy announced with an air of pride, and added rather dully, 'And the one hanging fainted on the horse is our Meidingu.'

'No need to go that far with lies. Once our chief approves my plea, I will keep all your skulls well-polished in my chamber. If Central, you will go on the top shelf,' Ranpui retorted.

'He is telling the truth, brother,' Leisatao spoke from the front. Ranpui kept shouting, nervous and angry for no reason.

'Shut up!' Ranpui yelled, 'Meidingu? So what? I am the chief commander of my clan. Soon you all will meet your death, no matter what. Shut up, you all.'

'Chief commander, huh? Now I get why you wouldn't believe us,' the pale boy said in a sarcastic tone.

Ranpui turned red with rage, but then he couldn't dare harm the retards from the valley without his chief's permission, so he gritted his teeth and continued to walk. I will have my moment when I skin their heads, he thought.

They walked quietly until Ranpui finally ordered the group to head inside the forest. It was already dark. The moon shone bright. Ranpui came through the secret path that Ningrei had found previously that day. There were boulders at each turn.

'A neat clearing within the forest,' the pale boy said, his bicoloured eyes curiously observing the surroundings. As if in a wild dream,

Ranpui felt like he saw the white iris of the boy getting bigger a moment ago. Freaks! This weird group will definitely end up as a bunch of dried skulls, he was sure of it. The boy asked coolly, 'Excuse me, Lord Commander, but are these giant boulders scattered in this path holy?'

'Holy? Why do you ask?' Ranpui didn't seek silence this time.

'The way I see it, these boulders seem like they are here for convenience. As if to help your clan out. None of the forests have paths and boulders as huge as these standing guard.'

Ranpui was baffled for a moment. The boy was voicing a doubt that he had had too. 'Alright, I will acknowledge that you are a smart young boy. But, move ahead onto this peak, my clan will be at the summit. Settle your fate there.'

The group continued on the trail in silence. Ranpui was exhausted with the cart and the horses, but was relieved to see the dim flickering lights from his small clan through the prickly pine branches. He saw the warrior guard standing near the large wooden gate of the clan.

'Oi! Brother Pou, behold,' Ranpui called with a grin. The guard definitely noticed the prisoners and his treasure trove. He came running, instantly.

'Who are these? And...and horses? From where?' the guard stuttered in excitement.

'Prisoners. And look, supplies. I got food and drinks. Look here,' Ranpui showed the cart to the guard.

'Oh, yes. But are they from the upper clan? If so, we might be in trouble,' the guard said timidly.

'No, they speak in the valley dialect. Call our lady. After all the heads they took from us, we might just have our first set of heads from the valley,' Ranpui said triumphantly.

The guard nodded and ran away. Ranpui pushed his prisoners further inside the clan's compound. Few clansmen began to gather around the strange bound prisoners, standing close together, one lying unmoved on the horse.

'Excuse me Lord Commander, but the lady you just mentioned, is she the chief?' the pale boy asked innocently.

'No, but bow before her, for she is our late chief's daughter,' Ranpui said uninterested.

'My dear fellow guardians, get yourself ready for we are about to meet our lady,' the pale boy turned to his companions and announced proudly. For some reason, all of them became ridiculously excited. They began chatting and murmuring among themselves.

'Oi, oi... You shameless rats! Our lady will be here. Stop your nonsense,' Ranpui yelled, but none of them seemed to care.

'For real? You are sure, right Laiba? We all will be safe then...' Leisatao was giggling along with the children.

'Oi, you funny man. Shut up! Behave!' Ranpui pulled out his spear from the cart and tried to threaten the animated group.

'Ranpui! What is all this about?' a sweet voice, yet one with a tone of authority, rang through the noise. Everyone became quiet. The gathered clansmen kneeled on the ground. Ranpui bowed as soon as he saw Lady Ningrei come up with the guard. The prisoners stood frozen in the middle. All eyes were fixed on the lady as if they hadn't seen a lady before.

'Lady Ningrei, I have captured these trespassers and seized their belongings. They were found loitering around the deep gorge. I shall plead to the chief for their heads,' Ranpui spoke proudly.

'Are you stupid? What if they were from the upper clan? Look at their clothes. They are in disguise and also mostly children,' Ningrei scolded.

'Lady, they speak in fine valley dialect. They are from the valley. The upper clan will be happy if they learned that we managed to behead these people from the valley. A small clan like ours taking heads despite calamity...' Ranpui snorted in excitement.

Ningrei walked closer to the captive bunch and observed all of them. They looked like an odd pack—a pale boy as white as a boiled egg with a pair of bicoloured eyes gleaming in the dim light from the torches, a fair tall boy her age with a high ponytail, a younger girl, an adult with uneven hair and expensive metal pins, and there was one who was already dead or unconscious. Another young boy around her age, with fine hair, slung across a beautiful white pony.

'Greetings to our great guardian. We have come all the way to meet you,' the strange pale boy walked up and spoke in clear valley dialect with a bow.

'Alright. Shut them up and haul them inside the chief's chamber,' Ningrei gave her order to Ranpui and walked away as swiftly as she came.

The captives broke up in confused chatter.

'...She didn't even seem to care...'

'...What if she refused?...'

'...Calm down. We will talk to her in...'

'...She looked tough though...'

'Oi! Oi! Shut up you all. Save your creativity; it won't work now. See, our lady has very little tolerance for nonsense. Move!' Ranpui pulled the rope and dragged all of them towards the chief's cottage.

'Yes, I can see why she doesn't seem to tolerate you either,' the pale boy snapped. He seemed disappointed, his snowy eyebrows frowning.

'Just wait until I get your head. You monster egg, *kakyel marum!*' Ranpui decided to let it slide and entered inside the large wooden chamber of the chief. The prisoners followed obediently. The unconscious one was dragged in by the guard.

The chief's room was lit with bright torches, with a regular decor of dried skulls of animals, ivory artefacts, huge festival helmets made of polished cane and fur skin tapestry. The chief sat on her sheepskin seat, her strong warriors standing guard on both sides. She adorned her elegant bright red-blue robe with a bullhead motif, a fabric of dignity. Her headdress was large with a fountain of expensive feathers on an ivory crown dotted with shiny cowries.

'Apai, they are the ones, trespassers from the valley,' Ningrei spoke, bowing to her grandmother.

'Ning-Ning, untie them,' the old woman said with a kind smile.

'What?' Ranpui asked, shocked.

'Apai, what do you mean?' Ningrei also asked, as she too was surprised by her grandmother's response.

'Thank you, oh great Chief. I am Lord Laiba, the head priest of the Kangla Palace and the one currently slumbered on the pony is our unfortunate Meidingu, who suffered a blow from your Lord Commander here,' Laiba said, looking at Ranpui with a smirk. 'And our utmost pleasure to finally meet our lady, Lady Ningrei, if I am not wrong,' Laiba bowed to both of them.

'Most welcome. Eternal blessings to the lord of the seven realms and the protector of the nine mystic ranges,' the chief bowed.

'Lord of the...protector...?' Ningrei muttered half-heartedly and yelled, 'These children?'

'Ning-Ning, they are just few years younger than you and there is one adult among them too. Return them your courtesy,' the chief kept her tone calm.

'Show them my courtesy? To these disgusting valley dwellers? And that too, the royals?' Ningrei demanded, looking at all the intruders with contempt.

'Respected Chief, these prisoners are mine. Royals or not, regardless. Please bless me the strength to take their heads as my reward. I have also seized their supplies, which will last us at least a few days. And, more fortunately, I will check with the upper clan if they are truly the Meidingu and his minions. They will be happier than ever if they realized that we have the head of the Meidingu.'

'I never thought I would be agreeing with you one day,' Ningrei sighed at Ranpui and continued towards her grandmother, 'Apai, I mean, respected Chief! Please understand the circumstances. This is not like olden times. Things have changed. Please remember our people that died in vain for their cause. Give Ranpui their heads!'

'Ning-Ning, I am not asking you to show your courtesy to them as an inferior clan. They have shown theirs and now you shall return yours,' though the chief said so with a smile, her voice was stern.

'Respected lady, my eyes, they are throbbing. Here, let me show you something...' Laiba stood up, stretching out his bound hands towards Ningrei.

'Get your hands off me!' Ningrei kicked the boy in the stomach. He fell curled on the floor. Both the adult man and the young girl cried out, the thin boy with the ponytail crawled forward in defence.

'Ning-Ning, since birth, you have never seen me mad at you, have you?' her grandmother asked with her usual gentle smile and said, 'If you do not untie them and show your courtesy, you will see a version of me that you have never witnessed before. An unpleasant one.' The tone of her voice became serious, her hand clutching tight on her sceptre lying next to her.

'Respected Chief...' Ranpui began, but the chief ordered, 'Chief Commander, lead our warriors out of my hall and stand guard outside. All of you, now!' She hammered her sceptre hard on the floor.

'Yes, Chief,' Ranpui genuflected and ordered the rest of the warriors in the hall to move out. Everyone moved as ordered without a word.

'I apologize for my granddaughter's regretful behaviour. Please forgive her for she is as blind as a termite. Maichou Laiba, are you alright?' the chief asked apologetically.

'I am fine. Just my gut feels turned and churned,' Laiba said, rubbing his belly.

'I can't believe she would just kick a child like that. That's too inelegant,' the adult man spoke, dramatically flipping his hair in anger.

'Apologies, deep apologies,' the chief bowed and said with a shy smile, 'Our Meidingu's companions. May I know your names? Starting from the eldest among all.'

'I am Leisatao of Luwang, and this girl here is Sana, a maiden from the eastern province, and this young boy here is Lungchum, the crown prince of the Moirang province. You already know Lord Laiba and our Meidingu,' Leisatao said, still giving a look of disappointment at Ningrei from time to time.

'The crown prince of Moirang? With our Meidingu? And you are from Luwang province?' the chief looked stupefied.

'What does this mean, Apai?' Ningrei asked suspiciously.

'This means you show your courtesy right now!' The chief finally sounded harsh, 'We are in the presence of friends from all corners and they showed us their respect. Ningrei, now!'

Ningrei was hesitant, but she had never seen her grandmother tense because of her before. She bowed at the prisoners and spoke, 'Greetings to our royals and their minions.'

'Respected Chief, since you have welcomed us against all odds, I believe you already know or have guessed our true purpose?' Laiba asked curiously.

'Maichou Laiba, I am afraid I do know a little,' the chief said with a weak smile.

'How come, our respected Chief knew about it and not our lady?' Lungchum asked doubtfully.

'Yes, that even I find strange,' Laiba agreed.

'Ning-Ning, untie your friends. They are here for you,' the chief said, taking a knife from a stand nearby and handing it to her granddaughter.

'Friends?' Ningrei asked, receiving the knife.

'Do it now. Serve them our sweet wine,' the chief then shouted a bit louder, 'Warriors, one of you come in here.'

'Yes, Chief,' a warrior showed up at the entrance instantly.

'Take the unconscious Meidingu towards the infirmary for treatment. Ask our healer to treat him with utmost care.'

'Yes, Chief,' the warrior picked up the Meidingu and carried him away.

Ningrei went towards the group and cut their ropes. She also took her grandmother's wine gourd and bamboo tumblers and poured rice *yu* for all of them. They all accepted a tumbler each with a bow. She served wine to the valley dwellers. She never thought she would do something as beneath her as that. What is my grandmother thinking? She wondered.

'Ning-Ning, sit here.' Her grandmother asked Ningrei to sit next to her and then she continued to look at Laiba, the pale boy with strange eyes, and said, 'Lord Laiba, you said you wanted to show my granddaughter something just a moment ago. Can you please show her that?'

'I am sorry, Chief. My eyes give some visions from time to time. But these are involuntary reflexes, and are mostly about particular memories of people and of places. I recently got a vision about our lady, but when she kicked me in my stomach, it went away before I could have a look at it myself.'

'Vision? Interesting,' the chief said thoughtfully.

'Apai, what is this all about? I want to know everything. Why are they here?'

'Ning-Ning. This will be a very long story.' The chief said with tears in her eyes, 'It was 14 years ago when you were five. Your late father and mother had gone out for clan wars as demanded by the upper clan. It was one of the fiercest. Some of the small clans were destroyed completely. Villages were burnt to ashes. Your father had returned heartbroken. He wanted peace, but without any sponsored help from other seemingly mighty provinces, a small clan like ours couldn't do anything about the frequent clan wars. But in that summer war with the eastern clan, my son, your father, decided, he had had enough and refused to slaughter all the defeated warriors and suggested killing only the war prisoners. The upper clan took this as a sign of weakness and came here at night-time, and took away both your parents and...and took their heads to set an example for the other smaller clans in the north. We all hated the valley for they ignored us, attacked us, even when we pleaded for help. Didn't we?'

Ningrei sat quietly and nodded. She remembered growing up feeling hatred for the people of the valley; also fearing the upper clan. If not for the sudden flux of famine all over the northern ranges, the terrors and horror of wars would have been even more rampant. At present, the only thing that they all cared for, the upper clan or the smaller clans, was enough food for the day.

'After your parents' death, you were my only hope to continue living. I looked after you all day, a weak child, that you were, Ning-Ning. Without your mother's milk, you became frail, my love. Always falling ill and refusing to eat anything most of the time. I thought I was going to lose you. The healers already consoled me and prepared me for the worst. I tried my best to...I tried my best...' The chief's voice faltered and she began to weep.

'Apai...' Ningrei called softly, more hurt to witness her forever-smiling grandmother cry so bitterly for the first time.

'But then, you left me. Ning-Ning left me,' the chief said grimly.

'I left you?' Ningrei asked confused, 'Apai, I am here.'

All the other guests sat quietly, listening to the tale with a heavy heart. Laiba said calmly, 'Please continue, Chief.'

'Yes, you are here now but...but 14 years ago, in the dark of the night, after all the healers of our clan left you to take your last breath, you gave up on me. Ningrei, my dear Ning-Ning, you died at the age of five. You died in my arms.'

'But that doesn't make sense, Apai. I am here. How...how?' Ningrei asked, shaking her grandmother desperately.

The guests were surprised by the last words of the chief. The person being claimed dead was alive and well front of them.

'It was just me with you, in my arms, dead. I cried so bitterly. Called the Mother Goddess and the forest gods for help. I cried hard and long. And through this very door,' the chief pointed her finger at the entrance and continued, 'a lady, tall and beautiful, came with her bamboo basket slung across her head. A chilled air followed her and she was wearing different kind of clothes and a bead necklace, not our clan's. I asked her who she was and she told me that she came looking for a body she could borrow. At that instant, I knew that the lady coming in was no human. At first, I tried defending you and asked her again if she was a god or a demon. She smiled and replied that she was a goddess. She answered calmly without any hesitation. I believed her instantly. I asked her why she came to me and why she was in need of a body. She sat next to me. Here, right here (she pointed to a spot in the hall), and she told me that she had come here for a task. She said she despised being born as a human, the trouble of entering a womb and hence came looking for an already born child to harbour her spirit. She asked me to offer your dead body to her, as it would be perfect for her purpose.'

Ningrei sat with a gaped mouth; she was lost for words. Her hands were trembling. She was already dead? A goddess took her body? It was too much information for her currently sensitive mind.

'This is very unexpected, Chief. But all of us here are also incarnations of gods and goddesses,' Laiba added. 'So, what happened then?'

'Yes, I asked her about her task and that was how I came to know about all of you. She told me that her companions would come one day to recruit her for some quest. I was desperate, but also suspicious of her. I asked her what would happen to my granddaughter if she took her body and to that she giggled and said, 'Nothing much, but you will have a granddaughter again.' She assured me that all she would do was seed her spirit into Ningrei and as a return gift for hosting her spirit, she promised to return Ningrei's life.'

'A neat bargain,' Laiba nodded.

'Ning-Ning, your heart beat again because of the goddess. She is one of the guardians, just like these guests here sitting in front of you. You wouldn't have existed if not for the quest and for that even the boulder spirits pledged to protect you. I told you that something sinister is at wake. Something is not going as per the course of nature, but Ning-Ning, it was because something divine was lost and you, along with your friends here, are supposed to find it. Ning-Ning, you are a destined hero. You were chosen to serve and to follow this path.'

'Why did you never mention of this before?' Ningrei asked meekly.

'You were young when it happened. Even though you were once dead, when you opened your eyes again after being given a second chance at life, you were just the same. I was afraid, Ning-Ning. I thought that you would wake up as someone else, but as the goddess had promised, you came back as you. My most beloved grandchild. Pure and innocent and incredibly stubborn. I never wanted to remind myself that I once held you dead in my arms. It was terrible to even think about it, Ning-Ning. I wanted to forget all of it. Then, not so long after you woke up, you got lost in the labyrinth of boulders. When you came back from that treacherous hilltop to tell me that the stones called for you, I realized you would one day end up following your path, regardless. I thought that it was better for you to learn it all when the time comes. And, now is the time, Ning-Ning. Atuchaga Kamatei, the holy stones, had always been protecting you. You will prove wondrous in this quest.'

'I understand how you must have felt, Apai,' Ningrei spoke after a moment of silence. Her eyes were thick with tears. Her lips quivered as she spoke, 'But, this is too much for me right now. I...' Ningrei stood up and ran out of the hall.

She ran towards the only place where she always felt most safe. The megaliths.

Ningrei ran up towards the stones. She didn't greet them as she did every day, but she could hear the faint whisper, 'It is time, it is time,' as she ran through the crowded structures. The boulders seemed too crammed, as she found paths that were too narrow even for her to pass. She was crying as she pushed herself through the rock creek to go somewhere deep within the never-ending hilltop of boulders.

'I thought you were the spirits of my parents. I thought Kamatei was Apa, the voice of the woman as Ama. But, you were just protecting me for a purpose, is it? I thought I was being loved and cared for, but it was like I was some kind of stock, to be used when needed!'

'It is time. It is time,' the voices continued to whisper through the air.

Ningrei fell on her knees and began to weep like a child. She remembered how the sweet voice of a woman had called out to her when she was small. She had assumed it was her mother; the woman had asked her to follow her voice towards the hilltop of boulders. And she had. She always thought that her mother used to called for her. And when she entered the labyrinth, she couldn't find an exit. The place became an endless field of boulders. She cried, but the boulder king entertained her. He spoke to her and pledged his duty to protect her. She was happy that she could finally feel the love and care of her deceased parents. She was always content with the thought. But all that had changed now. She was now to work with those, whose very actions led to the death of her beloved parents. Just for that, the boulder lord had been guarding her. The Meidingu of the obnoxious Central Province, with their tall claims of being divinely superior, did nothing of real importance for the peace of the realm.

'Lady Ningrei'—she heard a faint voice drifting through the cold breeze. The long grasses around the huge stone columns rustled along with the voice that called again, '...Lady Ningrei.'

'Wait, this voice, isn't it the white boy?' Ningrei stood up confused, 'But, how did he...'

'It is time...' the stones whispered again and suddenly a thick fog descended around the stones, covering everything in a milky mist, illuminated by the silvery moonlight above.

'Lady Ningrei? Is that you?' It was the pale boy now speaking from somewhere near her.

'Yes. Are you stupid? Didn't my grandmother warn you not to walk in here? You are lucky not to have got lost in here,' Ningrei answered, irritated.

The fog subsided rapidly and the stone columns came into view again, but they had somehow changed their positions. She was standing in the middle of a circular clearing, the white boy standing opposite her.

'I know of these stones, respected lady. The great founders of the northern clans once carried them on their backs to test their strength, to gain respect and to mark their names across these hills. Here, now they are enchanted, each carrying the spirits of all our ancestors,' the white boy said, looking around the boulders with pride.

'You speak well,' said Ningrei, but she wasn't impressed, 'Now, leave. Let me have some time to think it all through. I have to digest everything. More than 10 years worth of secrets and lies and ignorance...'

'Lady Ningrei,' the boy said calmly, 'if you want to unleash your anger, please feel free to kick me again, as many times as you want. I will be happy to receive your blows as long as you would believe us and accept us as your comrades. As a guardian, it is my only duty to guide you to your charted destiny.'

'My parents died because of the valley. They ignored our call for help. "Protector of the nine mystic ranges!" What did he protect? He only protects his sorry buttocks on his stupid throne. They want tributes, respect, to be hailed with high claim to divine rights—all these things are so pathetic. Your Meidingu, lord of the seven realms… Don't make me laugh. There are no more seven realms but thousands of segregated clans with chiefs, looking for an opportunity to breech the mighty island palace. Why? Because the very lord of the realms does not have the tiniest bit of decency to respect his subjects. He kept on losing his united power with his unfair and selfish deeds around the kingdoms. Boy, the list goes on.'

'I am not much aware of the subject, but one thing that I must tell you, respected lady, is that our Meidingu, who came here with me shall not bear the shame of the mistakes not committed by him. He has been very recently crowned and any political upheavals shouldn't be blamed on him. He came here trying to follow his destiny and help us save the world together.'

'We all carry our parents' blood in us and by that, their legacy. He can't act innocent of his parents' sins. His father, the late Meidingu, was the worst of all. His horrible death was a deserving end, a fair payment for his part in many crimes of ignorance.'

'My lady, sometimes, legacy is not enough. Sometimes, we carry their blood to alter their wrongs. You strive to be respected as much as your parents. You want to be respected for who you are and not because of who your parents were. Why don't you give the same chance to my king? He is the king of destiny.'

Ningrei looked at the small boy who spoke much better than most of the elder prophets in her clan.

'It is not going to be easy,' she said after a moment of silence.

She didn't want to believe in the quest or suchlike, but as her grandmother had disclosed, she herself was the very product of a curious miracle. She owed much to the unseen divinity now. She knew she had to force herself to let her bitterness slide. But it wouldn't be easy. She had hated the valley for as long as she could remember. It wouldn't be easy at all.

'I never said it will be,' the boy smiled innocently.

Ningrei stood up without a word. Few more voices, not the stones, came lingering in the air again.

'Respected lady,' the boy asked apologetically, 'my eyes led me easily to you through the labyrinth, but I think my companions are lost somewhere. Can you help?'

'You brought your companions along? And here I am, thinking you are smart,' Ningrei grunted.

'Sorry, my lady, but it's just that my companions were desperate to make amends with you, with whatever displeasures you hold against us, and they just ran in when I told them that you would be here. And you know these boulders; they do seem to be just a few from the outside.'

'Fine,' Ningrei snapped and turned back with her eyes closed and she chanted in her mind, 'Father, I mean... Kamatei, my Leige, lead the other beings here.'

The faint voices became distinct, 'Laiba...Laiba....'

'I am here,' Laiba answered.

Out of a huge column, all the other companions of Laiba appeared one after another. They all came out at the circular clearing and seemed awestricken.

'Unbelievable. I had been running around here just a moment ago, and it all seemed like some congested pillars of these huge rocks. And then, I felt like I heard a whisper and turned around and here...' the adult with shiny pins spoke excitedly.

'Same here, I was walking around, calling Laiba's name, but all I could see was an endless field of these tall boulders. Even I heard a whisper and then saw this clearing right ahead of me,' the young girl spoke.

'Me too. I even thought of turning into a dragon to fly out of here,' the tall boy with a long ponytail spoke excitedly.

'Alright. All of you. Calm down. This place is enchanted and is Lady Ningrei's treasured domain. Didn't you people say you wanted to greet her properly? She is here.' Laiba walked up closer to Ningrei and smiled at her.

Ningrei looked at all of them, one after another. She neither smiled nor frowned. She just looked at them standing together in front of her, surrounded by her boulders, the full moon shimmering in the night sky. A weird band, she thought.

Ningrei joined the rest of the guardians in the cottage of the brave, which had been assigned to them, for resting, by her grandmother. The guardians gave her every piece of information she demanded about the claimed task, and about the sacred scissor—what it was, why, who and how. She learned that Leisatao of Luwang was a dart-maker, a hero incarnate of the sun-slayer and Sana was the Supreme Goddess incarnate. One look at the frail girl and the thought of her as someone as splendid as the great goddess seemed bizarre. The tall boy was just 15 and claimed he was able to turn into a dragon. Prince Lungchum, his name...

'...But Iwan is still in the infirmary...' Prince Lungchum seemed worried. They all were anxious.

'Excuse me, but you people said there was supposed to be seven of us. Only six are here. Where is the seventh?' Ningrei inquired.

'Yes...that...' Laiba said with a smile, 'He sort of...kind of left the quest while we were on our way here.'

'Left? Isn't this destiny driven? Can he do that while I can't?'

'Please don't worry, Lady Ningrei. Laiba said he will return,' said Sana, trying to sound confident. She failed.

'Gothang wanted to join us, but he decided to find his mother first. He is such a sweet child. He will come around for sure,' Leisatao said, poised.

'Anyway, whatever your plan is, you will need your king to wake up first. Don't you?' Ningrei looked at Laiba.

'I will go visit him and check,' he said.

Ningrei looked at Laiba for a while, but answered calmly, 'Alright. Hope your king is feeling better.'

Laiba walked out of the cottage, across the hill slope, towards the infirmary. The northern ranges could still be seen as a long streak of dark blue and gray on the moonlit horizon. Laiba was about to reach the infirmary, but stopped when he saw a sudden spark of light in the far mountain forest. The view was distant, but the lightning bolts shooting out of the dark forest on the other side of the range were distinct.

'Prince of the sky, so you didn't go so far,' Lord Laiba said, his silvery iris getting enlarged and his golden one getting slightly dimmed.

THE MANGSORE

'What about the giants?' one dark entity, a skull-like face shimmering within the dark forest, asked in a hissing tone.

'Who cares,' the lady answered, with her bright, designed stole, red and white in colour, dragging across the floor, black and white striped sarong worn tightly, high above the knees, her long silvery hair wafting as if there were a mist around her, her gracefully long neck adored with thick layers of necklaces made out of glass beads and cowries. She smiled and licked her plump red lips, 'I just want to taste a sweet drop of blood. Oh, how aromatic human blood is. I still remember how my human husband tasted. He was sweet and his intestines were even sweeter.'

'We are indeed free,' a heap of dark clouds dispersed and the lady waved as if bidding farewell. She looked at the sky for a while, but then walked away swiftly. The forest was thick and the mountain high; she loved the shade and the ominous chill around the forest.

'All dead. All dried. Hmm...but I shall meet someone perhaps. I have waited for so long,' she garbled, lifting her thin fingers to pluck a few leaves from a nearby branch.

'Ah! Are these human footsteps I am hearing?' the lady smiled, her canines protruding out of her mouth. Her eyes sparkled as the footsteps approached nearer.

A blindingly dashing man walked out of the woods and stood facing the lady without a word. The man was tall and strong, but looked confused. He was gorgeous and his calm muscular face gave off a pleasant aura. The lady smiled ever so gently, 'What an incredible beauty, my first catch!' she talked to herself and then spoke a little louder so that the man could hear, 'Lost your way, dear?'

'No, but who are you?' the man seemed confused.

'Me? I am a lady, my love,' she giggled, covering her mouth with her slender fingers, 'And you are?'

'Gothang.' He replied and added, 'Anyway, are you from the nearby village? Have you seen a woman pass by? She must be around 40. She has shiny dark hair tied in a bun and...'

'I know no woman but me. You know no woman like me. Have you ever touched a woman? Do you want to touch me?' the lady ignored Gothang's inquiry and walked up close to him, her body rubbing against his.

'Wait, what? No, no. Lady, respected lady. What are you doing?' Gothang tried to step back, but the woman hugged him tight.

'Oh, you smell so good.' The lady sniffed around Gothang's thick muscular neck. It gave him the goosebumps and he struggled to free himself from her strong grip.

'I am...wait...respected lady, I came in search of my mother,' Gothang struggled, 'If you have seen her, kindly tell me the direction she went and I will be on my way.'

'No!' the woman almost screamed, but she let go of her tight grip and instead ran her hands across Gothang's chest and whimpered, 'Please don't leave me. I am scared.'

'What?' Gothang locked his eyes with the lady's and was mesmerized by her hazy, grey eyes. She was one beautiful creature, with a face as soft as the petal of a lily, her quivering lips as red as a ghost chilli and her silver hair as smooth as silk.

'I am scared, love,' she repeated, sticking out her long fleshy tongue and kissed him.

Gothang almost vomited, 'Your breath, it stinks!' He cried out, gagging because of the foul breath he had just inhaled from the strange lady. Why does the lady reek so much? He wondered. She smells like rotten meat!

'Huh?' The lady stood perplexed for a while but tried to smile and said, 'I am sorry, love.'

'I need to get moving. Have a good day, lady. Please excuse me,' Gothang stepped back and tried to run away quickly, but the lady stopped him again, her hands gripping him around his waist.

'Let go of me, lady. I do not want to be rude,' Gothang finally sounded a little cross.

'But I said I am scared. You will leave a poor lady alone in the forest?' she pressed up to him and he stood there defeated. He had never felt comfortable around women folk and now he had met the worst of their kind, he thought.

'What do you want? Shall I drop you to your village? How far is it from here?' He asked

'I want to be with you. Take me wherever you are going.'

'I told you I came searching for my mother. Please, lady. Have mercy and let me continue on my journey.'

'We will search for your mother together then. I can be your wife. Don't you humans want a woman like me to be your wife?' the lady asked innocently.

'Human? Wait.' Gothang stepped away from the woman and asked, 'Who are you for real?'

'I am a lady. Lost in the woods. Desperate. Now make love to me and make me your wife.' The lady tried to get close to Gothang, but he yelled, 'I respect your boldness, lady, but I have no interest whatsoever. I am not worthy of a wife yet!'

'Huh? Strange. It worked just fine the last time,' muttered the woman and then continued, 'Fine, love. Let me just be with you. Will you let me follow you?'

'Follow?' Gothang was not sure what the woman meant, but he didn't want to waste more time and just answered nervously, 'Whatever, lady, but please don't distract me or try anything funny.' He walked ahead and the woman followed him with a giggle.

Gothang looked attentively around the woods and was sure that he had seen the place in his dream. He reassured himself that he was getting nearer to his mother. 'Please be safe, mother. Your son is finally here. I am here.' Gothang prayed within.

'My love, it will be dark soon,' the annoying woman said. She had been following Gothang without a complaint and he decided to let her be as long as she didn't try her strange seductive tricks on him.

'I don't care. I need to find her,' Gothang said without slowing his pace.

'I know of a village nearby. We can rest there.'

'A village? Is it yours?' Gothang asked excited, thinking he could finally leave the woman in her village.

'No, but if you want, it could be ours. I can give you a village, a kingdom and so much more. We can stay there forever,' she ran up with a delightful smile.

'No thank you, but you can lead me to the village,' Gothang planned to think of a way to leave the woman behind.

The woman sniffed the air as she led them through the gradually darkening forest. 'We are near, closer to the children.'

'Chil...children?' the woman's words disturbed him, but he didn't want to chatter much and just followed her. And as she had predicted, he began to pick up the smell of burnt wood and a human settlement. Flickering lights and tall bamboo cottages with carved wooden fences came into view.

'We are here, love,' she sang.

'Right, I will look around for a place to stay here. Do you know anyone here? Which clan is this?'

'Doesn't matter. Equally delicious. Come, we will stay there.' She pointed towards a dark stable that stood ruined at the corner of the clan's compound.

'Let me go and greet the clanspeople first. You stay here if you like.' Gothang let go of the woman's arm and went ahead towards a house that was a little bigger, expecting to meet the clan's head or house leader.

'Anybody here?' Gothang knocked at the door. Petite voices could be heard from within. He waited patiently.

The heavy wooden door was finally opened and through the creek, a pair of anxious eyes stared at him. Gothang smiled politely as the door got opened a bit wider, but the person, who turned out to be an old woman, hit him with a sacred *tairel* (red cedar) branch.

'Oyyh! Oyyyh!' Gothang was surprised at the unexpected attack. He curled up and shielded himself with his arms.

'So, you are indeed a human,' the woman stopped whipping him and stood staring at Gothang.

'Yes, I am.' Gothang said, relieved. 'I came here in search of a place to stay for tonight. I also have a lady with me. She seemed lost too...'

'Sorry. No visitors these days. Too risky,' the woman tried to shut the door.

'No, wait,' Gothang cried, disappointed with such unusual conduct, 'Since when do we treat guests like this?'

'Uh, since the dawn of the last reign. Since the wake of the darkness. Leave or stay wherever you want, but sorry, we cannot entertain guests inside our house,' the old woman spoke apologetically.

'Fine, I will be at the ruined stable around the corner. What about the lady? You will entertain female guests, perhaps?'

'No, can't do,' the woman shut the door with a loud thud.

Gothang returned and the strange lady was there waiting for him at the ruined stable, leisurely lying on top of a heap of straw.

'Lady, you can stay here and seek the villagers' help in finding your way back home. I need to leave early tomorrow and you can't follow me forever,' Gothang said calmly.

'I can. Forever,' the lady reached out her arms for Gothang again. He stepped back.

'I am serious, respected lady. We will part tomorrow. You will stay here.'

'No, I will not stay. You are mine,' she slowly got up and cuddled Gothang again, touching him in a way that made him uncomfortable.

'Behave!' Gothang had had enough and pushed her hard. She moved back and fell quite inelegantly on the floor. He immediately felt sorry. 'I told you to behave. Please stop being so strange. Now get some rest. I am tired too.'

The lady stood up, looked at Gothang without a word, but he turned away to get some rest, without saying anything more. He really didn't want to face the lady any longer. First, he pretended to be asleep and eventually he really did.

It was his mother again. Now, running through a dark cave. Her hair was undone. With dirt-stained clothes and a smudged face, she looked exhausted, but kept walking.

'Mother!' Gothang seemed to call out, but she didn't look back. She kept on walking. Her feet seemed injured, lips were cracked and eyes were sunken deep. He felt deep pain to see his abandoned mother running cluelessly, waiting for him. My father is cruel, he thought. His mother ran deeper into the cave and vanished.

'Mother, wait!' Gothang screamed, but his voice echoed back at him. He began to weep and heard a sound from behind. He turned around and, to his horror, saw the strange lady standing behind him, her lips dripping with blood and in hand was the severed arm of a child.

'Ahhh!' Gothang woke up screaming. He looked around in the dark but didn't see the lady. 'Now, where is she?' Worried, he began to search for the woman within the deserted compound. The sun was yet to rise and it was difficult to see anything properly. Everyone in the houses within the clan were sound asleep; there was drop-dead silence all around except for his heavy breathing and footsteps thumping on the grassy floor.

At the far corner, Gothang saw a hut with its front door wide open. It was a small hut, but he felt a throbbing fear as he approached it. He heard the sound of bones cracking, reeking with the smell of blood and, to his dismay, as soon as he entered the hut, he saw the lady bending down and tearing up meat. It took him a while to distinguish things in the dark, but there were arms and legs lying around like pieces of flesh, just like in his dream. The lady was feasting on a human, a child to be exact.

'Monster!' Gothang ran in without a plan.

The lady stood up and attacked him, pressing her clawed hand around his neck, suffocating him.

'You would have been more delicious and it would have been less painful for you if you had let me to eat you as we cuddled.'

The lady had somehow turned incredibly strong. Gothang was pushed up in the air with one arm. He flailed desperately and unsuccessfully, the claws digging deeper into his neck.

'You were too handsome to eat just right away. I was attracted by your beauty but I was hungry, love,' the lady smiled with her sharp teeth drenched in blood, her silver hair flying around her like a thick fog.

Gothang began to feel numb, his strong arms almost useless and his thick legs dangling mid-air. A bolt of lightning streaked within the dark hut. Gothang was not sure what happened, but he fell on the ground. The lady screamed aloud. The room turned bright, his hands were on fire! Gothang looked at them, astounded. They were not on fire but engulfed within a bright flickering something. What is going on? He wondered, but he didn't waste much time and grabbed the screaming lady who was now trying to escape out of the hut.

'Lightning! Who are you?' the lady screamed and Gothang squeezed her as if she were a piece of wet cloth.

'A prince, they said,' Gothang uttered, as his hands continued emanating more glow, lightning bolts to be exact.

The bolts shot out in random directions; while the hut was only perforated, the lady got fully roasted within his grip. Gothang didn't loosen his hands until he was sure that nothing but the char of the lady was left.

When he let go of his grip, the lightning bolts subsided and he fell on the ground, unconscious.

Gothang slowly opened his eyes; there was a dim torch nearby. A thin lingering smell of alcohol hung in the air. He tried to move his head, but felt a sharp pain and stopped.

'Rest a little longer,' an old woman said.

He rolled his eyes and saw the woman sitting beside the bed with a bowl filled with water and a towel. It was the same woman who had hit him with the *tairel* branch earlier. The one who didn't welcome him as a guest. Who would blame her anyway?

'What happened?' Gothang raised his arms and looked at them. They seemed fine but the tips of his fingers were blackened, though he felt no pain whatsoever.

'That, I should be asking you,' the woman said dully and continued as she rubbed the towel around his stomach, 'Why would you bring a creature like Karaimei to our already unfortunate clan and then do the stunt?'

'Karaimei? Was that her name? What happened to her?'

The old woman explained that Karaimei was actually a celestial being. Gothang nodded, but let out a yelp when he saw the demon curled up inside a bamboo cage in the corner. He thought he had killed the demon!

'Karaimei is a munificent demon. If chastised right, she knows better than committing more trouble. You have roasted her well with your power. She will no longer be a danger to us as long as she stays inside the cage. In fact, if she stays here, maybe other demons will avoid my clan for she is respected and feared by the dark entities,' the old woman looked at Karaimei, who returned a bored look.

'So you are the prince of the sky, known by different names in the human realm; but up there, you are our celestial lord. I shall protect these humans because of your courtesy and respect for a woman like me. I shall bid you farewell. Take care, lord of the sky. The east is where all the monsters are headed,' Karaimei gave a smile of approval, though her words warned of the sinister affair.

Gothang asked about any caves nearby and the old woman told him about the large cave system in the east, the Mangsore. He decided to follow the path, quite sure that his mother went towards it.

Gothang gave a last bow to the old woman and Karaimei, and headed back to the forest, running fast towards the east with the sun sliding down behind him. If he could, he would stop the slithering sun and reach the cave before nightfall, but it was just wishful thinking on his part. The forest became gradually engulfed in darkness.

It was dead quiet in the forest with the moonlight slowly sinking over the tall treetops. Gothang was running still. He remembered Karaimei warning him of all the demons heading east. What if my mother is in danger? I need not rest, he thought.

Just as he was about to slow down to catch his breath, a thumping sound from someplace far echoed through the quiet forest. Gothang could hear his blood running hot in his veins. Now what! He tried to calm down, but the thumping sound got closer. An elephant, perhaps? The thumping sound approached him; he ran but the sound was distinctly following him. He suddenly stopped running and decided to face whatever was following him instead. He slowly turned his face towards the sound.

He didn't feel afraid; he was, in fact, ready for a surprise. A demon? Obviously, it will be a shocker. It wouldn't look or be normal. Karaimei

proved right. He took a deep breath and stood waiting for the source of the sound to reveal itself.

Out of the darkness, from the shade of the trees, there emerged not one but two large entities. Gothang readied for defence, his hands beginning to flicker with streaks of lightning. He had learnt of his power after his fight with Karaimei. However, there was no fight necessary. He recognized the creatures coming out of the woods. The moonlight was shining on them. The identical beasts that once attacked his pigsty were the ones that dropped him at the Central Palace. The strange looking beasts had bright red eyes and gold and silver antlers.

'Not again,' Gothang muttered. The beasts walked up to him. He couldn't ignore the majestic look of the beasts despite his fear. He waited to see if the beasts would attack him. They didn't. The twin beasts stood staring at him again. Gothang also hesitated to attack the beautiful creatures that didn't seem to harm him. Something told him that the creatures were looking at him as if he were a mystery, but he was on guard. They were animals, nonetheless. He still let his hands flicker with lightning sparks. The quietness settled back again.

Lao hei...lao hei...lao hei... A low hum suddenly filled the air and both the beasts snarled irritated, standing defensively in front of Gothang. He stood still and listened to the bizarre noise breaking up in the forest. It came like a swarm of flies.

The beasts began to growl and the hum turned into an unbearable scream of many things saying, 'Lao hei...lao hei...'

For a moment, Gothang wasn't sure of what was happening, but he began to notice the arrival of an army within the forest, along with the irritating chatters. The forest was rattling with footsteps and movements throughout.

Gothang saw the silhouette of the noisy entities heading his way, approaching him. One was hooded or maybe coated with some sort of fur, indistinguishable, running up to him and even tried to scratch him with its razor-sharp claws. Gothang was ready for defence, but one of the beasts bit the entity right on time and threw it up in the air. He then realized that the beasts were not there to attack him, but to protect him instead. But why? He would need to figure it out later, he thought, because swarms of terrible creatures with claws and fangs surrounded him. Both the beasts circled and defended him from the entities as much as they could, their powerful jaws biting the flying or jumping creatures and juddering them until they fell into pieces.

'What in the world are these?' Gothang wondered. He tried to throw the lightning sparks, but was not competent enough. He produced the sparks and tried to control them. The twin beasts opened their mouths wide and howled, and inside the open mouths, many of the dark hopping creatures seemed to perish. Gothang looked at them in amazement, admiring the beasts even more. He was defending himself well and the beasts were cooperating fine. However, the sheer number of the screeching creatures soon seemed to overpower them. Gothang and the twin beasts slowly got surrounded. This is not good, he thought, and tried again to shoot lightning from his hands. Few bolts did fly out and hit random creatures, but not as effectively as he had wanted. While he was busy trying to hurl his bolts, one of the beasts got attacked. A dark creature dug its sharp talons into the beast's rear and it spilled sparkling golden blood all over. The beast gave out a painful roar, but continued defending Gothang. These creatures should not get hurt for me, he thought. His hands began to feel a controlled tremble. Sparks evoked up between his fingers and before he knew it, he was up, levitating in the air, with both his hands glowing with lightning bolts. He threw the bolts around the creatures and they all screeched in pain caused by the burns. The whole forest lit up, and then he threw some more bolts. The dark entities vapourized instantly. Some got burned and charred while some flamed. The beasts stood obediently near him, witnessing the dance of lightning bolts within the forest, dark entities being burned with the slightest touch.

Gothang ceased his mad lightning carnival. The forest became quiet again. All the attacking creatures got smoked or burned. The two majestic beasts sat staring at him, with admiration.

'So, you two came to warn me of this?' Gothang asked the beasts. They both gave a happy woof as an answer.

'But why?'

His hands were still abuzz with strings of sparkling lights. He didn't feel good. It seemed like his body was boiling up.

Another woof came as an answer, and to his surprise, the giant creatures suddenly shrank right in front of his eyes and turned into small regular-sized hounds. The beasts ran up to him and licked his feet, their gold and silver antlers still shining charmingly on their tiny heads.

'Wait, you can shrink your size?' Gothang couldn't help but pat them. They were dangerously adorable. 'You guys left me at the palace. You guys know something. Don't you?' he ruffled their soft fur. The beasts licked his face in excitement. 'Why are you guys protecting me? Is this about the quest?'

He observed them more closely. They were completely identical. He hadn't seen any other pair of animals like them. They were like an elegant crossbreed between deer, lion and wolf.

'So, are you guys leaving?' He asked the beasts, but they just stood listening to him obediently. He smiled again, 'Alright, alright. Adorable...'

He dropped down to the ground, exhausted. The beasts ran up and stood guard near him. It seemed like they had decided to stick with him.

Gothang felt better instantly. He was a bit disappointed, thinking that the beasts might disappear again in the forest like last time. He smiled, 'Thank you. I was hoping you would stay.' He pondered for a while and added, 'What about your names? Can I give you names?' He asked and the beasts sat listening to him, as attentive as ever, their perky ears pricked up. Gothang thought for a while. He remembered the old tale that his father used to narrate while tucking him in to sleep—a story about how the southern tribe came out of the cave and how few people remained inside the subterranean kingdom like Chongja and Chongkim.

'Alright,' Gothang looked at the injured one and said, 'You will be Chongja.' The beast gave a delightful nod.

'Great. You love it. And you will be...,' he smiled at the other beast waiting obediently and said, 'You will be Chongkim.' It gave a big excited woof.

'I wouldn't rest for long; so, if you both are planning to stay with me, get some rest. Look here,' he slowly patted the injured one, the claw marks gleaming in gold, 'you got wounded because of me.'

Chongja licked its wound and, to Gothang's utter surprise, it got healed instantly, leaving only a faint claw mark.

'Incredible. Just incredible. You guys are...' He patted his new companions again.

Gothang lay down to rest a while, exhausted after the attack of the dark entities. His new companions curled up near him and he dozed off quite unwillingly.

His mother was now deep inside the cave. Gothang could sense her despite the darkness of his vision. His mother was panting heavily. Something was blocking her path. A huge boulder was blocking the cave tunnel. It seemed like she was chanting something...or was she singing? His mother ran her hands around the boulder as if caressing it and murmured something. Loud shrieks filled the air and Gothang felt like he saw a glimpse of something shiny and bright oozing out from the crack in the boulder. The dream shifted. Now, he stood in the middle of a vast valley edged by rolling hills. He looked around and, to his surprise, realized that he was not alone. He saw two children, one boy and one girl playing not so far behind. They were running around, chasing each other in the tall-grassed dale, dotted with pinkish lilies all around.

Gothang wanted to call out, but he knew he was dreaming. It seemed strange at first, but he knew it was a vivid dream that he dreamt quite consciously.

While he was contemplating about this new piece of dream, the boy and the girl stopped playing and stood staring at him.

'Wait, do they see me?' He wondered.

'Yes, Your Highness.' The small boy said with a little giggle. The small girl also smiled politely.

'Who are you? Where are we?' Gothang asked confused.

'You called me Chongja,' the boy answered happily. He ran up near Gothang and he noticed a faint claw mark running across his left leg under his brown cotton loincloth.

'And you called me Chongkim,' the little girl said with a giggle. She had long silky hair, a well-trimmed fringe and ankle-length brown cotton sarong wrapped around her tiny torso.

Gothang stood dumbfounded for a while. 'You two are the beasts?'

'We are here to guide you to your destiny.'

'Yes? My destiny? Which is?'

'Your Highness, you have successfully summoned your divine weapon twice in this human form. If you do it again, you will crumble before carrying out your task. To avoid it, the master told us to give you a handy weapon to avoid such a danger.'

The boy seemed to pull out a familiar-looking heavy *dao* out of the grassy ground.

'Master? Wait, isn't this mine?' Gothang examined the weapon and confirmed it was his. It had the same handle, embellished with the bullock crest of his southern clan and a broad blade shining as a mark of regular honing.

'Your Highness, wield the blade and summon the bolts and hailstones from the sky. Put no strain on your fragile human body. We will guard you with our life.'

'Wait, who gave this...'

Gothang woke up from his dream, both the beasts were still by his side, attentively standing guard, looking towards the dark forest around. The sky was glowing faintly, but the forest was still dark and cold in the pre-dawn air. Even in the dark, he knew something was beside him which was not there before. His *dao*. His weapon from the dream now lay right next to him.

'Chongja? Chongkim? Were you two in my dream? How did you get my weapon?' Gothang asked, desperate for an answer, but both the beasts turned around with happy faces and barked excitedly. He rubbed his face in disappointment. He would probably never know what it all meant. His destiny? Was it the quest? Or was it about his mother? Some master is looking after him? Sending the beasts by his side in times of need? He decided to waste no time and go after his mother faster. He saw her entering somewhere deep inside the cave. She kept running away for some reason. He realized he needed to find her and ask her everything.

A distant loud screech filled the air. Gothang sat still and listened for more. The forest went dead quiet again.

'Chongja, Chongkim! We better not stay here for long. Come, we will head towards the cave faster.' Gothang stood up, picked up his *dao* and ran towards the gradually brightening sky. The beasts followed him, running.

The northern forests were not familiar, but Gothang tried his best not to lose his path and followed earnestly towards the rising sun, climbing the steep rocky mountain. The thin air along with the reeking smell and foggy monstrous fumes made him aware that his path was indeed filled with dark entities as Karaimei had warned. Chongja and Chongkim seemed as excited as always, their ruby eyes watching alertly ahead.

He would have wanted to rest for a while, but the whole forest was humming. Not a leaf rustled, nor an insect buzzed, but it was the aggravating hum of those creatures of the dark. Gothang felt anxious with them being so close around him. In fact, it was strange to consider it a coincidence: his mother's whereabouts and the hordes of dark creatures concentrated in the same direction. He continued climbing, hoping that his mother was safe.

They were high up. The view of other far ranges and the valley could be seen among the low clouds.

'I need to find the mouth of the cave while there is still daylight. It wouldn't be easy otherwise,' Gothang said to his beasts.

Grrrr... Chongja and Chongkim began to growl irately, looking threateningly ahead. Their short brownish fur stood up around their spines, their furry tails erect.

'The cave is easy...' a voice hissed from a nearby tree.

'Who is there?' Gothang roared, terrified, readying his *dao* for defence.

Something sprouted out of the ground as if it were some bamboo shoot, quickly morphing into a woman. She was wearing a set of beautiful sarong and tight stole with incredible design patterns like the spearheads, tiger-tooth motifs and other sacred animals in a dark shimmering thread. If not for the way she sprouted out from the ground, Gothang might have had a hard time recognizing her as a demon, just as he had failed with Karaimei.

'Stay away, demon!' Gothang tried.

'I wish I could...' the woman hissed and stood facing Gothang. She was pale, her hair tied with layers of cowry diadem and glassy beads.

'I am a demon, but only to those who had not done their duty to serve your realm, with the gift of your strength. You are the one who lived your life in oblivion, coward; not worthy to venture into our sacred passage and more so for the chaos breached beyond the charted realm because of your denial.'

Gothang didn't understand a single word that the weird lady demon spoke in her difficult demon accent (a lot of hissing and grunting). He readied his weapon, but the demon continued as if a speech would make him less nervous. Chongja and Chongkim barked loudly, but the demon raised her arms and they both stopped, unwillingly as if forcefully muted.

'As a bearer of your proud clan's crest on your blade, I, your enemy of today, would have been your most impressed friend, to welcome you with joy, a nurturing companion onto the further realm, but I, Kulsamnu, shall now tear your soul apart and your mortal flesh with it.'

Gothang felt like his blood congealed when he heard the name of the demon, Kulsamnu. He flustered, but couldn't find a better reaction for the situation. Kulsamnu! The guardian of the door of death. Gothang knew of her well. The whole of his clansmen knew of her. She was neither a demon nor a god, but both. That was why they all performed their Sa-ai, Chang-ai extravaganza on time. Those who didn't, never got to enjoy Kulsamnu's favour. He never got to perform his. He was a secluded orphan who never took interest in hunting; no one taught him about the importance of rituals since infancy like other children in the clan who grew up determined to perform their Ai, so that Kulsamnu would bless them on their way to eternal rest. He learned about the Sa-ai's deeper relevance only after he saw his compeers' relentless effort to perform one and also intimidated by the requirement of it. Gothang had planned to conduct his, after he had gained enough strength as the chief's swine herder. There was no rush for the ritual because...

'But why are you here? I...I am not dead...' Gothang gathered all his courage to spit out the few words.

'You are not, but then here you are! The breached path has opened up like a sore wound and you are ready to follow the woman through it with these divine beasts as your companions. You cannot pass the gate without battling me, lord's son.'

'Wait...woman? So, my mother is in there for real...' Gothang smiled regardless of Kulsamnu staring sourly at him with her dark glossy eyes.

'Prepare, Your Highness. Kulsamnu will not be biased to perform the task with all the effort a demon can offer. I shall destroy you, unless your strength proves otherwise,' Kulsamnu seemed to smile, her fangs and pointed teeth visible within her crimson mouth.

Kulsamnu slithered like a snake and flew towards Gothang who barely got time to raise his sparking *dao*. Chongja and Chongkim seemed weakened somehow, both whining with their mouths shut and getting smaller in size. The demon was stronger than she looked, her human face shredded, revealing a feature that did not have a mouth, nose or eyes, it didn't have anything! Just a blob with woody spikes and bulges. The limbs were still human but hardened, and she was crushing Gothang as she grabbed him by his weaponed arm.

Gothang tried hard to summon his bolts, but the pain dimmed his consciousness and he couldn't help but cry. Kulsamnu flipped him up in the sky and then jumped up again to crush him with her massive weight. Gothang fell on the ground, her knee over his throat, crushed to die, but he somehow saved himself from the impact by guarding with his free arm. She was incredibly heavy and was getting heavier. The sky began to grunt and the wind readied for a storm.

Kulsamnu still overpowered Gothang amidst the tempest, nothing really seemed to bother this demon. She was determined to perform her task, to tear him up into bite-sized pieces. He desperately tried to free his arm to wield his lightning *dao*, but it was severely crushed, he couldn't even feel his hand anymore.

Chongja ran up and clouted Kulsamnu head on. The poor beast fell on the ground after its last effort to defend, visibly weakened. Chongkim was already down, its previous wound from the dark entities reopened. Both the beasts had shrunk considerably, now just the size of puppies.

Kulsamnu seemed startled just for a fraction of a moment, but Gothang knew it was all he could get. He freed his arm and jabbed it

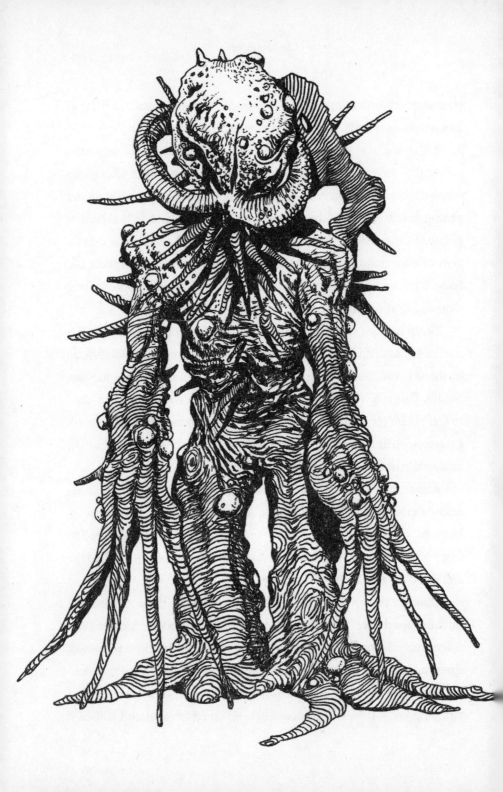

hard across the demon's chest. It clanked as if hitting a rock, but the impact threw her away. She somersaulted and landed on her feet, her dress and hair slowly merging with her formless prickly membrane.

Gothang didn't wait and summoned a heave of bolts and sent them flying towards the demon. The gigantic sparks went straight for the demon, but she raised her arms and stayed still as if quietly sucking it all in. The bolts didn't affect her. The battle didn't go well. Despite the pain, Gothang had to make sure that the demon didn't approach him again. Kulsamnu flipped and jogged through the mad lightning bolts as if dancing, slowly inching closer to Gothang again.

The crushed muscles were making him want to scream in pain; the summoning of the lightning was exhaustive. Gothang wanted to fall on the ground, but the demon was ruthless. She wouldn't even spare a minute for him to breathe.

Why does a sky prince need to be so mercilessly pulverized by a demon? That too when he came that close to actually finding his mother! Gothang felt a sudden bitterness in his pounding heart, his arms energized with anger. He jumped up and raised his weapon high. This time, there came no lightning, but the wind and the rain hurled around the blade. He twirled his *dao* up in the sky. The blade gathered more of the sky and condensed into a massive chunk of solid ice. He sent the gigantic hailstone flying towards the demon who tried to dash away from it but couldn't. The hailstone crushed the demon like an ant. Gothang fell on the ground near his unconscious beasts. The demon did seem defeated, finally. A loud crack thundered and he saw a huge opening within the rocky face of the mountaintop. The Mangsore.

'Chongja? Chongkim?' Gothang cuddled both his beasts in his arms. They blinked their eyes open but whined.

'I am so sorry...'

Both the beasts opened their mouth wide and jumped down from his arms. They both walked in a circle and conjured a loud howl. With it, they both enlarged into the size of a full-grown tiger.

'Great! I love you guys!' Gothang hugged them tight, always impressed with the way they could rejuvenate fast, but he spoke seriously, 'Now we are about to go inside the cave. With a demon like Kulsamnu loitering here instead of guarding some underworld door, it means that we cannot predict who or what we will run into. Come!'

Gothang ran inside the cave, slowly engulfed by the darkness. Chongja and Chongkim followed him cautiously, sniffing up the moist rocky walls. The path was rough and the darkness made the place more ominous. However, Gothang was most glad that the path was exactly how he had seen in his dreams. I am very near my mother, he thought.

As they advanced deeper into the cave, the tunnel became wider and luminous. Within the walls, there came a turquoise glow coming from strange veins running in wide branches.

Gothang could see shiny rocks, multiple colours protruding out of the rough walls. His beasts shrunk their sizes, and became as small as puppies and ran about the place in awe, chasing each other playfully. He looked up at the high ceiling of the tunnel and, to his amazement, realized that it was sparking with a thousand luminous wisps hanging as if they were frozen raindrops. The view was breathtakingly beautiful.

'Sure, I would not mind spending all day here...' Gothang said to himself, but he realized he was getting distracted.

'Chongja! Chongkim! I think we are letting our guard down. Let's go find my mother, quick. This place is only distracting us. Come.'

The beasts stopped playing, grew into their regular hound size again and ran after him. The tunnel seemed endless, branching out into many puzzling paths and chambers. Gothang began to feel confused. He would never know if he took the right turn.

After hours of walking, there came a huge chamber with a big boulder lying next to one of the many tunnels.

'This...' Gothang realized that it was the exact path that his mother had taken in his dream. In the dream, the boulder was blocking the tunnel, but now, it seemed to have somehow moved. Had his mother moved it? He would never know.

He ran down, desperate. He could protect his mother, finally. The beasts ran ahead of him, the tunnel became wider and wider with the luminous light becoming more intense, the sparkling crystals more congested.

At the end, Gothang came out into a vast valley with tall furry grass and small hills around the edge.

'Which place is this?' Gothang muttered.

Chongja and Chongkim grew enormous, roughly like full-grown elephants and roamed around the vast valley that seemed to spread endlessly.

He looked around for his mother. There was no one.

'Mother! Mother!' Gothang called out and the calm breeze carried his voice away. The feathery grasses were waving gently. No other sound but his voice echoed back at him.

He looked up and saw the oddity of the view above. Was it the sky? No. Too dark to be sky and he was already deep inside a cave. But the supposed ceiling was too high and luminous as if day was breaking, but there were no celestial orbs anywhere like in the real sky, it was a blank dome glowing in sunset orange. The place was strange. The air felt strange. The whole terrain was nothing like what he had ever seen before. How would he guess about his mother's whereabouts here? He wished she would come running to him.

While he stood wondering, Chongja and Chongkim barked and ran up.

'What is it?' Gothang cried and followed them.

He noticed the grass moving. Something was ahead.

'Chongja, Chongkim! Be careful. Might be another demon!' He warned, but the beasts ran faster and jumped towards the trembling grass.

The beasts wrestled right away, but Gothang was further behind and the tall grasses obstructed his view. He ran fast, terrified.

'God!' Gothang let out a cry. He reached the spot and, to his horror, realized that they were wrestling with a giant python with buffalo horns, adorned with feathers and an ivory headdress.

'Another demon?' He cried.

'I am...no...demon,' the monster python spoke as he wrestled with Chongja and Chongkim. 'I am Gulheupi, the giant, the majestic, the forever excellent peer of the realm of pythons.'

'Doesn't make a difference!' Gothang yelled as he readied his *dao* for defence.

THE WATER GODDESS

Iwan woke up, soaked in something pungent.

'Where am I?' he wondered.

'Ah! Meidingu, you are up,' Laiba walked in.

'Where are we?' Iwan asked and took a swift glance around. He saw the wooden walls lined with pots and jars, herbs and mortars, rows of cream cotton fabrics and an old woman squatting on the floor with a vessel, humming something.

'You seriously remained unconscious for the whole day. People here even called you "flower". I heard them referring to you as the Flower King,' Laiba said, crossing his arms across his chest.

'Shut up, will you?' Iwan rubbed his head annoyed, 'I think I had some wonderful dreams. I forgot most of it, but I think I was flying with Yangba and...'

'And?' Laiba asked excited, his eyes flashing wild.

'And...that's it. I was flying around and having fun...I forgot, anyway.' Iwan tried remembering, but he sincerely could not recall what the dream was about.

'Hmmm...Can you try recollecting it? It might mean something.' Laiba seemed disappointed with Iwan's carefree answer.

'Forget about my stupid dream anyway. Don't we have more things to worry about? Bother Gothang ran away...' Iwan looked down.

'Well, that…he is right there on the next mountain. I just saw him on my way here,' Laiba said dully.

'What!? You saw? In one of your visions or as in, really sighted him?' Iwan asked desperately.

'Call it sighting since it was not a vision. Anyway, he seems to have learnt some new divine trick. I told you we all have some in each of us. Your dream could mean something.'

'I said forget about my dream. Is Brother Gothang coming here?'

'I think he is heading towards the cave system. That's the only destination on the eastern hilltop. So, no. He isn't coming here. But now, we can go after him.'

'Don't we need to find our last guardian first?' Iwan asked, slowly getting out of the straw bed. He realized that he was naked underneath the blue and red cotton drape. 'Where are my clothes?' He looked around to spot them.

'We found our last guardian. You fainted through the whole process. Convenient for us all,' Laiba said, passing some fresh clothes from the nearby basket to his king.

'Wait! What? When? Wh...who...who is she? Is she here? How...how did...so what happened?' Iwan cried out, he didn't even see the clothes that Laiba was offering him.

'Long story. Anyway, what really matters is that she agreed to follow her destiny with us. Took a lot of persuasion on my part, but she is ready for our quest. She is here.'

'Alright! Alright. I mean, I will go and greet her,' Iwan headed out the door.

'Your majesty, it will be appropriate to present yourself with some clothes on. And also, you stink. Get your medicinal ointments washed off first. Our esteemed healer is here to help you. I will be in the adjacent cottage, resting. Come fast. We have a lot to discuss,' Laiba bowed at the healer and went out of the infirmary. Iwan followed the healer hastily.

Few warriors saw him coming out and running towards the Cottage of the Brave, though none greeted him as they were supposed to, but Iwan didn't pay much attention and burst inside the cottage where he knew his friends were waiting for him.

He opened the door wide to enter in style.

'Iwan!' It was Sana who saw him first and she ran up instantly with her arms wide open. Iwan hugged her with a smile.

'Brother, you are well,' Lungchum smiled, looking genuinely glad.

'Yes,' Iwan nodded, but then saw the lady sitting next to Leisatao. She was around his age, but with a serious look on her delicate face, a thin tattoo on her chin and all the way down to her chest. Her hair was tied into a high bun with a hornbill feather pin and rows of cowrie diadem, feather earrings, her lips were thin but pinkish, eyes light brown and almond-shaped. She was slender, but her firm physique made her look well sculpted out of the softest clay. Tanned and blushing, with a tight, striped sarong around her heaved torso down to her knees, she looked handsome and beautiful at the same time. She was prophesied as someone strong, but the prophecy didn't mention anything about her beauty.

'Even better...' Iwan maundered with a dreamy smile.

'Said something?' Laiba asked.

'Huh? Na...not. I mean no,' Iwan fluttered and greeted Leisatao, 'Brother Leisatao, I heard we already have Brother Gothang's whereabouts.'

'Oh yes, dear. The poor boy is heading for the cave system. Wonder what he wants to be doing there,' Leisatao said with a sad look on his face.

'And, my lady,' Iwan could feel his cheek burning up as he bowed to the lady and he also noticed the lady's face turning as red as his. He tried not to smile much.

'Greetings, Meidingu,' the lady turned away.

'Our Lady Ningrei, Your Majesty,' Laiba said, but dragged him away from the new guardian.

'Ningrei, nice name,' Iwan smiled, but he followed Laiba who pulled him by his hand towards the corner.

'What?' Iwan asked irritated.

'You know Lady Ningrei is not a very jolly person. I want you to mind your distance. You just don't know what I went through to convince her into this. Don't just look creepily at her like that. You are a brat, but this is not a good time to be careless. Alright?' Laiba whispered.

Iwan looked at Laiba questioningly.

'Maichou Laiba, so now what is our exact plan?' Ningrei asked aloud, her annoyance was already evident.

Laiba ran up and explained how all the guardians needed to unite first in order for the prophecy to be carried out.

'Will the scissor magically appear inside the cave once we unite?' Ningrei asked.

'My lady, I cannot guarantee, but I have the eyes of the Atingkok. Once we unite, I have a strong belief that my eyes will guide us all towards the scissor. First, to follow the prophecy, we shall unite,' Laiba answered cleverly.

'Speculation it is but, anyway, it's not like I have a choice here; so, we better discuss our trail. We have to cross the Lam forest, and I must warn all of you that the path has been growing unusual. The forest has been reporting strange incidents with people going missing, animals dying, wild trees withering and so on.'

'About that, not just the Lam. I feel the whole of the north reeking with dark auras,' Laiba said bluntly.

Ningrei stood up and looked at Laiba questioningly, but she seemed to decide not to inquire, 'Alright, people. First ray of morning, tomorrow. Have a few moments of rest for now,' Ningrei walked out of the cottage and towards her chamber to pick her choicest spears.

'She is incredible,' Iwan muttered, looking at the exit long after Ningrei left.

'Yes, she's pretty,' Lungchum nodded.

'Oh, Sana! Is something bothering you?' Iwan joked, walking up to her and poking at her cheek. He knew she was worried as always.

'Lady Ningrei is right. Once we unite with Brother Gothang, everything will fall on Laiba's shoulders,' Sana said weakly.

Laiba was scratching his back when he heard Sana. He stopped and smiled, 'At least my hypothetical wife is worried about me. Feel blessed.'

'I worry for all of us,' Leisatao said rubbing his head, 'Poor Gothang is running around some cave, chasing a ghost. We are all heading towards some mysterious forest tomorrow. I am worried for me, you and all of us.'

'But no point in worrying. We will be fine,' said Lungchum, flashing his smile.

It was still dark, but Ningrei was already at the gate with her long spear. Laiba greeted her with a yawn. He had only taken a brief nap.

Lungchum came out as energetic as always, flashing his smiley face for everyone. Leisatao came out with Sana, both looking worried sick. Sana did a little courtesy bow to Ningrei who reprimanded her. 'Sana, I saw you being casual with the Meidingu yesterday. Drop your courtesy.'

'Sure, I will not. Sorry,' Sana apologized immediately.

She looked at Sana for a while and said calmly, 'Anyway, you are one of the guardians. We should be comfortable with each other.'

Ningrei's face turned red with anger when Iwan came out with his horse insead of a weapon. She rolled her eyes and walked away, too exhausted to even comment on the inconvenience he was going to cause them all with his horse.

'I think she likes me,' said Iwan, with a shy smile.

'Wait, what?' Sana asked a little confused. Even Laiba's jaw dropped.

'And what made you come to that conclusion, Your Majesty?' Laiba asked, batting his eyes rapidly.

'You know, she kept blushing and all.'

Laiba and Sana stood together watching Iwan slowly heading towards the mountain forest.

'Should we tell him?' Sana asked after a moment of silence.

'Nahh...better keep him happy for a while. I didn't enjoy the last time he was sad,' Laiba said, fixing his big cloak that slithered down from his narrow shoulders.

Ningrei led the group, understandably, as one who knew the forest best. However, Laiba couldn't feel any less at ease with the thick fog that covered all treetops and the sky rumbling with thunder. He followed Ningrei close, hardly blinking.

Leisatao wanted to talk, but even Lungchum had been quiet since they had started climbing the mountain forest. He decided to stay as alert as everyone. Behind them was Iwan, struggling with his horse, and Sana trying her best to be helpful to him in any way, perhaps the only one willing to deal with Iwan's foolish idea of bringing his poor horse onto the rough course.

'Iwan, will Yangba be alright inside the cave? He already seems tired now in this steep forest,' Sana said, helping Iwan as he struggled to support Yangba.

'He will be fine. He will be...fine,' Iwan said, despite feeling worried for his dear horse. Yangba didn't complain, but he knew that the forest was a difficult challenge for him. Yangba was a palace horse; having spent his time in luxury, his hoofs did not know anything other than soft grasses. And he had been travelling with just few hours of rest and now was walking into one of the most testing challenges.

Sana realized that Ningrei and the others were far ahead. She wished they'd wait up, but knowing how Ningrei was, she knew Ningrei must be already annoyed.

'Iwan and Sana are still down there,' Lungchum said, looking back at the duo with the horse.

'Let them catch up. I don't want to dawdle here. I will advise you all to mind your own steps,' Ningrei answered coldly.

Lungchum looked back again; he had no choice but to walk close to Laiba. Laiba had been incredibly silent, his eyes staring straight forward. If something were to happen, he would be the only one who would be able to do something quick to protect them.

Leisatao had been breathing heavily, patting his face with his soft cotton towel. He wished Ningrei would slow down her pace, but the girl seemed to be made of iron. She didn't even shed a single drop of sweat.

'Ningrei, I will wait for Iwan and Sana,' Leisatao said, dropping his bag of *arambai*s.

'Yes, get them here, please. We will slow down too, but I am warning you all, we shall not linger here,' Ningrei said, nodding towards Laiba who didn't stop.

Leisatao set on the forest floor, watching the two kids struggle with the horse below.

'God, this will be the end of me. Where is the pitcher?' He rummaged through his bundle, retrieved a small gourd and drank some water. The thunder rumbled loud on top of the mountain. The fog seemed to be ascending, while the trees stayed silent except for the pitter-patter drops of rain. The exhaustion was making him feel dizzy, his vision blurring slightly. He wished he could just lie down for a while, but the kids were already up ahead and Iwan and Sana were also closing in on him.

'Kids, come on up. I am here under an excuse of waiting for you. Look, they are not planning to wait for us,' Leisatao grumbled, resting his head on the trunk of a tree. There was no reply. The forest went quiet. He closed his eyes and took a deep breath.

'Sana, Iwan, I am talking to you. Is Yangba alright?' Leisatao opened his eyes. He didn't see anyone below.

'Now, where are they?' he thought.

Leisatao stood up and looked around the dim forest. Sana and Iwan couldn't be seen anywhere.

'Did they leave without me? I saw them near alright,' Leisatao wondered. 'Sana! Iwan!' he called out.

No one replied.

'Did they seriously go without me? And here I am, waiting for them...or did I doze off here? But...' Leisatao was confused and also a bit uneasy. He saw both Iwan and Sana climbing towards him a moment ago. He looked up and realized the forest was no longer infested by fog. The treetops were sparkling with sunlight, the huge leaves stirring, calm breeze lingering and there was an aromatic smell of wild flowers around.

'Ningrei? Laiba?' He looked ahead, but there was no response from the other end either. The mountain forest was dead quiet except for the eerie gossip of gentle leaves.

Leisatao ran up on the mountain with his bundle swung across his shoulder, calling out all the names.

The forest began to get strange as he came upon an orchard and the supposedly higher part of the mountain somehow became less steep as if he was already heading down or reaching a plane top. This is the Lam—they said this forest has been appearing strange, Leisatao thought, slowly reaching for his bundle and taking out one of his lethal darts, the *arambai*. The orchard was heavy with ripe fruits, melons and beans. There were flowers and thick tendrils netting all over the forest floor. The sun was right above his head. It was not even properly morning yet when they headed out into this forest just a moment ago. He realized he had been trapped.

Sana and Iwan saw Leisatao sitting down near a tree, drinking from his gourd. Laiba was leading Ningrei and the rest further up.

'Guys, can you wait up?' Iwan asked guiltily, as his horse was slipping on its hooves as they struggled to climb higher. Iwan turned back to his horse to support the climb, while Sana also helped him pull Yangba up.

'Sorry, Yangba. I am really sorry. Why is this forest stupidly steep?' Iwan was beginning to get annoyed, particularly at Laiba as he went ahead without assisting.

'Stupid Laiba! You...' Iwan turned around to scold his head priest, but he realized they were already far ahead and out of sight. 'What the...! Did they really leave us here?' Iwan cried, frustrated.

'Iwan, we better catch up with them fast. I don't feel good,' Sana said, looking around. She realized something odd, and to add to her suspicion, she began to feel a throbbing sensation of malevolence around. Something was not right.

'Are they really crazy? We are supposed to go together. What in the...' Iwan was yelling, but Sana grabbed his arms tight and whispered,

'Iwan, Brother Leisatao was right there a moment ago. Something is not right.'

'They left us, Sana. Even I'm a bit hurt now. I bet, Ningrei is not happy with them treating me like this. I think...'

'No. Wait, Iwan. This is not right. Look!' Sana looked up and Iwan followed her gaze. The forest was no longer gloomy; there were streaks of sunlight sprinkled all over the spiky leaves.

'Oh, the fog subsided. And the storm too,' Iwan said gladly.

'In the blink of an eye, Iwan,' Sana said grimly.

Iwan looked around and began to comprehend Sana's apprehension. The forest seemed to glow up; the breeze hovering around them seemed scented, the unruly forest path was now smooth with moss and there was a bed of thick juicy herbs. The pinewoods were no longer in view, but some different fruit-bearing short shrubs dotted the sunny field. Field?

'Sana, we are in trouble!' Iwan cried out.

The sky came crashing down, with a grumbling storm and strong winds around the summit. Ningrei was attentively observing Laiba, how unbothered he was with the sudden wake of a tempest. He kept walking, with his eyes straight towards the rocky top where the mouth of the cave would be. Lungchum looked back for his friends, but he could not see any of them catching up.

'Lady Ningrei, look back,' Lungchum said, trying to sound calm.

'Laiba is acting strange. He hasn't blinked, not even once, and his eyes are glowing...' Ningrei couldn't help but expect something extraordinary out of Laiba's strange eyes.

'Lady Ningrei, I think the rest of our guardians are no longer following us,' Lungchum looked back again and he was right. The forest behind them was empty of any beings.

'What do you mean...' Ningrei turned around and stood petrified. She knew what was happening. Leisatao, Iwan and Sana were all down there just a moment ago.

'What should we do?' Lungchum checked on Laiba, but he seemed well possessed, not flinching over anything or responding to their worried chats.

'Wouldn't Laiba be able to do something?' Ningrei asked desperately. She placed her hand on Laiba's shoulder.

'I don't know, but let's try waking him up.' Lungchum tried to smile even though he was worried sick inside. He called out, 'Laiba! Laiba!'

Laiba was being pulled towards the cave as if by a magnet. His eyes were showing him strange lights and tunnels filled with gems. He also saw Gothang running deep inside the cave, but the vision was distorted and he woke up in the midst of a thunderstorm on the top of the mountain forest.

'Now what is going on here?' Laiba said, feeling a little lost. He realized that Lungchum had been calling out his name and Ningrei was shaking his shoulder. 'Why are you two distorting my vision? We are

about to reach the cave. We were this close...' Laiba cried, disappointed with the disturbance right when he was about to find a huge clue about the quest.

'Laiba, the rest of them are in danger,' Lungchum cried.

'What?' Laiba checked his surroundings and realized that Iwan, Sana and Leisatao were missing. 'Where are they?' he asked a bit tensed.

'They were right behind us a moment ago,' Lungchum said, looking back guiltily at the spot where he last saw them.

'It's the forest,' Ningrei said, giving a look of distaste around the pinewoods that stood innocently against the stormy wind. 'Laiba, can you do something? Can you see where they went?'

'I can't do that. I already told you I can't...' Laiba replied, but stopped mid-sentence and stared at Lungchum, 'Lungchum, can you fly me up? Let's see if we can spot them from above.'

'Lady Ningrei, can you step back a little?' Lungchum asked worriedly and she jumped a few steps back.

Lungchum closed his eyes, spread both his arms and took a deep breath. He began to grow tall, his skin stretching, his wings sprouting out of his back, his dark silky hair transitioning into a golden mane, glossy scales nascent out of his smooth skin, with his bright reddish yellow pupils glowing as he opened his eyes.

Ningrei stood enchanted, forgetting the howling wind or her despair over their missing companions. The majestic beast stood calm and listening. Regardless of the transformation, the dragon displayed Lungchum's coyness.

Lungchum growled and Laiba answered, 'Sure. I will be careful.'

Lungchum lowered his dragon body and Laiba climbed up quite comfortably and stood on the back, hands-free.

'Laiba, at least try sitting down or hold on to his mane. He is going to fly around for God's sake,' Ningrei could feel her fingers tingling at the sight of the reckless boy standing up proud on the back of a dragon.

She wasn't sure if Laiba heard her, as they flew away instantly. The sight was mesmerizing if not for the disturbing wind, fluttering dust and dirt off the forest floor. She blinked, but didn't want to miss the sight of the magnificent creature soaring through the sky.

Laiba stood calmly and looked at the vast forest beneath his feet. Lungchum swooped over the pine tops, hoping to spot their companions around somewhere. The raindrops began to turn ruthless; there was hail and thunder, with the dark clouds distorting their view underneath.

Lungchum gave a loud roar.

'I am trying, but my eyes are not cooperating. They keep showing the cave system. Lord! Why...' Laiba yelled and covered his silver eye with his hand, hoping that it would stop the haphazard vision of the cave and crystal tunnels that kept displaying in his head, disrupting his present sight. He stared down at the forest with his golden eye and saw a huge dark tendril approaching towards where Ningrei was standing down below.

'What on earth...' Laiba couldn't believe that they had been walking leisurely through the forest all this time without losing their life or worse. The extensive mountain range was infested with throbbing veins of portals that open and close like a thousand hungry mouths and rapidly multiplying. Meanwhile, the rain began to irritate him even more.

'Lungchum, Ningrei is in danger! Fly down!' Laiba shouted.

Ningrei stood staring at the huge golden dragon roving in and out of the dark clouds. Laiba seemed to be looking for the rest, but without success. She began to feel the air getting colder, her breath fogging up and her spear handle began to ice up. She looked around terrified, but there was nothing present. The rain joined the cruel wind. Ningrei instinctively whirled her spear and stood defensively, turning in a circle, expecting an attack from any direction.

She saw Lungchum and Laiba descending fast towards her. She knew that Laiba must have seen something from the top.

'Come out if you dare!' Ningrei cried.

A soft scented wind seemed to sweep past her face and before she knew it, a huge flat boulder sprouted out of the ground and stood in front of her. She was surprised at the trembling ground and the huge flat rock standing right ahead of her as if it had always been there.

More trembles and there came three more of the boulders shooting out of the ground and encaging her inside. She stood perplexed. Traps of plenty...a voice whispered in the air.

'Kamatei?' Ningrei muttered weakly.

To the cave...your destiny awaits...the voices continued.

'What about the other guardians? Where are they?' Ningrei asked aloud, running her hands through the stones.

To the cave...the voice subsided and one stone fell flat on the ground, opening up towards the direction where Lungchum and Laiba came flying in, probably to rescue her.

'Lady Ningrei! Are you alright?' Laiba cried.

Ningrei wanted to answer, but Lungchum flew in at an incredible speed and just picked her up with his clawed foot. She screamed at first, but soon realized that the dragon had held her gently and she began to see the mountain forest distancing away and vanishing under the dark clouds.

'Laiba! Did you find them?' Ningrei cried, trying hard to look at the boy but failing. All she could see was the giant belly of the dragon and its elegantly flapping wings.

'Lady Ningrei! We need to head for the cave. I will explain later!' Laiba shouted back. Lungchum roared and flew towards the Mangsore at a shooting speed.

'What do we do now?' Iwan cried, hugging Yangba around its neck.

'We need to calm down, Iwan,' Sana said, trembling. The blossoming field stretched far beyond the horizon.

'Calm? Here?' Iwan literally began weeping.

'I mean...' Sana gulped and kept scanning around, 'We should try and find our way back. They must be here somewhere.'

'Find our way back? Good luck to us. I think we are so done. I don't think we lost our way. This is it. The dark powers have finally won! We are going to die!'

Sana just kept licking her lips in apprehension and strolled back and forth around the field to think of something. She was never brave, but she also knew her king was even worse. With all the others gone, it was up to her to do something for real now.

'...I am thirsty.' Iwan finished his whining. Even Yangba seemed aware of Iwan freaking out. The horse stood bending its head low.

'Maybe...' Sana turned towards Iwan to console again, but she stopped when she saw the view behind Iwan. The terrain had changed and now there was a vast lake a little further ahead.

'Iwan, you need to turn around.' Sana said grimly.

'Why? Wh...what?' Iwan turned around slowly, but relaxed and cried, 'Water!' He ran up and Yangba followed.

'Wait! It could be a trap!' Sana yelled, but Iwan didn't stop and she had to follow them up.

'Don't drink it right away! We need to examine this strange place first. The water could be poisonous! Iwan!' Sana tried her best.

'What? I am thirsty!' Iwan turned around disappointed. They were already at the shore. Yangba seemed eager to drink too, but as a good horse, it stood waiting for Iwan.

'I know, but this place is not an ordinary one. We better try examining first. This lake was not here before, but appeared right after you said you are thirsty. Can you trust that?' Sana held Iwan's hand.

'But I am seriously thirsty and look, the water is crystal clear,' Iwan said gulping greedily.

'Fine,' Sana had to give in, 'but let me examine it first, just to make sure.' She went towards the lake, dipped her hand in the water and bent over to sniff. She saw the magnified bottom of the lake under the invisibly clear water. The bed was covered with zillion tiny pebbles. The water didn't seem dangerous and didn't smell anything funny, but she didn't want anybody to drink it. Sana sat quietly, playing with the water idly, pretending to examine it. Iwan stood near her, pressing his hands around his hips, drumming his foot impatiently.

'So?' Iwan asked.

'Fine...' Sana was about to stand up when she abruptly sensed something odd. 'Wait!' She dipped her hand deeper into the lake and she could feel the strong current. The surface of the lake lay as still as a mirror, but inside, a little deeper, Sana could feel that the water was churning.

'Iwan, step back!' Sana screamed, but the current dragged her into the lake without any delay. Sana didn't know how to swim. She kicked her limbs under the water, but knew it would be hopeless. The cleverest thing she could do was to preserve her energy, stay still, and hope that Iwan would somehow escape the enchanted trap and have their friends come for rescue.

...Sana? Sana? Is this you? A voice lingered in the water. It was Laiba's voice. Sana was surprised and confused. She looked around the water and, to her horror, the bed of the lake with its zillion pebbles had vanished and now she was drifting around an endless chasm.

She thought, was that Laiba?

'...Yes, it's me. There are raindrops in my eyes and that's how I found you. Where are you people right now?...'

'I have no idea. But we are trapped and...and what do you mean you have raindrops in your eyes and how...what does that mean?' She asked in her mind. She knew Laiba was speaking to her through telepathy.

'...You don't know? I am sensing you now in your elemental form. Didn't you change your form?...'

'What form?' Sana asked confused, 'I think I am dying. I am drowning.'

'...Drowning? Are you sure?...' By the tone, Sana could imagine Laiba's sarcastic eye roll.

Sana looked around the water again and, to her surprise, she could no longer see her own body now. She had gone invisible. She wasn't able to feel anything either. She felt as light as a feather, calm and chilled and refreshed.

'Laiba, can you please explain what is going on?' Sana asked nervously.

'...You are now in your elemental form. You are turning into Ereima, the goddess of water, another manifestation of our Supreme Goddess...

I don't know why you took that form, but you are doing good... I need you to find Brother Leisatao and Iwan and come towards the Mangsore tunnel... There are plenty of waterways there. It will be easy for you to travel in that form. Go and find them...'

'Iwan is with me. He is probably freaking out by the shore of the lake, thinking I drowned. So, alright. I am water now? So, wait, how do I find Brother Leisatao and how do I travel in this form?'

'...Every...drop...of water...in...this world is you! You better figure... out the...rest on...your own. I am running...out of time...here. Lady Ningrei...is in danger. I better...go and get her. We will...head towards... the cave. You will...know where...to...find...the...cave river....'

'Wait!' Sana cried out, but there was no longer any response. I am water? She tried to hopelessly make sense of it.

'Sana...Sana...'—she heard Iwan's muffled voice. It was not in her head, but a voice from above. She looked up and, to her surprise, saw Iwan lowering his face just an inch away from hers.

'You scared me,' Sana blurted out.

Iwan was kneeling by the shore, bending over the water, when he saw strings of bubbles that boiled up the word, 'You...scared...me...'

Iwan stood staring at the water where Sana had got dissolved as if she were salt just a moment ago. 'Sana, is that you?' he asked.

There came more bubbles with the response, 'Yes...I...turned...into... water. I...don't...know...how. This...is...strange...'

'What? You turned into water?!' Iwan yelled, 'Oh, good Guardians! It is my fault. It is my fault. I...I....' And Yangba neighed nervously.

Sana could hear Iwan blaming himself for everything. She just drifted buoyantly, remembering what Laiba said, how she was supposed to be able to travel everywhere.

'Don't worry, Iwan. It is not your fault. This is not a bad thing. I have to figure out something for all of us to get out of here,' she said.

I am water... Sana thought about it again. She imagined closing her eyes and tried to locate her vanished body. Where are my hands? She tried moving her fingers, her toes, her head...

Sana began to feel her pulses. Was it her blood? She began to feel her hair slapping the rocks on the great shores, her fingers sliding across the eerie waterbed of the grand lakes, million fishes and slimy creatures gliding across her navel. She took a deep breath and opened her eyes.

Iwan was mumbling apologies when he saw a translucent face forming on the water surface, it was Sana's. She looked aged, her eyes were unmistakably staring at him, her smiling lips distorted once in a while by the endless ripples.

'Sana?' He whimpered.

'Don't be afraid. I am Ereima now. This realm, we are currently in, is one of the most dangerous ones, filled with deadly enchantments. The presence of water in a meticulous death trap like this one shall be our blessed chance to escape. This place can change into anything we want to consume, but will trap us as soon as we guzzle a single thing. Giving water to quench our thirst was a great move to ensnare us, but it didn't quite pan out like that. The veins of these enchanted traps have punctured the real world with several holes, trapping victims like ourselves in an unending loop of despair.'

Iwan sat staring at Sana speaking calmly, the faint image of her face floating around the water surface. It was odd and disturbing to see, but she seemed collected and knew what she would be doing.

'And Meidingu, one more thing. I need to find our sun-slayer first so that we can all escape from this place together. Stay put until I return and do not touch or eat anything grown here. No matter how tempting it gets. Just stay here and I will be back with him in no time.' Sana smiled one last time and her face disappeared along with the ripples.

'How did...' Iwan's words of inquiry choked in his throat, but he knew she was gone and that he had to obey her. He sat quietly with Yangba. Now, it was just him being pathetic. Even Sana was about to do something wonderful now.

Leisatao was not sure how he ended up running around a field of crops, the sun unmoved from the spot. He had been cautious all this time, throwing his darts at any sound or disturbance he sensed around the strange orchard. He kept running but ended up moving in circles.

'So, will this be my end? I did shoot the sun once, didn't I? But then, this situation is entirely different. I am going to die for sure at this rate,' Leisatao began to sob. He was running out of ideas, alone, surrounded by plump fruits and crops that looked incredibly appetizing, but scary at the same time.

'...Brother Leisatao...Brother Leisatao...'

Leisatao seemed to hear a petite voice that sounded like Sana. He stood alert and tried to listen again. He wondered if he was imagining it, but the voice called again; muffled, unclear and faint, but he was sure it was Sana's voice,

'...Brother Leisatao...Brother Leisatao...'

'Sana!' Leisatao yelled and turned around frantically, 'Is that you for God's sake? Is that you?'

'...Yes...open your gourd...' Sana replied.

'What? Gourd?' '...Yes... hurry...'

Leisatao pulled out the gourd hanging on his side and removed the seal with his teeth.

'Brother!' Sana yelled from inside the gourd. Leisatao almost dropped the item in fright.

'Sana? Are you in there? But, how did you...why are you inside my gourd? Is this really you?' Leisatao peeped inside the gourd, but he didn't see Sana, only a pinch of water left at the bottom.

'Listen! I was terrified when I didn't sense any water body within your section of the realm, but lucky that you brought your own water. Thank the Guardians!'

'But what are you doing inside?' Leisatao peeped inside again, 'and I don't see you in here.'

'Listen brother, I am going to do something that I have never done before, but you have to trust me and not panic. Water is a part of human element. It will work, it has to... Laiba said it will be possible...' Sana's voice was clear and echoed from inside the gourd.

'What are we going to do, Sana? I will try to be calm, but I have been nervous and scared for a while now. You know, dear?' Leisatao wasn't that convinced with Sana's mumbling.

'Yes, I understand, but trust me. You need to stick your finger inside the gourd, tilt this vessel a little and touch the water. I will do the rest!'

'The rest?' Leisatao asked doubtfully, 'Alright, but can you tell me what you might be doing?'

'I said trust me, alright?' Sana cried desperately, 'I am sure this will work. I am new in this form, but I have sensed enough to perform what Laiba asked. Yes, it is going to be alright. Now, give me your finger. Hurry!'

'Alright! Alright!' Leisatao stuck his finger inside the gourd. The orchard began to rattle and hiss as if in disapproval, but before he could blink his eyes again, something strong began to suck him inside the gourd. He felt senseless and numb, but also imagined as if he were dispersing. What is going on? Leisatao wondered, but he could no longer see anything, it turned all blank, cold and quiet. A little hum began to surge ahead. He wanted to ask what was happening, but he couldn't; he slowly began to feel drowsy and lost all consciousness.

Iwan sat at the shore of the lake that began to shrink in size. He obeyed Sana's order and didn't move a muscle, but was trembling with worry. He sighed. 'I will be the only useless piece among us all now.' He reminded himself. His thoughts got disturbed when some familiar bubbles began to boil up at the lake.

'Sana!' Iwan stood up, worried.

'...Come...' Iwan could hear Sana's voice faintly from within the splash of water and, before he could react, the water hurled both his horse and him inside.

Iwan felt cold and numb for the rest of the journey.

Sana began her journey slipping through a thousand dimensions of water, her body and spirit scattered everywhere. As her first try in her divine form, she had to labour hard, trying to find the route of her course. To do it, the zillion particles of her companions drifting inside her were not at all helping. She concentrated hard for all the pieces of Iwan, Leisatao and Yangba travelling with her, for she knew that even missing a single drop of her passengers would result in some catastrophic outcome when she restored them again.

Sana delved deep into the creeks of the earth, dripping through rocks and layers of dirt. She sensed her spine coursing through a rough course in a rocky tunnel. It was on the eastern range, the Mangsore system. Alright, here we go, she thought.

THE GOLDEN SWORD

Chongja and Chongkim collaborated well in the battle, the monster python didn't even get a chance to turn on Gothang. Gothang had to wait for a suitable opportunity if he wanted to land a blow. He didn't want to hurt his beasts even by accident.

'Get your annoying pets off me. Aren't you a god? Fight me with pride!' Gulheupi, the monster roared in anger, Chongja and Chongkim still attacking him around the lower length of his body.

'Tell me where my mother is,' Gothang demanded.

'Mothe...grrrrhhhhhh...' Gulheupi got distracted as Chongja dug its sharp nails on the monster's scaly body. Chongkim bit its tail and the monster let out a yelp, 'Grrrrhhhhh!'

'Tell me...' Gothang began again, but the monster retorted angrily,

'What nonsense! What mother? Aren't you here to defeat us all? Try me first. Where are the rest? Come, all of you. Gggghhhhhhhh!'

The monster rose tall and stared with its angry eyes at Gothang. Chongja and Chongkim tried attacking, but it refused to slither about and now seemed determined to face him head-on.

'Alright!' Gothang stepped back and summoned more lightning as he took his leap. He jumped up high towards the monster's head and struck with his *dao*, but the monster defended with his hard, metallic buffalo horns. Gothang flew away with a loud clank, his thunderous lightning flying out elsewhere.

Gothang immediately attacked again. The monster laughed aloud as if growing high by the fight. It grew taller and stronger, throwing Chongja and Chongkim away with its gigantic horns. Gothang was not really skilled as a swordsman, but he was rapidly getting better with his weapon. He had come this far and was determined to defeat the monster at any cost. He attacked the creature without a pause, summoning bolts after bolts of lightning and charring the angry monster who kept fighting him even with its whole body burning up in flames. Gothang knew he was winning, but Gulheupi was insanely persistent; his body, even when falling apart, wouldn't stop darting his head for a fatal impact. Chongja and Chongkim came for the finishing bite, tearing the giant snake apart into pieces. It was a satisfying victory. Gothang couldn't help smiling—smiling at his beasts, smiling at his sparking *dao* and smiling at the burning pieces of carcass.

'Incredible...we are...' Gothang blabbered excitedly, but he couldn't enjoy his triumph for long. From the far corner of the strange sky came a shrieking sound and huge dark things flying towards him at an incredible speed. Now what? Gothang instantly felt vulnerable. He was already exhausted from the fight with the python monster, but now he saw giant things that could fly!

He swung his *dao* left and right along with Chongja and Chongkim standing in the front, ready for defence. The dark things flew closer and turned out to be those monstrous birds of tales and fables, the Kakyels. They looked vicious with their sharp-toothed beaks, burning lime eyeballs and their giant grey wings that boom with each movement.

They circled the high, sky-like ceiling, shrieking out and unwelcoming. Gothang was not sure how to stay sane, but even that little spark of optimism got smothered when he noticed something more. Far from the other end of the field, he could see giant creatures waking up and slowly approaching. They were incredible in size, their heads more pronounced than human heads, giant legs shaking the very ground with each step. The grasses hissed, several other unknown creatures or monsters were crawling towards him. He stood blinking, already feeling defeated.

Out of nowhere, came a spurt of fire. Gothang screamed a little in fright. He looked up nervously, but widened his eyes when he noticed the small bald-headed child riding the gorgeous golden dragon that flew in, casting a storm of fire towards the flying monster birds.

'Laiba!' Gothang yelled.

The dragon lowered near him and he also noticed that there was a girl within its claw. It let her go and the lady leapt out furiously, flashing a long spear towards the monsters around.

'So many?' She snapped.

'Brother Gothang, so we are not late to the party?' Laiba said as dully as he usually did, but he saw Chongja and Chongkim leaping around defensively and cried out, 'What on earth! Aren't these the celestial beasts? Majestic! How did they come here?'

'They came to my rescue, but anyway, how did you guys know I was here and...' Gothang noticed the missing members of the so-called team of seven guardians.

'They are all coming. Something is telling me that our scissor could be here. Why would the monsters group up here, if not?' Laiba covered his throbbing eyes with his palm for a while.

'Here?' Gothang wondered, looking back at the throng of demons and monsters closing in.

'We are about to complete our task, but while we wait for our ultimate reunion, we also need to stay alive by defeating all monsters who are here to spoil our quest,' Laiba said, uncovering his eyes. The dragon, probably Lungchum, was busy combusting the high ceiling, warding off the monster birds who kept trying to swarm over them.

'Sorry, I am Ningrei, but we better do something about all these things here first and hopefully pray for a time to introduce ourselves decently later on...' Ningrei said, as she ran up towards the crowd of monsters approaching them.

Gothang stood gaping. He hadn't seen a person as alive and intimidating as her. Assuring, he thought.

Lungchum kept spitting fire all around. Gothang began his lightning dance. Ningrei stood amazed for a while, but she also did something incredible herself. As she charged one of the giants with her spear, a giant boulder came flying in and crushed the monster. She knew instantly that it was the Kamatei. She summoned more giant boulders and they all flew in from whichever direction her spear would point. Yes! She yelled, summoning more giant boulders from all over. Some monsters were even beginning to realize that it was better to run away from the wild lady with the spear throwing giant rocks out of nowhere.

The war was clearly on, the subterranean valley was roaring with battle cry—of the monsters and of the guardians. Laiba stood firmly on Lungchum's back, meditating. He was conjuring the location of the divine scissor which he could now feel like his own heartbeat. It was very close. Very near... His eyes were burning up, but he knew he couldn't stop. Everyone was going to play their parts now.

Deep inside one of the many courses of the Nungkhong tunnels, a silent underground lake began to bubble up. Tiny bits of foam began to wash up on the shore and they accumulated inch by inch into frothy pulsating beings. It took time, but slowly, they bubbled up into fully formed humans and one horse.

Iwan woke up with a scream. He looked around his dim surroundings, rubbing his eyes in fright. The ceiling began to be illuminated faintly with a thousand sparkly dots. For a moment, he thought it was the night sky, but then he could make out the structure of the rest of the environment—the stalactites, rock pillars and crystals of some sorts around the edge of the sparkling water body, a cave system.

He noticed Leisatao and Yangba lying unconscious beside him, but what really froze his blood was the condition of Sana. The lower half of her body, which was supposed to be inside the lake, seemed to have dissolved away. Only her torso above the water lay peacefully hugging the slippery rock slab.

'Sana!' Iwan crawled up to her and tried to pull her out of the water, but to his utter surprise, realized that she seemed stuck inside the lake water from waist down.

'What is going on...' Iwan cried confused, 'Sana, are you alright? Sana, please wake up.'

He tried to pull her out of the water again, but her waist sucked up the water like it was some gelatinous extension. It looked extremely disturbing, but Sana, though unconscious, was breathing calmly.

'Please wake up. Please wake up!' Iwan prayed helplessly.

Leisatao began to stretch and moan beside him. Yangba woke up alert, looking pleased to see his master near him.

'Brother Leisatao! Are you alright?' Iwan asked, still holding Sana's upper body.

'Hmmm...' Leisatao blinked his eyes open, but cried as soon as he noticed Sana, 'Oh, good Guardians! Sana dear! What is happening here?'

'She told me she had turned into her divine form, but we are now inside a cave and she...I think half of her body is still water. I can't pull her out of the lake. I tried...' Iwan whimpered, trying to pull Sana again.

'Let's try together, alright...let me hold her here...' Leisatao went closer to Sana and held her hand. Yangba observed them innocently for a moment, but then moved away to explore the cave system.

The two tried hard but with little success. The effort had distracted them and they didn't see Yangba turning back in fright. The several tunnels diverging out of the lake were humming. From one of the many tunnel mouths on the other side of the lake, came a sinister laughter, echoing closer. Iwan heard it and knew who it might be, but wondered how he came here. It was fear that was stiffening him. He stopped pulling Sana. Always a coward, he thought to himself. Leisatao seemed oblivious of the sudden change in scenario.

'Brother Leisatao...I think we are in trouble...again...' Iwan gulped and said grimly, looking straight towards where the echo came from.

'You said something, dear?' Leisatao asked and followed Iwan's frozen stare. He too heard the echo of some crazy laughter.

'They are here alright. And my girl too,' a husky voice roared triumphantly and out of the tunnel came a creature that made Leisatao shriek in fear.

'Heinous! God!' Leisatao cried, covering his face with his hands. He tried to reach out for his darts, but stopped and observed more of such creatures coming out. There were also few indistinguishable creatures with long stretchy arms hopping forward. All petrifying and coming out in a huge number inside the enclosed chamber only made them feel worse.

'Keibu...Keioiba!' Iwan muttered, stepping back.

'So, we meet again, Your Royal Majesty,' the tiger-man growled excitedly, standing proud with his army that looked somewhat like him but smaller in size. What really shocked Iwan was that the smaller Keibu Keioibas wore the royal guards' uniform, the black and red attire. He knew that Keioiba had somehow turned his abducted soldiers into tiger-men.

'Have you met him before?' Leisatao fumbled.

'What have you done...' Iwan looked at the smaller tigermen.

'Oh, them? I took them to Keioibi Pat and dunked them for good. The cursed lake is out there too. Opened once again for good.' He noticed Leisatao making a disgusted face. The mention of Keioibi Pat made Iwan shudder. It was the infamous mythical lake where any human who drank or touched the water turned into a tiger. Keibu Keioiba must have somehow found the lake that was rumoured to be shielded by enchanted boulders.

'Oh, so you must be another guardian. And you look, hmmm... not so appetizing,' Keioiba said, mocking Leisatao, and turned to his companions with a laugh. They all seemed to be waiting for his orders. All the monsters stood growling, but not moving anywhere.

'And you look... I don't know why you have the head of a tiger. Your body is fine. Muscular, I admit, but your head, where is your head? I have never seen a human head with stripes or yellow fangs or...' Leisatao had little idea of what he was saying, but something told him that it would be smart to just chat away like this and give himself some time to calm his fear.

'Chitty chatty...' Keioiba didn't seem interested and stared straight at Iwan whose face already bore an expression of defeat. His thin cotton garment was dripping wet, his curly hair was stuck on his neck and eyes were welling up with tears.

'Hmm...I don't see the sword yet, so lady luck is smiling on me, again! And oh...' Keioiba saw Sana lying unconscious, 'My sweet lady. I am here for her, anyway.' Keioiba took a giant leap across the cave, hurdling across the wall and ceiling, landing smoothly in front of Iwan who instinctively stepped back.

'Wait...where are her legs?' Keioiba noticed Sana's unusual condition, 'Is she alright? Did you people fail in the quest already?'

'Don't...don't touch her!' Iwan managed to shout, but his voice broke up.

'Boy, go and cry to your mother. This is no war that you can win without this girl here. I am disappointed that you people exhausted my bride to death, but my friends here will take care of you piglets.' Keioiba kneeled before Sana and sniffed around. His friends on the other side of the lake began to growl noisily.

'He is scaring me, Iwan. What should we do?' Leisatao whispered, almost crying.

Iwan stood quietly. He clenched his fist, but didn't move anywhere. Keibu Keioiba looked stupid and confused beside Sana's half water body and Iwan wanted to punch him hard. Why do I have to be so pathetic always? He began to shed tears.

'I think my bride needs a little bit of rest; so, why don't you guys do your business with these two? I will stay here. She is safe with me...aha...aha... ahahahaha...' Keibu Keioiba's laughter shook the cave.

The creatures came crawling forward; they had lanky hands and were swimming across the lake with ease. The others who looked like miniatures of Keibu Keioiba leapt around and growled like many angry house cats.

Leisatao and Iwan jumped on Yangba's back and rode away through the nearest tunnel they could find.

Iwan could feel his face cold and wet with his tears. He had left Sana in the hands of some heinous monster. She had saved him and Leisatao, but he left her. He began to hug Yangba tight and was crying aloud.

'Iwan, we need to get out of here and find the others. They will know what to do, boy. She is a goddess. She will be fine...' Leisatao yelled from behind, but the monsters were getting closer and he seemed to know it was them in trouble and not Sana for the moment.

Yangba ran as fast as he could and Iwan just cried, not knowing where it would lead or how he was supposed to find an exit. The tunnel seemed to extend endlessly and Yangba was incredible for he did not slow down at all. The monsters got closer, their threatening roars getting louder.

'They are closing in... Iwan, they are...' Leisatao cried, but Iwan suddenly scolded back, 'Yes, I know. They are behind us! But you are the one with a weapon. You are one of the guardians too! Do something! I am always useless and have no weapon! You do something for God's sake!'

Leisatao was taken aback. He saw Iwan crying bitterly. He turned back and cringed at the sight of the monsters crawling through the tunnel behind them. He reached out for his *arambai* pouch and felt the last piece rolling around. He gulped. He knew his aim was accurate but the best he could hope to do even with that ability was shoot down one.

With Iwan snivelling aloud, he pulled out his poisonous dart and turned around to aim at one specific monster. There were many!

'Even killing one would be satisfying if we were to die here...' Leisatao prayed to a few gods before throwing his dart at the fastest running creature with lanky hands. The dart flew effortlessly and punctured the creature right on its heart. It dropped down dead immediately. He smiled excitedly, not minding the four more closing in, hands stretched out, nearly catching Yangba's tail.

'Emai... If only I had more...' Leisatao cried out and he felt his dart pouch shaking. He touched it and to his utter surprise, could feel the feathery ends of several darts inside. He looked down, saw his pouch glowing and stacked with more darts. Unusual—he had been expecting something peculiar to happen for a while now and finally it did. He knew what to do, but did not have time to explain to Iwan.

'Iwan...Go and find the rest. I will get Sana,' Leisatao yelled and leapt off Yangba. He fell down rolling towards the monsters that swarmed up on him like ants on honey.

All this was happening too fast for Iwan to process. Leisatao just jumped off the horse like a madman. He turned back but the tunnel took a turn and Leisatao, along with the monsters, was out of sight.

'Goddd...' Iwan blinked, too shocked to continue crying. He stared behind for a long time. Yangba kept on running.

The echoes of the monsters and Leisatao died away and Yangba slowed down after they crossed several turns and corners of the tunnel. Iwan understood they had been separated, and that Leisatao was far, very far from them. He wanted to go back for Leisatao, but he had told Iwan to find the others. Every one kept presenting stunts and now, even brother, Leisatao, could too.

'Yangba, you can stop now? Please?' Iwan asked meekly. He had been crying, exhausted, and quite depressingly ashamed of being alive. Yangba halted, but neighed nervously as if suggesting that they keep on moving.

'Oh, don't show off. You want to die running? You must be tired too. Just like me. Your pathetic brother of a man. Let's sit down here and think. We both are the worst. Even Brother Leisatao jumped off with some stupid confidence. Showing off. All of them, just pulling stunts. If something happened to him or Sana, I will be the one responsible. I left her. I am just good at losing people. That's all I am good at. Hiding, being scared and being a stupid coward!' Iwan began sobbing like a child again. Yangba stood staring at his master with sad eyes, it almost looked like he would have said something comforting if he could speak. He neighed kindly, but Iwan didn't even look up. He leant over the wet rocky wall of the tunnel and began to sob. How would he even get out of the tunnel, let alone find his friends.

'I think I failed them all. I will be the one to ruin everything. They all came for my kingdom and I will be the one to ruin everything. I should have died instead of my able father. What a shame...what...' Iwan was muttering to himself when he heard a faint footstep somewhere. Perhaps it was apprehension, but he almost felt his pulse racing, his heart as if coming up to his mouth. He knew the sounds were louder inside the tunnel with the echoes travelling far, but was sure that he heard a distinct footstep from somewhere nearby. He looked at Yangba and knew that he had heard it too. Yangba turned towards the direction of the sound, unmoved.

Is it them? Did Laiba find him using the power of his eyes? A fresh hope burst in his heart. Iwan almost smiled. He stood up instantly and ran towards the sound. The footsteps were echoing as if the person was running further away from Iwan. He almost called out, but the unusual events of the past had made him smart enough to not do so. If it was Laiba, he wouldn't be running away or at least someone else too must be with him. He realized the lone running footsteps could not be that of his friends. However, Iwan wanted to find out who came running that deep inside a cave. He quickened his pace with Yangba following him close. The tunnels had several confusing channels branching out on every turn and corner, but Iwan could easily follow the sound, disappointingly running away from him faster. He had to follow the pace, even though tired, leaving Yangba far behind, who had finally accepted his exhaustion. The tunnel took a sharp turn and to Iwan's disbelief, he saw a person. It was a woman with incredibly black hair flowing behind her. The sight was bizarre and more so because of the turquoise glow covering the woman's lower body as if it were fluorescent mud. It was quite dark to make out much, but Iwan noticed the striped lower garment, and thought to himself that she might not be just any woman. The woman seemed aware of Iwan's presence but didn't stop; she kept running away even faster. He wasn't even sure if the woman was human. It could be some demon too. But why was it running away from him?

Iwan would have followed the woman deeper if not for the sudden cry of his horse far behind. The sight of the woman had made him almost forget about Yangba.

'Yangba!' Iwan immediately turned back and saw his horse kneeling. He seemed to be in pain, 'Are you alright boy? Please don't die on me. No, not you...'

He kneeled near his horse and rubbed its head, feeling quite helpless. The horse began to twist and turn in pain.

'Yangba...' Iwan wept, looking around his dim surroundings, all quiet except for the sound of Yangba struggling violently. The horse began to gag as if suffocated. Iwan knew he would be losing him. He relaxed his hands and stared ahead blankly, crying was the last thing he wanted to do while bidding farewell. He blinked and thick streams of tears coursed down his cheeks.

Yangba looked at him and gagged harder. Iwan thought of turning his face away from the tragic sight, but something odd struck him. Yangba's gaping mouth seemed glowing. At first, he thought it was because of the strange lights glowing in the tunnel, but the beam on Yangba's mouth was like that of fire and not the light in the cave that was bluish. Iwan pulled Yangba's head to examine it, but his horse flung away in pain and gagged even more. The horse now sat up, throttled and his mouth glowed even brighter. Iwan was confused, stepping away, he wondered if his horse's soul was struggling to escape.

With a loud gurgle, Yangba vomited golden fluid all over Iwan. However, the real stroke of peculiarity was the long golden sword falling near Iwan's feet. He didn't mind Yangba's warm golden vomit dripping down his head and body, and picked up the sword real quick. He felt familiar with the handle. He knew it belonged to him even though he had never seen such a huge glowing sword in his life before. Finally, his own something divine, like the rest of the guardians. But why and how was it inside his horse? Iwan looked at Yangba and wondered but the horse was still struggling for something more. Yangba's body began to grow bigger and from the side of his abdomen, protruded fluffy giant wings as white as the northern snow. Yangba stopped its painful cry and managed to stand up erect, wobbly still, but looking calm and staring at his master with admiration. He seemed to like Iwan with his sword.

'You got wings?' Iwan stood staring at Yangba's wings that he flapped excitedly, scraping across the congested tunnel walls as he flailed them around, making the glowing dust flutter off the walls as if it were bluish fireflies.

The sword was light in Iwan's hand. He could also feel it grumbling and angry enough to slash something. Now his horse could fly, should there be any need. He felt something he had not felt ever before. Power!

***

Leisatao wasn't doing so great after his heroic leap. His *arambai*s were not effective for use in confined spaces like the tunnel he was stuck in, but the seemingly idiotic monsters kept on running straight at him, which made it easier for him to destroy them by using the darts as a knife. The glowing *arambai*s seemed more deadly to the monsters as compared to the regular ones. They perished even at the slightest touch. Regardless of his impressive weapon, the sheer number of monsters began to overwhelm him.

'Just how many of you uglies are here?' Leisatao cried and stabbed some six or seven monsters at once. The darts were clipped between all his fingers like extended nails.

Right when he thought his arms would fly off his shoulder, a bright big something swooped up from behind and started chopping up the monsters. They all perished as if they were clay pots being smashed. Leisatao squinted his eyes in disbelief, but he knew exactly what he saw. It was Yangba, now with wings, and he was flying, and on his back was the little boy king, not so little anymore, and with a huge golden sword, which he swung effortlessly, slaying a hundred monsters in one go!

'Iwan! And Yang...' Leisatao cried out before he fell on his knees, almost fainting, but he couldn't take his eyes off the sight. It was a flying white horse and a boy with a golden sword! You don't see such sights every day!

Iwan was always impatient, but now he felt like his sword was more so. The sword slit into the monsters, almost flying in by itself, hardly waiting for his muscular command. It took just a few moments for all to be turned into dust or whatever was left of the disintegrating monsters.

The sword calmed, and gradually Iwan felt its weight on his palm. Yangba stopped near Leisatao, who crawled nearer.

'Iwan... I thought we are done for...' Leisatao was almost weeping.

'Brother, let's go for Sana! Come on!' Iwan said, excited.

'Yea...yeah,' Leisatao breathed heavily and dragged himself up on to the horse. Yangba's feathery wings were real. Leisatao felt them as it flapped them uncomfortably near his thighs.

Yangba was ready to take off, but then stood frozen again, both ears straight like that of an alerted dog.

'Yangba? Go... You forgot the way too?' Iwan tried to nudge his horse forward, but it didn't move a muscle.

'Iwan, I think...' Leisatao wanted to explain, but there was no need. They all could now feel the hum coming at them. It must be the monsters again chasing them in multitude. Iwan readied his sword excitedly, but Yangba took a swift turn, almost making Iwan fly off its back.

'Yangba! What the...turn back! We need to go find Sana,' Iwan screamed, but his horse took a leap and flew away at an incredible speed in the opposite direction.

Leisatao looked back and realized Yangba was smarter than them. Not just lanky monsters and miniature cats, but now, giant slithering creatures, hopping about, and the others who had wings, were all chasing them down at an incredible speed. The tunnel was filled with those creatures as if rice inside a bamboo tube. He would never find another bamboo rice tube appetizing again! Ever!

'Iwan, your sword or my *arambai* wouldn't do much unless we find an exit, an open space!' Leisatao turned back shaken.

'Guardians! Why so many!' Iwan clenched his fist.

Yangba just flew swiftly through the tunnel, taking each turn and corner with clarity and confidence about which curve to take. Iwan wondered if his horse knew about an exit within the cave. He desperately wished so, because he was at his wit's end. The tunnel became dimmer and the speed of their ride confused him more. The roar of the monsters kept getting louder and his sword kept glowing as if it too was excited to slay more of them.

PAMBA KEIREMBA

Laiba's eyes began to glow even brighter. The sacred scissor was dangerously near them, summoning all monsters towards its trail to avoid its restoration to the palace. For some reason, he also felt more divine and his vision cleared more than before. Up ahead of the subterranean battlefield, he sensed the presence of an intricate system of tunnels.

Concentrating a bit more, he was able to penetrate his vision further.

'No way!' Laiba almost screamed out.

It almost felt like a huge slap on the brain. Laiba realized the chilling truth. He instantly knew where exactly they were. At the end of the tunnels was the eternal realm of ancient immortal humans, the Khamnung. They were dormant as if in deep slumber; their majestic forts and palaces deserted and a stretch of settlements without anyone living there. Laiba stared deeper and saw the humans, the ancestors, the charmers and the intellects hiding away in their designated compounds, some deeper underground and the royal priests and priestesses standing guard near the inner stone entrance, fully covered with white translucent silk, unmoved, that at first Laiba mistook them for some fancy statues.

'We are in Khamnung? But why would the scissor be here?' Laiba tried to surmise. The Khamnung, an underworld realm, was one of the most sacred realms. Laiba couldn't understand how a stolen divine scissor could be brought towards a realm like Khamnung. It didn't make sense to him. Something was not right; even though just a child, he had already learnt about the three great realms—the celestial, the earth and the subterranean. Khamnung was as sacred as any other realm, no mortals or spirits could pass through their entrance without their permission. The scissor, if stolen, guarded by such hordes of monsters, was expected to have been taken somewhere in the dark abyss and not inside another holy realm. And more surprisingly, none of the Khamnung citizens reacted to the onset of the war right outside their abode. They were powerful, mystic and brave. Their immortal kings and queens were worshipped as near-god entities. Why have they not helped the guardians retrieve the scissor if the monsters brought it towards them? The unanswered questions started to bubble up inside Laiba's head, but seemed to burst all at once with one single question. Laiba exclaimed, 'Wait...we can't be in Khamnung! This is impossible! Khamnung is sealed from the mortal entrance. All seven of us except Gothang are mortals. Who opened the enchanted door? No human or monster can do that. Even the gods were forbidden from the act. Who would open such a door and let all monsters run berserk through another holy realm and carry the scissor here?'

Laiba, for the first time, wished he were wiser. He tried his best to learn all he could from the previous royal Maichou, but he wondered if the ex-head priest would have known the answer to his doubts. Even while flying deep inside the cave, Laiba never imagined he would be crossing into another realm. He thought he would rescue Gothang and defeat some monsters while they reunited and restored the scissor. He had imagined it to be easy. He looked towards the sky prince, busy fighting off monsters with his lightning blade, his majestic beasts cooperating brilliantly. Laiba squinted his eyes. Wait a moment, why did Gothang dash here in the first place?

Gothang was glad that the guardians followed him all the way, but didn't think much about how he would explain his true cause. He was busy defending against all the monsters that kept coming out in multitudes.

'Brother Gothang!'

Gothang almost jumped up in fright when a loud voice exploded inside his head. What was that, he wondered, standing still for a while, Chongja and Chongkim defending him while he was distracted.

'It's me, Laiba!' the sharp voice replied.

'What is going on?' he replied aloud.

'I am talking to you telepathically. Since we are near the scissor, all of our divine powers are enhancing. Now, I can talk to all of you telepathically if I concentrate hard enough. You can reply back in your mind too,' Laiba said calmly.

'Alright, that sounds useful. Have you found the rest?'

'Forget about the rest! I am here to talk about something serious and important. You have to be sincere with me. Promise?'

'Is it about my mother?' Gothang predicted right.

'Your mother?' Laiba was quiet for a moment, 'Yes, maybe. What? Is she here? How did you know? How is she related to the scissor?'

'Related to the scissor? Is she related to the scissor?' Gothang stood still, monsters attacking him left and right. He would have been hurt if not for his beasts.

'I am asking you. Something is not right here. I need you to tell me the truth.'

Gothang looked up at Laiba. He was standing straight, well balanced on top of Lungchum who flew around at an insane speed, raining fire over the monsters ahead.

'I saw her here,' Gothang sighed.

'Saw her? Did she have the scissor? Did you see her enter here? How did she open the enchanted door?'

'I saw...' Gothang wanted to say in his dream but since he wanted Laiba to take him seriously and help him find his mother soon, he said, 'I saw her move a boulder but no... I don't think she carried...'

'She what?!' Laiba yelped.

Gothang wondered if he was revealing bad or good news because Laiba sounded like he was awestricken for some reason. He begged, 'Will she be in trouble? She looked already exhausted. Can we all go and find her first? I will definitely help out with the scissor later.'

'Brother Gothang, if what you were telling me is true, we might be in bigger trouble. All of us will be trapped here for eternity except for you,' Laiba said grimly.

'What? Why? Where are we?' Gothang cried back, charring few monsters on his way.

'We are in Khamnung! The realm of immortals. Your mother opened the forbidden enchanted door and we all happily walked in here! I think we are already deep inside! This is bad news!'

'I don't understand!' Gothang got more distracted, he wished Laiba would just stop freaking out in his mind.

'Your mother somehow opened the Forbidden Door of Death, the Ashi Thong! It is only one way and only dead people are supposed to use it to become an eternal citizen of the underworld!' Gothang never heard Laiba so frightened before.

'What...what will happen now?' Gothang didn't want to believe his long-lost mother would run around and perform such a felony.

'I don't want to sound dramatic, but we are all going to die!'

'Will you please calm down? Laiba? Please, there must be something we could do. Aren't we deities?'

'With the door of death open, mortals of earth will be sucked in here. The monsters and all these dark entities will toil on our realm for eternity...spreading calamities, famines or epidemics... Fighting monsters and restoring the scissor would be impossible if we are stuck here. Our realm will collapse anyway. We aren't supposed to be here. I am sorry but I thought I would know all. This part was never in the prophecy.'

'We failed the quest? What about my mother?'

'Your mother will be fine if she is strong enough to open a door like the Ashi Thong! Brother Gothang, please, from now on, pay more attention to the quest or we all will be in trouble. We need to get the scissor before it reaches the inner kingdom of Khamnung! I sense it within the tunnel system ahead. Just pray we aren't as doomed as I think we are or else our earth realm will have to restart from sticks and stones again...'

Lungchum and Ningrei were blissfully slaying monsters, unaware of the mental mayhem shared between Gothang and Laiba. Ningrei was effortlessly establishing herself into her new power, enhanced by the presence of the scissor nearby. She even used some large sprouting boulders to shuttle her up towards the flying monsters, stabbing them with her long spear.

Lungchum flew closer to her, perhaps wanting to collaborate, but Ningrei had never done anything together with anyone. She thrived in solitude. She went further ahead, approaching a particular spot at the far end of the field from where the monsters seemed to emerge. It was the thrill of danger that excited her more. She seemed invincible, the boulders hovering around her as if they were some celestial objects, protecting everyone around.

Almost flying through the monsters with the help of her boulders, Ningrei reached the far end of the field and to her surprise, noticed a section in the subterranean mountain filled with tunnel holes of several sizes; the monsters seemed to be coming out of the larger ones. What is this place? She wondered. She never knew the eastern cave system to be that enormous. Apart from the long journey while flying in, the size of the field and the extended tunnels made her wonder. Flying monsters and other crawling creatures were after Gothang and Lungchum, while the giants learnt that they were the only ones who were a bit of a challenge for Ningrei. They followed her slowly, grunting uncomfortably.

'These idiots still want to die at my hands,' Ningrei sighed and got ready with her spear.

The giants were getting closer but for some reason, slowed down and turned away.

'Hah! Yes, was calling you all stupid for not learning to fear me. Now, I guess you guys aren't that thick,' Ningrei flattered herself with a smirk. She stood proud but began to notice a noise from behind her. She turned back and realized the noise was coming from the tunnels nearby. She stood staring curiously, but dropped her jaws when she saw the white horse flying out towards her. She dodged the horse but was still in shock. It was the valley king and the cross-dresser. They were holding glittering weapons. Pathetically fancy as always.

'Where have you...' Ningrei tried to shout but Iwan grabbed her by her waist and pulled her up on the horse. It happened too fast. The boy king got stronger, did he?

'Hey...' Ningrei cried out, holding on to Iwan.

'Lady Ningrei, the monsters are following us,' Leisatao yelled from behind. Ningrei looked back and saw a swarm of unrecognizable monsters oozing out of the tunnel from where they flew out. These people vanished and came leading a troop of monsters!

'There are monsters everywhere. Let me down. We need to fight, not flee!' Ningrei snapped. The giants followed, their gaze on them as they flew through.

'Yes, you are right lady, but we need an open space like...yes... right here,' Iwan said as they approached the central part of the field. Lungchum spotted them. He stopped his fire for a while, observing them, but flew away towards the tunnel system, raging with bigger waves of fire. Laiba didn't turn around and flew away on Lungchum's back, still standing as if he were a stone statue, eyes looking straight ahead. Gothang didn't notice at first, but Iwan ran up near him and slaughtered some few hundred monsters at once with his new sword. Gothang turned and gave a weak smile. Iwan couldn't help but smile back. He noticed the giant beasts standing near Gothang.

'My pets,' Gothang shouted, throwing lightning bolts towards the monsters as they ran closer to each other.

'Save your happy reunions for later. Wait...' Ningrei looked around and asked worriedly, 'Where is the girl? Sana?'

'She is inside the tunnel. The tiger-man attacked us...we tried...' Leisatao began to explain in spite of the chaotic fights, but all the guardians began to hear a voice inside their heads. It was Laiba broadcasting telepathically,

'Guardians, we must enter the largest tunnel at the north-west end of this field. There is a huge change of plan now.'

What? Why? Huh? What plan? The realm of subconscious mind got noisy with the guardians' voices.

'Sana is still inside one of the tunnels, far behind. Keibu Keioiba got her,' Iwan said grimly. He sliced up a monster nearby into tiny pieces, probably venting out his anger and regret. Everyone went quiet.

'Keibu Keioiba, eh?' Laiba seemed to be in thought but replied quickly, 'Hate to say this but she will somehow be safe with that cretin for now. Let us first go towards the huge cave chamber ahead. I am sure the scissor is being carried towards the inner kingdom. Once it reaches there, we wouldn't be able to restore it. We need to move fast. We cannot let the scissor cross inside the subterranean kingdom. Come, guardians! This is it!'

All of them looked towards the far end of the field and saw the glittering golden dragon vanishing inside the enormous mouth of the tunnel.

'Ningrei can ride Chongkim,' Gothang pushed the northern lass up on one of his beasts and he jumped up on Chongja while Iwan and Leisatao nodded and flew away on Yangba.

The beasts were fast and ran with racing speed, Gothang and Ningrei both had to hold on tight to their thick fur, their spear and *dao* latched on their backs. Some monsters chased them and Ningrei got worried for a moment, but a school of darts rained down and disintegrated the monsters. She looked up and saw Leisatao throwing rows of darts from above. She smirked, impressed.

The guardians entered the colossal tunnel mouth and went further inside. All of them were captivated by the unusual terrain of the Mangsore. First, a meadow, and now, the tunnel, huge enough to have small hill ranges lined up at the corner. The rocks were multi-coloured gems of some sort, and the high ceiling adorned with glowing stalactites.

'Lady Ningrei, can you use one of your boulders to block the entrance to prevent the monsters from coming in? If not, they will keep following us.'

Laiba asked Ningrei and she looked back at the tunnel swarming with monsters. She jumped down from Chongkim, summoned a huge rock out of the tunnel wall and blocked it before the monsters could reach them.

With the monsters shut away for the first time, they all relaxed a bit to catch their breath. Iwan and Leisatao jumped down from Yangba's back and joined Gothang and Ningrei.

They saw Lungchum and Laiba hovering above, probably waiting. If Sana was there, this moment would have been the first time all seven guardians were united. Lungchum shrank from his dragon form into his original human body. Laiba jumped down to safety.

'Whoa, I had never been in the dragon form for this long. Good to see all of us safe so far,' Lungchum smiled at his gloomy friends.

'Now what?' Ningrei asked, impatiently.

'We shall pray for luck to be by our side. There's got to be some way,' Laiba said, looking at the distant entrance of the tunnel where the monsters were screeching and grunting to shatter the boulder.

'Will Sana be really fine? She was unconscious when we...left her,' Iwan said with guilt and unsheathed his sword again, flashing it at Laiba. He was dying to show it to him in particular.

'Impressive, Meidingu,' Laiba said rolling his beaming eyes, but continued in a serious tone, 'Keioiba wanted her as his wife. He wouldn't hurt her unless necessary and we know our Sana is way smarter than him. She will do fine for now. At this moment, we need to discuss our plan first.'

'Yes, what plan?' Ningrei cried out.

'We are not inside a cave, but inside a different realm altogether. We are in the land of death, the underworld—Khamnung—as the valley calls it.'

The guardians didn't say anything but gasped. The absurdities they had been through made more sense now. They just wanted to listen to Laiba while he continued.

'The scissor entered the inner kingdom but not deep into the royal square. I sense it unmoved on a spot not so far from here now. If we are lucky,' Laiba said calmly, 'it would mean good news for us. Whoever is carrying the scissor is powerful and not some mere thief. We need to defeat the person, retrieve the scissor before it is hidden inside the forbidden kingdom and then plan our way out. We need to try our best, regardless. We are not sure of what the thief of the scissor is capable of; so, this is going to be tricky, but at least the scissor is not moving around. Stay observant, cooperate and no hasty moves. Understand, guardians?' Laiba asked, more specifically to Iwan who seemed eager to show his skills with the sword.

'Thief of the scissor?' Gothang muttered.

'Yes, thief. The scissor was stolen and is being carried around, even crossing realms, brother,' Laiba said matter-of-factly.

Gothang nodded, but looked down in shame. What will his friends think of him when they realize it was his mother who caused all the trouble? He never had any friends before. This was the first time that people actually counted on him. He wished his mother had a good explanation.

'But Sana...' Leisatao muttered, nervously adjusting his dart pouch.

'Sana will be fine, brother, I promise. First, let us all go and capture the thief. We will need her to return home too,' Laiba said, turning away to lead the group.

'Lungchum, if you could please...' Laiba asked calmly.

'At your service...' Lungchum turned back into the dragon form and allowed Laiba on his back. They flew away and the rest of the guardians followed on their respective rides.

The strange landscape of the underworld stretched out farther as they travelled deeper. So many colours and light for a world breathing in the depth of the earth. The breeze was cold too.

Laiba did wonder if he should find Sana first, but focused back to the scissor that seemed too close as if just beneath his nose. He was determined to fulfil the prophecy at all costs.

The guardians rode as fast as they could, Lungchum and Laiba leading ahead. The subterranean scenery was pure distraction and all of them knew stopping to enjoy it would cost lives and more. The tunnel opened up again and this time, it revealed a small hilltop at the centre of a huge, mossy, cave chamber. The ceiling was netted with lines of red lava veins, glowing red and yellow. The guardians stopped their flight. Lungchum turned back to the human form. Laiba walked up slowly towards the central hill, his feet squeezing the mossy ground. This mossy part of the scenery was giving off a faint green glow. Bright red veins above and soft glowing greens below. No surprise, Khamnung is known for its geographical sophistication.

Gothang saw his beasts getting excited. He suppressed a smile, looking at the two, shrinking their sizes and loitering through the glowing grass-like thing. Ningrei stood puzzled. She never knew the underworld realm would be this miraculous. Iwan smiled, admiring Ningrei's awestricken face. Leisatao and Yangba stood close to each other. It seemed as if they had decided not to relax until the end of the quest.

Laiba ran up the hill and stopped when he saw what he expected. On the summit, inside a large, intricately woven structure of floating white curtains and drapes was the silhouette of a woman sitting straight.

Gothang stopped smiling when he noticed the presence of a person on top of the hill. His mother at last! He ran up the hill, tearing at the glowing grasses which produced a crusty sound with each of his steps. The rest also noticed the presence and approached cautiously.

The guardians were about to reach the woman but the sound of thumping footsteps stopped them. They froze, their eyes roving alertly. Chongja and Chongkim instantly grew back to their original giant size. Yangba fluttered its wings. Iwan could feel his sword throbbing. Leisatao went and stood closer to Ningrei who instantly flashed her spear towards the sound. Lungchum instinctively stood in front of Laiba.

From the other side of the hill, came two giants—one tall and a bit skinny and the other, short and fat. Their faces looked identical with big droopy eyes, a piggy nose and a thick-tusked mouth. They both wore earthy loinclothes, exposing the rest of their body that looked like it was made up of some grey stone with dark stripes here and there. They also wore a horned, feathery headdress, which must have been nice at some point of time, but was now mossy and looked fossilized.

'More giants?' Ningrei grunted. She was so done with giants. They were too stupid a creature to even fight a battle with. All they did was try to catch her as if she were a fly with their giant hands that moved as slow as a tortoise.

'Leave this to me!' Iwan yelled and ran head on towards the giants. Yangba flew in and he jumped on his horse for a fast ride. He wielded his golden sword and to his ultimate satisfaction, easily cut the giants into halves. It was so fast that the giants didn't even get the time to react.

'Hah! That was too easy,' Iwan scoffed.

The other guardians ran after him. Iwan jumped down from his horse and walked proudly towards them.

'Took care of them myself. No worries...' Iwan said, shaking the giant's blood away from his glowing sword, 'Who is that woman up there? Is she the thief?' He asked, looking towards the silhouette above.

'I told you not to act hastily...' Laiba scolded, but the rest of the guardians seemed pleased with Iwan's splendid performance, except for Gothang.

Gothang knew it was his mother on the hilltop. He couldn't see properly yet, but the silhouette was exactly how he saw her in his dream. He had been waiting for this moment all his life, but now, for some reason, he hesitated to celebrate the reunion. He stood behind, brooding in thoughts but noticed something odd. The blood dripping down from Iwan's sword didn't fall on the ground but flew back towards the slaughtered giants.

'Umm...guardians, I think something strange is going on...' Gothang called them and they all turned to look. He pointed at the blood drops drifting away and the body of the giants burbling up as if a fountain.

'God...' Iwan stepped back in fright.

The butchered giants began to grow back from their severed halves. Now multiplied in number, there stood four giants in front of them. Two tall and two short. Great!

'Did they just grow back alive?' Ningrei asked, disgusted.

'Oh no...' Laiba mourned.

'What? What are these?' Iwan asked, visibly frightened.

'They are the twin giants. The most indestructible of all giants. The tall one must be Tin-ngam and the short one, Lai-ngam!' Laiba cried out, 'They will multiply if they bleed! Do not, under any circumstances, do not cut the giants! Don't spill a single drop of their blood!'

The giants stood looking at each other for a while but then began to chase the guardians.

The guardians ran down not knowing what to do. Two Lai-ngams followed Lungchum who flew away with Laiba and Ningrei, each trying to crush them. Lungchum tried throwing fire, but the giant seemed unaffected. Ningrei shielded herself by summoning a boulder, but she couldn't make any attack. How could she attack without wounding the giant? The fat giant kept on punching Ningrei's flat boulder she was using as a shield, almost breaking it down. They were insanely strong too.

Two Tin-ngams, the taller of the twin giants, chased Leisatao, Iwan and Gothang. Gothang handled one with the help of his beasts, but even he was confused as to how to defeat the giant without spilling its blood. They just dodged attacks and kept running, clueless. Iwan and Leisatao handled one that seemed honestly annoyed with Iwan. It followed him with its black beady eyes. Helpless, they flew around the giant's face like a fly, making the giant even more irritated.

Laiba stood comfortably on Lungchum's scaly back. He looked down towards the woman over the hilltop. He observed that even the curtain was not made of a regular cloth material but of something shimering, a magical one. The giants were attacking in a peculiar manner.

'Hmmm... They are guarding the woman,' Laiba realized. Tin-ngam and Lai-ngam were twin giants, but they were also known for guarding divine things. They were not exactly dark entities. Why would they guard a thief? Were they manipulated? Tin-ngam and Lai-ngam, the great giants who once were given the task to dig up the great lake, Loktak. They were known for their loyalty to the gods once. And now they are loyal to the thief? Did the scissor also give some divine power to the one who stole it? With the presence of the twin giants, their quest seemed fated to be failing. Laiba tried hard to collect the puzzle, pieces that had been scattered everywhere since the wake of their adventure.

'Sana... Sana... Where are you?' Laiba concentrated hard, trying to catch hold of the fragments of Sana through his mind. No matter how impossible it all turned out, all the seven guardians were yet to reunite as suggested by the oracle. Laiba decided to put all his faith on that.

Deep inside the cave, by the lake, Sana woke up coughing. She found herself lying on the underground shore of the lake, on a smooth rock surface.

'At last, my lady, you are awake,' a happy voice greeted her.

Sana froze instantly. She knew the voice. Her weak body barely took the shock well and began to shake visibly.

'Don't worry, I will take you out of here safe. Only mortals are not allowed to leave, but creatures of the dark realms follow no such rules.' Keibu Keioiba walked closer to her and she cringed.

'Where...are my friends...?' Sana asked; exhausted to the bone, she couldn't even lift her head properly. The fear was taking its toll.

'Friends? The pathetic lot who called themselves the guardians? They left you here. Let's go!'

Keioiba tried to grab Sana, but she snuggled against the cave wall and cried, 'Stay away!'

Keioiba stopped. He noticed the lake water throbbing up to create huge waves.

'Lady, your quest has already failed. None of your friends will be able to restore the scissor back to the palace now. They will die trying, but you—I can save you.' Keioiba spoke, his hideous face relaxed, perhaps trying to smile kindly, but without much success.

'What do you mean we already failed? What did you do to my friends?' Sana cried but secretly peeped at the lake and was somewhat relieved that she could still feel the water. She wondered if she could fight Keioiba.

'I did nothing, sadly,' Keioiba said, sneaking up closer to Sana, cautiously.

'Stay away, Keioiba. You know I am not the timid helpless girl anymore...' Sana tried sounding courageous. She was sure she had restored Iwan, Yangba and Leisatao fine. She knew Keioiba must have done something.

'Calm down and you will know I have no desire to harm you. I want a bride. You. That's all,' Keioiba smirked disgustingly.

'Tell me first, where are my friends?' Sana said, inching a little closer to the lake, trying to make it look like she was rolling in fatigue.

'They are probably fighting monsters now. But the number of monsters summoned here by the scissor couldn't be defeated even by all the gods of the pantheon combined. Your six friends, some terribly late bloomers, wouldn't stand a chance...' Keioiba seemed to notice

Sana moving towards the water. He roared angrily and sprang up on her.

The huge clawed hands pinned hard on Sana's throat. She almost choked, but raised her hands and splashed a strong gush of water.

Keioiba flung back, some distance away, but growled angrily.

'...told you I am no longer weak...' Sana said, barely breathing. She looked at the lake, wondering for a way to defeat the tiger-man, but a familiar voice popped up in her head. She almost cried out in happiness. Keioiba stood up to attack Sana again, but she swirled her arms and shrouded herself within an emblem of shimmering water out of the lake. Keioiba circled the water cocoon helplessly.

'Laiba!' Sana answered in her mind, 'Can you hear me? Laiba!'

There was silence. She could see Keioiba trying to break her transparent water shield.

Sana closed her eyes and concentrated hard...

'...Sana...' Laiba called again.

'Yes! Yes... I, I can hear you!' Sana replied.

The voice became clearer, her water shield growing thicker and churning faster.

'Sana, are you alright?' Laiba asked.

'Yes, but Keibu Keioiba caught me. I don't know where I am right now. Did you find all of our friends?'

'Yes, I need you to come and find us soon. Sana, we need you here as fast as possible,' Laiba had an urgency in his voice. The boy had always been calm even in the face of the most absurd of events. Sana suspected something ominous.

'I want to, but how? What about Keioiba? I don't think he would be easy to handle even with...'

'Sana, I know something about Keioiba. I will share it with you through the dream realm. You will know what to do with him. He wasn't always a monster and I think he could be used to provoke your most powerful form!'

'What? Dream realm?'

Sana wondered, but Laiba took hold of her mind and she began to see a view. It was a small village alley. A group of children were playing. Sana saw them as if she was walking past them. The children ran around and played, not aware of her presence. She walked a little closer and could hear the children laughing, pointing their fingers and singing, 'Ugly ugly tiger-boy...ugly ugly tiger-boy...no girl will love...no lady will like...ugly ugly tiger-boy...'

Sana realized the children were bullying. She went ahead, but was struck with guilt when she saw the victim. Curled timidly in a corner, surrounded by the mean children was young Keibu Keioiba, wearing a cute loincloth, bead necklace and feather headpin. The view flickered and Sana found herself inside a dimly lit kitchen. There was a woman roasting meat on her earthen stove. She spoke, '...you must not listen to other people, Pamba. You will always be the most handsome boy to me. Now, one day, a lady will look at you the same way I do and tell you just how strong and courageous you are. She will love you, Pamba.'

'But mother, they said I am still ugly even with the necklace you gave me...' a tiny voice protested and Sana turned around to find young Keioiba snuggled beside the lady, his supposed mother. Sana had to admit that Keioiba looked cute as a child. His greenish eyes sparkled in the stove fire, his tiny canines protruding out of his pouting lips.

'Oh...ho ho...you shall forgive your silly friends for they are only gripped in a trap called "Envy". Sometimes, people act mean only to conceal their own feeling of inferiority. Back home, they would only think about how good you looked in your beautiful bead necklace.'

The words seemed to lighten up Keioiba and he asked innocently, 'Mother, will a girl like me for who I am one day?'

'Of course, dear.'

'I will bring a beautiful girl as my wife and will prove everyone wrong someday.'

'Always remember, Pamba, being different is what makes you grand. Not just girls but even gods and goddesses will respect you one day. Great things are not meant for the ordinary. Embrace your true self and that is how you win. You will be called the great Pamba Keiremba...'

The vision vanished and Sana came back to her present view, Keioiba roaring and scratching up her churning water shield.

Sana looked deep into Keioiba's eyes, even though they were now glowing green with hatred and coldness, she could see the small part of innocence deep within. She relaxed her hands and the water washed away slowly towards the lake. Keioiba roared but didn't attack Sana. He stepped back and observed cautiously.

'Keioiba...calm down...' Sana tried. She was thinking of doing something outrageous.

Keioiba didn't answer but snarled irately, kneeling in suspicion.

'I would love to be your bride...' Sana said, slowly trying to touch Keioiba's face, 'but you already know I am a goddess incarnate.'

Keioiba roared in anger and she had to cringe back.

'I said I want to...'

Keioiba began to get violent, but Sana was determined,

'I said I am a goddess! Pamba Keiremba!' She cried.

The mention of the name stopped Keioiba and he seemed confused for a moment.

'Pamba Keiremba!' Sana called out again. It seemed to work.

Keioiba stepped back, but still stared at her suspiciously.

'You are one strong spirit, a gift of nature bestowed with the wisdom of humankind and the strength of a beast. I will make the great realms equal and you will never suffer false judgement of pitiable rogues, but instead, will attain glory as the mount of the Supreme Goddess. Come, my brave, the great Pamba Keiremba...'

Sana caressed Keioiba's face. He didn't protest, but looked deep into Sana's eyes. He blinked and a thick teardrop escaped from the corner of his eyes.

She pulled up the lake water with a single swift movement of her hand and let it swirl through Pamba's body as if washing him off. The water danced its way from the torso that was of a tiger, towards the lower human half that slowly began to turn into that of a tiger. Pamba was no longer a half-breed but a full-grown tiger, majestic and regal and stood on all its limbs.

'You are indeed a beauty, Pamba,' Sana whispered. She couldn't believe her insane plan had worked, and at the same time, she also sensed a change in her feelings. She was suddenly sensing restlessness.

'Pamba, you are no ordinary tiger but my special divine mount. You will find no beast or monster capable of harming you. Find me the rest of the guardians! They have wasted enough time!' Sana said, almost yelling. There was anger too. Sana was surprised. She never got this annoyed easily before.

Pamba nodded as if he understood and lowered his body. She jumped up effortlessly, but was a bit surprised. The usual Sana would have hesitated. As soon as she settled on Pamba's back, she also felt a sudden surge of her blood, her heart pumping faster and her small dagger glowing up as if it were on flame. She pulled it out and it grew larger into a sleek black sword. She smiled at her evolved weapon. It fit perfectly in her hand. She would have admired the sword longer if not for the sudden screech of monsters nearby. She turned towards the sound and yelled,

'Alright, yes, go!'

Pamba sniffed a little and dashed towards a tunnel ahead.

THE WAYEL KATI

Tin-ngam and Lai-ngam ran havoc with the guardians. Gothang secretly tried to reach near his mother first, but with no luck. The giants were extremely strong. None of them were spared. Ningrei was engulfed by her stone shields. Iwan flew around madly with Leisatao. Lungchum and Laiba were up in the air too, chased by the tall giants.

'What on earth is going on here?' a loud voice thundered from the cave entrance. Even the giants stopped and stared towards the voice.

The guardians turned around and almost yelped in unison, 'Sana!'

Sana came out and into the brighter cave chamber. She seemed more mature and eye-catching, riding her huge tiger covered in black monster dust and blood.

'What happened to you...?' Iwan flew closer to Sana.

'The monsters on the way here...had to slay them,' Sana spoke, eyeing the giants.

'My dear, you got yourself a gorgeous friend,' Leisatao admired them from behind. One of the Tin-ngams now chased after them.

'Thank you and Yangba looks much better flying like that,' Sana smiled. Even her voice seemed louder.

'Ningrei, we need time to think. Will you be able to shelter all of us inside your boulder defence?'

All of them heard Laiba, broadcasting another telepathic message. Sana realized the guardians were finally united for the first time. The prophecy was supposed to play out in their favour, but something had gone wrong. She felt it too.

She saw Gothang running towards them accompanied by two beautiful beasts with gold and silver antlers, and Lungchum in his dragon form, carrying Laiba on his back. They saw Ningrei running up as if her whole life depends on it, and probably it did, as all the giants were now after her as she was the slowest amongst all.

'Quick! All of you, stand close. Brother Gothang?' Laiba looked at Chongja and Chongkim. Gothang nodded, hastily rubbed them, shrinking them back to their adorable puppy sizes. Lungchum shrunk into his human form too. Ningrei jumped into their reunion and the boulders encaged them right on time before the giants could touch them.

The boulders formed a dome around them and made a fortress that was strong and steady. Ningrei murmured to her Kamatei to protect them all. The boulders were thick, but the giants were pounding them hard, shockingly loud.

'All seven of us are here, finally.' Laiba said calmly and he looked at Sana and her tiger with a smile of admiration.

'Something went wrong, isn't it?' Sana asked and it wiped away the smile on Laiba's face.

'Yes, these are the Tin-ngam and the Lai-ngam giants. We cannot slay them for they will just multiply, but we also cannot defeat them otherwise as they are insanely strong,' Laiba sighed. All the other guardians looked down as if already defeated.

'The prophecy called for us to unite and this is how we are going to greet each other in our first union?' Sana asked irritated.

All of them looked up a bit surprised. She sounded more like Ningrei now. Even Ningrei raised her eyebrows.

'I think someone was on the top of this hill...' Sana wondered and Laiba replied,

'Yes, that is probably the person who stole the scissor. We not only need to restore the scissor, but also to find a way for us to leave this place alive. The thief might probably know the way and guide us, however unlikely that sounds.'

'The question is, how do we defeat these giants?' Ningrei looked at her spear, which had seemed incredible until recently.

'Now, Brother Gothang has these adorable beasts, Iwan has a sword, Yangba can fly, Sister Ningrei can build...this with boulders? Lungchum and Brother Leisatao with their dragon and *arambai*...' Sana summarized the changes quickly.

'Not just some *arambai* I have here, they are more accurate, can even fly in insane curves and multiply in any number I want!' Leisatao updated them about his weapons proudly.

'Which will be useless here,' Sana cut him short.

'That's true.' Leisatao gulped. He realized that he needed to adjust with Sana's new persona.

'So... If I may ask, where did you find this tiger?' Iwan asked, the tiger grunted annoyed.

'It's all right, Pamba. We are all in this together now,' Sana rubbed the tiger and it purred back.

'Laiba, Tin-ngams and Lai-ngams were once the guarding giants. I know that much from the tales, but how long do they take to regenerate from their severed body?' Sana asked Laiba, ignoring Iwan completely. He rolled his eyes, but Sana seemed too intimidating to protest.

'Not much time. They just start budding as soon as wounded. We are not supposed to shed any blood. Not a single drop of blood. They can grow into a full giant even from a single drop of blood,' Laiba answered, wincing at the sound of the giants pounding around them.

'Blood...' Sana tried to think of something, but the giants were too noisy; she wished she could just pulverize them all for good.

'Hold on, didn't the supreme deity have some legend of fighting a monster once and sucking all the blood away?' Ningrei looked at Sana, 'Can you do that?'

'Suck the blood from these disgusting monsters? Do I look like a leech to you?' Sana snapped.

Ningrei just blinked back. Snapping at people was her thing.

Laiba explained how Sana is now manifesting her warrior form, suggesting that they needed to accept more than just her cockiness.

'Whatever, but I can't suck blood. There are four of them. Did any one of you even count?' Sana looked around and all of them tried not to meet her eyes.

'Suck blood?' Gothang asked quietly, looking at Lungchum.

'There was once a monster as imperishable as these twin giants. The warrior goddess was at her wit's end when they battled because her sword wouldn't cut the rock-like skin, but she pulled out the tongue which was the only soft part, cut it and sucked the monster's blood until it shrunk like a dried fermented meat. That's what they are talking about now. She is known for knowing the weakness of all the opponents,' Lungchum summarized for the clueless Gothang, who nodded gladly at the little enlightenment.

'Uh, the details,' Leisatao stuck out his tongue, losing his appetite again.

'But she is right. She can't suck all the blood,' Gothang was worried that they were putting too much stress on Sana. She was the next youngest person in the group and he wasn't even done feeling sorry for Laiba.

'Considerate of you,' Sana nodded, appreciating Gothang.

'My fire didn't work either,' Lungchum said sullenly.

'Fire...' Sana mumbled and remembered that she could still feel her elemental form. Her formless body churning the deepest point of all the realms.

She looked back at her depressed friends and said with a smile, 'You all know that I can also turn into water, right?'

'Yes? What are we supposed to gain from it here?' Iwan wondered, but Lungchum seemed to get what Sana said. He nodded excitedly.

'I will need all weapon wielders to cut the giants into as many pieces as you can while Lungchum and Laiba can go up towards the thief and see what we can learn about the scissor,' Sana looked at her tiger and ordered, 'You will be witnessing something extraordinary now. I want you to go after these guardians and help them with severing the giants.'

'Alright,' Ningrei wondered what she meant by 'can turn into water' but didn't want to bother with unnecessary details and asked, 'Shall I release my boulders?'

'Please, sister. And do the very best with butchering,' Sana knelt down the floor and closed her eyes.

'With pleasure,' Ningrei smirked and swirled her spear. The boulders flew apart and the guardians emerged out of it with their weapons and rides.

Lungchum and Laiba flew directly towards the hilltop.

Iwan and Leisatao dashed in with Yangba and attacked the tall Tin-ngams. Gothang and Ningrei rode Chongja and Chongkim, taking care of the chubby Lai-ngams. Pamba helped them, attacking the giants in any way he could.

Sana sat quietly, the roar of the battle becoming more and more distant. She tried to find her body again. She sensed that she was somewhere deep under the ground. Her body was farther away. There were countless layers of earth and rocks between, the nearer presence was an entangled labyrinth of tunnels. She breathed in deep and almost screamed out, trying to haul out her element. She began to hear a rumbling. Her body became cold and lighter. She stood up slowly and spread her arms.

The guardians followed as Sana told them to and went all out, cutting up the giants into countless pieces. There was blood spurting out all over but none splashing away, instead, clogging to a blob and trying to grow back. Iwan mutilated some into micro pieces but was worried and looked back at Sana. What he saw made him jump off his horse and stand awestricken. He had never seen anything like it before. Sana was glowing as if she were the surface of clear water, on a bright moonlit night. Her skin slowly turning translucent and then completely transparent in the blink of an eye. She spread her arms and out of the walls, flew out waves of water that dissolved her completely. The tall wave of water came towards them as if to crash, but it only washed away the blood of the giants, leaving all guardians unharmed. The water encircled them like a thick wall, churning at a notably high speed. The blood of the giants made it look red, but after churning for a few moments, the water turned crystal clear again.

'Incredible. She dissolved the blood in water. Smarter than me, alright,' Laiba smiled when he saw what happened but he turned back at the curtained spot. With the giants no longer chasing them, Lungchum went lower near the hilltop.

'Stand close,' Laiba said as he jumped down.

Lungchum nodded and shrunk back to his human form.

The other guardians followed them.

Sana flushed all her water away and emerged out of it for a huge gasp of air. Pamba ran up to her and supported her to stand on her feet. She fainted last time, but now she was just slightly exhausted.

'Come on, Pamba. Whatever mischief that thief is up to, we should be ready to take care of them all,' Sana jumped on Pamba and they caught up with the rest of the guardians on the hilltop.

All the seven guardians stood together with their mounts behind them. Laiba stepped forward but froze when he heard the claps. The person inside the cloudy curtains was clapping. They looked at each other, confused.

'Whoever you are, we win and none of your monsters defeated us. Better reveal yourself. We are all gods. Forgiving is yet another one among our many virtues,' Laiba said, sounding as authoritative as he could.

Gothang clenched his *dao* tight. He would want to embrace his tired mother. What would she do when she realized that he was her long separated son? Wouldn't she reveal her true intention with the scissor? He gulped down, sweating and shivering for the first time. He wasn't this nervous even while fighting all those monsters on the way.

The person stood up, still clapping, and turned around. The silhouette was that of a woman. Laiba looked at Gothang and felt sorry for the man. He was almost crying, staring at the woman with quivering lips.

The woman lifted her arms and the curtains vapourized, revealing a splendid woman in her forties, clad in a striped silk, gold and bead jewels and the sacred royal cloak, Laiphi, wrapped around her bare shoulders.

'Mother!'

Laiba was expecting the cry from Gothang, but it came from Iwan. Everyone gasped. Gothang was about to call out just the same, but was shook by Iwan's sudden cry. He looked at him and saw the boy king, pale and shivering, crying out again, 'Mother!'

Gothang felt as if his heart was frayed, unrecognizable. She was never his mother. The boy king had said that his mother had gone missing. It all made sense now. His dream was never about his mother but the quest. He was too naive and had built his own outrageous assumption. He wanted to meet her so much; he still wished that the woman would correct Iwan and say that she was not his mother.

'I am not your mother,' the woman did answer in an echoic voice.

Gothang turned back at the woman, surprised.

'I simply borrowed the body of our queen,' the woman now laughed at Iwan, quite callously.

Iwan began to sob, dropping his sword and covering his gaping mouth. Gothang looked around nervously. None of them looked his way except for Laiba. He nodded his head and turned away. He rubbed his eyes in silence.

'Why would you do that? Who are you? Where is the scissor?' Laiba had to ask what needed to be asked, but he deeply pitied his poor king. He knew how scared Iwan was when his ministry discussed his mother's involvement. Turned out, not just involved but someone manipulated her and used her to open a forbidden door. Nothing was getting easier; things were getting even more puzzling.

'Oh, the bearer of Atingkok's eyes. The supreme incarnate,' the woman still sounded mean, smirking and blinking too much unnecessarily.

'Where is the scissor?' Laiba demanded louder.

'Who do you think I am?' The woman laughed.

Laiba didn't answer. All of the guardians exclaimed almost in unison. They knew what the woman meant. Of course, they were lost at how things would turn out, but they knew exactly what the woman meant. Laiba wanted to punch the oracle. Their quest was nothing like what was spoken of in the prophecy. It was all a game!

'The prophecy spoke of you being stolen and you are supposed to be an object. Care to enlighten us?' Laiba crossed his arms.

The queen looked at Iwan for a short moment, but shifted her eyes quickly towards the blazing lava veins above and spoke calmly, 'Yes, I was stolen. If not, the world wouldn't be as balanced as this.'

'This is not balance but the complete opposite,' Ningrei yelled. She felt intimidated too, but wanted to vent her anger before things became more serious.

'Quite right, the goddess of the mountains, Sampubi, you loved your humans just too much, but still refused to incarnate in one of their wombs. I always enjoy your irony. You of all the people must know my ways. I am called the scissor, the scissor of justice, but what I am is nothing but a bonded spirit observing the world as it balances itself.'

'Please tell us why, why all this? Weren't you created to balance the realms, to bring justice to the way of the world, to put order and restore peace?' Laiba asked, desperate.

'Peace? The humans always claim they love it, but all their lives, what they do is always the opposite. Peace was the way of the inert. We warned them that they don't deserve such tranquility. I am Wayel

Kati, the scissor that stood on the edge of all realms. But I do not bring judgement to anyone. Regardless of my name, all I really did was to just be present to alert the divine laws and flow of all energy. The real judgement, you all will be surprised, is always carried out by Nature itself, all by itself; there is no divinity involved.'

The guardians didn't understand the queen's prattle, but Laiba was the only one nodding.

'You are not an actual scissor. That much I can understand from her, sorry, our Royal Majesty's words,' Leisatao spoke uneasily.

'Oh yes, our sun-slayer. You are the one with pride. You always wanted balance too or else why would you create night by killing the elder sun, right?' The queen smirked at him.

'Never mind me, please continue with your scissor talk,' Leisatao tried to hide behind Ningrei.

'What did you do to my mother?' Iwan asked, blinking away in tears. He was biting his lower lip, trying not to sob anymore.

'Who would have thought, the gods would want the son to be the King of Destiny, but I am not surprised. Knowing the god of war, I knew he would want to be someone among the lofty lot. A provincial prince sounded just as predictable as his incarnation. But I am disappointed that you couldn't even summon your own sword until your mother dragged me into your path for the purpose. She knew my presence would awaken your divine senses. Your mother earned my respect. Even when completely possessed, she managed to look out for you.'

Iwan blinked and more tears rolled down from his eyes. He remembered the incident at the tunnel. The woman who ran away was his mother.

'Why her? Why would you do this to her?' Iwan cried out. Sana held his hand.

'Yes, your mother is one pure entity, all the more reason why I needed her for my travel. I am a spirit. I have no body, but when my bonded shield was broken, I was free to go just anywhere I wanted. All I needed was a body and I found your mother crying by the shrine. I lured her to the palace tunnel and possessed her.'

'Yes! That. Who broke your shield?' Laiba asked. He finally realized the prophecy was still playing out and it made him more restless.

'You wouldn't believe who,' the queen smiled playfully.

'Please tell us,' Lungchum smiled back innocently.

'Oh, our serpent king's proud egg. He is going to brag endlessly about you if you succeed in this quest. So untouched of human follies yet.'

'Please, tell us,' Laiba begged. 'Who broke your shield?'

The queen stopped smiling and looked deep into Iwan's eyes. Everyone turned to him.

'I didn't,' Iwan answered nervously.

'No, silly,' the queen said, 'not you, but it was your father.'

Sana cried aloud, 'What?'

'Yes, it was the king. He was the only one who could have stopped everything, but instead, proved himself much more ruinous. He wasn't the only one accountable, but sure, he did release me from my seal. I meant to leave anyway, but the previous kings on the serpentine thrones were all submissive to my dream warnings. Only our late king was foul enough to go against an ominous warning of the dream realm.'

'Dream warning...' Gothang muttered, remembering how he always saw the queen running in his dream.

'Yes, I did give the final touch in the form of a warning in his dream. You see, in today's world, we live in well-segregated guilds called kingdoms, but the earth realm is not for the humans. It never belonged to them. They merely exist as a byproduct of divine creation and now acting as if they were meant to be the prime creatures on earth. Destruction worst than in this era could not be expected.'

'So, you decided to leave because humans became awful?' Laiba narrowed his eyes, 'You know, you seem like you are giving the silliest excuse ever in the history of escaped spirits.'

'I already told you, I cannot exist in any realm out of tranquility. I was revered in the Central Province because your excessively proud kings assumed that I was a divine entity myself and that I would heedlessly protect all from the dark realm. Yes, I wasn't supposed to leave the earth realm, but why can't I come back to Khamnung, the best of all realms, if I got the chance? Chaos is not mine to defend. I'd rather please myself if I can.'

'See, I told you. You are selfish for a spirit too,' Laiba now nodded proudly. He was able to scold the notorious spirit, who had turned the quest upside down.

'I wasn't. That is why I gave those warnings to all the kings. If the very protector and warden of all kingdoms proved his felony, the seal was supposed to break on its own. Nature does not differentiate beyond these laws. Spirit or not, I was allowed to return home. It was the late king's fault. He set me free. He failed to heed my ultimate warning.'

'What warning?' Iwan asked even more confused.

'The golden deer he saw in the swamp. That was my doing,' she answered with pleasure.

Iwan closed his eyes. It was his father who had turned the world into chaos.

'As a king bounded by the code of the Kanglei throne, he was never to ignore divine commands and duties. My dream message to him was a divine command for him. I told him not to go after the deer. He did. Greed and arrogance overtook his heart and he perished in the trap that I had laid to set myself free. Nature in the earth realm extends to all needs, but the law forbade greed. The golden deer—why kill it when you don't need it? That very act is the beginning of all chaos for human existence. The monsters are just returning to their original realm. It is you humans who shattered the balance and shall pay the price.'

'If the gods knew of human failure, why are we here to defend them again?' Laiba sulked at the truth.

'Failure? It's not failure. You people just live in denial. That is why the so-called "gods" made you believe in a higher order to keep you grounded. That is why, you guardians are here. This quest is not just about restoring me or fighting monsters and being heroes, but the journey needed for you humans to understand the basic laws of nature, *watta padaba*...'

'*Watta padaba*, our prayer, to be blessed with enough but never more,' Leisatao understood what the scissor meant. Simply put, human greed leads to chaos. He realized that it all made sense now. The provinces were at war for a long time for wealth and power. The mountain ranges were also under similar chaos. None ever sat back and tried remembering their past or the bond they shared. They all just set the monsters free.

The scissor also explained how it was the generation of ambitious and power-hungry kings on the sacred throne that led to the darkness, with eyes looking straight at Iwan, as if to make him feel accountable for his ancestors' blunders.

Iwan looked at his mother in tears. She had been the only one trying her best to teach him the humble way of the realm. However, when the chaos broke lose, here she was, possessed by a spirit, feet filled with cuts and bruises, hair unruly and covered in dust, her clothes all stained.

'If we restore you to the palace, our world will have a chance to return to its course,' Ningrei said apologetically.

'All the guardians here are humans except me, but regardless of their divine power, granted by your presence, they are also individuals brave enough to stand up for the realm.' Gothang spoke calmly, 'The guardians have proved their worth. You can't refuse us.'

The rest of the guardians nodded.

'It's the throne that brings all of us to this suffering. The Central Palace is where we will need to begin our reforms...' Iwan bit his lips but the queen was already grinning. Her body began to glow. Honesty was a food for the spirit.

'With the seven chosen guardians blocking all the cardinal directions of my way, I, Wayel Kati, the scissor of justice, shall return to where the guardians take me,' the queen bowed with a smile.

'That's it?' Ningrei muttered. The scissor calmly agreed to return to its locker in the mortal realm, in such a suspiciously straightforward manner.

'The journey up till now is what the quest was about. Recruiting spirits isn't always tough, I learnt,' Leisatao nodded; he had been staring at the queen without blinking much since the beginning.

'One more thing, though,' Laiba said after a moment of thinking, 'we are deep inside the forbidden kingdom of the underworld. How are we supposed to leave this place?'

The queen stared at Laiba for a while and Laiba stared back. The other guardians observed them gazing at each other and wondered what the two were doing. It was quite obvious that they were conversing telepathically.

'I will make sure they are safe, whatever happened,' Laiba said nodding his head a little. The queen grinned but turned her face towards Sana.

'Our Supreme Goddess is in her most audacious form, the goddess of strength, the unbeatable. I, for I am a spirit, will have to be carried under a shield and therefore choose your cosmic womb as the safest medium for the travel,' the queen smiled triumphantly and looked at Sana who sat upright atop Pamba.

'You want to enter my womb? How?' Sana asked surprised.

'The seven guardians learnt of the deep truth of existence. The scissor of justice will now nestle back in the sacred human realm. Oh! Mother of all moving, queen of all living, in your rousing belly of all creation is where I shall slumber, for the guardians have united and Nature has conceded,' the queen sang in delight and opened her mouth wide. There was a thin wisp of smoke venting out from her throat towards Sana.

Sana inhaled it deeply and the queen collapsed on the ground.

She felt dizzy for a while and could feel a solid something embedded in her belly. She began to levitate and lost her consciousness.

The rest of the guardians watched in awe as Sana floated up with her body shimmering and her hands forming the inverted-hand triangle, *khoidou saba*, over her stomach that was giving off a soft golden glow. Her hair turned into golden ripened paddy, her skin hardened into earth, her dress morphed into a flowery phanek (with moving vines and leaves) and a thin translucent watery drape that covered her shoulders like a shawl. She hung in the air with her eyes shut and unmoved as if in deep meditation.

'This is her divine maternal form, mother of all living creation, the Earth Goddess, the one that nurtures all living beings,' Laiba said and bowed low as a show of respect for the evolved goddess in front of them.

All the guardians stared at her with concern for a while, but Iwan's cry distracted them and they all went towards the queen.

'Mother, mother, are you alright?' Iwan knelt next to his mother and cried.

'She is fine, look, breathing normally. I guessed being possessed for so long must have exhausted her. Calm down, she will be fine,' Laiba rubbed the sweat away from the queen and fanned her with his hands.

'So, this is it? The scissor is probably inside Sana's belly. We did it,' Leisatao said in relief.

'Yes, but there are still the monsters and the door of death to deal with. If we do not restore the scissor inside the palace, our kingdom will never be safe,' Laiba reminded them.

'Let's go then,' Iwan said impatiently.

'Your majesty,' Laiba said calmly, looking at his king with a sad smile, 'before we leave, I should tell you that you are the best king ever born in this realm. You will be the one to bring back the glory of our ancient blessing. More than a king, you will be revered one day as the true guardian.'

'Why are you praising me all of a sudden?' Iwan was blushing. He pretended not being flattered and scoffed, 'I promised the Wayel Kati to follow the rule of Nature. It is our sole duty now. You don't have to praise me specially. I am just glad we all did it. And my mother is safe.' He embraced his unconscious mother tighter.

Ningrei gave a smile at Iwan for the first time.

'Alright,' Laiba did his sarcastic eye roll and turned towards the rest of the guardians, 'the Ashi Thong is not meant for mortal travel, so I will have to cast a strong spell on all of you to puncture the subterranean magic veil. Sana will be dormant while she bears the scissor inside her so we need to protect her until she reaches the Central Palace. The scissor will restore itself once she reaches the palace; so until then, Ningrei and Pamba will protect her. Brother Leisatao, Brother Gothang and Prince Lungchum should use their ultimate strength and push the monsters back to their dark realm. Our Meidingu will carry our queen on Yangba towards a safer place; first, go for the Koubru mountaintop. Once the scissor is restored, the divine shields will rejuvenate. Everything will be back to normal. Do we understand the plan?'

The guardians must have had a lot of queries but they didn't get the time to raise them. A loud rumble filled the chamber and they heard the monsters storming towards them.

All the guardians immediately jumped to do their assigned tasks without much thinking.

Laiba stayed calm and poised. Both his eyes were burning up.

THE NEW CHAOS

Gothang rode Chongja and trotted out of the mouth of the Mangsore, chasing a horde of monsters towards the dark abyss. Leisatao followed with Chongkim, throwing his multitudes of sparkling lethal *arambai*s at the flying monsters. Lungchum flew out as majestic as ever, jetting across the sky and towards the dark abyss into the horizon of the mountain folds. Ningrei caged Sana inside her stones and levitated them across the valley, meanwhile fending off the few monsters with the help of Pamba, the giant tiger. Iwan flew out with his mother on Yangba towards the Koubru mountaintop, hoping to keep his mother inside the shrine until the restoration of the scissor. He too had slain a few monsters on his way, but there were not many left loitering as the guardians had successfully chased them all back towards their dark realm.

Deep inside the Khamnung tunnel, Laiba stood at the stone entrance of the Ashi Thong. He put his hands on the giant boulder and began his spell. The stone moved, flickering with sparks of light here and there, the enchantment of the door reviving and the underworld ready to be shielded off forever again.

Ningrei reached the palace. There was no one around the vast island. Pamba lowered himself as if suggesting that she climb on his back. She did. The tiger rode inside the palace and towards a secluded grove where a small abandoned shrine stood in the middle. The giant ball of stones that contained Sana flew behind them. The wooden shrine was encircled by white sacred flags, the trees dressed in Laiphi, a thin starched cotton stole.

Ningrei could feel her stones rumbling and she waved her spear. The stones flew out at once, revealing Sana in her meditating state.

Sana still seemed unconscious, but her hands moved away from her belly and the golden fumes flew out of her nostrils and towards the shrine.

Ningrei watched in awe as Sana returned to her original self, her hair turned black, her dark glossy skin restored along with her plain white bodice and red phanek. She opened her eyes. Ningrei ran up and caught her before she fell.

'Laiba...' Sana wept.

'Everything is fine now. We did it,' Ningrei cried.

'Yes, but Laiba...' Sana wept bitterly.

'What?' Ningrei looked at Sana and stopped smiling.

The dark realm was shielded. The monsters trapped inside the deep dark abyss. The storms and dark clouds subsided. Citizens of the realm came out of their hiding for the first time. They saw the bright ray of the sun on the eastern mountain. It was daybreak.

Gothang, Leisatao, Lungchum and Iwan came riding their mounts towards Ningrei and Sana.

'We did it!' Iwan cried out. They all were smiling.

Gothang patted his good boys, Chongja and Chongkim, feeling proud as if he were their father. Leisatao rearranged his hair, giggling. Iwan almost embraced Lungchum, but stopped awkwardly midway. Lungchum jumped and hugged him anyway.

Ningrei stood still. She tried to smile, but looked at Sana and sighed heavily.

'Sana, you did wonderfully well...' Iwan ran up to her, but she gave a painful smile.

'We did save the realm...' Sana began shakily. Everyone stopped their revelry. They all turned to Sana with searching eyes.

'Where is Laiba?' Iwan demanded after a moment of silence.

'The door of death...the Ashi Thong...it needed to be shielded and that could only be done from the inside...' Sana tried to explain, but she broke down into a bitter sob.

Everyone looked down.

'But...he is my head priest. I...I need him here,' Iwan mumbled. He realized he wouldn't be seeing Laiba ever again.

***

The six guardians were assembled on the Koubru mountaintop. There were already seven thrones of grass, thrones made literally out of sacred grasses that grew into the shapes of thrones. The thrones of grass in the Koubru mountain was long considered a myth, but none seemed surprised to find them waiting for the conference. They all took their seats, while the middle one remained empty. It belonged to Laiba. All the kings of the provinces and the chiefs on the nine mystic mountain ranges came together for the new re-establishment. They encircled the guardians, kneeling along with their clan members. The queen, having recovered elegantly, stood near her son for the first time since her disappearance. The ministry also joined the crowd, standing in isolation, unable to look up, their heads bent low.

'My heartfelt greetings to all the kings and chiefs present here today. I welcome you with my heart to bless this new beginning,' the queen spoke calmly, looking perhaps a little tired but standing proud. 'My husband might have failed to serve the sacred throne, but the guardians came to our aid when in need. As your queen, I shall vow to serve the realm of nature, as nature seems fit, and to follow the code of the sacred order wherein our human anomaly is cultured into compassion. I vow to our guardians,' the queen genuflected, followed by the rest of the crowd.

The queen had always been a woman easy to adore. She looked regal as always, in her striped silk phanek, fresh floral ornaments, thinly starched cotton stole, necklace made out of shiny chaning seeds and glassy beads around her graceful neck, and her dark hair tied into a low bun with feather pins.

The guardians smiled and bowed to the people. Iwan looked at the empty seat in the middle and gulped. He seemed to tear up every time he thought about the little pale boy, Laiba—his head priest, forever trapped in the underworld. He knew he wouldn't be able to forget the annoying head priest with his sarcastic eye rolls and prophetic speeches that never matched his age. Sana reached out her hand and patted Iwan before she stood up to speak,

'The world was at the brink of collapse and yet we thrive and pave the way to our own success. This realm is not ours to meddle with. We are not its owners but mere guests. Our forests and animals are not ours to destroy for our sports and desire. As your Meidingu, the lord of the seven realms and the protector of the nine mystic ranges, it was the duty of the sacred throne to protect and to serve all the realms under the divine law, but generations of spite and greed consumed us all, sadly, including our recently deceased king. Our queen bore the price. The divine scissor of justice, Wayel Kati, took her humble body hostage and tried to escape our realm when the sacred balance was disturbed. We were mere human children, ordinary people, when the divine quest was thrust upon us. But we won. Humans will and shall always find a way to commit to our humble existence. We may lose ourselves at times, but we will always find a way to serve the verdict of nature.'

Everyone seemed to forget that Sana was a mere 13-year-old, with her black slim sword slinging down her waist and blood and dirt all over her phanek and cotton bodice; the speech seemingly touched everyone's heart.

A big roar of acceptance thundered across the mountain.

'Hail our king, hail to the divine throne...' The ministers began to cheer, but Meidingu Iwanthanba interrupted,

'And there is one more alteration in the conduct and order in the Central Palace. I, hereby announce—that Pongba Tara, my royal ministry of 10 noble officers, will be adjourned indefinitely. The throne will be advised and heeded only by the institute of royal scholars, heads of priests and priestesses and the heads of all essential royal departments.'

The ministers broke up into confused murmurs.

'But we are an essential part of the throne!'

'This cannot be...'

'The king is making another grave mistake again...'

'A Meidingu cannot exist without his Ponba Tara!'

Meidingu Iwanthanba calmly listened to the chatter and cleared his throat. Everyone went quiet again. The ministers looked at the Meidingu with sorrowful eyes.

'My beloved ministers, I have taken this decision not because I despise your presence at the palace. I do, in fact, revere your supervision.

However, with the newly reminded obligation of the divine rule over our heads, I fear that your heart as a minister will find it hard to accept the changes. Hence, I am humbly asking you all, my beloved ministers, to leave this office and be at home with your family and appreciate the little things in life. Your duty to serve me is not more important than smiling over your child's first horse ride, appreciating your wife's skilled weaving or helping your neighbour in the field. We are in for a great awakening and I want you to wholeheartedly accept it first.'

The ministers didn't dare argue with the Meidingu in front of the whole crowd and nodded their heads in agreement. Their dream for a great empire shattered at that very instant. Minister Nongthomba stared at the crown prince of Moirang, Prince Lungchum, who was standing with the southern bastard, Gothang, as equals and as if they were friends. If not for their divine powers, the two would not have stood together.

'A mere minister shall not disobey the direct order of the Meidingu, regardless of how regretful it may turn out in the future. I, on behalf of the whole Pongba Tara cabinet, will take our leave and shall depart from this glorious sacred mountain at once,' Minister Nongthomba said with a painful smile spread across his sweaty face and stood up.

'I shall be forever grateful to my ministry for guarding my throne till this day. I will anticipate the time when our ministry resumes with altered motives and principles that justify our divine law. Farewell,' Meidingu Iwanthanba bowed back to the ministers who descended down the mountaintop.

All the chiefs and kings of the realm assembled. Gothang smiled while he noticed Lady Kilungshi wearing the chieftess's headdress. Even the northern clans were there, cheering for Ningrei. They knew that the time of wars and conquests were finally over. The existence of the guardians was the proof.

'I have something to say,' Iwan spoke with a genuine smile for the first time, 'My father left the throne to me, but I think there is someone even more capable here.'

Everyone looked around. The sacred throne was meant to be taken by the one who most deserved it. It had belonged to many from different clans and dynasties since ancient time.

'It is my mother,' Iwan said. There was silence, but every eye was on the queen brimming with love and admiration.

'But, son, no queen has ever ruled our sacred throne alone,' the queen answered.

'Your Majesty,' Leisatao spoke gently, 'we have witnessed your virtue and your legitimacy. Say what, guardians?'

'I think it is true. My northern brethren and I shall acknowledge,' Ningrei bowed and the rest of the guardians joined.

'We shall hail our queen and all of the realm,' Lungchum leapt up and bowed.

The rest of the guardians stood up and acknowledged and the whole mountain erupted with cheers and praises at the restoration of the realm.

'Leima Laithonghangbi shall be the one true queen of Kanglei!' Leisatao exclaimed.

Queen Laithonghangbi genuflected on the ground. Her head touched the cold grass and the crowd roared in unison. They knew she had earned it.

The guardians returned to the Central Palace from Koubru. With the royal duties finally resting in his capable mother's hands, Iwanthanba fooled around his friends as usual. He pretended to hide his sadness over losing Laiba, but Sana noticed and consoled him by assuring him that Laiba was safe somewhere in the underworld. All the guardians laughed and talked with each other like a family, enjoying the warm fire and wondering how their lives would move on. Their divine powers also seemed to be dissipating slowly. Ningrei could no longer summon her stones, Leisatao couldn't multiply his *arambai*s and Chongja and Chongkim turned into shadowy figures and disappeared right outside the entrance of the Kanglei Palace.

'What made us guardians is our commitment to prove our worth and doing what is right. It was never about just the divine duties. We are still guardians with our virtue,' Leisatao said, feeling proud regardless of losing his powers. Pamba also went to the forest as a majestic and free beast. Without a human body, Gothang was the only one feeling the growing fatigue. He needed to return as well. He looked at his companions with a sad smile, contentedly but also poignantly. He knew he would miss them.

At daybreak, Gothang walked out of the palace with his small bundle. He didn't wake up anyone before taking his leave. He assumed that it was not needed as they had already discussed at length about his departure the night before.

The Queen of Kanglei was returning from her morning homage at one of the shrines, but stopped and called when she saw him.

'Gothang, my lord, are you leaving the palace?' The queen asked innocently.

'Yes, mother,' Gothang said, his heart heavy just like when they had met for the first time in the underworld. For months, he had chased her, thinking she was *his* mother.

'I heard you are from the southern ranges. I will arrange a...'

'Mother, it is alright. I'm not heading back to the mountain, but somewhere nearby. I shall take my leave,' Gothang bent to bow but the queen stopped him.

'What are you doing, my lord? Even though I am the queen, you are still a god incarnate. It is a profanity to bow before mere humans like me.'

'No god or spirit is greater than a mother. Allow me to pay my respect to you as a mother. I always wanted to,' Gothang smiled and even shed a few tears with pride.

'Alright...' The queen embraced the sky prince and said, 'you are indeed like a son to me regardless. Take care and always remember us, love.'

Gothang went to the Konthoujam clan. His mother's shrine was inside a grove, under a huge banyan tree that branched out into five more giant trees around. The stone inscription narrated the tale of his mother. While he stood reading, a bright light cast down from the sky. He looked up uninterested and saw the sky lord in his blinding attire, descending from his famous golden stairway.

Gothang knew it was his divine father, coming to take him back.

***

Back in the Moirang Province, Prince Lungchum was about to be crowned as the new king of Moirang. He was excited to invite all his guardian friends in the realm. They hadn't met for years since the quest.

'I heard my brother, Iwan, and Lady Ningrei will be coming together. Brother Leisatao and Lady Sana should preside over the ritual for more blessings...' Prince Lungchum kept blabbering to himself. He grinned, thinking about the reunion that would take place sometime soon.

'Your Highness, there is a man out there who is requesting your audience,' one of his guards disturbed his happy thoughts.

'Who? Why don't they wait until the court hour? Is it urgent?'

'He told me to give you this,' the guard gave him a piece of cloth.

Lungchum took the fabric. He was a bit confused, but felt a sharp pain in his heart when he saw the pattern on the cloth. It was the tiger motif worn by his mother in the vision that Laiba showed him long ago and also the cloth that was wrapped on him while he was a baby. Someone who knew about his mother was there to meet him.

'Let him in at once!' Lungchum yelled.

The nervous guard ran and came back with a middle-aged man, who had a familiar face.

'Who are you?' Lungchum asked impatiently.

'What's more important is who you are.'

'Dear stranger, tell me why you are giving me this piece of cloth?' a confused Lungchum demanded, and he also remembered who the stranger was. He had met him before.

'Aren't you one of the Kanglei ministers?' Lungchum asked.

'Yes, I am the former Minister Nongthomba, but that is not my name now. I am Lamtakpa, the crusader of the new Kanglei realm. I am here to reveal everything about you.'

Lungchum shook his head and stepped back, but Lamtakpa came closer and whispered the very words that Lungchum had been trying not to think about.

'None of your so-called friends were truthful to you. The guardians were just using you to fulfil the quest. They are not your friends. That pale boy, Laiba, manipulated your true story with his ocular power. Your mother was brutally tortured by her clan, for getting pregnant with an unknown man and your own grandfather tried to murder you. Your father abandoned you willingly... Your mother was falsely informed of your death while you starved in the streets like a lost dog. Your mother's clan is your enemy and your real name is Tangja Lilha Pakhangba, the new Pakhangba of our new Kanglei... Meidingu Iwanthanba is not worthy of succeeding the Kanglei throne and yet he gave the throne to a mere woman. He has marred our dream for a great empire with what most civilizations are trying to build now. You cannot trust your friends. They are not your friends... I will make sure that you can turn into a dragon again; not exactly a dragon but a

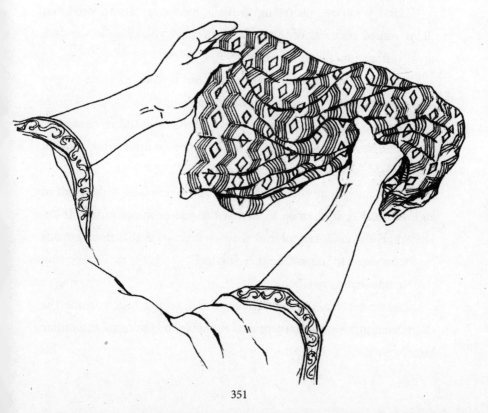

serpent just as your father did. You will be your father. You will be the true king of Kanglei...'

Prince Lungchum tried to scream 'Liar!', but the man threw a concoction on Lungchum's face, making him unconscious.

Lamtakpa took the prince inside a secret chamber and kept him bound.

Prince Lungchum swore to kill all who participated in such a profanity as abducting a provincial prince.

'I am your humble servant, my lord,' Lamtakpa would whisper in his ear regularly.

There came more of the former ministers inside the chamber, circling Lungchum and asking him to submit to their cause.

'Liars! Why are you trying to make me betray my friends? You all are fouled creatures of the dark. I will shove you all up in the dark abyss!' Lungchum screamed angrily.

'Nongthomba, I support your cause, but holding a prince captive seems too extreme,' one of the ministers said.

'Fumthakcha! You are always the doubtful one, and in our cause, there shall be no one who whimpers,' Nongthomba unsheathed a sword and stabbed Fumthakcha right then and there.

Prince Lungchum screamed in horror. The minister dropped dead and the mad Nongthomba looked at the rest of the ministers, 'I am Lamtakpa, the great crusader of the new Kanglei era! Is there anyone here who wants to suggest anything better?'

No one dared say anything.

Regular torture and manipulative counselling began inside the chamber. Lungchum secretly prayed for his friends to come and rescue him. None did.

Lamtakpa brought an unidentified strange seer, dressed in an unrecognizable manner, who grabbed his head and instilled visions just as Laiba once did, but in a more painful way. The new prophecy showed Lungchum on the Kanglei throne, ruling as the most feared king. The vision also shared his past where his divine father left his weeping mother and his mother was tortured by her own clan. The painful vision was repeated again and again until Lungchum couldn't take it anymore.

More visions were rendered, and in another prophecy, Lungchum was assassinated by a group of men in the Khaba clan's attire. Lamtakpa was convinced that they were the descendents of Iwanthanba.

Lungchum cried for help, but the new crusader invaded his mind. The constant torture finally dissolved Lungchum into a monster that Lamtakpa had wanted to create. Lungchum stopped struggling.

He accepted his new name as the Tangja Lilha Pakhangba. He began to believe that he was the actual serpent king. The rest of the ministers joined the effort and helped Lungchum perform the rite to bring back his divine ability. Lungchum regained his power, but Lamtakpa insisted that he cut off his wings and legs to become the golden serpent king. Lungchum did as told. With his large golden wings and legs chopped off and blood spewing all over, he came out determined to obliterate the new establishment of Leima Laithonghangbi and the ardent faith on the nature's way and replace the royal bloodline with his own line of succession, rewriting history with him as the real serpent king—a new beginning.

As Tangja Lilha Pakhangba howled in anger, his serpentine body gleaming gold over the scarlet backdrop of his own blood, a new chaos was born.

EPILOGUE

Laiba was sitting quietly over the edge of a high crystal cliff, the crimson sky of the underworld above him.

He saw the immortal humans leisurely working in their sparkling fields and farms below. He had been accepted as a new citizen of the underworld, but he felt like he didn't really fit in.

'Laiba of the upper world, our king has asked for you,' one of the servants of King Thawarel called out.

Laiba stood up and headed towards the Khamnung Palace without wasting any time. He had already learnt that the underworld king was the most impatient.

As soon as Laiba entered the grand palace hall, King Thawarel cried, 'Laiba, I have some news for you.'

'Bad news? Your Majesty shouldn't have taken the trouble of rendering it to me personally,' Laiba said with a bow.

'No, come here. Sit with me. It is not bad news, but neither is it a happy one. It is about the upper world.'

The mention of the upper world instantly made Laiba run up to the king.

'What happened to them? They succeeded in the quest. The Ashi Thong is successfully shielded. What else is there?'

'Our seers felt a new chaos infesting the earth realm. Divine establishment will be completely eradicated. A chaos conceived of the human vanity is at the verge of ignition. The restored Wayel Kati will be destroyed and humans will slowly evolve until their own conceit consumes their existence.'

'But why? Did Iwan fail in his promise to maintain the course of nature?' Laiba asked, disheartened that all his effort and sacrifice seemed to have gone down the gutter.

'It is not Iwan but someone else. Someone is to rise unexpectedly and engulf all with his manipulated will...'

'Everything I did, what we all did was for nothing then? Why did we even take the trouble to embark on the quest if this is the ultimate result?' Laiba almost yelled out of frustration.

'The human realm is chaos incarnate. They will always lose their way with time. That is the reason why the guardians were chosen to be revived each millennia...'

Laiba rubbed his head and sat down on the ground. He pondered quietly for a while and asked the king with a sad smile, 'Will the chosen guardians be reunited if the chaos breaks lose again?'

'Yes,' the king answered easily.

'What?! For real?' Laiba asked, excited. He always wished to be reunited with his friends.

'The guardians will always reassemble when the world is on the verge of ultimate collapse. You will one day reunite with the rest of the guardians to restore order again.'

'When will that be?' Laiba asked impatiently.

'May take thousands of years or longer, but since the chain of chaos is prophesied as disrupted, it will eventually happen. The ultimate collapse of the sacred realm. The humans forgetting their own names, hatred revered and truth punished. The realm disconnected from the glory of their own past, infested with abhorrence and bigotry...'

'Do I have to wait for thousands of years here as the realm disintegrates at leisure?' Laiba asked, a bit disappointed.

'You have to, until you are summoned back in desperation. Even though all the entrances of Khamnung are shielded, Achang Thong, the door of the living, is still an entrance for transporting the summoned living spirits. You will be summoned through that door one day. It will happen for sure. And here in this immortal underworld realm, waiting for a few thousand years is not a big deal anyway,' King Thawarel grinned.

Laiba quieted down again for a while, thinking many thoughts at a time.

'Your Majesty, will I still be Laiba when we, the guardians, assemble again? Who will we be in our next incarnation?' Laiba asked.

King Thawarel smiled and whispered, 'Seekers!'

ACKNOWLEDGEMENTS

I express my gratitude to all who have contributed to the making and shaping of this book, for providing inspiration when I needed it the most and constant encouragement for seeing it through. I am aggrieved that I will not be able to mention all of them, as then it will extend into a long list, so I will console myself by mentioning the few names that this page will allow me.

I would like to thank Th. Thumbu Maram, D. Tallu Maram, Khangba Anth, K.C.Kabui, A.S.W. Shimray, B. Kulachandra Sharma, Sarangthem Boramani, T. Chingzaman, Usham Rojio, Dr N. Nara Singh, Chanam Hemchandra, Dr N Saroj Nalini Paratt, Mangpu Killong, D. Athuibu, Dr N. Pramodini Devi and Dr Ngangom Ekashini Devi for their dedication and commitment in preserving the cultural knowledge of Manipur in folk performances or written archives, allowing a cultural enthusiast like me to explore them during my writing journey.

I would also like to thank my editor Arunima Ghosh for her patient and diligent involvement in turning this manuscript into a book.

Yaiphahenba Laisham, a patient artist who worked tirelessly for months on the illustrations, envisioning and transforming the many images from the tales into art for the first time.

My utmost gratitude also goes to the many well-wishers and advisors in my field of work, for contributing endless support and encouragement. Your names are forever engraved in heart and soul.